The Curse of the Radiant Opal
By Anskar Thorston

This book is dedicated to the diggers who have flung their youth into a hole in the Outback of Australia in the impassioned pursuit of their fatal stone. May they rest in peace, free from the Curse of the Radiant Opal

Published by Thorston Books

© 2011 Jack Stuckmayer

ISBN 978-0-578-09187-7

First Edition

Cover design, layout and art by Bob Buckner

Editing, proofreading and critiques by Harvey Hagman,
Carly Horner, Sandy Buckner and Jean Haskell

www.thorstonbooks.com

CONTENTS

vi

C O N T E N T S continued...

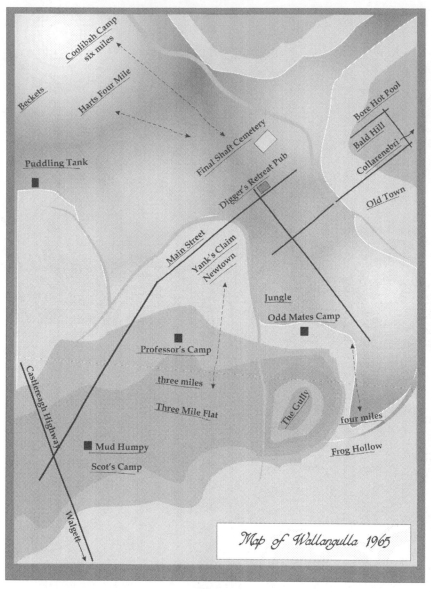

Map of Wallangulla 1965

"These are the stones that steal men's souls. Stones that men live for, kill for, die for. The ancient Aboriginals feared and avoided these sparkling gems flashing reds, golds, greens and yellows that lay on the ground and winked at them enticingly in the sunlight. They believed them to be the eyes of the half-devil, half-serpent, Ooluhru, who lives in a hole and lures men with flashing colored shafts of evil magic. This demon has the power to dominate, curse and destroy"

The Professor

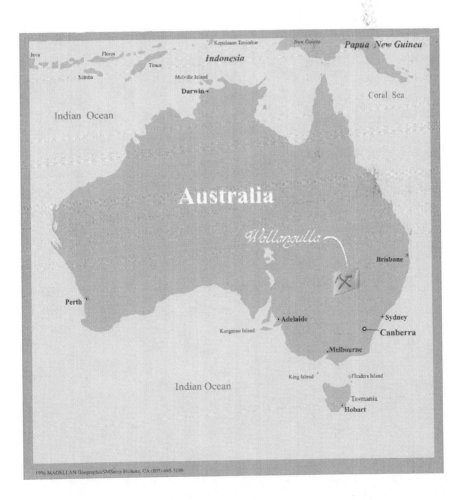

Prologue

Anskar and I were college roommates in St. Paul, Minnesota, during the late fifties and early sixties. We became good friends. After graduation I accepted a job in another state, and we lost contact. I never saw him again. Consequently, it was a surprise when several years later, I received this manuscript which had been sent to me in care of the college.

After a glance I put it aside. It was a busy time in my life. Years later, at a class reunion, someone asked me if I had stayed in contact with Anskar. My curiosity was aroused. I dug out the old manuscript and read it. What a story! This young man with a job, a fiancée, a promising life surrounded by friends and family in a community he loved, gave it all up on a whim to "see the world."

He left everything, promising to return in a year or so. That might have worked, but he stumbled into an extraordinary place. Anskar was enticed and enchanted by it and little by little became entrapped by powers beyond his control that took him from ecstatic heights to the brink of madness.

I will make his story known. It is a fascinating tale, as the metamorphosis of his life was constant and subtle.

Here, then, is The Curse of the Radiant Opal, as told by Anskar Thorston in his own words, in his own way.

JS

Preface

Then one day, 30 feet underground, as I was driving through the clay below the opal dirt with my heavy pick, a lump fell out. It was lower than nobbies were normally found. I rubbed off some clay and saw a glint of color. Then more clay off, more color. I wiped it hard and a burst of colors shot out. I rubbed it, licked it and held it close to the candle. Brilliant flashes of violet, gold, red, green, yellow and blue leaped out in the candlelight. Sweat poured into my eyes, my heart raced. This was the stone I had been searching for. A loner, there all by itself, waiting for millions of years for this moment; waiting for me to bring it into the world, to let the light shine on its brilliance, to give it life.

And it waited to give me life. At last we were together, fated to be united. I clutched it tightly in my hand. I had been put on earth for this moment. I was filled with delight. It is mine! Mine alone! No one will ever take it from me! No one else will ever see it! This was my stone!

All wants, lusts and passions were sated. All hatreds were avenged. I needed nothing more; not love, wealth nor power. Everything I longed for was in my hand. My life was fulfilled. I had been placed on earth for this moment. My Radiant Opal had been predestined for this moment. At last we were together, to be together forever!

Anskar Thorston

Chapter I
Noodling

May 19, 1965

First Week

I was noodling, poking through piles of tailings[1] left by the old miners, hoping to find some potch[2] and color, maybe even a nobby[3] that would cut[4] a stone. Most likely just a mug stone;[5] the old miners didn't miss much. They were looking for big nobbies and passed over the little stuff.

Why it is called noodling I have no idea. It could just as easily be fossicking, probing, rummaging, searching, prospecting, scouring, examining, seeking, ransacking, combing, raking, prying, scrutinizing, fishing, excavating, nosing, hunting, pursuing, digging, exploring, canvassing or dinking.

But it's noodling.

I was noodling on Pom and Marco's claim. I had met Pom and Marco at the Digger's Retreat, the local pub and my first stop in Wallangulla. The Outback Aussie pub is the font of wisdom and knowledge and anything else that can be explained after a few beers by an enlightened bloke to the less informed – or the gullible. There is always someone who will give a dissertation. Have a question? Something you don't understand? John Calvin's treatise on predestination? Mention it and a bloke at the end of the bar will look up, make an appraisal as to whether or not he can hold his own with you if it comes to a bluey,[6] and began explaining the concept in terms maybe, but not necessarily,

1 Tailings – The dirt dug out and left by the miners, usually around the shaft

2 Potch – Common opal chunks, black or white, that have no value if they lack color

3 Nobby (nah'bee) – A hard lump that may be worthless potch or valuable opal

4 Cut – Worth polishing and shaping into a gemstone

5 Mug Stone – A poor quality opal that only a mug (sucker) would buy, usually worth less than ten quid ($22.50 American)

6 Bluey – Fist fight

theological. You may listen politely or disagree; those around you will do the same. These dissertations sometimes lead to a lively discussion and often to a bluey. Aussies like a good bluey; it's the national sport. After it's over they'll all have another pint together and admit they were totally wrong, which might lead to another bluey.

I stepped into an empty spot at the horseshoe-shaped bar, next to a hairy bloke who was being shouted at from the other side of the bar.

"They ain't no sech thing as a Radiant. I've been here 15 year and ain't see one yet." The bloke across the bar – Wee Willy, I later found out – had to stand on the bar foot rail to eye up to the other drinkers.

The hairy bloke retorted, "Buy Two-Bob Bobby a beer. He'll show you his."

"I ain't buyin' no beer for a bludger.[7] He's got a fortune in gems, but they ain't no Radiants. If they was, he'd be off to somewhere chasing dingos."[8]

The hairy bloke tried again. "Jest how do you account for Lizard Larry? He found his Radiant."

"Yeah, and ain't nobody seen him since. That 'us a Royal Gem[9] black opal, not a Radiant. He left for the Big Smoke[10] to sell it. No mystery there."

"The Big Smoke is east. He drove west across the desert into nowhere. 'E's gone mate, gone with the curse."

Wee Willy summed up his argument, "Radiants is nonsense, no sech thing," and went on muttering into his beer.

The hairy bloke turned to me. "Don't pay him no never mind. He's got the Wallies. I'm Harry Hutchen."

I shook his hand and asked, "What do you mean 'gone with the curse?'"

He smiled. "There's a lot of silly nonsense about gem-quality black opal bringing bad luck."

"And the curse?"

---

7 Bludger – Panhandler, beggar

8 Chasing dingos – Pursuing something hard to find and impossible to catch like the wild dogs of the Outback. Running after a dream

9 Royal Gem – Top quality black opal, but less precious than a Radiant

10 Big Smoke – Sydney or Brisbane

"Some say Radiant opal has a fatal curse. Don't pay any attention to these wild superstitions." He then went on to explain to me, a gullible visitor, how opals were formed millions of years ago, when the seas receded and shellfish and small animals were left trapped in the clay.

"In time silicon dioxide filled in the shells and bones. Geyser activity caused them to color and create gemstones. That's what we're looking for, mate. That's why we're 'ere. Most of these creatures don't exist anymore. Some of them never did."

The two blokes on my other side were smiling. Harry went on, "I buy and sell opal." At this he pulled out a small tin of opals. He opened it and placed a half dozen small stones on the bar, none larger than my little fingernail. Can these tiny stones be what men spend their lives looking for? I was not impressed, having never before seen an opal and not knowing what to look for.

"Sarah, bring the Yank a pint," Harry said, and laid a two-bob[11] piece on the bar. I believed that by this time I looked, talked and smelled like an Aussie, but he cadged me right away. Sarah looked about 50, one to whom life had not been kind, but capable of handling things.

"See blokes of all kinds come through here, but not many Yanks," she said as she set my beer on the bar. "One was here a few years back. It got too hot for him. Went back to Yank land, 'e did."

"This one is no dill,[12] Sarah, he'll hang in there. Aye, mate, You just might hit it right and make a fortune. It happens all the time, ah reckon."

I was somehow deep in the receiving end of a conversation that was none of my doing. Harry said, "I met a lot of Yanks during the war, mostly in blueys. Yanks got shipped down here while we were being sent to France. Why they just didn't send the Yanks over there, I don't know. Anyway, they kept messing with our sheilas.[13] Constant blueys. The Sydney coppers roped off a whole city block, and we went at it. What a time," he said with a distant look in his

---

11 Bob – Shilling, Two Bob – Florin, two-shilling piece, less than twenty five cents American

12 Dill – Idiot

13 Sheilas – Girls, women

eyes, "Went on for a week. Yep, I like Yanks, always good for a bluey." He turned to me again, "Yer gonna like it here."

"Ah, no," I said. "I'm just passing through on my way to Alice Springs and then to Darwin. I heard about Wallangulla when our ship made a stop in Tahiti. It sounded like an interesting place with the opal and all. Thought I'd stop by and have a look."

"D'yer hear that, Sarah? The Yank says he saw an ad for the Digger's Retreat in a newspaper in Tahiti and couldn't wait to get here." Then to me, "Glad to have yer, Yank." He held out his hand. I took his hand, but before I could introduce myself he said, "The first bloke to yer right is called Marco, his father was an Itie.[14] Nobody knows his first name; his last name is Polo, which is why he's called Marco. Make sense? It's the Wally way. Next to him is his mate, Pom. He's from England. We call them the Odd Mates because they're different; Pom says little, and Marco's an ear basher."[15] He laughed. "Yer'll need a place to camp, I reckon. Those two blokes'll be glad to have you. They're camped in the Jungle, plenty of room."

Before I could do more than nod at the two, Harry went on, "This is a milky." He pointed at a white stone with a few little flakes of color, next a jelly, clear with some color, then another stone that was oddly shaped with dull color. "Now," he said, "I could let you have this one for 20 quid." He picked up the best looking one, which had a little flash of color but was mostly dead. A bloke on the other side of the bar, snorted, "Careful, Yank. He's still trying to get even for the blueys he lost during the war." Harry scowled.

I said, "Thanks, mate, but I'm not ready to do any buying yet." Harry looked a little miffed. Then it struck me: He's a bull artist.[16] He put his stones back in the tin, and I asked Marco if it would be okay to camp with them for a few days.

"She be right,"[17] he said with a little smile. "It's a big jungle." He could see I was puzzled. "Not a real jungle, just a few trees.

---

14 Itie – Italian

15 Ear basher – A bloke who tells you more than you want to know, and then some

16 Bull artist – Braggart, boaster

17 That'll be fine

Diggers exaggerate. We're leaving in a bit. You can follow us back to camp."

I parked my minivan at the "Odds" campsite. The mini was too small to sleep in comfortably, so I rolled up my jacket for a pillow and slept with a blanket on the ground, under the gum tree near the firepit.

Pom, I realized the next morning, needed watching and careful handling. I awoke to a gunshot and found a slug hole in the gum tree three inches above my head. I jumped up and looked at Pom, who was laughing wildly. "We woke the Yank up, Edward," he said to his dog, who was running around expecting a bird to fall out of the tree. "We sure woke the Yank up that time." He was a crack rifle shot, I later found out, and could hit a penny at a hundred feet. I also found out that he was privately called the *Mad* Pom and was well into the Wallies, the Outback madness that afflicted many of the diggers, at least to some degree.

Marco and Pom boiled a billy over the open fire. After a cuppa,[18] they left for their claim on Newtown. I boiled a couple of eggs and walked around the jungle a while, just to get the feel of the place. Several abandoned campsites indicated better times. I wondered how many of these men had left broke or with a fortune.

I drove to the Newtown mining area and found Pom's pickup by their claim. I yelled down the shaft and made my way below using toe kicks in the sides, hanging onto the rope. They were working 25 feet underground, gleaning the old dirt left during the rush 60 years earlier. Not digging new ground, just going through the tailings that hadn't been taken to the surface. The drifts were pretty much filled with tailings. The Odd Mates were busy digging in one tunnel. I didn't want to disturb them so I took a quick look around and started back up. I really didn't fancy squatting in a dark hole lit only by a candle stuck in the clay wall.

Once above ground I talked to some locals. Newtown mining area is a quarter mile from the pub. One helpful soul told me, "Just take a stick and poke around, mate; yer might hit it. Or use

---

18 Cuppa – cup of tea

a pick and shovel. Or just kick the pile and knock out a big one. Anywhere yer want. All open to noodling. No restrictions 'ere, mate, 'less the claim is posted, and most ain't." Advice on how to noodle was free, frequent and humorous. The resident diggers were either puddling[19] or digging underground.

Opal was first discovered in Wallangulla around 1887 but wasn't considered valuable until 1903, when the first parcel of gems sold for 15 pounds. The price quickly went up and attracted a rush of miners.

Getting here was a chore in itself. Wallangulla is located 470 miles from Sydney on nearly impossible Outback roads. It's so rough that the few drivers there keep moving away from the designated road on either side, going either way, driving next to the road until that surface also becomes too rough, and then moving out farther.

The "Castlereagh Highway" departs Sydney as a wide, smooth tar road that narrows and roughens at Orange. Two hundred miles inland, at Dubbo, it becomes a gravel road, over a 100 feet wide in some places. Doesn't matter; the Outback is flat for miles in all directions. Another 50 miles and it became a dirt trail. I doubled back to see if I had missed a turn, but there's only one road into and out of each town. That was it. Thirty miles per hour top speed. The last 40 odd miles from Walgett was the worst. The front bumper of my tiny Morris Minor fell off. I just tossed it into the back and kept going. The trip from Sydney took five days, but I got here.

I noodled, but ah, what a place to noodle! The designated mining area called Wallangulla is 5 by 35 miles and open to anyone who cares to poke through the piles of tailings, called mullock heaps, around mineshafts that had been abandoned as much as 60 years earlier. You could stake a 100-by-100-foot claim if you wanted or reclaim an old mine with the shaft already dug. But few of the current 50 or so miners bothered staking a claim. With more than a thousand abandoned shafts to choose from, each surrounded by piles of tailings to explore, there was no need to settle on any particular one unless it showed promise.

Day after day I noodled. At lunch time – "dinner," as it is called in Wallangulla – I had a pork pie and a pint at the Digger's Retreat,

---

19 Puddling – Separating dirt from nobbies with a machine

maybe at the same time as the Odds, maybe not. It didn't matter to them or me; we weren't mates. The pork pie was served on a sheet of toilet paper. Sarah thought napkins were too expensive. I bought a frying pan at the general store. With my coffee boiler and one other small cooking pot, I could now cook a piece of meat from the general store and whatever vegetable was available. I never was too fond of Dinty Moore beef stew or Spam.

The first three days I covered a lot of ground, going from pile to pile, poking through tailings that hadn't been noodled to death. I sometimes found a nobby with a bit of color showing. Each evening I brought back a few nobbies. Marco showed me how to snip the nobbies around the edges, looking for color. I found nothing that looked like it would cut a stone. The fourth day, noodling around the Newtown mining area, I came across a nobby the size and shape of a Hershey's candy kiss. I brushed it off and saw color. Red. Any experienced digger would have immediately licked it to let the color out. But I was new, not yet ready to lick dirty stones, and kept wiping it.

"Aye, mate. Yer've got a china hat nobby. Shaped just like a china hat." Marco licked it and held it up in the sunlight. "Let's snip it."

I wanted to say, "It's my stone, mate. I'll snip it," and grab it out of his hand. But I didn't. Already I was feeling the pull of the opal.

He snipped a bit off one edge. "Real color there. Might cut a little stone. Take it to Chuck the Cutter. Yer've 'ad a bit of luck. Yer won't be leaving now," he said with a grin.

"We've got a Yank for a new campmate, Edward," Pom added. "Mind yer manners. Don't bite him 'les he bites you first."

I thought they were joking about my staying here, but this had happened hundreds of times over the years. I was not the first to be hooked on opal and wouldn't be the last. I recall having heard once that the first shot of heroin is free. So is the first opal.

Next morning I drove my minivan the three miles into Wallangulla and found Chuck in his cutting room. He was just a cutter. Didn't noodle, didn't puddle, didn't dig. Just cut and polished stones for four bob[20] a nobby, regardless of the stone's quality or value. I watched nervously while he secured my little

---

[20] Four bob, two shillings = 45 cents American. One Aussie pound = $2.25 American

china hat nobby to a stick and started grinding away at it on his wet wheel. Grind, look. Grind, look. Grind, look. "Stop!" I wanted to shout. "There won't be anything left!"

Finally he showed me a very small black opal, about one carat, less than half the size of my little fingernail. Reds, yellows and greens shot out from a black backing. A rush of adrenaline hit me. Chuck smiled. He knew from pub gossip that I was the newly arrived Yank.

I had seen opals handed around the horseshoe bar in the Digger's Retreat. The light was dim, and I didn't look at the stones carefully, but I was not impressed. It was common practice for diggers to get their mates comments on newly cut stones so they could set a price for the buyer, who would nod "yes" or "no" and maybe bargain. It was said that one time a parcel of nine stones was passed around the mates at the bar, and only eight made it back to the owner.

But this was *my* opal. *I* found it. *I* possessed it. *I* held it in my hand. It was beautiful, the most beautiful thing I had ever owned.

"It's a nice little stone," Chuck said, "but not worth anything. Two tiny sand pits in the face make it unsalable." He pointed at what I could barely see. It didn't matter. I wasn't going to sell it. Far too precious. My find. My opal. I thanked Chuck, paid him four bob and went back to camp, delighted.

"Nice bit. Good color. Too bad about the pits." Marco smiled. "There are bigger ones out there just waiting for you, mate. Now you know what you're looking for."

"No, this is just a souvenir. I'll be leaving at the end of the week. I'm on my way to Arnhem Land." I was going to the Northern Territory to visit Nardoo, an Aboriginal friend I met while working on the Khancoban Dam in the Snowy Mountains.

"Hear that Edward? 'E's not staying. Don't like us all that much. Don't get too attached to 'em," Pom said with a smile. Edward danced around as he always did when he heard his name.

They were convinced I would stay. I was sure I would be gone in five or six days. This was mid-May 1965, a nice time of year in the Outback, 90 to 105 degrees Fahrenheit during the daytime and down to 50 for a couple of hours at night. Not the 110 degree plus heat of January and February that I had gone through in the Snowy Mountains, when flies are so thick you can't tell the color of a man's shirt. Just nice weather. I felt comfortable cooking over an open fire and sleeping on the ground with just a blanket. Now I had fried bread and coffee for "breaky" and maybe "styk 'n eggs" for supper if the general store had a bullock hanging that day.

A friend of Marco's brought back a lamb's fry[21] from Walgett. Marco sliced it and fried it in butter for supper and invited me to join them. It was the most delicious liver I've ever tasted. Afterwards we sat around the firepit and had a cuppa. Remembering the pub conversation the day I met them, I asked, "What's a Radiant?"

There was a pause, and Marco said, "Best quality black opal." Another pause. "Most beautiful of all gemstones." Another pause. "Said to glow in the dark. I've never seen one."

Pom said, "Aye, but if he had one, Edward, he'd be off chasing dingos." Edward got up and looked around expectantly.

Marco and Pom got up and left for the pub, leaving the question only partially answered.

Wallangulla consisted of the pub, a petrol station, general store, small café, post office and 8 or 10 houses along one side of the street, leftovers from more prosperous times. None of the buildings had ever experienced paint, just exposed gum tree hardwood that endured the climate. An anticyclone had wiped out the other side of the street 40 years earlier. The pub, post office and petrol station were reliable. The general store offered limited groceries but usually had Spam and Dinty Moore beef stew. Lenny's café was slow: "Bring a book; it's going to take a while."

One day I got back to camp before the Odd Mates and decided to do them a favor in return for their hospitality. The tea billy, about the size of a three-pound coffee can with a handle, was black from sitting over an open wood fire for months. Black inside and out, covered with thick charcoal. Disgusting. To think they were drinking tea out of that mess! I cleaned it. Shiny, clean metal looked so nice. It was quite a job, but I got it all off and proudly set the billy on the fire grate.

Marco noticed it first. "Aye, mate, yer've got yerself a billy now that yer've decided to stay," he said with a smile.

---

21 Lamb's liver

"No," I said. "That's your billy. I cleaned it up. It was a real mess. Took a lot of scrubbing to get rid of that eighth inch of black carbon and tar, but now its as good as new."

He looked stunned, picked it up and looked at it. "Yer've ruined our billy. It took a year to mature. It was just now coated enough to make a decent cuppa tea. Now we'll have to start all over again." He shook his head in disgust.

Pom, meanwhile, was walking around in a circle with his arms tight against his sides, staring at the ground. "Bloody coffee drinking Yanks, Edward, think a tea billy is the same as a piss pot. You scrub the one you piss in, not the one you drink from."

In the Old West you didn't mess with another man's horse, and, as I found out, in the Outback you don't mess with another man's tea billy. Marco was willing to live with it. He filled the billy with water and set it on the fire grate, but it was full of tiny holes. The carbon buildup had kept it from leaking. He said nothing, pulled out a vegetable pot and boiled the tea water in it.

They both went to the pub that night. Didn't invite me. The news would be out. Everyone would hear about the Yank who doesn't know a tea billy from a piss pot. I would be a marked man, maybe even earn the nickname, "Piss Pot Yank." So be it, I was leaving in a few days anyway.

I sat down on a log, and Edward and I spent the night gazing into the gum wood fire. It was pleasant and thought provoking. This was a far different world from any I had ever known – quiet, serene, relaxed, open but with different customs and conventions. Already I felt I would miss it.

Next day I bought them a new billy at the general store; the subject of the old billy was never mentioned again. I also bought myself a billy and made the effort to learn the ritual of making billy tea. The tea ritual must be observed if a visitor should drop by your camp. This will establish you as an okay bloke or a hopeless battler[22] faster than any other act. First, bring the billy to a rolling boil over the open fire. Next throw in a handful of rough tea leaves and let it boil for just a minute. Then remove it from the fire, drop in a hot coal, stir with a crooked stick, and let stand for five minutes. After the tea has steeped, pour in a little cold water, and rap the side of the billy to settle the leaves. Serve with milk, if

22 Battler – Tries hard but never gets anywhere

available, in a dented tin cup. With a good fire and a log to sit on, your visitor will say, "Nice cuppa, mate. A bit of awright, it is." I quit coffee. Completely. When in Rome…

I was starting to settle in. At night as I lay down to sleep, gazing at the sky made me a little uncomfortable. The southern hemisphere's unfamiliar constellations took a lot of getting used to. But sleeping on the ground is pleasant. You drop off quickly, wake up rested and get right up, no point in lying there. The Odd Mates, in their separate tents, slept later. Usually I had a bit of fried bread and a cuppa and was off noodling before they got up. An old pick and shovel they loaned me made my foraging easier.

Potch is common opal, milky white, grey or shiny jet-black and of no value without color. Most nobbies I found were milky white. I carted them back to camp and snipped the corners looking for color. Chuck cut several of my small nobbies and handed them back to me without comment. They were so tiny that when I showed them to the Odds, one flew off as I blew the dust off my hand. We couldn't find it. No matter, they were all worthless.

With my new tools I covered a wider area and scraped the tops off many mullock heaps,[23] not just on Newtown mining sector, but also on Old Nobby, the first field worked, and New Nobby, a more recent rush. The old diggers left hundreds of mullock heaps. On my eighth day of noodling, longer than I had planned on staying at Wallangulla, I found a promising looking milky white nobby with green showing on one edge. I licked it, rushed back to camp, and snipped it carefully. Yes! Color all around!

By now Chuck the Cutter was getting to know me. I was less apprehensive, trusting his skill. Grind, look. Grind, look. Grind, look. Then he handed me a jelly opal, not as valuable as black opal, but still gem quality. "It's 4.7 carat, oval shaped, round domed, flake pattern with predominantly greens but also yellows and blues. Nice stone," he said. "Too bad it has a sand pocket in the center, but that doesn't show unless the light is behind it." All this, cutting and appraisal, for only four bob.

"Yer'll want to show this one to Shadow, 'e'll know what to ask for it," Marco said. He knew Shadow from the pub, where Marco worked some nights, maybe for pay or free beer, but he

---

23 Mullock heaps – The piles of tailings around each mining shaft

spent a lot of time there. Shadow had earned the reputation of being the biggest crook on the Wally. I had met and talked to several diggers in the pub or on the mullock heaps. Shadow was known. He and his brother had worked a claim on Three Mile Flats and left the nobbies in a coffee tin in the main drift. One day the tin was gone. Just gone. They looked everywhere. For a long time after that Shadow had wonderful luck noodling, found many good nobbies. Jake the Wasp said, "Any bloke that'll swing a stone[24] on his own brother is a real rotter." Shadow had lived in Wallangulla for almost 30 years but now worked alone; no one trusted him.

Marco introduced me. I showed Shadow the stone. He was lean, like most diggers and had a deeply wrinkled face. I instinctively distrusted him but hoped he would give a fair appraisal. "Nice bit of light stone," he said. "Ought to be worth 50 quid[25] even with the sand pocket." Good news.

"How do I sell it?"

"Three houses down on the left. Bernie Bingo. He's the main buyer. His brother Benny comes and goes most of the time and does their selling. Just rap on the door."

I thanked him and headed down the street. When Bernie answered the door, I showed him the opal. Bernie was overweight, looked like he had never been down a shaft or wielded a shovel. His fat hand turned it over and around.

"What've yer got on it, mate?" Bernie asked.

"Seventy quid," I said, hoping to bargain.

"No way, mate, nobody will buy that sand pocket." He handed it back to me and closed the door.

The Bingo Brothers, I later found out, knew about every stone Chuck cut, and Shadow was their crony.

The Bingos wanted to put the Yank in his place right from the start, making it easier to deal with him later; Shadow priced it high hoping it wouldn't sell and I would get discouraged and leave without taking his opal. He was local and therefore he was one of the rightful owners of the whole field. Marco recommended Shadow hoping this would help him in his pursuit of Shadow's 19-year-old daughter, Dovey.

---

24 Swing a stone – Steal an opal from your partner
25 Fifty pounds Australian, $112 American

Word gets around fast through the pub. The next day I took the opal to Hairy Hutchen. (Since meeting him the first time, I had learned that "Hairy" was his moniker.) He glanced at it disdainfully and said, "It ain't worth 12 quid, mate."

Now I had two unsalable opals. They were beautiful, and I cherished them. But I was the sundowner[26] who didn't know the rules.

I had to rethink everything. I had been here 10 days, longer than planned. I had good luck noodling, found two nice opals, and now it was time to leave – only I didn't want to go. I wanted to see Nardoo and venture into the parts of Arnhem Land normally accessible only to Aboriginals, but I could forgo that trip. My teaching job in Minnesota didn't start until September. Minnesota, the United States, seemed so distant and long ago. I still had two and a half months left in Aussie, and I wasn't finished here. I felt there was more opal where these came from. Maybe a lot more. Maybe a fortune!

I kept both opals with me at all times, snapped in my shirt pocket during the day and in my rolled up jacket pocket at night. I took out my little black opal and held it up. One and half carats, flake pattern, four colors leaping out. I was hooked. I held it in my hand, turned it in the sunlight as it changed color and pattern. Then I gazed at my jelly opal – flashes of greens, blues and yellows and quickly came to the realization that with opal so easy to find, after a couple months I could forget about teaching and retire to a Pacific island or live in Paris, or anywhere. A fortune was under my feet just waiting for me! I had heard the stories: Didn't Sam the Barber leave just a few years ago after selling a valuable parcel? Didn't Wally the Piano Tuner move into Sydney and buy himself a Bosendorfer? Yes. I had almost three months free time. If I didn't find anything I could still make it back to Minnesota by September. I decided to stay and noodle with more commitment than anyone.

That evening I told the Odd Mates that I would stay for a month, until the end of June, thinking I'd be tired of the whole thing by then and still have time to get to Arnhem Land.

---

26 Sundowner – Here today, gone tomorrow.

This set the Pom off on another conversation with Edward. "The Yank's staying, Edward. He's going to make a fortune noodling. He really needs a puddler. Puddling's a lot faster, and he's in a hurry. Yanks are always in a hurry. Should we tell him, Edward?" Edward was dancing around expectantly. "Should we tell him there's a puddler for sale? A working puddler just waiting for shovels of tailings to sort through?"

I was eavesdropping on a private conversation between a man and his dog, aimed at me. I took the bait and jumped in. "Who has a puddler for sale?" I asked.

Chapter II
Puddling

May 29, 1965

Second Week

The Odd Mates selected their claim after many hours in the pub talking to the older diggers about the richest mines of the past. They were coming up with enough opal to make it worthwhile. Some diggers spent most of their time in the pub buying beer for the old-timers, then digging for a few hours a week in a rich area.

Pom was from England and had once been married. I didn't know how he ended up on the Wally[27] and didn't ask. He was going bonkers; getting the Wallies, the local name for those who had been too isolated too long. He faced Edward when communicating with me. It was irritating. Sometimes Pom talked directly to Marco.

Marco was fond of American-style bowling, called ten pin bowl in Aussie, and he was sometimes called Ten Pins. How those two got together was a mystery. They probably met in the pub. They were different, but mates[28] just the same. Neither of them was passionate about opal, drifting through each day with as little effort as possible. I suspected they were here escaping from some failure. Both were lean enough to get up and down the shaft easily, but not muscular. Pom had a good frame and would have filled out nicely with exercise, but he was thin and frail looking. Marco had the look of a bartender, pale and fragile. By contrast most diggers were lean and muscular.

King Tut, a mate of Pom's from the pub, had a puddler for sale. I wanted to have a look at it. It dawned on me that I could go through 10 times or maybe even 50 times as many tailings with a puddler than with a shovel. King Tut lived with his wife and three small children on the Three Mile Flats. His wife was a

---

27 Wally – Short for Wallangulla
28 Mates – Close friends, working partners

skinny, rugged, smiling woman capable of cooking over an open fire and raising a family in a tent. The children played on mullock heaps surrounding open shafts 50 feet deep. "Not to worry; we told them to be careful," she said. She invited Pom, Marco and me to join them for the noon meal, a delicious Irish stew of lamb and carrots with a few potatoes, cooked in a Dutch oven placed over hot rocks in a hole and covered with hot coals.

Tut was a small man and had earned his sobriquet, King, by a tendency to strut with his head held high. "As a kid I wanted to be a jockey, but a trainer noticed my hands were too large, indicating I would be too big as an adult." He showed me his puddler made from a small car, like my Morris Minor van. I had noticed the dust from puddlers as dirt was being shoveled into them but had never seen one up close. All that was left of the original automobile was the motor (no hood), the steering wheel and a ragged driver's seat. A three-foot-high perforated cylinder about the size of an old washing machine sat over the back axle with a rotor at the bottom that churned the tailings. Dust flew as tailings were shoveled in, leaving only the hard nobbies to be removed and snipped. I liked it. "What've yer got on it, mate?"

"Ought to be worth a hundred quid,[29] I reckon," King Tut said with a toss of his head. A hundred quid. That seemed reasonable for this unique, handmade machine that could bring me thousands in gemstones. All I had to do was park it by a rich claim and shovel.

"Righto, mate. I'll have it."

I peeled off 10 ten-pound notes and drove it back to Newtown where Pom picked me up. This cut deeply into my remaining cash but could return 1,000 percent in a few weeks. My second vehicle from the Morris Minor line.

I puddled all day and snipped and rubbed nobbies each night while learning about life in the Outback. Lying on my side with my pile of nobbies by the light of a lantern, I'd often hear a rattling noise and look up to see a small army of scorpions coming toward me. At first I thought they were attracted to the light, but when I stood up to get out of the way they slowly kept moving through. I was curious as to where they came from and where they were

---

29 $225 American

going but not curious enough to take time away from snipping to follow them.

After the Odd Mates returned each day and had a bit of tucker,[30] Marco brought me up to date on the latest pub news. "Jimmy the Snake Catcher[31] says he may have to find a new wife," Marco said with a smile. "She's been crook[32] for three days, and Jimmy is worn out from having to do all the work himself. He's spent the last two days in the pub."

"Sarah told Two-Bob Bobby not to come into the pub again until he is ready to stand his shout.[33] The diggers are getting tired of his bludging."[34]

"But he can't shout anything, can he, Edward?" Pom said. "He ain't got a quid. Won't part with his stones. We could live in London and have a servant with just one of his opals, couldn't we, Edward?" Edward danced around, looking at Pom.

"Vertical Bill bottomed on air again," Marco continued.

"Just fell through the last two feet of clay, didn't he Edward," Pom added with a laugh.

"What does that mean?" I asked.

"Lot of blokes named Bill on the Wally. But Vertical Bill is afraid of cave-ins and won't work underground. So he just sinks shafts, hoping to bottom on pay dirt. Horizontal Bill won't sink a shaft, too much hard work. He just digs in old claims. This can be dangerous. The good claims have four-foot-by-four-foot pillars of opal clay left to support the ceiling. If you dig these out, the mine caves in. Horizontal Bill had some close calls, but he's been lucky so far. But to get back to Vertical Bill. He sinks a new shaft over an area that has produced good opal in the past. Problem is these areas have been dug out, and after a week or two of hard digging, sinking a shaft through sandstone, he most often is over an old drift and falls through. That's when he comes to the pub looking buggered. All this could be prevented if he had an offsider[35] to

---

30 Tucker – Food

31 His sobriquet acquired from his former trade of catching poisonous snakes to be used for medical extractions

32 Crook – Ill, ailing, not feeling well

33 Buy a round of beer when it's his turn

34 Bludging – Sponging off the other diggers

35 Offsider – Friend, pal, mate, helper

crawl down and have a look under where he where he plans to dig. He's a bit balmy. But then we all are," Marco said with unusual introspection.

The stories were endless. The Wally was filled with characters living alone in tents or humpies (shacks) scattered over a large area. Some had elaborate stone fireplaces. One bloke was making his humpy out of beer bottles – no lack of these on the Wally. A few bark and mud humpies dotted the area. Eccentricities flourish in the desolation of the Outback. Each man is free to live or die as he pleases. If you want to risk your life, it's your business. Not even Archer the Cop will prevent you from doing something stupid.

The Wally had none of the class distinctions and animosity I had noticed while working on the Khancoban Dam. Everyone here was working class, except the Professor, the Banker, and maybe a couple others I hadn't heard about. Outback Aussies were equals in this world where men hurl their lives into a hole, with only hope for sustenance.

Descriptive, earned monikers were common. Jake the Wasp digs narrow drives he can just fit in, using a small pick to avoid moving a lot of dirt. He once got stuck. His mate dragged him out by his heels. Hungry Hank the Hatter is malnourished, living on bread and treacle,[36] and well into the Wallies; with a Radiant in his pocket he won't sell. The Goat Colonel, a little man, stands at attention when anyone passes, a habit carried over from his military days, and stinks like a goat; or maybe it has to do with the rumor that he got caught in a sex act with a she-goat. At any rate, "Don't stand downwind of the Colonel."

High-Rise John built his abode on 10-foot poles; his wife was afraid of snakes. The Piano Tuner, the Dane, and Flint the Ratter, were all distinct characters. Some diggers didn't know they had a sobriquet. I was called the Yank. No one asked my real name. No need. I don't know how they referred to me in the pub, I hope not Piss Pot Yank.

Newtown seemed a promising place to puddle; it had yielded a lot of high-quality opal. I took out a miner's permit, not really necessary, but I wanted to be legal in case I found something big. A week later, after moving from mullock heap to mullock heap, shoveling tons of tailings through my puddler, sorting and

---

36 Treacle – Molasses

snipping dozens of nobbies and finding only a few with color, I started having second thoughts. A couple of mug stones were all I had to show for my labors. This was discouraging, but I wasn't about to give up.

Then two Slovakian immigrants who were working a claim close to where I was puddling decided to leave the Wally and put their claim up for sale for 100 quid. The price was high ($225 American) but the claim had produced good opal. I climbed down the 25-foot shaft, from toe kick to toe kick, hanging onto a rope, and had a look. The Slovakians had taken more than 3,000 quid worth of opal out of here in the past six months and now wanted to go to Sydney to gamble and carouse. They had sunk two shafts 50 feet apart, which could be connected for good air passage. Three drives radiated out from the primary shaft, the longest one 15 feet. The drives were clean and clear, four feet wide – safe from cave-ins. The cribbing at the top of the shaft was well timbered, leaving a lot of room for tailings. Good, neat miners. I could work here comfortably. I wanted this claim! I would find the money somewhere and buy it!

The excitement of knowing that tomorrow I could dig into a patch of opal worth thousands of dollars filled me with energy and desire. Where else could a man go, armed with a pick, shovel and 10 bob for a mining permit, and expect to make a fortune? I had been seduced the same as other miners. We were all here in the pursuit of beauty and wealth. Failure was not a possibility. I would work hard for long hours underground.

Most diggers puddled old tailings, hoping previous miners had missed something valuable. I now realized that the big finds were still down there. It would only take a week or two, a month at the most. I still planned to puddle a couple hours a day just for mug stones to pay the bills, but a fortune awaited me underground.

Marco said, "Why do you want to buy a claim when there are hundreds of shafts free for the taking? Just stake a claim and start mining."

"The Slav claim is new ground. I want to have first look. The old miners found the really good gems. I don't want to rework old ground hoping to find something valuable that they missed. I want to make a fortune, not just enough to exist."

"In new ground you also have a good chance of finding nothing. Then just existing can be difficult. But it's your bob." Marco shook his head and walked away.

I was caught up in opal mania. Time was running out, but I still had two months to go. Without dilly-dallying I went to the public telephone in the post office and called my friend Willis in Pennsylvania, waking him up in the middle of the night. I asked if he would like to be a partner on a new claim. Yes. He would send $400 the next day. He was working and could afford the risk, with the prospect of making a fortune. I knew I wouldn't disappoint him. This was a sure thing.

Chapter III
Digging

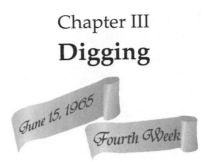

June 15, 1965

Fourth Week

Of the 475 quid (more than $1,000 American) I had saved working at the Khancoban Dam, $250 went for the Morris Minor van, which had a slight knock. After an oil change it needed a new engine, $225. The mechanic said, "He must have shoved a dozen bananas in the crankcase to quiet that knock." Used car salesmen are the same here as in the States. The puddler took another $225. Travel and other incidental expenses left me nearly broke. Willis' money made the Slav claim possible. This claim could yield a fortune. Or nothing. It came with a tent, a cot, two 12-gallon water tanks, a water cooler bag and a cupboard, all of which I moved back to the Odds' campsite. There also was a windlass and bucket at the claim to haul up the tailings.

Archer the Cop gave me the forms, which I filled out. "What'd yer call it, mate?" I thought for a minute but before I could think of a name he had written in "The Yank's Dig" and handed me the sheet for my signature. I became a full-fledged resident with a 10 bob miner's license and a registered claim. I had squandered my savings foolishly – a lifelong pattern. Maybe I could redeem myself by hard work – a lifelong fantasy.

I pitched my umbrella tent; eight by eight with one center pole that had four arms radiating out to the corners, which were secured by guy lines, making it possible to walk upright anywhere inside the tent. This was far superior to the Odd Mates' wall tents that you could barely stand in down the center. The cot fitted nicely along one side, and the new cupboard gave storage space. What a difference a few conveniences make. I no longer slept on the ground, and the Slavs even left me a pillow. The water bag hanging from the gum tree kept my bacon, butter and eggs cool. The two 12-gallon water tanks would last two weeks before I had to haul them into town for refilling.

Our three tents were spaced about 50 feet apart. Hourglass spiders, similar to black widow spiders and just as poisonous, spun delicate webs in the upper tent corners. They caught insects. I didn't bother them, they didn't bother me. A $5 metal locker from a surplus store in San Francisco, a chair I had picked up somewhere, a kerosene lantern, a small rug by my cot, and a mantle lamp were my entire worldly possessions. Life had gotten better! I felt at home and quite comfortable. Especially since I was on the fast track to riches.

My days quickly became routine. I laid in a supply of sandalwood, which burst into flame at the touch of a match. With this over a base of four-inch gumwood faggots, I could cook faster than on an electric stove. The first few days I had eggs and fried bread with a rasher of bacon for breakfast, but this became less frequent as I got wrapped up in the pursuit of opal. More often I would make a stew out of whatever was available and bring it to a boil over the gumwood fire twice a day to keep it from spoiling when set by the firepit all day. The stew became breakfast and supper. The second day it got so black I couldn't tell a potato from beef or chocko.[37] By the third day it was glop. But food was unimportant. I was after opal, obsessively. Stew, bread if I could get it, and billy tea was my main diet.

After breaky, I drove the three miles to Newtown and climbed down my claim. I found that four hours at a time alone underground was all I could stand. I needed to come up for some fresh air and sunshine. At noon I might go into the pub for a pork pie or back to camp for a bit of fried bread and a cuppa. Then underground again for another four hours. After that I spent a few hours puddling, then back to camp for some stew and tea and a couple hours snipping nobbies in the hopes of finding color. One nobbie in 20 or 30 might have a bit of color, and one in 10 of those might cut a stone. One in 20 of these might be gem quality. I was enthusiastic.

A normal drive, tunnel, is four feet high and four feet wide, roomy enough to work in and still be safe. Usually more than one drive radiates out from the bottom of the shaft to explore in different directions. When a drive connects to another shaft, it's

---

37 Chocko – A green vegetable that looks like a fruit

called a drift. Twenty feet from the shaft in a drive is about as far as a digger can go without hanging a windsock at the top of the shaft to channel air downward. But windsocks only work in a breeze.

I knew nothing about mining and questioned everyone. Going down into the Odd Mates' claim a couple of times had been my only experience underground. They did as little work as possible and climbed over piles of muck rather than remove it. It was too cluttered to move comfortably. I decided to work hard, do things properly and keep a clean, safe dig.

Sinking a shaft[38] is the most difficult part of mining, starting with two feet of shin cracker, similar to cement, and then 15 to 30 feet of hard sandstone to dig through before hitting the opal clay level. Fortunately the Slavs had already dug two shafts 50 feet apart that I hoped to connect for good ventilation. Lots of new ground awaited my pick. Life was full and promising.

I bought a heavy driving pick and two small shaving picks, which I kept razor sharp. Then I laid in a supply of a dozen candles and four "spiders" (candleholders) to stick them in the wall. I wanted my drive bright. My first project was to connect the two shafts with a four-by-four drift. The free flow of air would make it possible to run drives in every direction. I started slamming my pick into the clay, knocking out a fistful with each swing. Next I shoveled the muck back down the drift toward the shaft and then shoveled it again and again, until it was under the shaft. Fill the 15-gallon bucket, set the hook in the handle, climb up the shaft, wind up the bucket weighing 100-plus pounds by cranking the windless, lift it out of the shaft, dump it and let it back down. Climb down the shaft using the rope and toe kicks and start digging again. This heavy work builds all the body's muscle as a unit. After a few weeks I was stronger and felt better than any time in my life.

It took a week before I felt comfortable alone underground. I had never been in absolute silence. It was unsettling at first, but I grew to like it and finally to prefer it. With a digging mate some noise is generated, but alone there is absolute silence except for the

---

38 Shaft – The two-by-four foot vertical hole that leads down to the opal clay level

sound of tools. Pick striking clay makes a dull thud that shatters the silence. The shovel scraping tailings and muck dropping into the bucket fills the drive with noise. But overall silence reigns, a silence that almost hurts your ears. After four hours of digging, I always felt the need to come up for a breath of fresh air.

Above ground, the Outback is quiet, peaceful and serene. The breeze flowing through the trees, the songs of birds, the rattle of scorpions marching and the clicking quills of echidnas are not obtrusive or offensive, but comforting. But the total silence underground opens the mind to another world. I don't think a man who is not at inner peace with himself could endure it without going mad.

For a break I enjoyed a hand-rolled cigarette. Tobacco, ready rubbed or rough-cut came in two-ounce tins slightly larger than a snuffbox. The rough-cut had to be rubbed between the hands. I preferred the ready rubbed. Just take a pinch or two, lay it in a cigarette paper, lick and roll. What delight! Somehow this enjoyable tobacco fit right in with the clean, fresh, pure air of the Outback. Draw gently, inhale and relax. This rich full-bodied tobacco was satisfying. I smoked three or four cigarettes a day.

Most diggers worked with mates, a lot easier than going it alone. One bloke shovels the tailings down the drive to his mate, who throws them the rest of the way to the bucket. One fills the bucket; the other winds the windless and dumps. Much easier, much more efficient. But I had heard so many stories about blokes yielding to the temptation to swing a stone that I didn't want to trust anyone I didn't know well, and I didn't know anyone well.

I got around this somewhat by buying a trolley from the local blacksmith, Gentle Mike; a 15-gallon drum cut in half lengthwise and mounted on wheels to facilitate moving the dirt down the drive. I had him make a grapple hook (three hooks welded together) and purchased three more tailings buckets. I never could quite understand why Gentle Mike, Chuck the Cutter, Archer the Cop or anyone else was content to work at a regular occupation with a fortune under their feet. The thought that they knew something I didn't never occurred to me.

On Newtown, opal was usually found within six or eight inches of the roof or ceiling, just under the sandstone. The lower three feet I dug out with my large driving pick; the top foot I went after with the smaller, razor-sharp handpicks that sliced the clay a sliver at a time. A slow process, but I had less chance of missing a nobby. The muck that piled up in the drift I loaded into the trolley, pushed back to the shaft, and dumped. After shoveling this into four 25-gallon drums with loop handles, I climbed up the shaft, snagged the handles with a grapple hook on the end of the windlass cable, cranked the buckets to the top with the windlass, dumped them and let the empty buckets down again. This had to be done two or three times a day.

I gleaned information from anyone who would answer my questions. I quickly adjusted to life in the Outback and grew to love it. The main impetus is opal, always there, just ahead in the drive you are working. Opal waiting quietly for a million years, just for me. Maybe tomorrow, maybe just a few more feet. Dig, shovel, tote, haul. Dig, shovel, tote, haul.

Chapter IV
Two-Bob Bobby

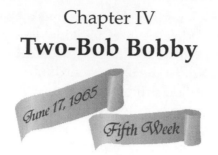

June 17, 1965

Fifth Week

    I sometimes went to the Digger's Retreat pub to have a beer and pork pie for lunch, but it's a tricky business if you want to get back to work that afternoon. Diggers often, after working a few hours in the morning, will spend the rest of the day in the pub. "Nobbies don't come to those who work the hardest or the longest, just to those who are in the right place," was the general sentiment. But I wanted to dig, not stand at the bar all day.

    I couldn't just have a pie and a pint and leave. A bloke who drinks by himself is said to be "having one with the flies" and is considered "a bit off." And if you get caught up in a *mob*, you have to "stand your shout." If a few blokes standing around a table invite you to join them, only a *dingo*[39] could refuse. This, then, is your mob. No escape. Each bloke stands his shout, that is, buys a round of beer when it's his turn. You can't shout ahead of your turn and leave early, and you can't leave before standing your shout. "A bloke what stands his shout[40] is fair dinkum.[41] Only galahs[42] gink out." (He who buys beer when it's his turn is a true Aussie. Only cheats leave before it's their turn to buy.)

    If your mob consists of five or six blokes, it could be an hour or two before it gets to your shout. By that time, after five or six pints (20 ounces each), I'm in no shape to go back to work. I tried to avoid this by joining Wombat and Skinner at their small table. Skinner supported his unsuccessful mining operation by skinning out dead sheep for the local station. This worked for me. No one wanted to be near the stinking skinner, and the most beer I would

---

39 Dingo – The native Aussie wild dog. Outback slang – someone who does
    not accept his social responsibilities

40 Stand your shout – Buy a round of beer when it's your turn

41 Fair dinkum – True, genuine, one of us

42 Galahs – Noisy, worthless parrots

have to drink before standing my shout is three pints. I could endure the stink long enough to have a pie and a couple pints.

One day as I approached the table, Wombat told me, "Hungry Hank the Hatter has a bluey for you. Yanks rubbished 'is stone."

"What?"

"Aye, mate. Hank the Hatter was showing some mug stones to a Yank tourist and his wife," Skinner said. "She told him he was asking too much, they weren't worth it, hoping to haggle. The Hatter took this as an insult and cussed them out in fair-dinkum Aussie. They didn't know what they were being called and backed off. Now the Hatter wants to get you for their insult."

"That's nonsense. He must be dill. I don't know these Yanks. I can't be responsible for what they say."

"Hungry Hank want bluey. Wombat do not lie."

I don't know where Wombat acquired his quaint speech. I sipped my beer slowly, wondering what I was getting into. Before I could think about it, Hungry Hank showed up at our table. "

"Yanks are rotters,"[43] he proclaimed for all to hear. "Bloody, no good rotters." Then he tossed out a string of obscene Aussie expletives I had not heard before, culminating in "Ratbags."[44]

I threw up my hands and said, "Look. I don't know these Yanks and have no idea..." Before I could finish I was flat on my back. I had never been in a fistfight. It wasn't part of growing up in Minnesota. He had hit me square on the cheek. This lean, hungry digger had floored me. I reacted automatically, rolled over, got on my knees, rose and drove my shoulder into his gut. We hit the wall, seven or eight feet away; with him slamming into it head first. Without thinking I looked down at Hank, laying as still as a piece of shin cracker, then looked around at the other diggers, eye to eye, with false bravado, as if to say, "If any of you wants to get into this, I'm ready." They all went back to their pints. It was over.

I said nothing to Skinner and Wombat but held up four fingers to Sarah. When she brought four glasses for the three of us, I downed my pint, put the extra glass on the empty side of the table and said, "Tell the Hatter the Yank stands his shout." I nodded toward Hungry Hank, still on the floor, and walked out.

I didn't want to get into another bluey, but it's a part of pub

---

43 Rotter – No good
44 Ratbags – Despicable people

life. But how could I avoid it? Skinner's odor was getting to me. He stunk like a dead sheep. For this I took the word of those in the know, having never smelled one myself. The question was how to avoid blueys, the mob and Skinner?

There might be a way I could do this and learn "Outback Aussie" at the same time. My first encounter with Outback idiom, or jargon, had left me wondering if I would ever be able to communicate with the locals.

"G'day, mate. Ah've been flat out all week. Me sheila's crook, and I been off me tucker. Me mate got'n a bluey and's gone off to the Big Smoke. I might come a cropper."

Translation: "Good morning. I've been working hard all week. My woman is sick, and I've lost my appetite. My friend got into a fight and left for Sydney. I may not be able to handle everything myself."

Two-Bob Bobby hung around just outside the Diggers Retreat, and greeted anyone new with, "G'day, mate" (pronounced g'dye, myte), "I'm a bit short on a quid. If a bloke 'ad two bob for a pie and a pint she'd be right, and I'd show me stones." (I'm broke. With two shillings for a meat pie and a beer, everything would be fine and I'd show you my opals.) I had heard stories about Bobby, but had never talked to him. He was a fair-dinkum Outback Aussie.

I had tried to stand at the bar and not get caught up in a mob, but often got invited because I was a Yank and some bloke wanted to talk about America. Now I was hoping to get a table with Bobby. We wouldn't be invited to join a mob because he can't stand his shout. That's why Sarah wouldn't let him come in alone; he was a bludger. Most of the diggers had bought him a pint at one time or another, had seen his stones, and knew if he even sold one he would never have to think about money again.

"I ain't shout'n 'im. Let 'im sell a stone and shout the house," I'd heard them say.

Sarah gave me a disagreeable look as Two-Bob Bobby and I stood at a table of our own, but she knew I was standing the shout. I gave Bobby a two shilling piece and paid for the pint and a pie for each of us.

His story of finding the gems was long and rambling and had

become more elaborate with each telling. He had been scouring in an old mine dug 50 years earlier. The old diggers left pillars of clay posts every four feet to support the sandstone ceiling, but this claim was dug out without leaving enough pillars.

"I's 'avin' a bit of a look around when I see's 'em, in a pillar 20 foot off the shaft." He knew that a sandstone ceiling that open might collapse if he took out a pillar, but one of the pillars had crumbled and exposed a nobby with a bit of color.

"Reckoned I'd nip in, 'ave a quick dig and be out 'fore it fell. I didn't make it, mate. I had me stones, but it crashed on me leg before I could gink out."

He managed to dig himself out and crawl up the shaft, but one ankle was crippled. Since that day he has been afraid to go underground, hasn't had any luck puddling, can't work much and won't leave the Wally, the home of his beautiful opals. He was stone poor – had a fortune in his pocket but no cash.

"But I 'ad 'em, I 'ad me stones, and now she's right, mate, she's right."

Once we were back outside in the sunlight, he showed me his stones, which he kept in his shirt pocket. Incredible black opals. Two true gems. Radiants, beautiful flashing purples, reds, greens and golds. Bright and clear rolling flashes on one, flake pattern on the other. Worth, by the estimates of those who had seen them, at least 30,000 Aussie pounds, more than $65,000 American, a small fortune owned by a man who was skin and bones, broke and barely surviving. He was obsessed. He would not part with them and would die with them in his hand. I, like everyone else who had seen his Radiants, had the urge to grab them and hold them. I leaned in to get a better look and he pulled back; I was getting too close. He turned them slowly in the sunlight to show the flashing colors and then put them back in his shirt pocket.

"Ta,[45] mate," he said. "Ta." I resolved to buy Two-Bob Bobby lunch from time to time. I liked him, and it was a sure way to avoid the mob. He was animated and passionate, a man obsessed with his precious opals.

I crawled back down my shaft with a new outlook on life. Would I do that – starve to death with a fortune in my pocket? What is the value of life compared to the value of opals? What

---

45 Ta – Thanks. Thanks for the beer

does it mean to possess beauty? What is worth living for? What is worth dying for? Why was I here?

The class I had taken on Immanuel Kant's "Critique of Pure Reason" didn't help. I never did understand Kant. Kant's view of life was theoretical and objective. Opal is real and personal. The Bible I had been brought up with also didn't answer my questions. "What shall it profit a man if he gain the whole world but loose his own soul," concerned wealth and power, not beauty. I was beginning to understand Bobby and the mesmerizing, captivating attraction of opal. What could he buy that was half so precious as that which he had to sell?

Chapter V
Daily Life

June 21, 1965

Sixth Week

The Odd Mates camp that I was now a part of was located in the area called the Jungle, so named because it had trees, rare in the Outback, but not dense enough to be called a woods in Minnesota where I grew up. You could swing your arms freely anywhere and never hit two trees at once. Still, you couldn't see 100 feet distant. Since Australia has no indigenous deciduous trees, bough sheds are used for shade. Four upright poles, eight feet tall, eight feet apart, with leafed branches strung across the top, give shelter from the sweltering sun. The leaves never fall off. Our campsite had a bough shed. This made life more comfortable.

Diggers had been coming and going for 70 years and left many things besides bough sheds. Fire pits, and stone fireplaces were scattered throughout the Jungle.

During the Aussie winter the temperature in Wallangulla seldom went over 100 degrees and was cool at night. In summer, December to February, 130 degrees was not unusual with 90 degree nights – but I would be long gone before that. Underground the temperature was a constant 70 to 75 degrees, no matter what time of year, a nice place to spend the day.

Life became as unchanging as working on an assembly line or in a corporate office. My daily schedule varied little. I believed hard work would pay. The harder I worked, the more clay I dug, the more clay I moved, the better my chance of finding opal. Sounded logical to me. But luck had a lot more to do with it. Digging in the right place is everything.

I boiled my billy and had morning tea before the Odd Mates were up. Then, after digging for four hours I either had a meat pie in the pub or came back to camp for a jam sandwich, if I had bread. If the Odds happened to be in the pub at noon, we just nodded. They were usually in a mob, something I wanted to avoid. Evenings, after my puddling, we sometimes ate together if they had driven the difficult 40 miles into Walgett and picked up some groceries. They went every fortnight. I didn't. My tires were so bad I had to carry two spares, and my Morris Minor shook violently on the rough road. I avoided driving myself and rode with the Odds when necessary. The road was only soft enough after a rain to be graded, maybe once a year.

Pom spent some of his evenings at camp reading by the firelight and sometimes went to the pub with Marco. I seldom went to the pub at night, too much of the same talk, and I really don't find drunks amusing. Also, every night brought on a bluey or two. One bluey was enough for me. Pub fights usually last only a couple of minutes. One man goes down, and it's over, and the combatants have a beer together, but sometimes blueys erupt into a barroom brawl. I preferred snipping nobbies and reading.

Books of all kinds floated through the Wally, as well as old magazines, from pub to post office, camp to camp. I preferred my kerosene mantle lamp, which gave as much light as a 100-watt bulb, to the firelight. I offered to share the lamp, but Pom preferred the firelight. We had little conversation; he was quiet by nature. Speaking to Edward was his way of avoiding direct conversation. But sometimes, after a few cans of beer, he talked about growing up in England during World War II.

"The Germans dropped mini-bombs wrapped in colored paper to look like candy. We didn't dare pick them up. We spent a lot of time in bomb shelters during the raids. The shelters were crowded but okay if you didn't get next to the shit-can-man." He smiled at my puzzled look. "Outhouses didn't have holes in the ground, just a square can under the seat that had to be emptied every week. The man who pulled it out, slung it over his back and dumped it into the slop truck was called the "shit-can-man." Even after he took off the protective leather cape on his back he still stunk. Everybody avoided him. The bomb shelter was poorly vented, and no matter how crowded it got, the shit-can-man had plenty of room to himself."

He smiled again. He had a weird sense of humor. "'Get in here and wash up, or you'll smell like the shit-can-man,' my mother used to say. It didn't seem like such a bad job to me. He was paid more then anyone else we knew, and I liked the idea of people staying their distance." He pondered for a minute. "I mentioned that to my mother. She told me not to even think of it, or she would disown me."

I liked to hear him talk; he had a very resonant voice and could have been a radio announcer. I was starting to like Pom, but he was strange. After a pause, he said, "I get cold at night and have a hard time sleeping."

"Don't you have a sleeping bag?" I asked, never having been in his tent.

Giving me a quizzical look, he said, "Of course."

I had only a cheap sleeping bag but was warm enough. Now, in winter, the temperature got down to 50 degrees or less at night, but only for a couple hours. It was important to keep dry in a sleeping bag.

"What do you wear to sleep in?" I asked.

Another "What kind of a dumb question is that?" look.

"Just as I am."

I now realized Pom was not out of his dirty, sweaty clothes for days, weeks or even months at a time. Water had to be hauled from town. Pom had a five-gallon bucket and was welcome to use my water but never did. Washing clothes was a difficult project and had to be done by hand with little water. Most men had a second change of clothes, so one set could air out and dry a little. He evidently didn't. I didn't dare tell him I slept in my skivvies; he would think I'm a poofter.[46]

He seemed to have withdrawn from life, existing from day to day, week to week and year to year. Why was he here? For many blokes Wallangulla was the bottom rung. The last stop. No place else to go. And his mate, Marco, whom I knew almost nothing about and saw little of; how did they come to be working together? No answers, just questions. But my thoughts were more focused on opal. I too was withdrawing into myself.

Marco came back with a checkerboard one day and left it by Pom's tent. I asked Pom if he played checkers or chess. We cut up a shovel handle and painted chess symbols on it. It was

---

46 Poofter – Homosexual

immediately evident that he was a poor chess player. I let him win the first three games and then thought it would be all right for me to win one. Through a series of clever moves, I managed to force the capture of his queen with my bishop. He stood up, hunched over, arms stiff at his side and walked around in circles, muttering, "You deliberately exchanged your bishop for my queen without cause," which is exactly what I had done, thinking it a clever move. It took a while for him to settle down.

That was the end of the chess games. I became more cautious and a bit apprehensive. He sometimes went off into the Jungle with his gun and Edward.

Then one evening after tea, while I was seated on the log sipping my last cuppa, he leaned in close and said, "I know what they're saying about me. I know they're talking about me in town. I'll get them. Just wait and see. I'll get them. I'll take care of them."

I nearly dropped my tin cup but managed to stay calm. It didn't help knowing he was a crack shot. He could easily slip over the edge and start blowing people away. I vowed that if I started to develop his symptoms – lethargy, animosity, acute withdrawal and paranoia – I would immediately head for the Big Smoke. It wasn't an urgent avowal; I would be here only another six weeks or so and was in no danger of getting the Wallies in that short time. But I must keep up my guard and stay alert. Also I must keep a close eye on the Mad Pom, and be careful what I said and did around him. When the time came, I didn't want to be in his gun sights.

Sometimes he seemed and acted like a normal person. One day I noticed a refrigerator standing some distance away in the trees.

"What on earth is that doing in the middle of the desert?" I asked curiously.

"It was here before me, and I've been here a year" he said. We got up to look at it. It was a kerosene burner, and someone had hauled it all the way out here from Sydney. Someone who was tired of roughing it and wanted to "smooth it" instead. Inside was a half-eaten tin of strawberry jam that had been opened roughly with a jackknife can opener. He stuck his finger in the can and licked it.

"That could be poisonous," I said.

"No. Jam doesn't go off. It has sugar in it."

I took his word for it but didn't try any myself. We decided to drag the refrigerator back by our tents and light it up. It held a gallon of kerosene, and, incredibly, it still worked. I was thrilled at being able to keep food cool in something larger than a canvas water bag. However, my excitement was short lived. It burned a gallon of kerosene per day. Far too expensive. Back to the canvas bag hanging from the gum tree.

For all the time Pom and I spent around the same firepit, we didn't talk much, and when we did talk, he talked to me through Edward. One night I said, interrupting his reading, "I would like to know more about opal. Are there any opal books floating around?"

"Aye, Edward. The Yank wants to know about opal," he said to Edward as though he, the dog and I were carrying on a private conversation. "Well, he wants to have a yarn[47] with the Professor, he does. That'll set him straight. We've walked past the Professor's fireplace many a time, haven't we, Edward?"

The next day I made it a point to talk to Harold Blake, a local who also had a claim on Newtown. He had a house in town and had somehow not acquired a sobriquet; he was just known as Harold Blake. He must be normal. If so, how did he end up on the Wally?

After a round of "G'day, mate, 'oweryergoin's" and "findin' any color?" I asked him about the Professor.

"Aye mate, we all know who he is but no one knows much about him. Been here a few years, I reckon, leaves for weeks at a time, doesn't puddle, seems to just poke around in old claims and noodle a bit. Doesn't need the quid and enjoys lecturing. If you ask him a question and he's had a bit to drink – 'e drinks the hard stuff – you'll find out more than you ever wanted to know. He's lectured the whole pub. Slammin' Sam[48] once threatened to throw him through the window if he didn't shut up. It's rumored that he taught at a college in Canada and was kicked out for some sexual indiscretion, whether male or female is not speculated. But

---

47 Yarn - Chat, talk

48 Slammin' Sam – Huge man. Strongest underground pick driver on the
   Wally, six feet a day. Can keep three men behind him busy just clearing,
   shoveling, hauling up and dumping

that's just rumor, not the sort of thing that a bloke would ask him about. Thinking of doin' a dig with him?"

"No. I just wanted to talk to someone who knows about opal and the history of opal mining. Life on the Wally gets quiet sometimes. Just curious, that's all."

"Aye, e's your bloke, mate. Ee's a bit of a dag[49] but 'e knows his stuff, I reckon."

---

49 Dag is the dirty wool around a sheep's rear end. It has to be cut and processed separately. The expression, bit of a dag, applies to someone who is different, interesting – usually meant as a compliment

Chapter VI
The Professor

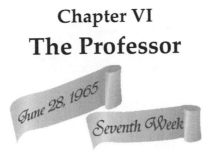

June 28, 1965

Seventh Week

There are no dung beetles in Australia. With few privies in the Outback, it's left to the annual rain to clear things up. As I started out in the general direction Pom had indicated to find the Professor, I noticed discarded toilet paper and old newspaper cluttered the ground around current and abandoned campsites. Not that it mattered much with all the discarded beer cans, but I thought that burning used toilet paper and picking up trash could easily be done by everyone. These blokes were concerned only with opal. I could hear the reply, "She'll be right,[50] mate. The rain'll clear it up. Carry on."

Brilliant sunshine by day and a sky full of bright stars at night are the Outback norm. Days are shortest in June. It was getting dark by 6 p.m. I carried my kerosene lantern and hoped the Professor had a fire I could see. After a good half hour, I came upon two men under a large bough shed next to an elaborate fireplace, sitting on chairs and playing chess on a small table. One was heavyset and wore a shabby Harris tweed jacket. That has to be him, I thought.

"G'day, mate. 'oweryer goin'," I said, in my best Outback Aussie.

He didn't look up. "What's that bird called that laughs all the time?" he said.

"What?" Why would he ask a stranger about a common, obnoxious bird? "You mean the kookaburra?" I asked, thinking he must be drunk.

"You're the Yank. I've been wondering when you'd pop by. Have a cuppa and a log. I'm just in the process of checkmating

---

50 She'll be right – Common term with various meanings: Everything will be okay. Don't worry about. Don't bother me. I'll take care of it. Whatever

Artie here. He tried Fried Liver and it didn't work against a master player like me." Artie smiled. "It's not over yet. Check."

I poured a cuppa from the billy, white, with milk in it; the way tea is served in Sydney. The stone fireplace was waist high; I didn't have to bend down. I glanced inside his large tent, piled with racks of books. I like this bloke, I thought.

"Well, that's it for me," Artie said as he laid his king over. "I have to get back to *Hamlet* and *Macbeth*. G'day." He nodded in my direction. "See you again mate."

I was pleasantly surprised – two intellectuals, playing chess and speaking the Queen's English in the middle of the Outback. The Professor got up, poured a shot of rum in my tea, did the same for himself and sat down.

"How are you getting on with Ten Pins and the Mad Pom?"

"It's iffy. I don't know Marco very well; he spends most evenings at the pub. But Pom is getting the Wallies, and I'm apprehensive about what he might do."

He nodded. "Not that unusual. Just in the time I've been here we've had two or three suicides, three or four accidental deaths and three or four murders. Archer the Cop has a hard time determining which is which. That number, out of fewer than 80 men, gives us a higher casualty rate than Vietnam. The Wally attracts men who want to get rich quick or escape from something. That's why everyone has to sign in with Archer the Cop; he checks criminal records. But there is no law against being half insane." He smiled. "One digger, after a few pints, took off his clothes, rapped on the bush nurse's door, spread out his arms and said, 'What do you think of that?' She wasn't impressed. Archer hauled him off to the insane asylum at Orange. Orange has gained many inhabitants from the Wally. Several go over the line every year. The combination of opal megalomania, poor diet, desert heat and beer can be a fatal one. Many who stop by to noodle for a weekend end up permanent residents."

He looked at me.

"I just came to Aussie on a working holiday," I said, "to see a little of the world before I settled into 40 years of teaching high school." He nodded understandingly. I continued, eager for the chance to talk to a North American after a year and a half away. "I'll be leaving in August. I worked my way to Aussie scrubbing latrines and peeling potatoes on a German freighter. We made one stop in Tahiti. I got into a conversation with two Germans on their way home after working in the mines in Aussie. They talked about Wallangulla and said if they came back again they'd try their luck at opal, so I made a mental note of this and, after six months in New Zealand and several months working in the Snowy Mountains, I stopped here for a few days on my way to visit an Aboriginal friend. I found a couple of small opals and decided to forget Arnhem Land and stay here till the end of August."

"And now you're a permanent resident."

"No, no, I'm leaving in six weeks, win or lose."

He smiled a knowing smile, and poured another shot of rum in each of our mugs. Aussies are beer drinkers. I can't keep up with them at beer, and now I'm drinking the hard stuff.

"Go ahead, ask me," he said.

I thought for a minute. The rum was already having its effect. "Well, I sought you out because you're the opal expert, and I know very little."

"Ask the other question."

I pondered this and finally said, "Why did you ask me about the name of a stupid bird?"

He smiled. "It's a game I play. I wanted to know if you were a local, a visitor or a foreigner."

"I named the bird. How did you know I was the Yank? Don't all Aussies know about the kookaburra?"

He leaned over the table, "Yes, but they pronounce it like an Aussie. It's a word that only native-born Aussies can pronounce, with the exception of a few linguists. It's a sure test, and there's no need for you to attempt Outback Aussie. Just speak Yank. It's perfectly acceptable."

I poured more tea, and he again topped it off with rum. He got up, went into his tent and came out with two books. One was about opals and the other was a book on mining opal. "Here, these will fill you in on opal. Bring them back when you're finished." Then he walked around and took on a different posture, the stance of a college professor.

"Gem quality black opal is the most beautiful of all stones," he began, as though addressing a public meeting. "Emeralds, rubies, sapphires, diamonds are all *one look* stones. Once you've had a good look at them you've seen it all. You've seen one diamond you've seen them all, so alike are they. No little hidden flashes of fire or color, no subtle surprises. It's a one-shot deal. To get someone to look at your diamond again you must mention the outrageous price you paid for it. But a gem quality black opal, like Beethoven's Ninth or Shakespeare's Hamlet, offers something new with each encounter. I have looked at my opals for years and see something different each time. Something new, something exciting."

He was walking around, gesticulating as though lecturing a class in literature and poured more rum into my tea and his.

"Opal is one of the most common stones in the world and has for centuries been cut into jewelry. Some opal, like that from the opal mines in Andamooka or Coober Pedy, comes from a whole tree that has opalized. Many have nice color but don't move when turned in the light, just lay there flat and dull. These massive chunks of rough opal are sold by the pound, sometimes by the ounce. Wallangulla opal sells by the carat, 140 carats to the ounce, a huge difference in value."

"Black opal is found only in Wallangulla. Gem quality black opal is more precious than diamond; rarer and more beautiful. It is named for the black potch under the facing colors of the gem, which causes the brilliant colors to flare out."

"Light opals found here vary in color from pale cream to milky white or clear. The latter are called jelly opals and can also be gem quality but not as valuable as the black. Opals come from siliconized seashells or bones of small animals trapped, individually or in small pockets, when the sea surged over the land and then receded."

"Emeralds are beautiful but like other gems can be made artificially. Some years back a genuine emerald could be identified by its imperfections, called garden. Synthetic emeralds did not have gardens and were easily detected, an unusual way to judge the authenticity of a stone, but now synthetic makers have learned to implant imperfections. The Spaniards brought jade and emerald from the New World but had difficulty distinguishing one from the other until someone discovered that jade could withstand a hammer blow. Trouble was the emerald was destroyed in the verification process."

"Diamonds are artificially valued," the Professor continued. "You can buy a diamond and walk down the street to another jeweler, and he will offer less than one third of what you just paid for it. An opal's value is in its beauty. The owner might be offered two or three times what he paid for it if it catches someone's fancy."

"In the 19th century, before Cecil Rhodes monopolized the market, diamonds were plentiful and cheap. The real value was industrial, for abrasives and glass cutting. When Rhodes, now DeBeers, gained a monopoly and based the number of diamonds released for sale each year on the number of wedding engagements in each country and created the tradition of diamond engagement rings, a fortune was born. Synthetic diamonds, Wellingtons and even zircons are as beautiful or more beautiful than diamonds. Still, customers who are caught up in the scam perpetuate the market. It's now tradition. A 10 year supply of diamonds is always kept in reserve so the market is not flooded. On a supply-and-demand basis, diamonds would sell for 5 or 10 dollars a carat."

He was indeed a professor, and I was quite enjoying this new information.

"The value of black opals is simply in their beauty. Price is determined in the eye of the beholder and the knowledge of the seller. They are not permanent, and, like us, will in time disintegrate, thus adding a sense of urgency to their fragile elegance. A hardness of three, as opposed to the diamond hardness of nine, makes them more vulnerable to the vicissitudes of life. Each stone is individual – cut, dome, pattern, color, size, shape, brilliance, flare – and so unique and intriguing that a miner, for the rest of his life, can identify every stone he has ever found and recall where and when he found it, and why, regretfully, he had to sell it. Opals are dug and sold daily, but every digger you meet will have a few stones in his pocket to show, not necessarily gems, but stones he favors and will keep till he's short on a quid."[51]

"Basic opal stone is called potch and can be white or black. It has no value. Potch with color may cut a mug stone, worth little.

---

51 Short on a Quid – Out of money. Broke

Next in rarity is precious opal with a variety of patterns: Pin Point
– tiny little points of color; Flake – larger patches of color; Flame –
streaks of color like fire; Flash – colors that change when stone is
turned. All of these come in different patterns, shapes and sizes,
making opal difficult to value. Every buyer will offer a different
price for the same stone. Gem quality black opal is more brilliant
and very rare. Radiants are the rarest of all."

This was fascinating. I sipped my tea slowly, trying to
remember everything, and thought the lecture was nearly over.
But no, he was just getting warmed up.

"Miners look at their finds three times a day, or more, and at
least once at night in artificial light. Some stones are fantastic in
the daylight and dead at night, and vice versa. The sun should
come over your right shoulder for the morning observation and
over the left at sunset to see the best characteristics. Each turn of
the stone gives it a different character, every angle a new look.
Black opal cannot be successfully photographed because it's a new
stone in a new light and has different colors at different angles
and must be turned and twisted to see the depths and patterns. A
backing of black potch gives the colors brilliance, hence the name
black opal, but the stones themselves are multicolored. So rare
are these that not one person in 1,000 has seen a precious opal.
And, I would guess, not one in 10,000 has seen a gem quality
black opal."

Now the Professor leaned in close and looked me right in the
eye. "But the rarest and most beautiful of all is the Radiant opal,
the most exotic, beguiling and magnificent of all gems. These are
the stones that steal men's souls. Stones that men will die for, live
for, kill for. A man with his Radiant in hand has touched the stars.
This earth will never be the same to him."

He poured us more rum and walked around distractedly,
then turned on me,

"If you find *your* stone, your Radiant opal, flashing brilliant
purples, violets, golds, reds, greens, and yellows, the prize gem
you have spent weeks, months or even years underground
searching for – *your fatal opal* – it will come to possess you and
ultimately take your soul, your life and your sanity if you do not
sell it, give it away or destroy it immediately. Immediately!" he
shouted, throwing his hands in the air.

A bit extreme, I thought, but there's no end to the superstition that surrounds opal. Was he speaking from personal experience? Did he have a Radiant in his pocket? His tent? Buried under his table? Or was it still in his imagination, waiting for him underground. I was shocked back to partial sobriety at the passion of this intellectual mind. Drink had taken its toll, his speech was becoming slurred, but he continued.

"The ancient Aboriginals feared and avoided these sparkling stones that lay on the ground and winked at them enticingly in the sunlight. They believed them to be the eyes of the half-devil, half-serpent demon, *Ooluhru*, that lives in a hole and lures men with flashing colored shafts of evil magic and has the power to dominate, control and destroy. They took great pains not to disturb or loose this beast. As legend goes, to appease him and neutralize his power, they placed a curse on anyone who disturbs Ooluhru. But now miners who covet the beast's eyes are plucking them at their own peril, flirting with the Curse of the Radiant Opal, the Scourge of Wallangulla."

I interjected, "Surely you don't believe this curse of the ancient Aboriginals has anything to do with us. This is primitive superstition." He ignored me and went on with his lecture.

"Some think of it not as a curse but as a punishment from the gods for the greed, avarice, covetousness, rapacity and lust that these stones arouse, hence the terms, *fatal opal* and *fatal stone*, used to describe the effect a Radiant opal can have on its finder. Fatal in the sense that once you yield to it, you can never escape." I wanted to question this, but couldn't get a word in.

"If you have the bad luck to find your Radiant, your fatal stone," the philosopher said with an intense look in his eye, pointing his finger directly at me – we were sitting by the open fire with stars shinning brightly over head in the clear Outback sky – "If you have the bad luck to find your Radiant, your fatal stone, you will not part with it. It may not kill you or cause your death, but it will irreparably alter your life. You will not be able to sell it, and you probably won't leave with it. Some have tried but have had to return. You *can* leave without *it*, but *it* will never leave you. Your stone will haunt you until both you and it are again united underground."

His lecture was bordering on nonsense, probably the effects of the rum, but he had my full attention and made me think. I was not sober enough to take all this seriously. He does get a bit carried away with this curse business. I could see why Slammin' Smith threatened to throw him through the pub window. The Professor was about to fall down in exhaustion, I thought. But no, he continued. His classes must have been exciting, especially if he had a couple drinks ahead of time.

"In the court of Louis XIV, opals were considered bad luck, as they were by Queen Victoria. Endless tales abound about the misfortunes caused by opals. Sir Walter Scott's novel, *Anne of Geierstein*, is one. Anne's grandmother, Hermione, possessed a Radiant opal that reflected the lady's moods: bright when happy, dull when sad and flashing when angry or excited. This opal was apprehensive near water. When after many years a drop of holy water fell on it, it shot out a brilliant spark and became dull and colorless. Hermione, at the same instant, fell to the floor in agony and died. This gave birth to the legend that a Radiant opal looses color and brilliance at the death of its owner."

"An opal is blamed for the plague of Venice that took two-fifths of the population. And King Alphonso of Spain received a magnificent opal ring as a wedding present from a former mistress, who, unbeknownst to him, was seeking revenge for being passed over. He slipped it on the finger of Mercedes, his new queen. A few months later she died of a mysterious illness. He then gave the ring to his grandmother; soon she also passed on to the eternal world. Next, to his sister who died of the same mysterious illness. His sister-in-law asked if she could wear the ring, and she also succumbed to the same fate. Finally he placed the ring on his own finger and was soon encompassed by the mysterious illness that had claimed so many of his family. Wisely, the new queen, Christina, attached the ring to a gold chain and hung it about the neck of a statue of the patron saint of Madrid, the Virgin of Alumdena, where it still may be found. Pure chance? Willed vengeance from his former lover? Bad luck? Or the dark curse?"

The Professor looked at me intensely. I made no comment, and he continued. "Pliny, the ancient Roman, said 'The opal is made up of the glories of all the most precious gems, which places it beyond description.' He goes on to relate the story of Nonius, the Roman senator who possessed what seems to have been *his fatal opal*. Mark Antony coveted this stone and offered to buy it from Nonius with the intention of presenting it to his beloved Cleopatra. Nonius adamantly refused. Mark Antony insisted and brought such pressure to bear on Nonius that Nonius fled Rome. He chose exile with his stone rather than live in the luxury of Rome without it."

"Mark Antony proceeded to Egypt without his magnificent gem and, after a year with Cleopatra, committed suicide. Was all this brought about by obsession for an opal that he had not been able to possess? Had he never seen *his fatal opal* would it all have ended differently? Would the history of the world have been altered?"

He was asking me questions I could not answer. Let one of the other students put up his hand; there must be 40 or 50 of us who can easily hear the lecturer, I imagined through my somewhat inebriated consciousness. I looked around. No, only me. I was the whole class. *Another shot of rum? No thank you, just tea for me, please.*

"And the Curse of the Radiant Opal? The Scourge of Wallangulla? I know many diggers who have mined and sold beautiful, valuable black opals with no ill effects. Fatal stone? Is there such a thing? Perhaps only in another sense, like a femme fatale. Lola Montez, the bewitching 19th century courtesan, refused an enormous sum for one night's affection from an English lord who consequently committed suicide. Was she a femme fatale? Or was he just a weak, stupid man? Few men could resist her beguiling charm, but most survived, perhaps never quite the man they were before having met her, but survived never the less."

His arms were waving, hands opening and closing. I was entranced. "Is this what happens with the enticing, seductive, beguiling, enchanting Radiant black opal? A man would rather die than part with it? I have not met the digger who could resist the allure of his black opal gemstone – to hold it, to own it, to possess it; not Radiants, just high-quality gems." He paused again. "The beautiful flashing colors are captivating and enchanting but are not fatal. If a digger regretfully has to sell his favorite gem, it doesn't kill him. He goes on digging, hoping to find another. Can he survive parting with it? Yes, perhaps in an altered state, not quite the man he was, but able to move on."

"But the Radiant grabs a man's soul and will not let go. The fatal opal. The stone that changes a digger's life, permanently. Does the opal, the vulnerability of the man, or the curse cause this?" He was gesticulating wildly, walking around the large rock fireplace. "The one stone. The stone he can't part with or live without. The stone that haunts him forever? Yes, there is such a stone. But is there a curse? Or is this a silly superstition used as an excuse for uncontrollable emotions?" He looked into my eyes. "The decision is yours. Take care!"

He sat down with his head in his hands. The lecture was over, and I realized I wouldn't make it stumbling through the Jungle back to camp. After some time he looked up. "I'll drive you home." Anywhere else I would refuse this offer and sleep on the ground. But here there's nothing to run into except a few trees. Once past them it didn't matter if you were on the road or not. The desert is flat for hundreds of miles.

He staggered some but once seated in his old, dented Land Rover, following my directions, he maneuvered the long way around back to my camp, staying on the road much of the time.

We made it. Edward gave one small bark. I crawled out of the Rover, mumbled "Ta," stumbled into my tent and fell onto my cot.

Chapter VII
Wally Justice

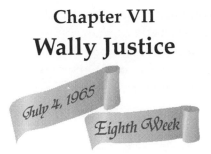

"No use looking for the Yank, Edward. He had a yarn with the Professor last night. He won't be rapping his billy 'til after noon. Walk softly."

Marco laughed. The Odd Mates were up. I heard them build a fire and make tea, but I had no desire to get up. My head ached, and my body hurt all over. Had I been that tense? I dropped off to sleep again. God only knows how long. Then, when I finally awoke and had a cuppa, I sharpened a pencil with my penknife and proceeded to write down everything the Professor had told me.

It all rang true, but I still had doubts. Is there such a thing as a fatal stone? Was the Professor speaking from personal experience? What brought him here? Why does he stay? Has he found his fatal stone? Is there a Curse of the Radiant opal? Two-Bob Bobby, Hungry Hank the Hatter and the Goat Colonel all have valuable stones they won't sell! Are these fatal opals? Do their stones possess them? Will they die of rapaciousness, consumed by greed? Am I susceptible? Will I end up like those three, unable to feed myself but unwilling to part with my opals?

No, I am not superstitious! I didn't believe any of this, no matter how much it had permeated my thinking. Only those who are weak and greedy are susceptible to the Curse. I appreciate the beauty of opal and want to acquire many stones, a fortune if possible, and keep a few nice ones. But a fatal stone? A stone that I would die for rather than part with? No. Impossible. Besides, it's already July, and I have only six weeks left. Get to work or you'll go back to Yank land with nothing but a pick and shovel.

Most of the day was gone. I had only a couple hours left to puddle, half-heartedly, and was back in camp before the Odds returned.

"Well, Edward, you'll have to go along next time. You've never heard the Prof's lecture or tasted the hard stuff he gives out to his students," said Pom. Edward wagged his tail.

Okay, I was not the only one to have heard the Prof's lecture. Most of the pub regulars were familiar with the Prof's ranting.

"He gives diggers something to think about," Marco said. "If they can't get him to shut up, the discussion goes on for hours. Good for beer sales. Sarah should hire him to come in twice a week, but sooner or later Slammin' Sam – after too many pints – will throw him through the window."

After three weeks of digging in the Slav claim, now the Yank's Dig, I had found nothing. Not even a nobby. Puddling yielded only a couple of mug stones, not enough to buy food. I was spending what little money I had left. I bought a 12-volt generator, thinking a string of light bulbs was better than candles. Wrong. Too noisy and too expensive. Electrical surges kept blowing out the bulbs. Back to the candles.

Day by day my knowledge increased but not my wisdom. I had the blacksmith sharpen my two small picks for scraping the top foot of opal clay, where the nobbies are located. After roughly digging out the bottom three feet with my driving pick to a depth of six inches, I carefully sliced away at the top foot. With sharp picks you slice a bit off the nobby without breaking it. Many stories are told of valuable pockets of opal ruined and smashed by an enthusiastic pick man, but so far I hadn't found any opal to ruin.

The blacksmith had a puddler standing off from his outdoor forge. "Your puddler for sale?" I asked.

"Not mine, mate. Bloke left it in my safekeeping 10 years ago."

"After that long he's probably not coming back. You could sell it."

"Reckon I can't do that, mate. Not mine. I'll let it stay till he sorts out what he's up to."

"What d'ya reckon it's worth?" I persisted.

"Probably 25 quid or so. You paid way too much for yours. The Mad Pom and the King lurked[52] you, I reckon."

I was surprised and disturbed by this revelation. This news no doubt came from the pub. After a few pints, everything is

---

52 Lurked – Cheated

divulged. My private life was known to blokes I had never met. So Pom and King Tut couldn't wait to tell about buggering[53] the Yank. I could hear him say "Aye, we really ginked[54] the Yank that time, didn't we, Edward?"

By the second week of July, I had about a month left to go. When I find my pocket of nobbies, we'll see who laughs, I thought. How many are in on this? Marco? Shadow? The Bingos? Chuck the Cutter? Have your laugh. It's not over yet.

I needed a lunch with Two-Bob Bobby. Next day I found him outside the pub as usual and invited him in for a pint and a pie. Two pints. I had to clear my mind and talk of other things. I realized I knew nothing about Two-Bob, where he came from, why he was here or where he was camped.

"How long have you been on the Wally, mate?"

"Ten years, I reckon."

"Before that?"

"Spent a bit o' time as a jackaroo[55] Back o' Burke.[56] Then did some shearin'. She's a right life, mate, humping me bluey from station to station, followin' the season." He looked up at me. "I never was a swagman or a sundowner.[57] The Bingos started that story. I was a shearer, mate, a shearer."

Bobby usually had a pleasant, almost happy, expression, not mean or angry. But when he mentioned the Bingos, it changed to a dark troubled look, and he put his hand on the shirt pocket that

---

53 Buggering – Cheating

54 Ginked – Cheated

55 Jackaroo – Ranch hand

56 Back o' Burke is the desolate Outback that makes the Mojave look like the garden of Eden. Also referred to as Behind the Black Stump

57 Swagmen are blokes who tramp across the country with a few possessions carried on their back in a swag, a bag. They manage to arrive at stations (ranches) looking for work but hoping to avoid it by getting there after the shearing season. Their way of life, moving from place to place carrying a swag, is called Waltzing Matilda as in the song. It's also referred to as humping the bluey or on the wallaby. The law of ten, ten and two (ten pounds flour, ten pounds bully beef, two pounds salt) requires the station owner to provide them with enough provisions to tramp on to the next station. Sundowners are a little more sophisticated and often arrive by automobile late in the workday, also looking for work; but after a good evening meal are off the next morning before anyone awakes

held his stones. I was getting to like Bobby, and this troubled look worried me.

I changed the subject. "On the 500 mile drive up here from Sydney, I drove at night to avoid the hot weather. From time to time I noticed little glows that almost looked like fires way off in the barren desert. Was someone out there?"

"Them's the Abos.[58] They go walkabout and live off the land. Doesn't look like anything fit to eat out there, but she's right for them. They build a little saltbush fire, mate, and are all over it. They laugh at the white man who builds a huge fire and stands back away from it. It's their land. They live out there with nothing and love it."

I wanted to ask him where he camped and what he thought about the Curse of the Radiant Opal. While I pondered how to say this, a big bloke at the bar started shouting and waving his arms.

"Someone ought to shoot that bloody bastard," he said. "I'd like to blow his head off myself." Sarah, the publican's wife, tried to quiet him.

"Calm down now, Niggly. You're not going to blow anyone's head off. Fair go, mate."[59] He stood there looking angry, but he stopped shouting.

"What's he on about?" I asked Jake the Wasp at the next table.

"That's Niggly Neville. He's always on about something. That's how he earned his name. He just heard about Cocky[60] Bowman's dog. Cocky had a dog that didn't follow his car like the rest of his dogs when he went off to tend his sheep. He drives 30, 40 miles an hour across the desert sand. They have to follow or get the strap. This new dog just quit and went back to the house and lay down. Got the strap good, she did. Two days in a row. Cocky told us the story, right here in the pub. 'The third day I drove back, tied a rope around her neck and connected her to the back bumper. She followed. Followed all day she did.' He laughed when he told us this. 'Set an example for the rest of 'em. Wasn't much left of 'er but they saw me dig a hole and put 'er under. Got the message, they

---

58 Abo – a frequently used but derogatory term for Aborigines
59 Fair go – Calm down, be reasonable
60 Cocky – Farmer, rancher

did.' He laughed again. 'I won't have a worthless dog or any other critter chowin' me tucker[61] without doing his job.'"

"When did this happen?"

"He told us about it couple days ago, laughing all the time. The diggers thought that was no way to treat a dog; but it's his dog. He's the stationmaster out from Collarenebri. Tends 20,000 sheep. He has a reputation of being cruel with animals, but he overdid it this time. This got to blokes who don't even like dogs."

"I know Niggly. 'E'll blow Cocky's head off," Two-Bob said quietly.

"No, he's just letting off steam," Jake said. "He and Cocky usually get on fine. This'll pass." Two-Bob said no more.

"Why doesn't Niggly report him?" I asked.

"To who? For what?" Jake seemed puzzled at the naivety of my question. "It's up to the station owner, and he's right with it. His dogs, his station. How's a bloke like Niggly, who can hardly stand his shout, going to tell him how to run things."

Niggly was carrying on but no longer yelling. "That's no way to treat a working animal. No reason to act like that. He's a cruel man and deserves to be..." His voice trailed off. There were murmurs of "hear, hear" and mumbles of agreement.

I said "Ta" to Two-Bob and returned to my claim, glad to get away from the din of the pub.

A few days later as I was boiling my evening stew, the Odds came back to camp. "It was a terrible accident, terrible," Marco said as they got out of the pickup.

"Well, Edward, did he deserve it? Did he get what was coming to him? You're lucky not to be Cocky's sheep dog. Or a sheep," Pom said laughing. Edward danced around as always, awaiting something that never happened.

"It was an accident," Marco repeated. "I saw them drinking together and laughing all night. Niggly agreed that dogs have to obey. They left together, arm in arm, both drunk, to shoot some 'roo[62] that Gunther the Kraut had seen on Shearers Rush, just past Thorley's Six Mile. Niggly felt awful. He said the gun went off accidentally. They spotted the troop of 'roos, and he jumped

---

61 Tucker – Food

62 Roo – Kangaroo

out of the truck pulling his gun with him. It must have caught on the seat or something and went off, hitting Cocky in the head. He was dead immediately. Terrible accident."

"What do you think, Edward?" Pom asked. "Should he be shot for dragging a dog to death?"

"Is Archer the Cop going to arrange a trial?" I asked, finding this all a bit bizarre.

"No. Archer said it was obviously an accident, and he'll report it as such."

"But I heard Niggly threaten to blow Cocky's head off. Isn't that exactly what he did?"

"Niggly has a temper and gets in blueys after a few pints, but he's not violent. He'd never shoot anyone. A dozen diggers all agreed that it was an accident. Niggly said he was sorry. That's it. It's over."

That was the end of it. Outback justice. Two Bob-Bobby knew Niggly would keep his word, as did others. Many felt the same as Niggly about Cocky Bowman's cruelty to dogs and probably would have shot him themselves. Australia had been the dumping ground for England's criminals, some given life sentences for stealing a loaf of bread. Aussies remember what law did to their ancestors. They know that law brings lawyers and lawyers bring injustice. Outbackers don't care much for law or lawyers.

Later Harold Blake told me the story. "Cocky never had any mates. He was a drongo,[63] ruthless with animals and tough on drovers. Nobody liked him. Archer the Cop discussed the case around the horseshoe bar with 10 or 12 of us. Niggly was the only witness. He had tears in his eyes."

"'We had a few pints too many and decided to shoot a few 'roo. Gunter had seen a herd on Shearers Rush. We were dodging between the mullock heaps on Thorley's Six Mile when I spotted 'em, 40 or 50, I reckon. I stopped, grabbed my rifle and jumped out. It was awful. It just went off and hit Cocky in the head. Awful. He died instantly. Nothing I could do.' He put his head in his hands. We all agreed, after a few pints shouted by Archer himself, that it was an unfortunate accident. Niggly was innocent."

Archer's report simply stated "accidental death by shooting." Justice served. Case closed.

---

63 Drongo – Less than human.

Chapter VIII
Learning About The Wally

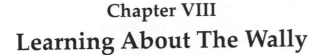

July 15, 1965

Ninth Week

"Cut off whatever they bite, mate — finger, toe, foot, hand — without giving it a thought. Our snakes are the most poisonous in the world, and you've got only a few seconds to act. Death is imminent if you don't." This advice came from Jimmy the Snake Catcher, who should know. He's lacking one forefinger at the knuckle. Good advice. Very disturbing. Hope I don't ever have to use it.

"Knock out your boots and shake your underwear," he continued, "a scorpion bite is very painful, and bull ants can get you twice." Scorpions like to crawl in boots and underwear for some reason. Bull ants, two inches long, have jaw pincers and tail stingers. Cut in half, they bite and sting themselves.

"Those cute little six-inch long red and silver centipedes have poison sacs in their small delicate legs. Brush them off you the same way they're crawling, or the legs will bite into your skin and poison you."

"Hourglass spiders, like black widow spiders, are poisonous but usually not deadly. They don't come looking for trouble; they stay in their own web waiting for dinner to come to them. But the brown recluse is deadly."

I rarely saw snakes, and it's easy to forget they exist. But you have to stay alert. One night I got up to relieve myself and, not owning a flashlight, nearly stepped on a black snake with my bare feet. He was sluggish on this cool night, and I dispatched him with a shovel. How close was I to losing a toe? Or a foot? Or my life? I became more vigilant.

Wallangulla is about 500 miles from either Sydney or Brisbane. Ninety percent of Aussies live within 100 miles of the seacoast. Beyond that, the Outback stretches for thousands of miles. Aussie is rich in minerals: gold, silver, mica, iron ore and opals. Mining many of these minerals is open to the public. Mining areas are often located on stations (ranches), some of which are larger than Rhode Island. The Wallangulla designated mining area is about 35-by-5 miles of land that can be claimed, 100 feet square per digger, and mined by anyone who is willing to pay ten bob ($1.15) for a miner's right and another 10 bob for a registered claim. The miner can use the land as needed, cut trees for firewood and mining, dig as necessary and have access to water if there is any, but he must not interfere with the station's sheep, cattle, goats, dogs, or horses, which can sometimes be a nuisance.

The number of miners varies. During good economic times there are few; in bad times many. The number of residents, town and camping, is probably 50 to 60, but some say 100. The pub is the center of Outback life, much like churches in the settling of the American West. The first thing the Americans did was to build a church. For Aussies it was the pub. There is no church in Wallangulla. The Digger's Retreat, where most worshiping goes on, is located at the end of the main street. Forty years earlier an anti-cyclone wiped out the other end. After 1,000 or so miners left, it was not rebuilt. The few who stayed managed to find enough opal to keep from starving. Then little by little the numbers increased until once again it is a community with a few families living in rough houses. No plumbing.

The government sunk a 3,300 foot bore well a mile out on the Collarenebri Highway. Anyone can use the hose hanging from a pole to fill tanks or buckets. At the bore site is a pool available for dipping, but the water is so hot you can stay in only a few minutes. The artesian well water comes out of the ground at 190 degrees. With no humidity, sweat evaporates immediately and clothes don't get drenched.

Australia is heavily governed. Few decisions are left to individuals. Hundreds of kangaroos are shot and skinned, their bodies left to rot. Some egg producers drag the carcasses home and let the chickens feed on them. The yolks of these eggs are blood red and taste terrible. I went to a local cocky who raises chickens with the intention of buying eggs directly from him; he feeds them chicken feed. But he can't sell to individuals. All eggs must be sold through the government. The producer is not even allowed to put his name on the carton. The buyer gets potluck. This negates caveat emptor.

To ship an item from Sydney to Walgett by rail takes three days. One day by air. But an item shipped by air cannot arrive faster than it would by rail, so the airline has to hold it up for two days before delivering it. It's considered unfair competition for air service to be quicker, even though the government owns and controls both rail and air. The privately owned airline, Ansett ANA, is profitable while the government airline loses money. Private companies making a profit go against the socialist grain. When I worked on the Khancoban Dam project for Kaiser Engineers, the government inspectors said, "Kaiser's made a lot of money on the Adaminaby Dam. We are here to see that doesn't happen again." Socialism.

The price of petrol in Wallangulla is the same as in any major Australian city; it's unfair to charge more, even though the petrol has to be hauled 500 miles farther. This ultimately hurts everybody. It's about control, not fairness or equality. Fortunately, on the Wally, individuals still had the right to do something stupid and kill themselves if they chose to.

Rabbits, imported from England, had no natural predators in Australia and overran the country. After years of fencing, shooting, poisoning and trapping, their numbers declined somewhat. The Mad Pom ran over one, skinned it, gutted it, and boiled it in the billy for a full day. We ate it. Wasn't bad. Had just one broken leg.

Most of the time life was pleasant, quiet and peaceful, so I was surprised when Edward's barking and running around woke me up. I got up and lit my lantern to see what was going on. He had his head turned sideways, biting the quills off an echidna that was digging himself straight down into the hard clay. Aussie dogs have learned to chew off the quills rather than bite straight into them. The echidna, a small, quilled animal similar to a porcupine was digging straight down while flat on his belly.

Pom also got up. Having been through all this before, he tied Edward to the gum tree. We dug around the echidna, pried him out and managed to get a loop of rope around this strong, determined little animal. I tied the other end of the rope to a shovel handle and, holding the echidna out the car window, hauled him a mile away to let him run free. This happened several times. If Edward had learned not to bark, he could have had supper on the hoof.

The Odds made fun of the Yank in the pub, but they treated me like a mate from time to time. I even liked them, despite Pom's deceiving me on the puddler and Shadow's misinformation on the opal. One day Marco said, "Want to go fishing?"

"Sure."

Off we went in Pom's pickup. No poles. No lines. No hooks. There are no rivers near the Wally, and the swamp-like billabongs often contain no water. But we were going fishing. Fine!

Rain is torrential when it comes. I had heard that the water doesn't soak into the hard red clay but runs off forming pools and even creeks for a few days, weeks or even months. We arrived at one of these pools about 100 feet long and 20 feet wide, the remains of a creek. Marco took a roll of chicken wire out the pickup and unrolled it. We pulled it through the water from one end of the pool to the other, gathering up all the fish. There were a lot of them. We picked through them, selecting the good ones and throwing the rest back. None looked familiar to me. What a way to fish! Beats stringing worms on hooks and sitting in a boat all day like we do in Minnesota. I was impressed but couldn't help thinking about natural selection. We had taken all the good eating fish and left only the undesirable to reproduce.

We were on station land. I noticed a calf, stuck in the mud that was obviously starving the death. "We have to pull him out," I said. "He'll die if we don't."

"No. It's not our calf. It'll look like we're going to steal it."

"But it will starve to death."

"No, we'll just get into trouble if we get caught."

In the States no one would give this a second thought. Just do the right thing and save the calf. Finally I said "Look, I'll take the blame if we get caught. I'll say I did it alone."

They didn't like the idea, but we got a rope out of the pickup, tied it to the calf and pulled him out of the mud. It saved the calf's life.

Back at camp we gutted and scaled the fish. I built a hot gumwood fire and put a generous chunk of lard in the cast iron frying pan. Marco dipped each fish in egg and flour and fried them in the hot lard. What a delightful meal! I hadn't tasted fish in months. Another pleasant culinary surprise was the arrival of a bloke who came around twice a week in his minivan, selling fresh vegetables, potatoes, carrots, chockos – more variety than at the local general store. Where he got the veggies and how he found us, I do not know.

The center of camp life is the fire. I always had a pile of firewood cut, both gumwood and sandalwood. My chore. I didn't mind. Wood was plentiful. Sitting by the fire calms all anxieties, soothes all forebodings and gives complete relaxation. The exception occurs when a wayward breeze blows smoke at you relentlessly, no matter how often you move. But for the most part the Outback air is still and quiet, broken only by the clatter of a frill-neck lizard going after a scampering insect. Here I wrote letters, kept in touch with the outside world, telling my friends about life in the Outback and the pursuit of opal.

Cleanliness is not of prime importance in the Wally. Having been brought up among Norwegians in Minnesota where cleanliness was mandatory, I regularly heated water in my billy, poured it in a hand basin and took sponge baths with a washcloth and soap. This reminded me of the old Minnesota farm joke about the woman who told her doctor that people said she stunk. Her house didn't have running water so she used a basin. Putting the basin on the floor she washed up as far as possible. Then placing the basin on the table she washed down as far as possible. "And still they say I stink," she said. The doctor thought for a moment and said, "Go home and wash possible."

I let my beard grow. It was quite long and had to be washed regularly or it gave off a musty smell. I tried to wash my underwear once a week, pants and thin shirt less frequently, all by hand. Cleanliness became less important as I became more acclimated.

My life was the same day to day. Days were getting a little longer now in mid-July. The sun set a little after 6 p.m., and it was dark by 6:30, not much time to puddle after coming up out of my claim, but I still came away with 20 or 30 nobbies each day. After a meal of three-day-old stew and a cuppa, I dumped the nobbies on the ground, lit my kerosene lantern and snipped the hard white lumps, which were no larger than a half dollar. I snipped first around the edges, carefully just in case, then deeper into the center, looking for color. Sometimes I uncovered a lump of black potch. Snip, snip. That, too, was valueless without color. Finding nothing, I finally snipped the whole nobby in two to make sure. My luck at puddling was not good. I found a few mug stones that Chuck the Cutter handed back to me without comment. I had done better just noodling. At least the two stones I found noodling had character. I sold the mugs to Hairy Hutchen for a few quid.

After snipping I spent the rest of the evening reading, writing letters or walking with my lantern to visit the Professor. Some distance off I announced myself, "Kookaburra," if I saw a fire. "Ah, the Yank," he said with a laugh. If he was in camp he was usually reading, but he was often gone. We became friends, never mates. I already had heard his lecture so we played chess or talked about Schopenhauer or Dickens. He was good company and enriched my life. Marco was always at the pub. My only other associate was Pom and, as the Professor said, if it weren't for Edward, Pom would be speechless.

Chapter IX

Bernie Intimidates Two-Bob Bobby

July 21, 1965

Tenth Week

For four weeks I dug day after day, finding nothing. Not a single nobby. Not even a mug stone. I didn't do much better puddling, just three mug stones that I sold for a total of 15 quid, enough for food for a couple weeks, but not enough to cover my modest expenses. I moved the puddler to a new mullock every few days. I thought, "Is this just bad luck, or am I doing everything wrong? Is anyone else doing as poorly as I am?"

Only a few of us were digging new ground. Harold Blake, also on Newtown, the field on a gentle slope near the pub, was one, but he was local. He had made a big hit years back, bought a house in town and could afford to explore. But me? Time and money were running out. I had to leave in mid-August, one month away, to catch the P & O ship back to the States in time for the fall semester. I'd have to send home for money if I didn't hit pay dirt soon.

Whether you eat tomorrow depends on your luck today. Pursuing black opal is an obsession, a madness filled with hope and expectation that makes everything else unimportant. But "not to worry," as the Aussies say. "Still plenty 'o time, and with a bit 'o luck she'll be right, mate."

My main drive now extended more than 20 feet from the shaft, and I had to hang a windsock to pull down fresh air. Mining is hard but not backbreaking work. Picking, shoveling, windlassing up and dumping makes a man fit. The buckets of waste weighed 125 pounds. I lifted and dumped them with little effort. I was now strong, like most diggers, felt good, and carried not an ounce of fat.

The work is routine, tedious, and automatic. To pass the time in silence underground I called upon my four years of music study while in college in St. Paul, Minnesota. Who did I want with me underground? Mozart is good anywhere anytime. His music appeals to everyone, learned or not, and is all joy. Mozart liked life and would have fit right in here. "C'mon, mate. Let's have a pint and smoke a Dr. Pat." I mentally replayed his choral music.

Bach's counterpoint is too complex for the simple Outback life. Palestrina and Monteverdi are too esoteric. Haydn would have worked, but I didn't have enough of him in my head. Beethoven, the greatest of all, was too ponderous. Even the *Fourth Symphony*, the gentle Greek Goddess – situated between the Norse Giants, *Eroica* and the *Fifth* – was too unwieldy to carry down the shaft. *The Choral Ninth* that I had sung joyously is too laborious. "You've made your point, Ludwig; now ease up a bit. We're only mortals." Mahler and Wagner, two of my favorite composers, were out of the question. The horns and trumpets alone would crash the walls down. The passion of Verdi? Yes! What better than the slave chorus from *Nabucco*? "Val pensierro," I sang, accompanied in my head by the Minneapolis Symphony.

While pondering composers hour after hour, I finally perceived the one who belongs here, underground in the Outback, pursuing the elusive opal: Hector Berlioz, that arrogant, proud, self-centered, self-righteous early 19th century French composer. By pure chance, or maybe divine intervention, I had been assigned to analyze his *Fantastic Symphony* as my senior project.

Berlioz fell in love with a Shakespearean actress, Harriet Smithson, who was playing Ophelia. She wisely rejected his advances several times. His ego was wounded. He wrote the *Fantastic Symphony* to tell of this rejection, and placed his story of the rebuffed lover on each seat in the theater. She heard the symphony, was overwhelmed, relented and married him; only to find out he was really in love not with her but with her character, Ophelia. They soon parted.

This was his greatest work. In my opinion, once his passion was dissipated his compositions suffered. An orchestra of 1,000 instruments was his desired size, roughly the size of his ego. But his obsession was similar to my opal obsession.

The *Fantastic Symphony* contains an l'idee fixe, a fixed idea. This theme of the beloved one recurs in each of the five movements, but in a different disposition each time, lessening as the beloved one becomes more distant. No matter how beautiful the music, the fixed idea stomps into each movement and takes over. An obsession. In the developmental section Berlioz intermingles the stated subject throughout the orchestral instruments in half time, double time, upside down and backward, milking every subtlety to offer full comprehension to the listener. But the fixed idea swamps it all, leaving that obsession fixed in your mind rather than the beautiful music.

A digger lives in the physical world, but the pursuit of opal is dominant, his reason for living. All thoughts and actions become subservient to this pursuit. If he finds his fatal opal, it bankrupts his life and leaves no room for anything else. Some diggers are quietly possessed and live secretly with their fatal stones.

I took Hector Berlioz, the megalomaniac, underground with me, the perfect companion. He understood obsession. I went over the *Fantastic Symphony* in my head, day after day, note-by-note, hearing all other themes shot down by the obsessive fixed idea. The happy waltz in the second movement has dark, ominous undertones, rightly so – there's no escaping the obsession – and this whole movement succumbs to the interloping fixed idea.

I was after opal. Obsessively. Compulsively. Urgently. Compellingly. Berlioz understood obsession and portrayed it musically. That was a comfort to me. We worked together, Hector and me, both slightly mad.

One evening, desiring the company of someone a little more rational, I returned the books to the Professor, always a pleasant walk, even by lantern. He wasn't at camp, and his tent flap was tied securely. I took the liberty of letting myself in and browsed through his library of books. Why would a man with this much knowledge choose to live in a tent in the Outback? A good place to ponder life without the clutter of civilization? A hankering for solitude? Was he writing a book? Or, God forbid, had he found his fatal stone and was now under the curse of the half-devil, half-serpent demon of Wallangulla? I selected a volume of Schopenhauer and *The Count of Monte Cristo*, left a note, retied the flap and sauntered back to camp.

I looked forward to lunches with Two-Bob Bobby, always a pleasant occasion. He and the Professor were the only two people on the Wally I knew well enough to talk, relax and feel comfortable with. How much he got to eat depended on how many tourists came to the pub and felt sorry for him. He was skinny, small and frail and had a noticeable limp, but he was always smiling. As his donors found out, one glimpse of his stones was worth the price of a pork pie and a pint.

The horseshoe bar at the Diggers Retreat could stand 15 blokes easily. Several standees' tables for up to five or six blokes took up most of the rest of the large room. The ladies' tables with chairs were in the far corner. Ladies were not allowed to stand at the bar or at the tables. Sarah wouldn't have it. They sat and were served. If she lowered the standards, where would it all end? But the few ladies who lived in town, a half-dozen or so, didn't spend the day in the pub.

Bobby and I found a table, and I nodded to Sarah. She brought us two pints, a new beer for Two-Bob and a middy[64] for me, and two meat pies. A middy is half new and half old beer. Sarah remembered what every digger drank and was able to pick up seven glasses from a mob's table and keep them in the proper order, bringing each digger back the same glass with the right beer in it. I never mastered the variety of glasses and beers available in Aussie: ponies, schooners, middies, butchers, handles, fives, sevens, pints. In a pinch I just pointed at someone's glass and said, "I'll have what he's drinking."

Bobby's smile was strained today. He was pleasant but troubled. It occurred to me that I didn't know anything about his current life: where he was camped, if he had any mates, if he got enough to eat, how far the walk to the pub. He looked up after a drink of his pint. "'E's after me stones. 'E's a drongo, Bernie is." There's that term again, a word rarely used, carefully saved up to describe the worst rotter a bloke can know. Jake the Wasp used it to describe Cocky Bowman. Now Two-Bob Bobby used it to describe Bernie Bingo.

"'Just like to 'ave a yarn,'[65] 'e said. 'Meet yer at the café.' I

---

64 Middy, new, old – designate the type of beer
65 Just want to talk

'aven't had a bit of café tucker[66] in months. So I went. Nice bit o' tucker it was, too, styke 'n eggs 'n chips. 'E 'ad a bottle, gave me a nip o' whiskey. I was feeling top on it when 'e asked to see me stones. I said 'no.' 'Just a quick glance,' 'e said. I've 'eard so much about 'em. Just curious for a look.' 'No,' I said, and got up to go. 'Then pay for your own bloody tucker, Bludger,' and grabbed me arm. Lenny (the café's proprietor) said 'Let 'im go, Bernie. You invited 'im, you pay.' I said, 'Good on yer, Lenny' and made for the door. 'E's after me, wants me stones, 'e does. Lookin' 'ere right now."

I saw Bernie at the bar, eyes on us. He was a heavy-jowled, pudgy man, out of place in the midst of lean, muscular diggers. I smiled, wanting to let him know Bobby was my friend, without offending him. Who else could I sell opals to?

"Not to worry, Bobby, she'll be right," I said, but I was unsure how I could help.

Opal, not intrigue, was my goal. I just wanted to dig. The Bingos were a nasty pair with far more power and influence than I had. I could threaten to physically beat the tar out of Bernie if he didn't lay off Bobby, but that would have little effect. One of his mates would call me out.

I ordered another pie and pint for Bobby and said, "G'day, mate, I have to get back to the underworld," and left. As I walked up the hill to Newtown, I heard a puffing sound behind me.

Fat Bernie caught up with me. "He really should sell those stones, starving as he is. He could have a comfortable life with what I'd pay for them, and I've never even seen them. They're top, I hear."

I nodded in agreement wondering what I was getting involved in. This Bernie was different from the one who degraded my stones. Now he was obsequious. "Anything you can do to help would be greatly appreciated," he told me. "Quite a few quid involved here." He smiled conspiratorially, gave me a quick, knowing pat on the shoulder and went puffing down the hill.

Repulsive. A drongo to be sure. Shadow, Marco, Pom, Chuck the Cutter and others – all Bernie's mates – were in on the cut. Bobby had a ruthless con man after his stones, and now I was in it. I really just wanted to dig.

---

66 Tucker - food

Chapter X
Goat Colonel Visits The Queen

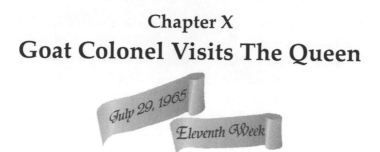

July 29, 1965
Eleventh Week

A few days later we were having a pint and a pie, Two-Bob Bobby and me, when the Goat Colonel marched in dressed in his army uniform, tie and all. I had seen him before only in dirty shorts. Standing erect, he laid a five-pound note on the bar and said, "Beer for the house. Drinks are on me, gentlemen. The Queen has called me home." This caught everyone's attention, although no one crowded around him; he stunk nearly as bad as the Skinner. "Hear, hear," a few murmured, raising their pints. Sarah had a puzzled look on her face, but the money was on the bar so she went along with the joke, if it was a joke, and busily filled glasses with beer.

"He's really got the Wallies," Old Sam the Bot[67] said at the next table. "I always thought he was a little bonkers, but a free pint is a free pint."

"Gentlemen, I give you the Queen," the Colonel said as he raised his pint. We all smiled and toasted the Queen, wondering what the Colonel was on about.

"The Queen has called for an inspection of my regiment. I must drill them. Time is short." Then he slammed his empty glass on the bar, called the entire pub to attention in his military voice, and saluted. We all returned the salute. He marched out the door like a commanding officer and was gone.

"Archer will have him off to Orange before the week is out," Wild Denny said.

"He seems harmless enough. Didn't have his rifle," Brady offered.

Speculation continued, good-natured for the most part. After all, the Colonel did shout the pub.

---

67 Bot – A drinker who can't stand his shout but always manages to stay drunk

Bobby said, quietly, "You won't see 'im again. 'E's on 'is death march." Then, after a pause, "Not to worry, mate; she'll be right."

I went back to my claim and didn't think much more about it.

Three days later the Odd Mates pulled up in Pom's pickup. I was lying on my side, snipping nobbies by lantern light. Marco said, without directly looking at me, "The Goat Colonel went walkabout last week. Told the pub blokes he was off to see the Queen. Nobody thought much about it. He had the Wallies, but who doesn't?"

"We don't, do we Edward?" Pom interjected, looking at his puzzled dog and smiling. "We don't go walkabout without water."

Marco continued. "Roo hunters found him 25 miles out, stiff at attention, laid out on the sand two miles off the Collarenebri Highway. They told Archer the Cop. They brought in what was left of him, dried out in the sun. His fist was closed tight. Bernie had to pry it open with a screwdriver to get the stone out. I had seen it once, a large, irregular-shaped, flat black gem with a beautiful violet and green rolling flash, worth a small fortune. Bernie was eager to get his hands on it. He and Archer pried the fingers back one by one. Bernie had been trying to buy this stone for years. Now he finally got it out of the Colonel's grasping fist, only to find it colorless. Worthless. Once it was a valuable gemstone Now it's nothing. The rolling flash was still visible but no color. Bernie cussed and threw it, just flung it down the street. Wombat retrieved it, laughing at the disgusted look on Bernie's face. 'He gave the stone life,' Archer said 'and the stone took his life. Queer things these opals.' They say that when the finder dies, the stone goes pale," Marco explained. "Maybe from lack of warmth, is one theory, but no one knows."

My thought was maybe only fatal opals die when the owner dies. "Was he going to walk all the way to Walgett?" I asked.

"Nobody knows. He was getting crazier all the time. Someone said he's been living on bread and treacle for the past month. But he didn't sell his opal. Bernie waylaid him several times, but the Colonel wouldn't sell. Wouldn't even talk about it. Just shook his head and walked off. He'd rather starve to death. Strange character. I can believe the goat story."

I surmised the Odd Mates could never have a fatal opal. Lack of passion? Desire? Joy? And the Goat Colonel? I never got close enough to smell him, never talked to him. Don't know if he had a mate. Probably not. Don't know when or where he found his stone, but he died with it. He died with his fatal Radiant opal, and his stone died with him. This touched me. Something about it seemed right, just and honorable. He's gone. His opal's gone. Another suicide, another story to be pondered over a pint of bitters.

That won't happen to me, I thought. I'm not going walkabout without water, clutching my stone. I don't even own a stone that's worth clutching, but I do carry my stones with me and look at them several times a day, never tiring of their beauty.

Next morning as I arrived at my claim, I saw a half-dozen diggers in white shirts on the Diggers Final Shaft, the local graveyard, situated on a slight rise 100 yards north of the Diggers Retreat. White shirts! I haven't seen a white shirt in months. The Colonel should have been buried yesterday.

"G'day mate, 'oweryagoin'. See that white sheet on the pile of dirt? That's the Colonel." Harold Blake had seen my puzzled look and came over to talk. I could barely make the body out, off to one side of where they were digging. "That's the Goat Colonel," Harold said. "'E won't get planted today, I reckon." I gave him a puzzled look. He laughed. "The diggers hit potch and color at four feet and kept goin', hopin' to hit a pocket. I had a look in this mornin', they were close to eight feet deep then. The Colonel ain't preserved, should have been under yesterday. 'E stunk like a dag[68] when he went walkabout. Yer ought to get a scent of 'im now after a few days curin' in the sun." Harold laughed. "They're starting a drive. If a few nobbies turn up they may dig up the whole graveyard. At least then the Goat Colonel won't be the only one lying above ground and probably not the worst smellin' one." Harold laughed again, obviously enjoying the event.

I climbed down my shaft thinking about the Goat Colonel. He had lived alone. Like so many diggers isolated on the Wally who lose all contact with the world they left, he couldn't leave. The pursuit of opal replaces family, community, wealth, love,

---

68 Dag – Dirty wool around a sheep's rear end

companionship and everything that normal people need and enjoy. He had his stone, and that was it. That was all. That was everything. I would have liked to hear the story of how he found his fatal opal. There is always a story.

Pick, thud. Pick, thud. Chunks of clay the size of a fist fell out with each strike of my pick. Thwack, whack, thump, clump. The lumps of clay built up in front of my knees. Berlioz deserted me. The goal of my digging left me. I thought of the Colonel, distasteful smelly bloke that he was. He had found his opal and had no place to go, no desire to live. So he walked into the great never-never of the desert, just like the Aborigines. But it is the Aborigines' home, where they live, where they love to be. For the Colonel it was the last stop, the place to be when there was nowhere else to go. And soon he will be underground. Will they bury his stone with him? It would be the decent thing to do. But I doubt it. Bernie flung it away, no value to him. But still, they should by rights be together – dust to dust and returned to dust.

Thwack, whack, thump, clump. I don't have anyone to talk to, not even a dog. No mate, no offsider, no cobber.[69] I've been so intent on digging and puddling, so obsessed with opal that I have made no friends, except for Bobby, and then only for lunch. And the Professor, but he's often gone, and I don't think we have enough in common to be mates. I am temporary, but I've already been here for ten weeks and have nothing to show for it but two small unsalable opals. The Odd Mates are fellow campers, but not my mates. Pom is from England, and Marco's family came from Italy when he was a child. Marco relates stories from the pub but never carries on a real conversation. And if Edward ran off one day, Pom wouldn't say anything at all. They scam me at every opportunity and go on like it's the normal thing to do. I'm sure the pub has had many laughs at the expense of the Yank. Both of them harbor resentment for America. It's a game. No true Aussie would do that to a camp mate.

Get a hold of yourself and dig. You've only a few weeks left and have to justify being here when you get back to Minnesota. Just dig, shovel, haul up and dump. Don't get philosophical.

---

69 Cobber – Working or drinking partner, offsider, mate

Soon it was noon. I walked over to the Final Shaft burial ground and looked into the grave, 10 feet deep at least. Horizontal Bill and his mate, Brady, were still digging. Bill looked up with a big smile "Still getting nobbies with color, mate. She'll be right, I reckon. We're starting a drive. Hope we don't hit any bones, but you never know." He laughed. I wondered whether you could stake a claim on a graveyard. Most of the graves from years past are unmarked. In theory, I suppose, you could move the graveyard to another site. It would be ironic if the hole dug to bury a stone-poor miner yielded a fortune in opals.

Bobby came up beside me. "G'day mate. They won't find anything 'ere; it's all been dug."

"I reckon yer right," I said, and we started back for the pub. Bobby walked slowly because of his limp. "Did you know the Colonel?" I asked.

"Aye, a bit. We cleaned and puddled a hole on Three Mile Flats a few years back. Never liked 'im much. 'E did stink." Bobby smiled. "A bit odd, 'e was. One dig was it. No stones. Never partnered 'im again. But 'e's straight, (trustworthy) I reckon 'e's straight."

Before we had finished our pints and pies, Horizontal Bill came in and joined the mob at the next table. "I's pickin' in real good just under the eight-foot sandstone level when an arm fell out. Just fell out with a big chunk of clay. All shriveled it was. Brady reckoned it must belong to Old Weber, planted here a couple years back. I said 'That's it, Brady. I'm packin' it in. I don't want to know what 'is skull and legs look like no matter how many nobbies we hit.' I climbed out, and we dropped the Goat Colonel in, no bloody ceremony or nothing. Just dropped 'im in. Plunk. Brady's finishin' shoveling 'im under now. I need a pint o' new beer," he said, nodding at Sarah behind the bar. "Been dealin' with too much old stuff."

He and Brady had spent the whole night in the graveyard. We never did find out whether or not the nobbies cut stones.

Bobby's face became dark again. He didn't see the humor in the Colonel's burial. I decided to tell him about Bernie Bingo. "Bernie followed me up the hill the other day. He wants your stones, but I don't think he'll do anything drastic. The Bingo Brothers are bloody rotters but not violent as far as I know. Let me know if they get onto you."

Bobby smiled. "Yer a fair dinkum[70] Aussie, Yank." This I consider the highest compliment I've ever received. And it came from a frail, done-over, limping battler I started drinking with just to keep from getting caught up in a mob. He continued, "Yer me mate." This last statement was serious. Mates stick together through thick and thin. Mates share good fortune and bad. Mates die with or for each other if necessary.

"Right, mate," I said, wondering what it was he was going to ask me for: money, a place to sleep, food, transportation to and from wherever he camped? Any of which I would have gladly given. But I had to be careful not to do anything that could make him feel uncomfortable or infringe on his independence and make us unequal. He looked at his pint seriously. I caught Sarah's eye and nodded for another round of pints and pies. I didn't want my first real mate going hungry or getting too sober. I knew it was important, whatever he was going to ask me.

"Aye, mate. Will yer shovel me under when the time comes?"

I spilled my beer. I looked at him to see if he was joking. He wasn't, he was dead serious.

"Do you mean..."

"Right mate. Me 'n me stones, together. See the Colonel. Took 'is stone they did and dumped 'im in a hole, alone. Alone, mate, without 'is stone! I don't trust 'em. I don't trust any of 'em. Gigs and ginks,[71] the lot of 'em. I want to be deep and well covered. Away from the rotters, away from the Bingos, away from the whole bloody mob. Away where they'll never find me. Me 'n me stones."

I was astounded. What is he planning? How can I do this? I'm leaving in three weeks or less.

"I'm going back to America in a couple weeks, mate. You'll be around for a long time. I won't be here to do this task."

"Yer ain't found yer stone yet. Yer won't leave 'fore that. Yer'll be here at the time, mate."

---

70 Fair dinkum – True, real, genuine, honest
71 Gigs and Ginks – Scoundrels and cheats

"Bobby," I said. It sounded strange to me; I had never called him by his Christian name. "Don't do anything rash. I don't want anything to happen to you. You're me mate."

"Aye. Not to worry. Just when the time comes, when it happens. Will yer? If yer still 'ere? Will yer do it?"

I paused for a moment. "Right," I said. "If I'm here at the time, I'll do the lot. She'll be right, mate. She'll be right." I raised my glass, Bobby smiled a big smile, and we drank to it.

I didn't like the implications of this and changed the subject. "Who are those blokes?" I nodded at a table with two young, nice looking blokes laughing and having a pint. "I haven't seen them before."

"Scots. Been here a few years. Young fishermen from the islands came over to make their fortune. Two more just like 'em, all together. Right blokes.[72] They stand their shout." Nice to know. I took a good look at them.

Thoughts flooded my mind. I said g'day to Bobby and left to climb back into my hole. That night I went to see the Professor. He understood the ways of the Wally. I sat down and moved pawn to queen's four without saying a word. He countered the same. Next I moved queen's bishop's pawn to four, a risky gambit. He looked up.

"Oh, you're puzzled," he said. He stood up and fetched the rum and two glasses. Then after I took a deep draught he said, "The Colonel had a vision. A vision from his stone. A vision brought on by the curse of the Radiant Opal, the Scourge of Wallangulla. A vision of returning to the best happening of his life, when the Queen reviewed his regiment during the war – his proudest moment, his happiest time. He died with his fatal opal in hand and a smile on his face, and the opal died with him. A valuable Radiant now worthless. A digger now dead."

I took another swig. "This is all superstitious nonsense. I don't believe any of it. He just went bonkers and walked out across the desert without water. Suicide, yes. But a curse? A vision? The Devil Serpent reclaiming one of his eyes? The Colonel had no choice but to die with his fatal opal? The Colonel dies being knighted by Her Majesty? Nonsense. Absolute rubbish."

---

72 Right blokes – You can trust them to do what's right

The Professor moved a piece, and I in turn did the same. We didn't talk for a long time. He devastated me. I tipped my king over in submission after only 15 moves. I poured more rum and sat back.

"Be careful," he said. "The curse is very powerful. Very powerful, indeed." Then I thought he said, "I know," but I'm not sure. We were both quite out of it by this time. When he drove me back to my camp, I still was pondering the mysteries of the Wally.

Chapter XI
My Stone

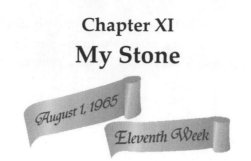

August 1, 1965

Eleventh Week

For six weeks, day after day, I dug 30 feet underground, seldom seeing or speaking to anyone, with the exception of Two-Bob Bobby, with whom I had lunch a couple times a week. I often was alone at night when the Odd Mates went to the pub. My only thoughts were of opal. When I happened to meet someone, we talked about opal. At night I dreamt about opal. In Wallangulla, with just a pick and shovel, you can make a fortune or dream a fortune. So dig, dig, dig. I never tired of the hard work; it was invigorating, and I never missed companionship. The pursuit of opal was my life. I never doubted that a fortune awaited me underground. I was going to be rich! After all, I was one of the few digging in new ground, no leftovers for me. All I had to do was keep digging. The lesson from my early upbringing was the harder you work the more successful you'll be. Would they lie to a little kid?

The opal obsession is far worse than gold fever. Gold is refined, poured into ingots and sold for money. Opals are beautiful. Possessing them is a goal in itself. You can boast of the money made mining gold, but you can display opals, carry them with you and show them. More exciting, more significant. But I wasn't finding anything, not even black potch or nobbies. Time was running out.

On the fourth week the sandstone ceiling over my four-foot-wide, four-foot-high drive started sloping downward. A ceiling change is considered a good sign; opal often is found in roof deviations. Now the drive face was more than 35 feet from the shaft. My windsock directed air downward for circulation. Dig, dig, dig.

Fifth week. Roof still getting lower. Shoveling the tailings out is more difficult as the drift slopes downward. I am making less progress. Then an odor, not a good odor and not necessarily a bad odor, but a distinct and unusual odor filled the drive.

"Right, mate, you can smell 'em when they're close, I reckon," Jake the Wasp had said. My candles started burning brighter, with flames a foot high. This was curious, but I couldn't be bothered thinking about it. I was getting close to opal. Down, down went the ceiling, more than two feet lower. Then the slope leveled off, and the ceiling went straight in for a foot before turning upward. This work consumed several days. It got more difficult to remove the tailings. I came back to camp excited at the end of each day but dared not tell Marco and Pom that I was "on opal" for fear they might rat[73] my claim or tell someone else who would. I no longer trusted them.

At this point the dirt just under the ceiling became gritty, almost sandy. Then I hit a few small lumps. The odor became stronger, and the candles burned brighter. I was on opal! The ceiling now took a steep slant upward so I had to lie on my back to dig with the small hand pick.

Pockets of nobbies are often the size of a football, with the smaller nobbies around the outside and larger ones in the center. The first few nobbies were peanut size without color. I pried them out with my jackknife. It is a very slow process, and great care must be taken not to break a stone. Pry, dig out the face dirt, move the muck back, shave more opal-layer dirt, then pry again. Sweat ran down my face, my heart raced, my hands trembled.

The nobbies were getting larger, hazelnut size, then almond. I licked each one looking for color. (It is said you can tell an opal miner by the hole in his tongue.) Then I snipped off a corner. Shiny, beautiful, clear black potch. No color! Pry, pry, shave, shave, shovel, shovel. Ten, 15, 20 beautiful black nobbies, some the size of walnuts, of absolutely no value. No color.

Then, lying flat on my back looking upward, straining in the candlelight to see, my pick sliced a tiny corner off a nobbie. Click. Bright colors that had been pent up for millions of years came flying out. My heart raced wildly, sweat poured into my eyes, my hands trembled. I pried it out ever so carefully, rubbed the dirt off and licked it. The flashing colors leaped out brighter than the candlelight. It was a true gemstone. This was clear to an

---

73 Sneak down my shaft at night and steal my opal

untrained eye such as mine, even while the opal was still in the rough. A thin layer of porcelain covered the face of the stone, but when licked a multitude of colors came flashing through: gold, green, orange, red, blue, yellow and chartreuse.

This was my opal! I grasped it in my hand, held it, looked at it. It was mine! Mine! Mine! For six weeks what I had worked and searched for was now in my hand. After millions of years we were finally together, my opal and me. Life was complete. All love, lust and passion were sated. All hatreds were avenged. I needed nothing more. Everything I ever desired was right here in my hand. My life was fulfilled. I had been placed on earth for this moment. My opal had been predestined for this moment. At last we were together!

I was too excited to work any more that day. I shoveled muck into the face to hide the pocket in case a ratter should happen by and climbed up into the sunshine to see my gem in daylight. I held it in the sunshine and experienced the thrill of seeing and possessing an incredibly beautiful stone still in the rough. Mine! Carefully buttoning the prize in my shirt pocket and looking in all directions to make sure no one was around, I drove back to camp.

However, there was a problem; I had eaten the last of my stew and didn't have a shilling left to buy food. I wouldn't borrow from the Odd Mates; I didn't want to be obligated to them and didn't know anyone else well enough to ask for a loan. "But not to worry, mate, she'll be right now I've got me stone," I said to myself. I wasn't yet through the opal pocket. Bound to be more good stones in there that I could sell. But not my prize. Not my beauty. That's not for sale.

Marco and the Mad Pom came back to camp briefly before going to the pub. I tried to be casual and not look smug. "G'day mate, 'oweryergoin?" I said.

"Been flat out all day, got a good dig in. Pom's off 'is tucker but a middie'll set 'im right. Jimmy the Snake Catcher and his sheila got a bit of color. Reckon we'll hit the Digger's and 'ave a look. Ta."

I enjoyed being alone by the fire that night. The dancing flames were comforting and thought provoking. Watching a fire is never boring, especially now while I looked at my rough gem in the firelight. Edward just lay there. I slept with my treasure closed in my fist and woke up several times assuring myself it was there.

Early the next morning I was back at the claim. I cleared the muck out and went at the pocket, prying, scraping, digging, snipping, mucking. I carefully dug the entire pocket out with my jackknife. Fifty-two black potch nobbies were in that pocket, some the size of walnuts, but only one had color. I would have had a fortune in opal if they all had had color, but only one did. One out of 52! The rest were just black potch. I was crestfallen, but I had my one beauty. I looked at it several times that day; it was brilliant in any light, even with a covering of porcelain.

Only tea left. No food that night or the next day and the day after that as I dug out all the ground around the pocket to make sure I had gotten all the opal. Then I had to make a decision. I needed money immediately for food although I was no longer hungry. My body seemed to say "I've been telling you for three days I need food, and you've ignored me. I give up."

I could sell the puddler for maybe 25 or 35 quid, enough for another fortnight of food. Or I could sell my stone. Unthinkable! Yet the more I considered it, the more I convinced myself that my claim was loaded with opal and I had found just one pocket of many. Yes, it was just one opal of many. I could sell my gemstone and replace it with a dozen more just like it in a week or two.

After much thought I showed the rough opal to Marco and Pom. I had seen several of their stones and was not impressed. They had found some good opal but no real gems, and I had not seen enough opals to judge quality. After turning it in the light they thought it might be worth a few quid if no sand showed up in the cutting.

I took it to Chuck the Cutter. After working on it a long time he handed me what looked like a fantastic gem. Ring size, just less than six carats, a cabochon.[74] Four broad bands of color running the full length of the stone, each band changing hue individually as the stone was turned. Six distinct colors in all, and shades of others. Gold, green, orange, red, yellow, chartreuse. Incredibly beautiful. Chuck handed it to me casually.

---

[74] Cabochon – Oval shaped, high domed. Most desirable shape

"Nice stone mate." Four bob was the cutting price, but I could pay him later.

I took Marco's suggestion and showed it to Shadow, by now his future father-in-law and still the biggest crook on the Wally. I did not know any other miners who could give me an appraisal. And I had been three days now without tucker.

Shadow casually looked at it, turned it, and examined it. Then said, "Right, mate; nice bit 'o color, ought to be worth close to 200 quid, I reckon." No one seemed to be too exited about the stone but me. I went back to camp, had a cuppa, and examined it for a long while, turning it in the sunlight, my fantastic gemstone black opal. I talked to Edward about it for some time and then went into town to sell it.

Selling opal is an involved ritual. I had already asked too much for the small stone I found puddling, and it was dead on the market; no one would buy it. In the established process the seller showed the stone to the buyer who, after looking at it said, "What'er yer got on it, mate?" The seller stated a price, maybe "50 quid." The buyer might say, "Too much, mate," and hand it back. This means he won't buy it at any price, and the seller has to find another buyer. If the amount "got on it" is a little high, the buyer makes a counter offer, and they agree on a price somewhere in between. During my time on the Wally, I never heard of anyone getting the full price he had asked for a stone.

Shadow, Chuck and the Bingo Brothers were all locals and lived and dealt together. The thought of seeing Bernie Bingo again repulsed me, but he was the only buyer I knew who could afford to buy more than mug stones. Fortunately, I had not offended him the other day. I approached Bernie Bingo apprehensively. As I hadn't eaten for three days, I was eager not to kill the sale. He looked at the stone, not me, and said, "What'er yer got on it?"

"A hundred eighty," I said, which I hoped was a reasonable price, less than Shadow had reckoned.

"Right, mate," he said, pulled a huge wad of bills out of his pocket and counted out the cash. This seemed strange, no haggling. He paid just what I asked. No smile, no thank you. A real drongo. I took the money, already regretting parting with my beauty. The price was the equivalent of $405 American; almost two months pay at that time.

I immediately went to the general store and stocked up on provisions: steak, eggs, bacon, potatoes, bread, butter, cream and cheese. Back at camp I built a fire, buttered a couple slices of bread and fried them and a rasher of bacon in my cast iron pan. Next I fried a large steak and scrambled four eggs. What a wonderful meal! My first in days. Fortunately the eggs had yellow yokes and were not blood red from chickens eating 'roo meat. I tossed the bone and scraps into Edward's dish, poured a cuppa, rolled a delicious Dr. Pat cigarette and sat down to think. As the smoke curled above my head I pondered, Was this meant to be my fatal stone? I had a belly full of tucker and an empty heart.

Then I contemplated. Bernie had barely looked at the stone. He knew exactly what he was getting ahead of time. Undoubtedly Chuck had described it to him in great detail and probably Shadow, too. Were they all in on it? The Odd Mates too? Was this just a game with them? That he paid what I asked meant I had priced it too low. But how much too low? Could I have gotten the full 200 quid that Shadow said it was worth? Maybe 250? Perhaps I would never know. My magnificent stone was gone forever. Where would it reside? On the finger of an Oriental ruler? A corporate CEO's wife? A New York socialite? A London courtesan? I would never know.

Now I had to get back to Minnesota. It was August 5, 1965. I had to leave next week or, for sure, in a fortnight. The pressure was on. Still, I didn't feel my life here was over.

That night I dreamt in color for the first time; beautiful flashing colors dancing in the sunlight, illusively evading my grasp.

Chapter XII
Day After

August 6, 1965

Twelfth Week

I spent a fitful night without my stone. My fist, my opal's normal nighttime residing place, was empty. I checked it several times during the night. With little sleep I reluctantly got up earlier that usual, ate a couple slices of fried bread and had my morning cuppa. I had a strange, empty feeling of having touched the stars and then been thrown back to earth. I was a king, held life, wealth, fulfillment in me hand and then found myself just another mortal, all because I had come up short on tucker!

I left for my Yank's Dig with little enthusiasm, knowing I had to leave in a few days, leave to spend the next 40 years teaching high school children how to sing, play instruments and read music. It would be expedient to marry my sweetheart, buy a new car, find a house and become a part of the community and live a normal life among people I loved.

Just a year earlier I was looking forward to this life. The chance to influence young lives, to inspire them to do great things and maybe open the door of musical opportunity for a talented teenager, to meld young voices into a choir, instrumentalists into a band, to know the joy, as I do, of being in the center of a chorus singing Mahler's Resurrection Symphony with a full orchestra, and feel the tears of jubilation pouring down one's cheeks. What can match that ecstasy? What can fill the heart and soul with such euphoria? What else can bring life to this height of exultation?

Finding a chunk of stone in the dirt 30 feet underground in the desolate Outback of Australia! That's what!

I stood by my mullock heap wondering what to do with all my equipment, the windlass, air sock, picks, shovel, ladder and buckets Give it all to Two-Bob Bobby, came the immediate answer. He could sell it and take a few days off from bludging. And my claim? I would transfer ownership to him and let him sell that, too. Should bring a good price now that it's proven. 'E's me mate.

Harold Blake came up, smiling. "'Oweryagoin' mate. Ta for the beer." I gave him a puzzled look. "The Bingo Brothers shouted the pub last night – never did that before and won't do it again, I reckon. Showed your stone 'round, they did. Said they were lucky to get it for less than five thou. Yer sold too cheap, mate, it's worth five times that."

My jaw dropped. They got it for less than 200 and even lied about that. Five thou! Five thousand quid! I really got taken! Shadow and Chuck the Cutter both knew its value. The Odd Mates knew. It is a game. A game they're good at. And how could my camp mates do this to me? Well, neither one of them is a fair-dinkum Aussie. Shadow and Chuck? Just ginks. Every place has some, even the Wally.

I now had much more to ponder than just what to do with my equipment. I smiled and tossed it off lightly. "There's a lot more where that came from, mate. Findin' any color?" I asked, wanting to change the subject.

"Just enough to keep a bloke goin'." Diggers don't give out a lot of information. We chatted, and he walked back to his claim.

I really didn't know anything about the value of opals. How could I? By standing at the bar in the pub looking at the latest finds? Yes, that would do it. But I don't like the pub or drunks enough to spend hours on end there. And the blueys. Every day at least one. Aussies love to fight and have a pint afterwards. Don't last long. One bloke goes down, and its over. But even innocent bystanders get caught up in it and lose a tooth or get a few broken ribs in the process. Too high a price to pay. So then how could I get to know the value of opal? Make friends with someone honest and knowledgeable. Too late now, mate; it's over.

I climbed down my claim using a rope and toe kicks. This would be easy for a ratter now that word was out I was on opal. Well, the next pocket is still a ways off. They could dig all night and get nothing. In fact it would probably help me. What am I talking about? I have to leave. After lighting the candles I sat back and rolled a Dr. Pat. Unscrew the circular tin, tear out cigarette paper, drop in a few pinches of sweet smelling tobacco, lick the paper, roll and light up. Then sit back, breathe deeply and inhale. Tobacco has been a part of the civilized world since Sir Walter Raleigh brought it back to England. It stimulates the mind and activates the body as the nicotine courses through the bloodstream, bringing pleasure and contentment. One hand-rolled cigarette does all this. Two or three a day is enough to satisfy the metabolism and quiet the soul. But today my mind was working feverishly, trying to come to grips with the vexatious information Harold had just given me.

I had arrived here on the Wally three months past, an innocent, out to have some fun and adventure before settling down. After uncovering a small stone I was driven to find more. Then another stone, and I was hooked – puddling, digging, snipping, always hoping, desiring. Finally the gem quality beautiful black opal. In my hand, in my possession. And now gone. I had grown in experience and knowledge but am no wiser. I have grown in strength and stature but am no better able to cope with the world. I will return to Minnesota richer in experience, changed for better or worse.

I finished my smoke, climbed out of my hole and walked slowly toward the Digger's Retreat. Bobby was, as always, at the pub door, smiling and greeting the tourists, "G'day, mate. I'm a bit short on a quid. If a bloke 'ad two bob for a pie and a pint she'd be right, and I'd show me stones." His expression sobered when he saw me. Obviously he had heard. I put on a big smile, "'oweryergoin', mate," I said. "What say we hit Lenny's Café for steak and eggs?" His face lightened up. "Right on, mate. Good on yer. Styk 'n eggs is nice, it is."

He said nothing more. What could he say? He had had the same decision to make and kept his stones and went hungry. We sat in a booth, and I ordered steak and eggs for both of us. In Aussie you don't specify how you want your eggs. They come sunny side up. The first time I ordered eggs in Sydney I said "Over easy" to the waitress. She gave me a peculiar look. The eggs came sunny-side-up. "Excuse me," I said, "I ordered over easy. The cook just flips them over in the pan and fries them another minute or two on the other side."

"I'll tell him," she said. "He ain't going to like it, having a customer telling him how to cook."

I watched as she took my plate back to the kitchen. The cook's face appeared in the door window. I smiled. My eggs came back, after five minutes, turned over. I thanked the waitress only to find out he had let them get cold and turned them over on the plate. When she came back she said, "We don't go for fancy stuff here. This ain't Ameriker."

You order a steak and it comes as it suits the cook. Makes life a lot simpler.

I looked at Bobby. "I sold my stone, mate. I'd been three days without food." He had gone hungry for months without selling his stones. "I need the money to get back to America."

"She'll be right," he said. "We're mates." He pulled one of his stones out of his shirt pocket and put it in my hand.

"No!" I almost shouted. "No, that's your stone. Please don't. I'll be just fine. It belongs with you, forever. Keep it safe. I'm leaving next week." With a look of sadness and relief, he put it back in his shirt pocket. I was astounded. He had offered me his most precious possession, sincerely and almost casually. I felt my eyes water.

"Aye, mate. If yer ever need it, it's 'ere." He patted his shirt pocket.

We sat in silence. When the tucker came we ate with zest. I, too, now had some idea of hunger. It'd be nice to top it off with a beer, but the café wasn't licensed, and I didn't fancy going into the pub. I put two 10-pound notes in Bobby's hand. "We're mates." I didn't dare give him more yet. Charity between equals has to be carefully measured; it can easily destroy a friendship. "Ta," he said simply with a sad look in his eyes. He would miss me although we met only three or four times a week and then only for an hour or so. And I would miss him. We were mates.

I drove back to the campsite. Edward wagged his tail, but didn't get up; this was his naptime. I boiled me billy and rolled another Dr. Pat to help me sort out my life. To find and sell my opal was one thing, but to find out its value was something else. How much would they sell it for, this beautiful gem they got essentially for nothing: 5,000 Australian pounds, 10,000, 15,000? This was one opal out of 52 large nobbies. What if they all had had color and cut gems? Five thousand times 52 equals 260,000 pounds! Over a half-million American dollars!

It could have been. And still might be. I needed to walk and think. I finished my cuppa and cigarette and started out through the woods. It was still early. The sun wouldn't set until almost 5:30, and even then it would still be light for another half hour. This was the first time I had walked to the Professor's without a lantern. My senses were heightened. I observed things in a new light. The number of men who had arrived in Wallangulla seeking riches was evident from the abandoned campsites. I walked past a lonely huge stone fireplace. Had its builder been a stonemason? Did he live in a tent temporarily and plan to build a stone house? Plenty of rocks scattered on the ground. How long did he stay? Did he leave with nothing? Or had he found a pocket and left to spend his wealth? If he had found just enough to survive, maybe he would have finished his humpy and still be here.

Another camper had started his humpy out of beer bottles. It was over four feet high, bottles set in mud, with a door opening and a half-finished window. What happened to him? Had he found a few stones, decided to stay and then run out of luck? Who knows? So many stories that will never be told. The characters are gone. Back to being stonemasons, brick layers, carpenters, bankers, laborers? Back to the wife and family they left in pursuit of wealth?

There were many abandoned fire-pits with tins strewn about, symbols of dashed hopes, shattered dreams. Wallangulla had had its big surge just after the turn of the century. A hundred or so miners, some with families, walked 400 miles across the desolate desert after the White Cliffs opal field was mined out, a difficult and treacherous march. Only a few miles per day were possible in the dry heat with little water. Some didn't make it. But Wallangulla had rare black opal. A few stones had been found in Hungary and some in White Cliffs, but here they were the norm. Wallangulla opal moves and dances when turned in the light. Stones from other sites are stagnant. Hopes shot skyward. Dreams overcame hardship.

So it went. There were several surges of miners coming and going for more than 50 years. How many sneaked away quietly with a fortune? How many died trying? How many left destitute? Fewer than two dozen locals remain, and that many or more were camped in the area. Have some decided to stay even though they have enough money to live in comfort somewhere else? How many carry a fatal stone in their pocket and can't leave because of it?

As Two-Bob Bobby says, "Aye, me stones like it 'ere mate. Don't care for the Big Smoke."

I stopped many times along the way to examine the clues of mysteries past and wondered if any hint of my having been here will be found in years to come. No matter, I'm leaving and won't be back except maybe as a tourist some 50 years from now. I may want to show my grandchildren how I once lived in a tent and dug for nobbies.

I saw the Professor's camp and was jolted back into the present day. I said, "Kookaburra," walked up to his chess table and moved king's pawn to king's four. He laid down the book he was reading. "Nietzsche's final rational act was to throw his arms around a horse's neck that was being severely beaten by its master and plead for the man to stop. Then he lapsed into insanity and spent the rest of his life in the care of his mother and sister. May have been syphilis; he was only in his forties. Pity. He is the most enjoyable to read of all the philosophers, and he admired both Schopenhauer and Wagner. You might enjoy him." I felt bad about interrupting his study but was not in the mood for a philosophic discussion. He got up out of his reclining lawn chair, a new acquisition, and moved king's pawn to king's four. I made the gambit, king's bishop's pawn to kings' bishop's four. He smiled and said, "I know how you feel." I played an aggressive and reckless game using my knights impetuously. I like knights leaping over everything and not having to move in a straight line like other pieces. He thought seriously and made good countermoves. He was a better player than I, but he had foibles that let me win a game now and then.

It is possible to learn more about a man by playing a few games of chess than by hours of conversation. Fears, hopes, joys, past triumphs and failures, desires, intelligence and aspirations all become apparent. The Prof had been through difficult times but was not beaten. He was intelligent, had unfulfilled expectations and at least one lost love. But he was still in the game, still alive and up to life's struggle. Why he was here I did not know. Escaping? Taking a breather from the world of culture and manners? Hoping to make a fortune? Of the last I think not. He didn't dig that often, if at all. Had he already found his stone?

My wild gambit paid off. I won but knew I would not be allowed to do that to him again. "Up for a cuppa and a shot of rum?"

"Righto, mate. Sounds tops."

He dropped a handful of tea leaves into the boiling water. "You did the right thing. That was a beautiful stone but not your Radiant."

"How do you know?" I asked. "I only sold it because I hadn't eaten in three days and didn't have anything else of value to sell."

"If it had been your fatal opal you would have starved rather than sell it."

"Nonsense," I said. "I can control my emotions. That won't happen to me, I'll sell the damn fatal stone for a fortune when the time comes."

He knew the whole story. The Wally is completely isolated, with no current newspapers nor magazines, no radios, one telephone in the post office that seldom gets used, and only the bush nurse has a two-way radio. Essentially isolated. Yet news travels throughout the area via the pub network. Whatever happens, every digger hears about it.

"There are larger forces at work here," he said, rapping the tea billy with a stick to settle the leaves. "Some power acting on your behalf. Why did you run out of food at the same time you found your stone? Why did your stone show up just as you are planning to go back to America? Why not two months earlier as it easily could have? Is this predestined? Or is it pure chance?"

Is he some kind of mystic? "Are you implying that this might have been my fatal stone? That the opal god Ooluhru almost had me? That I have escaped the Curse of Wallangulla? Nonsense! It just happened, coincidence. If supernatural powers are involved, why did they let me sell my stone for one-twentieth of its real value?"

"Oh," he said, more seriously. "I didn't know the Bingos got to you that badly. They really are a nasty lot." He dropped a dollop of rum in each cup. "Supernatural is too strong, but the longer I live on the Wally, the more I come to believe we don't direct our own lives as much as we think. So what are you going to do? Pack up and head back to the States? Tell your folks what lousy luck you had? How slick opal buyers deceived you? Can you explain the curse so it makes sense to your people? Are you finished here? Did you accomplish your goal?"

"I didn't have a goal," I said, somewhat irritated and ready to tell him to mind his own bloody business. "I just took a year off to see some of the world before settling down to a normal life. I stopped at Wallangulla because I had heard about it from two men on their way back to Germany at a chance meeting in Quinn's Bar in Tahiti. And once here, by pure luck I found a small opal and then another and decided to spend the remainder of my vacation right here. Nothing supernatural about that."

Another dollop of rum, a little more tea. "Perhaps from the very beginning your quest was a spiritual one. Why didn't you just settle down to a normal life? What were you hoping to find? What did you hope to accomplish? Something in your life must have been unfulfilled, unsettled."

I thought of my girlfriend, Sonja, my fiancée. It had happened to me like, I'm sure, it had happened to thousands of others. We dated, liked each other, and kept on dating until, after a year and a half, it was assumed that someday we would marry. Both our families thought it was a good match. That was it, a normal process. No sex. Sonja wanted to be virgin at marriage. Once, I now remembered, when we were sitting in my car with our arms around each other, she said, "Won't it be nice, after we're married, to just go home and crawl into bed together." She snuggled up close. I had not seriously thought about marriage before this, as we were both still in school. This brought on what I later realized was a panic attack, an anxiety attack. I had to roll down the car window and stick my head out. My whole body felt tense and anxious. I wanted to escape, to flee, to get away. "Are you all right?" she asked.

"Yes," I replied, lying. "Let's go for a walk." I did love her. Sonja had a sense of humor but no musical ability. Standing next to me in church, she sang loudly, off key, knowing full well how much it irritated me, and then laughed about it. I thought at the time I would have to teach this tone-deaf pretty lady to sing on key or shut up, but neither one seemed a likely prospect. It was too late to change partners. We were a designated pair, and that's the way things were in Minnesota. Could this be why I wanted to take a year or two off and travel? To find some way out of this commitment? Or was it the dour prospect of teaching uninterested teenagers for the next 40 years?

The Professor had filled his pipe and sat quietly while I pondered my future. He had a satisfied look on his face; he had made his pupil think. It was getting dark. The fire crackled from the green gumwood, and stars shined brightly overhead, clearer and more luminous than ever. The uncluttered air of the desert made the heavens reachable. For the first time since the sale of my stone, I felt relaxed, untroubled. I realized what I had to do.

I reset the chess pieces. "I ain't humpin' me bluey, mate,"[75] I said. "White or black?"

---

75 I'm not leaving. In Outback lingo: I'm not throwing a swag over my back and marching out across the desert

Chapter XIII

Settling In

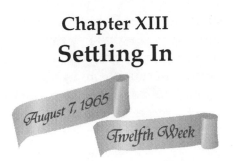

August 7, 1965

Twelfth Week

Another day without digging or puddling. I just made the most important decision of my life, so it seemed, and could afford to take time off. I can put off teaching and marriage for another year. Now I must write letters to explain my decision. Will my family and friends, who are part of a friendly, happy community, understand? "Why do you want to live with foreigners? You belong here with us," I can hear them say. "What do they have that you don't have right here at home?"

"Opal" is my only answer.

"Why on earth do you want to live in a tent in the desert and eat three-day-old stew cooked over an open fire when your sweetheart could be cooking your meals?"

"Opal" I said out loud. Fortunately the Odd Mates were off to their claim so only Edward gave me a puzzled look.

I could hear my family so clearly. "And the teaching job? Jobs like that don't grow on trees, taking charge of the junior and senior high school music departments. Pass this up, and you might not get another chance. What will you do then?"

"Opal."

My mother will say, "Do what's best for you. Be careful. We love you."

My father? "All that work you did to get through college, now wasted. You'd be better off back working at the meat market. Wasted education. You're just a bum!"

My roommate at college, Bernard, had very carefully looked over prospective employers' retirement plans. "With this company you can retire at 62 with three-quarter wages. Think of it! Then you can do whatever you want."

What would I want to do at 62? Sit in a rocker and rock, like Old Man Wells? Fish winter and summer, like the Anderson brothers? Or tour the country in a recreational vehicle like the Meyers? "But, Bernard, you have to pay the price for that luxury," I told him. "The price is 40 years of your life down the tubes."

I want to live now! This minute and every succeeding minute. I want the excitement and adventure that comes with pursuing opal. Opal, right under my feet just waiting to be dug up. I want to find a fortune in beautiful opal. Opal, that's what I want. "Hear me, parents, friends, family, and world: My answer is opal, opal, opal."

And to my fiancée? "Dear tone-deaf pretty lady; either learn to sing on key or shut up. If you don't do one or the other, it's all over between us." Too harsh. I'll write her later. We never were formally engaged, no ring, no announcement. Our friends and families assumed so, as we did, but the whole thing was unsettled and a long way off. When I left on my long trip, we agreed to go out with others and enjoy life.

"Dear Mom and Dad, here are two opals that will help you understand what I am about."

"Dear Superintendent of Schools, I don't want to spend the best years of my life teaching stupid students who are going to grow up and be just like their parents." No, that won't work. "Dear Sir, I regret to inform you that I will be unable to accept the teaching job at this time..."

"Dear Willis, it's not over yet. I'm staying a few months more and hope to find opal. We're not rich yet but on our way. Your investment is safe. I'll send money soon or maybe opal. P.S. Don't quit your job just yet."

This reminded me of Olan, a high school classmate and star quarterback on the football team who couldn't keep his pants buttoned and his girlfriend, the head cheerleader, who couldn't keep her legs crossed. They had to get married at age 17. He quit school and got a job to support a wife and child. "A tough row to hoe," his father said. "Mate in haste," they used to say, "and repent at leisure."

Was I doing something just as foolish? Seeking immediate gratification? Was I following my emotions, not my brain? It takes years to build a chorus and band; you can't start and stop.

Will I lose my abilities? My training? My voice? The Twin Cities has dozens of choirs, bands and orchestras. As a music student I was often asked to sing solo parts in local performances or on local television but always without pay. A lot of work without compensation, but good experience. Conducting is fascinating, but you are so alone up there in front. I must admit I prefer to be in the center of a 300 voice choir behind a large orchestra performing Beethoven's Ninth, Brahm's Requiem or Mahler's Second. Ah, what music.

The pressure was off; I no longer had to hurry. I was home, my home a tent, a firepit and a log to sit on. I could relax, work or think at leisure. Would I ever sing, play piano or conduct again? Of course.

Well, maybe.

The fourth movement of Brahm's Requiem was going through my head. I picked up a small stick, stepped up on a stump like a conductor and beat 6/8 time in the air with my imaginary baton while singing the words. Edward sat there looking somewhat puzzled, watching me intently. While keeping the beat with my right hand, I leaned in with my left shoulder, signifying the rubato, rubbing my fingers together crisply to indicate precision to the orchestra. I sang out, "Thy dwelling place O Lord." Edward turned his head to one side. "Pay attention, Edward; we're coming to the good part. 'O Lord of Hosts.'" Edward gave a little bark. I looked up to see a bloke walking some distance away. He had a puzzled look. "G'day," he said and kept moving.

My improvisation came to a halt, hands in mid-air. No one usually walks by here. I'm used to being unobserved. I had never seen him before and hoped he was just a blow-through, a passing stranger, but he looked like a digger.

I could imagine the pub conversation:

"I's walking by, I was, and saw this bloke standin' on a stump wavin' a stick in the air and singin' to a dog. Singin'! To a dog! Must be daft."

"What'd 'e look like, mate?"

"Just an ordinary, medium-size mutt, mostly black wi' a bit o' white on the nose."

"No, you dill, the bloke. What'd the bloke look like?"

"Ah. Big red beard and light hair."

"Sounds like the Yank. Yanks are a bit odd. 'Overfed, oversexed and over 'ere,' as they say. But I never 'eard of one waving a stick and singing to a dog before."

Marco and Pom had said nothing about my opal sale and didn't mention anything they heard about me in the pub. Acted like nothing had happened, nothing had changed. Marco did relate little tidbits like: "Barceau Jack came up with a shriveled hand when he was cleaning out an old drive on Three Mile Flats. Took it in to Archer the Cop. 'That thing's 50 years old,' Archer said. 'Probably some ratter got caught pinching stones and was buried. Throw it down a shaft. I don't want to be bothered with it.'"

Marco did mention that Shadow and his wife went into Sydney for a couple weeks. Didn't surprise me. He must have collected a few quid from the Bingos for setting me up. I wouldn't be surprised if Shadow and his missus took a trip around the world.

I got my letters written and into Petula at the post office. My diet was a little better now that I had a few extra quid. The fur-like buildup on my tongue subsided. I planned how to work my claim. First drive through to the other shaft for good air circulation. Next follow the ceiling channel both ways, looking for the blowhole; opals are found where there has been geyser action. Then dig carefully around the blowhole and follow ceiling deviations and hope to find another football-sized pocket of nobbies.

I was now home, healthy, had a few quid and a worthy struggle filled with promise. This is happiness. This is life. No time to dwell on those who had bilked me. As the Spanish say, "Living well is the best revenge." I will concentrate on finding opal. I also need a mining mate and a different campsite.

Meanwhile, I had long-term plans to think about. For comfort and a concept of justice I read *The Count of Monte Cristo* before turning in each night.

I dreamt in color.

Chapter XIV
Bruce The Banker

August 11, 1965

Thirteenth Week

My little panel van was not up to the 45 mile drive to Walgett so I asked the Professor if I could ride with him. I didn't want to have to ask the Odd Mates for any favors now that they had lurked me. The Professor's Land Rover was badly dented but in good running condition.

The pressure was off. I didn't have to make my fortune in two weeks or two months. I could relax and explore my domicile. I sometimes casually walked through the Jungle. One day I met two happy blokes in the process of creating a large pile of empty beer cans. They invited me to join them. I moved on. Next I saw a small camping trailer by a bough shed. Too cramped, I thought, but to each his own.

"G'day, mate, 'oweryergoin'?" Bruce and I got into conversation over a cuppa and a Dr. Pat. He talked about his 10 years as a bank employee.

"One day, mate, I analyzed my life. I could transfer from town to town – Sydney, Canberra, Coonamble and Tamworth – but would still see the world only from inside a bank, counting bills, making loans, and cashing checks. I liked the idea of mining and in my spare time had been poking away at a gold claim that belonged to my friend's father. It never produced much. Then one day I just chucked it all in, bought my little trailer and drove to Coober Pedy to try my hand at opal."

"The miners and their families live underground. It was too hot in my little trailer. Coober Pedy opal is low quality from larger plants and animals, sometimes a whole tree. Sold by the ounce, not by the carat[76] like Wally gems. Coober Pedy and Andamooka opals don't move when you turn them. They all look alike, just

---

76 140 Carats per ounce

flat. Dead. Not brilliant. Not gems. You may find a whole opalized tree and make a fortune, but like gold, it's just for the money."

He shook his head in disappointment. "I wanted to find something beautiful, something I could hold in my hand and cherish. Then I heard about Wallangulla, and here I am with a pick, a shovel and a couple dozen books." He pointed to his bookshelf. "Have yer read Jack London's *Valley of the Moon*?" I hadn't but made a note to borrow it from him. "Wish I had a sheila like he did and could just wander around looking for the ideal place to settle. But I'm here now and might come up with a *pahsel*[77] and do just that."

Bruce was a fair-dinkum Aussie, a pleasant bloke but not Outback. He had grown up in a small town near the coast. "About a quarter of Aussies are pro-English," he told me, "Another quarter are pro-American. The rest of us are Aussies. We are what we are, mate, and the hell with the lot of them." He smiled. "The government's letting in too damn many wogs.[78]"

Bruce, whom I'm sure will become known as Bruce the Banker, might just find his fatal opal and never leave the Wally. He was working old diggings on the Three Mile Flats. I asked if I could spend a day in the digs with him. He agreed, and we decided to do this the next day.

I brought a small shaving pick, not expecting to do any serious digging. I knew little about Three Mile Flats, the largest named area. Bruce filled me in. "Fifty years ago the flats were the most intensely worked section of the Wallangulla designated mining area. At one time more than 1,000 diggers worked this field. It consists of hundreds of old abandoned claims. Some of the old miners cut support props from trees and drove them in with caps, split one-foot-long shims. The support fits tightly to take some weight off the roof and prevent a cave-in. Cutting and fitting supports took time, so most diggers just left four-by-four clay support pillars every four feet to support the ceiling, even

---

77 Pahsel (parcel) – A collection of opals sold together. The buyer might say, "I can't buy that stone alone but will take it in a pahsel"

78 WOG – During the nineteenth century the English colonials referred to native people by terms that were not always complimentary. To combat this the term, Worthy Oriental Gentleman, was created to replace all derogatory epithets. This was shortened to WOG and, in time, also became a derogatory term

though they may contain nobbies. That's what I'm after, the clay pillars they left."

He parked the pickup, grabbed a coil of rope from the back, tied the rope to the support cribbing of the nearest shaft hole, smiled, and started down, hand over hand on the rope, from toe kick to toe kick. About 10 feet down he stopped and lit a match, then went down another 10 feet and repeated the process. At about 30 feet deep he motioned for me to climb down. "What's the match business about?" I asked.

"To test the air, checking for oxygen. These old mines have dead air. If a match goes out, I come back up. If it doesn't light, I come up quickly or not at all." He smiled.

"What do you do then? Go to another shaft?"

"If the claim looks promising and I want to get into it, I crumple a bunch of old newspapers, light them on fire and drop them down the shaft. The fire moves air up the shaft and draws fresh air down. Sometimes I even hang a windsock, but that's a lot of trouble."

Many of the claims connected underground. We went from claim to claim with lanterns, just poking at the pillars. Opal mining is safe if done properly. If the dugout area is four feet or less, it's considered safe. One claim must have been rich because an area 30-by-30 square feet had been cleared and timbered every four feet. No clay pillars left. It didn't look safe to me. Some of the supports had started to lean, but the area had all been dug out so we had no reason to explore it.

As mines dry over 50 or 60 years, the clay starts to crumble, the sandstone ceiling cracks, and the pillars give less support. The crumbling pillars that nobbies fall out of were what Bruce was interested in. We gathered up a handful by noon, but no color.

"If you find color, what then?" I asked him as we had sandwiches and beer he thoughtfully had packed for lunch.

"I might dig out the whole pillar if I think I can get out before it caves in."

"Seems like a risky business to me. You could cut log supports and drive them in."

"Ah, mate, it'd take me all day to drive out to the trees, cut supports, split shims, come back, toss them down the hole, cut them to the right length and drive them in securely with a maul, just to dig out one pillar. Cave-ins don't usually happen right away, and I look and listen for any movement, ready to gink out quick."

They don't usually cave-in right away, I thought apprehensively. That's what had crippled Bobby. I preferred the safe, new ground of my claim. But it's his shilling, his neck. I was impressed. He had thought it out and knew what he was about. He was a good bloke but not a potential digging mate; we were too different.

After lunch we drove to another area he wanted to explore.

"Heard about this in the pub. The story is that this is the richest field of all," he said as we parked. "The nobbies were so thick they dug them out with jackknives, brought a bucket full into the pub and dumped them on the bar. All with color." He became excited. "Good black opal. A buyer took the whole works for a bob a nobby. One shilling per gem! The partners got almost 10 quid each. A lot of money at that time. The buyer had a fortune in black opal gems, but no market for them. They were believed to be cursed, bad luck. Might be true. There's nothing left down here, all dug out, but I just want you to have a look at it."

We tied the rope to the cribbing and started down the shaft. The toe kicks were badly worn away. I climbed down just behind him. At 30 feet everything was caved in. We looked around through the gaps in the shaft. "They didn't use supports, just kept digging and moving," Bruce said. "Maybe a few blokes are still down here buried. Who knows? Accidental cave-in. One less to share the profit. A lot of tales that will never be told."

He enjoyed exploring abandoned mines. "I'm really interested in the Gully, but let's have a look at Frog Hollow first." Frog Hollow was at the southeast corner of the three mile, near the Gully. We crawled down a shaft he had been down before, one not more than 10 feet deep. I took my lantern through a narrow drive and saw sparkling color on the floor and picked up a few pieces. "Look at this," I said, "color all over. Might be some good nobbies here." He laughed.

"That's what many a digger has thought. These drives gave plenty of hope and encouragement. Look at the pieces carefully."

They were small, broken and cracked. "Looks like someone wasn't very careful with the pick."

"Didn't matter how careful they were," he said. "Frog Hollow nobbies crack on exposure to air. Maybe not the first day, but always within two or three days. It's the unusually high moisture content of this field. Several diggers thought they had a small fortune in a tin full of nobbies, but most cracked as soon as they were cut. The story goes that one bloke many years ago managed to cut and polish a passel himself and get it to the buyer the first day. Got a few quid, nothing to brag about, and ginked out. Every stone cracked. That's why buyers always like to know where a stone comes from. The story goes on. He came back a few months later and worked another claim, but no buyer would buy from him, and no digger would shout him. He got in one pub bluey after another and finally left. His lurk[79] made it difficult for everyone."

"Were there a lot of buyers here years ago?" I asked.

"They say the old days had a dozen regulars plus several that made the long trip from Sydney regularly. Now we've only got a half dozen, only two, really, who buy big stuff. A couple more show up from time to time."

"Two? I only know about the Bingo Brothers."

"I heard about your deal with the Bingos, a nasty bunch. You really have to look out for yourself here; the locals are closely connected. Angus the Scot is an outsider, only been here a few years. He stands his shout.[80] You might try him next time."

Next we stopped off at the Gully and climbed down a hole Bruce had been working. "Whoever had this claim started several drives, filling each one up with tailings when they switched to a new dig. I've found some mug stones and a few grays[81] here. I'm thinking about hauling some up to puddle. You have a puddler; you interested?" I thought about it.

"Sounds like a bit of all right. I've got a channel to follow, but maybe in a fortnight or two." After poking around an hour or two, we called it a day and went back to his camp. "I'll show yer me stones." He pulled out a tin from a shelf in his sleeping trailer that had half a dozen nice stones, better than mugs, precious opal but

---

79 Lurk – Cheat

80 You can trust him to do the right thing

81 Light opal and jelly opal can be gem quality but not as valuable as black backed opal. Gray backed opal is in between, some very nice

not gems. He was finding enough to keep in tucker. Obviously he wasn't worried about leaving them in the open. I had not heard of any thievery from humpies, just claims ratting.

I thanked him, bid g'day, and went back to my tent full of new information. It had been a good day. I had a new friend and was becoming a permanent part of the Wally. I had only a few mug stones, no gems to carry, show, or look at. But now that I'm a fair-dinkum Aussie, I'll act like one, "Not to worry, mate. She'll be right..."

Next day I stopped by Petula's post office. A letter from my recently intended said she had decided to go to teachers college and was going to date other men seriously. I was off the hook, free to pursue opal.

Chapter XV
The Swede

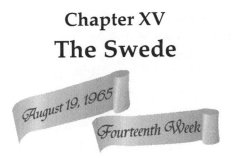

August 19, 1965

Fourteenth Week

The Professor yelled down the shaft, "Hallo down there, Yank." Startled me. I climbed up and invited him down. He hesitated finding the toe kicks. He wasn't lean and muscular but made it down. I demonstrated my mining method using trolley and grappling hooks and showed him the sloping roof and the channel I intended to follow. He was not comfortable underground. We climbed out and started for Walgett.

The road was too rough to drive on, even in his Land Rover. He picked a lane 30 feet off the main trail and followed that. It hadn't rained for nearly a year, and grading the hard, dry surface was pointless. Few cars traveled this road; it was an event to meet another car. From time to time we saw a pile of discarded beer cans along the road. The Professor said, "That's evidence that two or more Aussies met and, weary of the arduous journey, stopped, pooled their beer and had a yarn. No need for them to pick up the cans." He smiled. "Plenty of space left. It'll take decades to trash it all."

Walgett was a thriving community of a couple thousand. The main street was lined with businesses. The airport had daily flights from Sydney and Brisbane. Two airplanes from the two airlines arrived and left at the same time.

A local justified this duplication. "Aye, mate. It wouldn't be fair, would it, to give the Ansett ANA monopoly rights to all the business? That's why the government airline gives us a choice. They fly at the same time to the same place for the same price. Means the profit goes to us and not the capitalists," he said with a satisfied look. Later I found out that the owner of Ansett ANA made such a profit that he wanted to drastically lower the airfares, but the government wouldn't allow it. The government was losing money and wouldn't allow the privately owned airlines to charge less. I was beginning to get an idea of how socialism works or, in this case, doesn't work.

The Professor had a few errands to do so I wandered down the street looking into the various shops. I chanced upon the barbershop. Good idea! I'll just nip in and get a haircut. I was shocked to see my image in the large mirror. Did I really look like that? How did I smell? I hadn't taken a sponge bath for days. Or weeks. However, this is the Outback, not the Big Smoke. Nobody is spotless. He cut my hair short and trimmed my beard. I looked and felt much better. As I came out of the shop I nearly bumped into a 6-foot-3 blond woman in her twenties. She was window shopping.

When I came out of the meat market, there she was again, looking in the window. Then the grocery store and the bookshop. We crossed inside this time, never making eye contact. This was too much of a coincidence. She couldn't be interested in a ratty miner like me. Well dressed, nicely proportioned and neatly made up, she had an air of gentility. In Sydney I would have chatted her up, but not here. We were leaving within the hour. Still, interesting to ponder.

We packed our meat, groceries and books into the Land Rover and started back. I told the Professor about the sheila. He, too, had noticed her. "Must be a tourist, probably with a group," he said. A tourist? A group? In Walgett?

The drive back was just as arduous. I vowed not to make this trip any more than was absolutely necessary. Once back at camp I ta'd[82] the Professor, built a gum and sandalwood fire, sliced the lamb's fry (lamb's liver, the main joy of a trip to Walgett), boiled some eggs, fried a couple of slices of bread and enjoyed a delicious repast. My timing was good; the Odd Mates weren't back yet. They arrived after I'd washed up and was having a cuppa and smoking a Dr. Pat. I greeted them politely, lit my mantle lamp and settled in my tent for a night with *The Count of Monte Cristo*.

After my opal sale ordeal, I should have been bitter and angry, but I wasn't. I felt confident and optimistic and for now put off any thoughts of reprisal. Puddling had yielded a few good mugs, and I was making headway toward the second shaft, digging

---

82 Ta'd – Thanked

for speed. The faster I got to the other shaft, the sooner I could get back to the channel and my fortune. And then? Who knows? "She'll be right, mate."

I thought the next day would be a good time to have a pint and pie with Bobby. The money I had given him hadn't changed his way of life; he still bludged the tourists at the pub door. I think he had settled in and liked it. He's naturally friendly. Bless him, that's fine with me. I was also settling into a way of life and enjoying it. We were mates. He had his stones, and I dreamt in color every night – beautiful flashing colors dancing in the light, elusively evading my grasp.

The next day, over our pint and pie, I said, "Bobby, would you like to go into the Big Smoke or somewhere else for a holiday? We can afford it now, you know."

"Aye, no, mate. Me stones like it 'ere, don't care for the mobs."

"Righto." I let it go at that. I had no idea where he went at night or where he slept. He'd tell me if he wanted me to know. The Wally was his home. He wanted to stay here with his stones.

As usual we didn't talk a lot, just tipped our pints and listened to the pub chatter, which didn't interest me much. Then Old Sam the Bot came to our table with a story, thinking I'd be good for a pint. I nodded to Sarah, who brought him a midi. He laughed as he told the latest news. "Vertical Bill hit the big lolly.[83] Shouted the pub, 'e did. First time he bottomed right in a year. Brought in a coffee tin of nobbies and dumped them right on this table." He hit his hand on our table. "The color fairly jumped out of the nobbies, it did. Looked like she'll be right for old Bill."

I sipped my beer and waited. Bobby also smiled and waited.

"Took the lot to Chuck the Cutter and came back for a few pints himself, grinin' ear to ear, 'e was, with everyone sayin', 'Good on yer, Bill. Top 'o luck to yer.' I used to think he was a no hoper,[84] the way he dug. Now looked like I was wrong." He stopped to take a long pull on his pint.

---

83 Lolly – Sweet, candy. Had good luck

84 No hoper – Battler, someone who never gets anywhere, struggles but has no success

Get to the point of it, I wanted to say, but just smiled and sipped. "Well, wasn't mor'n a half-hour, I reckon, when Chuck comes in. Serious he was. Had a handful of color chips and a handful of sand. Just shook his head. 'Nothing but sand and chips, Bill, sand and chips.'"

"Bout killed 'im it did. 'E sat there starin' at the pile of sand and color. After a long, quiet time the diggers felt bad about his hard kack[85] and chucked in, some a few bob, some a quid. Piled coins and bills right on the table for poor Bill. Spot on, it was. 'E 'ad twenty quid fore it's over." Old Sam drank most of his pint, hoping I'd shout for another. "But still not right, I reckon, all that work and not come up with a Zac."[86]

"She'll be right, mate, 'e's still diggin'," Bobby said. I set my empty glass down and smiled. "That's about it for me," and I started for the door.

We came out of the pub, and there she was, tall, blond and well proportioned. Not beautiful, but elegant. I immediately pictured her at the bow of a Viking longboat, sword in hand, reaching out over the waters. Another thought crossed my mind; I have been here too long and am getting the Wallies, conjuring up wild illusions. She was looking the other way, toward the Diggers Final Shaft graveyard. She must know someone on the Wally, but why is she always alone? And what is she looking at?

Aussie men don't cater to sheilas like Yanks do. Aussie sheilas like men, working men, strong men, men who can laugh, drink and get into a bluey. Men who can pick them up and carry them off. The first time I saw an attractive Aussie sheila hanging happily on the arm of a drunken bloke who was talking nonsense, I wondered what the attraction was. *He was a man.* The sheilas I met first looked at my hands openly, even physically examining them. I had started working young and had strong hands. I once saw a well-dressed young American male knock on a door in Sydney. He had scrubbed, clean, delicate hands and was carrying a bunch of flowers. He's got Buckley's Chance,[87] I thought. He'd

---

85 Hard kack – Bad luck

86 Sixpence coin. Not worth much

87 Buckley advertised in newspapers for partners for his Back 'o Burke mining operations. He always returned with minerals but without his partners. They never returned; he left them buried in the diggings. Hence Buckley's Chance means no chance at all

be far better off half drunk and laughing. The typical Aussie sheila would politely put up with him for the evening but be too busy for a second date.

This blond enchantress had my curiosity. I looked her over for a minute and then started up the hill to my Newtown claim. Bobby was already back at his station outside the pub door, ready to smile and greet newcomers.

I was at my windlass deep in thought about the drive, tailings, opal and mining, before I noticed her behind me.

"G'day," she said in Aussie. No smile, just a cordial expression on her pleasant face. "I'd like to 'ave a look at yer diggin's if I might."

She didn't seem Aussie, her stance was wrong. Aussie sheilas are relaxed, without fear or concern. "This is me, like it or not" comes with a smile. This young woman was conscious of her appearance and the impression she made.

"What's the name of that bird that laughs all the time?" I asked. Now she looked puzzled and cocked her head to one side. "The kookaburra?"

The Professor had taught me well. She wasn't an Aussie. She was casually dressed in slacks and light blouse.

"Righto. You have other shoes?" I asked. "Yes," she said and went to her car. She had driven her Volvo up the slope between the mullock heaps. She must be Scandinavian, not many Volvos in Australia. Her boots were stylish but made for rough use. The slacks fit her well, and the color of her blouse suited her complexion. She had good taste; it even impressed me, and I hadn't seen anything sophisticated in months.

"Follow me," I said and started down the shaft.

She moved nimbly down the shaft. I looked up at her rounded thighs and felt my chest tighten. My pulse increased. I felt a tingling that I hadn't felt during my time in the Outback. I had forgotten the tension that attractive women arouse.

"Have you been in a mine before? Underground?"

"No."

"But you feel secure?"

"As long as you do," she responded with a smile.

She moved slightly and stumbled, falling against me. I took her arm, helped her up and realized I was near a woman for the first time in God only knows how long. Looking into her beautiful blue eyes I said, "Miners think it's bad luck to have a female underground, but I always make an exception for tall blonds."

She smiled. "What's your name?"

"I'm called the Yank. And you?"

"Helga. I've been working at the Swedish Embassy in Sydney for the past three years and thought I'd take a trip through Australia before returning to Sweden." She spoke British English, not Aussie or American. She leaned against the shaft, and a ray of light illuminated her soft cheeks and fine bones.

"What's your given name?" she asked.

"Anskar Thorston." She seemed nice. I lit four candles on spiders, candleholders, and stuck them in the walls.

"My family is Norwegian. I grew up with Scandinavians in Minnesota. My grandfather ran away from his home in Oslo at age 14, worked his way to America on a ship and settled in Minnesota. You and I have common Viking ancestors, barbarians who raped, pillaged and plundered," I said as a joke.

"They also settled: Ireland, England, France, Russia."

"But they left no culture. They loved battle and were bored with peace. The sagas said they fought bravely and died cheerfully. Their goal was to die a heroic death in a hopeless cause."

"You've read the sagas," she said, looking pleased.

"Some. There are so many, it'll take me years to get through them all."

She looked contemplative. "The Vikings were seafarers, and started pillaging out of necessity. They really had no culture to impose on the conquered. They sometimes lived with them and became more like them, being conquered by the conquered. They built beautiful boats and loved poetry. All of this ended when King Olav, in the tenth century, drove them out of Norway into Iceland. There, without wood to build boats and the forced conversion to Christianity, their raiding and pillaging ended."

I got the impression she missed the old days. I did, too. "Scandinavians are peaceful and avoid conflict. In Minnesota the bravest thing these Viking descendents do is to eat lutefisk in Lutheran churches at Christmas, just like in Sweden. My bravery doesn't extend that far."

"Oh no," she said, looking surprised, "We don't eat that stinky fish any more. It never was a Swedish tradition, just a dried fish that kept well over winter that we had to eat when times were bad. Now we ship it to America. We have goose for Christmas. I never cared for lutefisk even as a child when that was all we had."

What a surprise. Swedes don't like lutefisk any more than I do. "Well," I said, "somehow it became a tradition and now we're stuck with it. Fortunately there is always a choice. It's served with meatballs and mashed potatoes."

I thought for a minute or two, and then went on, "It must have been exciting to be a Viking."

"Yes, yes, indeed," she said with a somewhat distant look in her blue eyes.

We crawled through the drive, and I showed her the sloping ceiling and the channel where I found my gem black opal. I felt compelled to tell her every facet of my discovery. I enjoyed her company. "I plan to follow this channel both ways once I connect with the other drive for air circulation. Now I'm digging to connect."

"I'll help," she said, and picked up a small shovel.

"Fine." I smiled and started digging out the clay with my driving pick, and she shoveled it into the trolley.

"You love this. It's an adventure for you, isn't it?"

"It started on a whim, then became an adventure. Now it's an obsession, my whole existence. My life. There's a pocket of opal waiting for me. Just for me, placed here millions of years ago. " I reined in my thoughts before I got too carried away and smiled as though it was all a joke.

I showed her how to dump the trolley by the shaft and went back to digging. This was nice. My first visitor underground. She was strong and enjoyed physical work.

"I've never been anywhere so quiet," she said.

"You get used to it. It is so easy to think down here, no noise to interrupt. But it's too quiet. I have to come up after four hours."

"I can understand that."

"It doesn't have to be quiet. We can sing. Do you know *Halsa Dem Dar Hemma*?"

"Of course." We sang this lovely sailor's song. I knew the words in English and Norwegian; she knew them in Swedish and Norwegian. It was good to sing again. I had not sung underground. The compact drive and rough walls blended our voices closely together, a delightful experience. She sang like an opal shines, with radiance. We each sang our favorite folk songs, alone or together, like *Lili Marlene*, which exists in all western languages, and *Gamla Mor*, strictly Swedish.

"Opal mining is very safe in new ground as long as the drive is less than four feet wide," I assured her. "You have to be careful in old claims where the clay pillars are crumbling."

I was eager to talk to this woman. How long had it been? Several months. How long can a man live without the softness of a woman? Not sex, but the gentle female nature. I was so wrapped up in my pursuit of opal that I, like the other diggers, had forgotten the outside world.

"We grow up with the sagas and Scandinavian literature in Minnesota. Have you read Knut Hamsun's *Growth of the Soil*?"

"Oh, yes, of course. He is Scandinavia's greatest writer. I read him in the original Norwegian. We are taught all three Scandinavian languages plus English. Knut had strong feelings about the war."

"He's difficult to understand but interesting. Sweden and Norway get along okay now?" I asked. "Second-generation Norwegians in Minnesota think Sweden abandoned Norway to the Germans during the Second World War, staying neutral while Norwegians fought."

"Norway had also declared itself neutral, just like Sweden. They also wanted no part of the war. Then an influential member of the Storting, C. J. Hasbro, ceded to England the right to block Norway's ports. Knut called this the English invasion. Hasbro immediately fled to Sweden, leaving Norway vulnerable to the German invasion, which otherwise would not have happened. Knut hated England, loathed communism and never understood why the United States, a Christian nation, allied with Stalin. He already had killed 30 million Christians to make Russia Bolshevik."

This was interesting, but I didn't want to get into a discussion about World War II with an attractive woman 30 feet below ground so I changed the subject.

"Did you major in history?"

"Yes," she said. "I plan to do research and write a paper, maybe a thesis on the ancient Oskulden Flicka."

"Oskulden Flicka? I've never heard of them. I've read what Snorri Sturluson wrote about the Viking warriors, but I don't remember his mentioning the – who?"

"Oskulden Flicka. Virgin girls. Valkyrie. Richard Wagner wrote an opera about them, part of his Ring Cycle."

"Oh," I said, "The Valkyrie. I thought they were just myth. They were real?"

"Neither Snorri nor the other saga writers wrote about the Viking female warriors. It's as if they didn't exist. But their story has been passed on from mother to daughter for over 1,000 years. I've saved enough money to visit the Icelandic islands, the fiords of Norway and the isolated hills of Sweden to gather information. It's difficult because it's all oral history."

"Now you have my curiosity. Were the Oskulden Flicka the real Valkyrie? "

"It's a long story."

"I have time."

"Well, Oskulden Flicka means young girls, virgin girls, now called Valkyrie. Wagner said they were the virgin maidens who brought the dead and dying Viking warriors back to Valhalla to await the day of Ragnarok."[88]

"They picked up the battle dead, right?"

"Yes, and we tend the wounded. It gets more complicated. Shall I go on?"

"Please do. Sounds fascinating." It sounded especially fascinating since she used we in the present tense.

"For years young Viking men pushed off in their longboats and left the young girls behind to wait and hope for their return, which didn't always happen. In the tenth century the girls from one village got impatient and asked the men to let them come along. 'We can row and paddle and cook,'" they said.

"'No,' the men insisted. 'You'll just get in the way.' But these girls had planned ahead. Instead of just waving goodbye from the shore, 15 or 20 of them boarded a longboat and followed."

"They knew how to sail?" I asked.

---

[88] Ragnarok – The final battle between the forces of good and evil. It is foretold that the Vikings will lose

"Enough to get started, but it was risky. Each flicka selected the man she wanted. He would be hers forever. To make a long story short, it worked. They each dragged a wounded man off the battlefield, put him in their longboat, tended his wounds and brought him home. The warriors were content to stay with their own flicka the rest of their lives. Word got around, and soon many Viking longboats were followed by flicka boats."

"Quite a story," I said. I found my mind wandering, Helga's presence overcoming me in this close space. I liked hearing her voice, savoring her intelligence. She was as intent about her flicka as I was about opal. We cleared the face of the drive and hauled all the clay chunks back to the shaft.

"Now what?" she said.

"We'll take the diggings to the surface, dump them and call it a day."

We traded off loading the buckets and winding the windlass. It was good to be in the open air again, but I missed her closeness. We finished, and she smiled. "This was an adventure for me. I hope you don't think I was too inquisitive or too forward."

"No. I was happy to have your help and conversation." She smiled, thanked me, got into her Volvo and went off down the hill, fading away in a dusty trail between the mullock heaps.

I didn't puddle that day. I went back to camp, built a fire, heated my stew and thought how nice it was to have female company. Someone said there are three levels of dialog: personal, things and ideas. The first quickly becomes boring, the second is a little more interesting, but ideas are invigorating. She dwelt in the third level. I knew nothing about her, except her fascinating love of the ancient Vikings and their Valkyrie. I should have invited her back to camp for three-day stew to get the feel of the Outback. She could meet Pom and find out about the Wallies. I was bemused and wanted to see her again. But I was here for opal. She was just passing through.

Chapter XVI
Helga

August 20, 1965

Fourteenth Week

I tossed and turned for hours. Sleep would not come. When it finally did, I fell into a sleep so deep that I was caught between the real world and the dream world when I awoke. Helga dominated my dream and became more real than she was in the drift, talking and working with me.

I built a gumwood fire and boiled a billy. I had a cuppa and a bit of three-day stew with fried bread and left for my claim while the Odd Mates continued to snore. I was in a trance as I climbed down my shaft and encountered lit candles. She smiled at my surprised look.

"G'day, mate. 'oweryergoin'?" she said in her best Aussie. I hadn't seen her smile before.

I was delighted but tried to be nonchalant. "Your Aussie's good. Thinking of taking up mining?"

"No, just woke up early and felt like having a dig. I'm here for a few days then off to Queensland."

"That's what I said three months ago. I had the bad luck to find a couple of nobbies, and now I'm a permanent resident. Be careful."

"I want to get to work on my thesis. Been planning it for the past three years."

"Tell me more about your Valkyrie ancestors."

"The Valkyrie were young virgins. They dressed in scarlet corselets and carried spears for protection. Each selected her warrior, and when he was wounded in battle she dragged him off the field to the longboat, took him home and nursed him back to health. If their man was killed, they had to pick another or go home alone. Some Vikings thought they could choose their own female and take her by force. Valkyrie maidens did their own choosing, and several warriors learned that lesson by tasting the spear. The men went on raid after raid, but a Valkyrie stopped going once she had her man."

"The wounded warriors gave up raiding and stayed with their Valkyrie, contented?"

"Yes," Helga replied. "The Valkyrie healing power and devotion won the men over, and they vowed to stay together till the day of Ragnarok. They might return to their own village or go off to a new settlement, maybe to one of the Icelandic islands where they could raise a family away from the domination of kings and nobles. They raised sons to be brave warriors, wise, kind, knowledgeable, trustworthy, loyal..."

"You're running out of adjectives," I said. "What about the daughters?"

"The same, but also with the healing arts. Our mothers taught us to find our own wounded warrior and heal him."

Again she spoke in the personal.

"What if the wounded warrior should die?" I asked.

She looked up and stared into space for a moment. "Then we die also and go to Valhalla to be united until the day of Ragnarok."

This was getting too personal and a little spooky. I realized her mother had raised her to be an Oskulden Flicka, a Valkyrie. I needed to get back to the Vikings.

"The Vikings raped, pillaged and plundered," I said, as a joke. "Did your Valkyrie join in that?"

"Not in the raping," she smiled. "But it wasn't quite like you think. Imagine you are a 12 or 13 year old English girl living in a coastal town. You know your father will soon sell or give you to a man you may or may not know or like. One less mouth to feed. You know you will have to tote water, wash clothes, cook meals and produce a dozen children. You also know that in 15 years you will be a worn-out old woman like your mother."

"Then one day a Viking longboat appears on the horizon. Then another. Your heart leaps. This is exciting! The villagers run for safety and admonish you to follow them. But you admire these lusty men storming ashore, swords in hand, and you realize this is your chance to escape. You run toward them and fling you arms around a warrior's neck, pleading, 'Take me with you. Take me away. Please, take me.'"

"Did this really happen?" I asked.

"Often. The invaders had to physically break free of these girls, or they might get killed themselves. After the battle the defeated townsmen were gone and the women stayed in hiding. Again the young girls flung themselves at the invaders. Rape? Conquest? Seduction? Hard to call when the victims flung themselves on their attackers."

"How did your Valkyrie ancestors respond to this?"

"They were interested only in their wounded warrior. The rest didn't matter." She paused. "But sometimes things took a different turn. Not many girls followed the longboats, but those who did were strong and determined. Are you familiar with the term 'berserker?'"

"Sure, the bare-shirters, the Vikings who tore off their shirts in the heat of battle," I replied.

"Yes," she said. "They flung down their shields and threw themselves wildly into the fray, not caring if they lived or died. A type of madness. But not only the men. One village in England had raised an army against the Vikings and had them surrounded. The Oskulden Flicka always stayed back and watched the fighting, but this time the possibility of losing their men so enraged them that they grabbed their spears and ripped off their corselets." At this point she became so animated that she tore a button off her blouse. "Sorry, I get too carried away. They ripped off their corselets and ran into the battle to keep their chosen warriors from getting killed. You can imagine what the English felt, charged by a horde of screaming, spear carrying, bare-breasted, berserk female Vikings. They dropped their weapons and ran."

"Amazing," I said. "Did the Viking men later ask them to join in battle?"

"No, but some did anyway. They earned the name 'the virgins from hell' which stuck for 100 years. Now we refer to them all as Valkyrie. This group settled with their rescued warriors on one of the small Icelandic isles. I hope to visit their descendants."

For the first time in months I was thinking about something besides opal. Digging had slowed, but we had enough tailings to haul up and dump.

"I have an idea," I said. "What say we clear the drive, have lunch at Lenny's Café and puddle this afternoon?" She gave me a puzzled look. "Puddle?" "Shoveling tailings through a machine that separates the nobbies from the dirt," I explained.

"Oh, I've seen the dust. That'll be fun. I rent a room from Lenny's wife and had a yarn with them last night. They told me about Wallangulla. Did you know there are more than 30 diggers here, as well as 30 locals who mostly also dig?"

"Sixty? I heard more than 100."

"There was, sometime back, but now things are better in the outside world. More work available." She was full of information. That explains the many deserted campgrounds and so few miners. Sixty might be about right; blokes would show up in the pub at some time, and I'd never seen the pub overcrowded.

I was impressed with Helga's strength and abilities. Any Minnesota farmer would love her. "Marry a big woman," the father of my farmer friend always said. "They're healthier, work harder and can produce a lot of children."

Helga had walked up to my claim so we walked back down to Lenny's and had lunch, leaving my car at the claim. The puddler was close, parked on lower Newtown by a mullock heap that I thought looked promising. After lunch I started the puddler up, and Helga shoveled tailings into the cylinder with the whirling rotor at the bottom. Dust flew out as the dry clay rattled around in the cylinder, sorting the nobbies from the clay. After a few hours we had a tin of nobbies.

"What do we do with these?" she asked.

"Snip them."

Fortunately we got to camp before the Odds returned. Edward gave her a quick sniff and backed off, not used to having a stranger in camp, especially a female. I laid a base of gumwood, piled sandalwood on top and boiled a billy, showing her the whole tea ritual. She had never had billy tea. I rapped the side of the billy and let it settle. A hanging cylindrical canvas bag, half filled with water to keep bacon, milk and eggs cool, all of them in the water itself, caught her attention. This seemed like a good time to introduce her to Outback gourmet stew.

"What is it? I can't tell by looking."

"It's called three-day stew. I made this one yesterday so it will still be good tomorrow. I boil it morning and evening to keep it from spoiling and let it set on the side of the firepit. It has meat, potatoes, chockos,[89] carrots and any other vegetable available. After the first day you can't tell one from the other. I'll feed you after we snip."

I gave her the snippers and showed her how to start on the edges and carefully go around each nobby, then, if no color shows, snip it in half just to make sure. A few showed color. I showed her how to rub them on the wet stone. Three showed promise.

"Next we take them to Chuck the Cutter, but no hurry."

She politely ate the stew and had a tin cuppa. I took out my Dr. Pat and showed her how to hand roll a cigarette. She did quite well but didn't inhale. "This is life in the opal field," I said.

"A bit of all right it is, mate," she declared.

Chuck went right to work in his cutting room handing back the two mug stones in less than 20 minutes. The third had sand pockets and was discarded. I paid him eight bob. The two stones were similar, flat, solid color, no flakes or flashes, not worth much, maybe 5, 10 quid each. "Now you have a souvenir."

"We'll each keep one," she said, giving me the choice. I picked the blue, leaving her the nicer light green, and smiled. We each had a keepsake.

Back at camp the Mad Pom was sitting by the fire reading and didn't look up. I imagined him saying, "The Yank shouldn't be bringing any bloody sheilas into camp, Edward. Take her to the pub."

I lit my kerosene lantern to avoid snakes, and we walked into the woods without saying a word. I didn't want to sit in the pub, and Pom was not fun to be around. For the first time she was silent. As we walked I told her about arriving here, meeting the Odd Mates, finding two opals, getting hooked, deciding to stay and finding and being cheated out of my first gemstone. "Now I am a permanent, hoping to make a fortune. When the time is right I'll settle accounts with the Bingos, Chuck, who just cut our stones, Shadow and the Odd Mates. But that can wait; for now I'll just dig."

We had come full circle, from the world of ideas to the world of opals, to my personal life. Stars shone in the clear sky amid the

---

89 Chocko – A green vegetable that looks like a fruit

stillness of the night. I blew out the lantern and we leaned against a large gumwood.

"I've wanted to be with you since the first time I saw you in Walgett," Helga said.

"Why me, an unbathed digger in dirty clothes with a full red beard?"

"You are a Viking," she answered, "Your flaxen hair and blue eyes. You look like Bjorn Fair-hair, the mighty warrior who was also wise and kind. Ah, what might have been were we born a thousand years earlier?" She paused. "Maybe we were. I feel like I have known you forever."

"Am I your wounded warrior?" I asked jokingly.

"Not yet," she said with a smile. After some thought, she continued. "I planted myself directly in front of you several times, hoping you would notice." I squeezed her soft waist between my thumbs and fingers and looked up into her eyes, this blond, blue-eyed Nordic.

As I clasped my hands behind her back and lightly pulled her to me, I realized that we had never really touched. She wrapped her arms around my shoulders, bent her head down deeply and kissed me.

Picks, shovels, clay, rock, wood and windlass – all the lifeless things I had handled the past three months; none of them were soft, pliant or warm. As her body pressed tightly against mine I remembered the pleasures of the world I was escaping. We had sung together in harmony, exchanged ideas and swapped cognizance. For a seemingly endless time we stood there, wrapped in each other's arms – cheeks pressed together as I pulled her to me, mixing ethereal fervor with our unified minds and erotic bodies; for the moment, one.

"I'll be leaving tomorrow," she said, still holding me tight. I had anticipated this and already regretted the loss. I couldn't ask her to stay on with me and dig; she was here on holiday. After a quiet moment she continued, "I'm leaving tomorrow for Queensland. Come with me. We'll snorkel on the Gold Coast and surf the tides. We'll walk the beaches and bathe in the sun." She smiled and pulled back. "Come with me for a week. Come with me for two weeks." Then, "Come with me – forever."

My mind flooded with images. Her voluptuous body encompassing mine on a grassy knoll. Her lovely voice describing abstract ideas. Singing together in harmony. Her beautiful deep blue eyes melding our spirits. Her smile at dawn, her caress at night, her mind and body always near.

The stars shined brightly. Arm in arm we walked slowly back to camp in silence. I left the lantern by the gum tree – snakes be damned. A week, two weeks, forever. My brain reveled in ecstasy, floating in sensual and intellectual delights, darting between the stars.

Then other thoughts crowded in: Shadow and the Bingo Brothers ratting my claim and Marco and the Mad Pom selling my puddler, tent and equipment, then shifting camp and claiming some bloke stole everything. And my opal, my Radiant opal, buried for millions of years, waiting for me to bring it to life, to carry it into to the sunlight and make it sparkle. How can I tell my sensual Nordic goddess who has awakened dormant passions in my heart that a greater, all-consuming obsession overwhelms me and has taken possession of my body and soul?

We walked until the flickering glowing embers greeted our eyes. The Mad Pom had retired, his tent was dark; Edward was quiet. We stopped at some distance. I turned toward her.

"I can't," I said, with tears welling up in my eyes. I lapsed into Outback Aussie, "Aye, mate, I can't hump me bluey.[90] I ain't yet found me stone."

She hung her head in thought for a moment, sighed, smiled slightly and nodded with understanding. Then she grasped my weapon hand in her weapon hand, palm to palm, at neck level, and pulled me close in the ancient Viking farewell, used between lovers before a long, dangerous sea journey, before going into battle or when parting for what might be the last time. We stood palm to palm, pressed tightly together with the stars sparkling so brightly I could see the blue of her eyes. Now, in the same way Viking lovers had parted a thousand years earlier, we stepped back and held our heads high. Then, in a moment, she was in her Volvo and off into the night.

I sat on a log, stirred the coals and stared into the luminous embers. Drawing deeply on a Dr. Pat, I asked, "Does a digger

---

90 I can't leave

get a second chance at a fatal stone? Will Ooluhru, the half-devil, half-serpent Aboriginal god of the opals, cast two curses at the same bloke? Will I find another gem to replace the one I had held in my hand for a few days?"

The embers gave no answer.

I asked again, "Does a digger get a second chance at consuming love? Will Freya, the Viking goddess of passion, again give me Helga, my flicka[91] whom I had held for only a few days?"

Again the embers gave no answer.

I knew only that I would pursue opal, whatever else may be. That is my goal, my life, my existence. I tossed the cigarette into the fire. I am home. I am here, a part of the Wally, and here I will be until – until my pick finds the future.

And then? "It's all in the diggin', mate, all in the diggin'."

---

91 Sweetheart

Chapter XVII
My Valkyrie

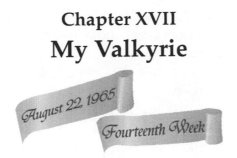

August 22, 1965

Fourteenth Week

Between opening my fist and awaking to find it empty and dreaming of Helga and awaking to find her gone, I slept fitfully. My only memento of her, the flat, plain blue mug stone on the footlocker next to the mantle lamp, reminded me of my lost opal and my lost love. I had a rasher of bacon with eggs and fried bread, and tried to divert my thoughts.

Isolation brings a new awareness. My compulsion to work eight hours underground and another two to three puddling was ebbing. The regular appearance of different birds and their elaborate songs marked the hours. First the Screechers, little green birds with outsized yellow bills, shrieked at the dawn. Heralded by one, a multitude followed, noisily chirping for a few minutes and then flying off. The following interlopers were quieter but still announced their presence. Group by group they came throughout the day. I never saw a lyrebird. They stay to themselves and can mimic any sound, filling the air with unusual, imitated warbling, trilling or cheeping. I once heard a freight train chugging through the gum trees. "Where's the nearest railroad track?" I asked Pom.

"He's leaving us, Edward, thinking about climbing a freight, he is. Well, don't wait up for him; he'll be off to Walgett." I didn't tell Pom I had heard a freight train; that would be too much to explain to Edward.

The laughing kookaburras and parrots that sound like a crying baby are disconcerting. One little bird, a loner, sang a long elaborate song, half a minute or more, which I tried to remember without success. His beautiful, plaintiff plea went unanswered. I had not yet seen an emu, the largest and ugliest Aussie bird. The apostle birds caught my curiosity. They are mottled brown, plump, black-billed, and blue-topped ground feeders who arrived in groups of 12. I counted them often. Not 8, 10 or 13, always 12. I asked whenever I had the chance, if that always was the case. "Ain't but 12 apostles, mate; read the Bible." But, I reasoned, somewhere in the great Outback there must be a group of apostle birds of more or fewer than twelve. It was momentous thoughts like this that occupied my leisure. The rattle of a frill-necked lizard chasing an insect broke my reverie.

Helga was on my mind. Once again I thought, "How long can a man live in comfort without the softness of a woman? How long before his soul longs for tender, comforting words? And his body cries out for gentle caresses? How long before he realizes something essential is lacking?"

The only women I had seen were Sarah, the publican's wife; King Tut's wife; and Jimmy the Snake Catcher's wife. Sarah was a lean, tough broad who could throw any man through the door if necessary, although she had Archer the Cop handle the ruffians when he was in the pub, which was often. The other two women worked like men, were female but had developed Outback strength and endurance; they were not soft. My life was opal. I must learn to live with my memories of Helga.

I did make it to the Digger's Retreat for lunch with Bobby. "'oweryergoin,' mate?" He smiled and confessed, "It 'us me, mate. I aimed 'er at the Yank's Dig. Bit o' awright, she looked. She stand 'er shout in the dig?" I pondered what he meant. Was he asking if she was a good helper or something else? But I didn't want to discus Helga with anyone, even my mate. I nodded to Sarah, and she brought pints and pies.

I had been giving Bobby a few quid from time to time, enough to eat at Lenny's Café if he wanted, but he stayed near the pub. He liked showing his stones and talking to the few tourists who came through. This was his life. I noticed his mood changing as the weeks went by, still smiling but showing more concern about something. It was always good to have a beer with him. "Yer got any kin, mate," I asked.

He shook his head. "All gone, long ago." I waited in silence for some time.

"The Bingos on yer, mate?" I asked.

He looked a little apprehensive. We finished our pints in silence. The Odds were at the bar. About a dozen blokes were scattered around the bar and tables, talking about the richest old claims and their latest finds. Brady was handing a stone around for appraisal. "Nice light jelly," Jake the Wasp said to Brady, turning the stone in his hand. "Just needs a bit 'o black backing to be a gem."

I was unsettled. We finished our pints. Bobby went back outside to await new visitors. I was not ready for work. The puddler and claim were still filled with my images of Helga. I drove back to camp, meandered through the Jungle for a while, and then just sat by the fire with a cuppa and a smoke, cogitating. I visualized her at the bow of a Viking longboat in a flowing robe, sword arm outstretched, pointing to the horizon, one breast exposed to show how casually Vikings faced death. And me? I am with the King's Berserkers, ready to plunge into battle and have my wounds healed by my Valkyrie. Ah, if only we had been born a millennium earlier, we would have been Vikings, lived the sagas and dreamed of Valhalla where we could be together again, preparing for the final battle of Ragnarok. Images flooded my brain. Once again I thought, perhaps I have stayed in Wallangulla too long. Am I succumbing to the Wallies?

I took another long walk, to the Professor's. He was gone again. I set the chess pieces in place and moved pawn to queen's three. If we didn't meet, the least we could do is keep a chess game going. The days were getting longer. It was still light when I returned to camp, and the Odds had already left for the pub. Still and quiet, not even a shifting breeze to blow smoke in my eyes. I petted Edward a bit, something I didn't normally do; he's Pom's dog and that's that. I had a bit of stew and a cuppa, still thinking about Helga. By the time I crawled into my sleeping bag on my little steel cot it was all clear in my mind, just how it would be in Valhalla preparing for the battle of Ragnarok.

The images were vivid as I dozed off to sleep: The battle raged. On my right Skarp-Hedin and the Vikings who fought with him were charging a swarm of Niebelungen, swords bloodied and leather shields slashed. To the left Egil and his berzerkers had a carpet of Skraelings to walk on in pursuit of the fleeing enemy.

I fought my way toward Skarp, wanting to learn. His fighting technique was the best. No matter that Egil had once burst into King Otto's banquet and lopped off the head of the honored guest sitting on the king's right and then asked the king's pardon because the decapitated one had once offended him. The mighty warrior not only received the pardon, but also was made chief of King Otto's Berserkers. But Egil was difficult to follow and too erratic.

I plunged in behind Skarp, slashing left and right with my short sword. The Niebelungen, metalworking dwarfs from the underworld, had longer swords and stronger shields. Short swords were easier to handle but a disadvantage unless you were right on top of your enemy. Our leather shields were easy to lacerate and render useless. But the choice of weapons was not mine; it was a tradition from the Viking's past. They would have to do. Skarp was well ahead. I tried to catch up and learn his style, but the dwarfish gnomes closed in behind him and encircled me. My sword bloodied and my shield completely chopped away, I slashed in all directions. There were too many of them. They outnumbered us 10 to one, 20 to one, 100 to one. "Come; I can take you, you vile Skraelings." I would fight bravely and die cheerfully as a true Viking.

She would come soon, my Helga. Ah, but she was too small for my fantasy: 6 foot 3 and 170 pounds. That will never do. Wagner's Valkyrie often top 300. I will make my Helga a 6-foot-6, 250 pound spear-wielding alto. Yes! That's it! My dream. My Valkyrie. My Helga. Wagner's music.

Blood gushes from my wounded body. Will my Helga get here in time? Hark! I hear it now, the music; Wagner's *Ride of the Valkyrie*. Violins swoop in on the first glissandos: zzzhooop – zzzhooop, zzzhooop – zzzhooop. Then the first four horns set the stage as the Valkyrie mount up: bum bum bum, bum bum bum, bah, bum bum bum, bum bum bum, bah. Next horns five and six blast out the fierce cry: pa pa pa pah, pah, pa pa pa pah, pah, pa pa pah, pah, pa pa pa pah.

While the horns are blasting away, the rich, full-throated trombones make their majestic fortissimo entrance. Then the third trumpet soars into the heavenly sphere to announce the Valkyrie. Now the whole orchestra makes the earth tremble as our Valkyrie maidens mount their steeds and charge through the celestial sphere to reclaim the fallen warriors.

They pass overhead, Bruinhilda and her troupe, singing, "Hy Yah Tow, Ha, Hy Yah Tow Ha," on their way to collect Skarp-Hedin, Gunner, Flossi, Egil and the rest. My Helga swoops down to me on her magnificent winged black mare, Voltronga. She leaps to the ground, both arms outstretched, still screaming in her full alto voice, "Hy yah tow ha, Hy yah tow ha," then charges towards me brandishing her spear, impaling and scattering Niebelungen. She stoops over me, smiles, brushes the hair from my eyes, kisses my forehead and gently touches my wounds, which stop bleeding immediately. I am still weak as she gathers me up in her strong arms and carries me to Voltronga, who is stamping and snorting impatiently. Helga, holding me close, my head reposing on her heaving breast, mounts and commands her mighty black mare – "Fly, Voltronga, take us from these Skraelings! Fly swiftly to Valhalla. Wotan awaits us."

Voltronga's mighty wings pierce the air and carry us soaring into the firmament, leaving the Niebelungen for another day. As we approach Valhalla my strength returns, and once inside the walls, my Valkyrie and I leap off the black mare to join our fellow Vikings in the great hall. I am cured.

Wagner's *Gotterdammerung* pervades the air. Ah, what he does with horns, trombones, trumpets and tubas! I hack off a slab of wild boar turning on the spit over the great fire, pierce it on Helga's spear, then slash off a chunk for myself. I fill our stoups with mead and we raise toasts: "To Wotan, Skula! To Thor, Skula! To Freya, Skula!" My Helga, my Valkyrie, always at my side, arms quick to embrace, lips eager to caress, spear ready to impale should the Niebelungen break through.

In Valhalla we hone our fighting skills to prepare for the final battle of Ragnarok – Vikings against the forces of evil, the Niebelungen. We must acquit ourselves well, knowing we will lose. It is foretold. Our gods will be destroyed, Valhalla will crumble, we will all die. Life is a heavy burden for Vikings, who are restive if not fighting. Our goal is to die a heroic death in a hopeless cause. The thought of playing a harp in a heavenly band eternally is more disparaging than any concept of hell. "Fight us, kill us, but don't bore us."

After many stoups of mead and toasts to the gods, we gather in the center of the great hall for the final tribute: "To Wotan, chief of the gods! To Ragnarok, the final battle between good and evil! To death, an end to it all!" With our mead filled stoups raised high, we shout, "Skula, Wotan! Skula, Ragnarok! Skula, Dauoar!"[92] and smash our emptied stoups into the great fireplace. Sleeping where we fall, arm in arm, my Helga and I awaken refreshed the next morning ready to again battle the Niebelungen.

With these images filling my mind and soul and Wagner's music permeating my consciousness, I slept, dreaming, in the arms of Helga, my beloved Valkyrie.

---

92 Dauoar – Death

Chapter XVIII
Dynamite Dan

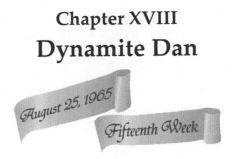

Sleep was sounder when dreaming of Helga and opals. By morning I felt rested, ate a good breaky and went to my claim as if nothing had changed. After a short day's dig and a little puddling, I snipped nobbies and found a few with color. I needed Angus the Scot and his stonecutter. Bruce the Banker knew where they are.

I walked leisurely through the trees toward Bruce's camp, following a roundabout way. Twenty minutes out I came upon a camp enclosed by a four-foot high palisade of branches with leaves that enclosed a tent, a waist-high stone fireplace, a small table and a stool. A rifle leaned against the tree. I stood staring for a minute, wondering about its inhabitant. A bloke came quietly up behind me, ready for a bluey.

"'Oo the bleedin' 'ell are you, and whater yer pokin' around after?"

"Fair go, mate," I said. "Just blowin' through, havin' a look. I'm the Yank."

He looked closely at me and then relaxed. He looked like the 3rd century Saxon invaders of England, lean, fair-haired and light skinned.

"Aye. Righto, mate. I heard about it. They got you, too, the bloody Bingos. Grab a stump, I'll put the billy on."

I looked around. A case of dynamite sticks seemed to be the only place to sit, except for the one stool.

"Go ahead, mate; it's safe. Takes 60 pounds of pressure and a spark to set it off. Needs a blasting cap and fuse. If you drop a stick of dyno on the fire it just burns, but it sure gets blokes movin' after a few beers." He laughed.

I sat down but didn't feel comfortable sitting on a ticket to the next world. I looked at his fireplace and added that to my list of aspirations. Why the dynamite? Some diggers blast through the shin cracker and sandstone when sinking a shaft. It's faster than a pick but leaves the sides cracked and broken, and chunks fall off. It also cracks the fragile nobbies if you're not careful.

"Sinking a shaft?" I asked while he set the billy on the grate.

"No. Protectin' me stones. They ratted me. The bloody Bingo bastards ratted me claim and stole me pocket 'o nobbies." He uncorked a bottle of whiskey and offered me a drink.

"Ta, mate," I took a swig and handed it back. I hoped I wouldn't end up drunk, but I didn't want to refuse his hospitality nor miss his hostility.

"Used to hit the boozer,[93] but ain't been back since they ginked me, the mangy ratbags. Now I do the hard stuff." He took a deep swig from the bottle. "I was there the day they lurked you." He got off his stool and tossed a handful of tea leaves into the billy and went through the tea ritual. Finally, he rapped the billy and poured me a cup. Perfect Outback etiquette. I could get to like this bloke. I waited quietly as he went on with his story.

"The Bingos came in, both Bernie and Benny, and shouted the pub. 'Beer for the lot of 'em,' they told Sarah. She looked suspicious; the Bingos don't shout anything for anybody. 'She'll be right, Sarah,' Bernie said and slapped a five-pound note on the bar. 'Australia has received foreign aid from America. The Yank's buying tonight, mates; its all on him. Raise your glasses to our Yank allies.' The Bingos laughed and called for another round. Then Bernie said it was a hooly-dooly,[94] but I suspected they had it fixed. He showed your stone around, a real beaut, it was. Jake the Wasp said it was the best he had ever seen. The colors flashed even in the dim light o' the pub. 'We got it for under five thou,' Bernie said. 'Under five thou!'"

I jumped up and sloshed my tea. I had heard the details before, but it still hit me hard. Marco hadn't mentioned any of this, and neither he nor Pom ever talked about it again.

"They got it from me for under two hundred," I said. "The bloody bastards." I told my new acquaintance the whole story, why I had to sell and how Shadow had put the price on it. For the first time my anger exploded. I wanted to rip into them.

---

93 Boozer – Local pub, the Diggers Retreat
94 Hooly-dooly – Unexpected treat; favorable turn of events. Serendipity

"Have another hit, mate, and I'll tell you how they lurked me."

I took a deep swig and sat down, my anger growling.

"I was new, just like you, and diggin' fresh ground. After several weeks I smelled opal clay and knew I was close. Then I hit some nobbies with good color. It was late in the day, and I wanted to find out right away if they was good, so I climbed out and took them to Chuck the Cutter. 'E roughed them in just a half hour while I waited. 'Nice bit o' color,' 'e said, 'Be worth a few quid.' I said this is just the start. I've got a whole big pocket waitin' to be dug out."

"'Oh?' he said, 'What say to a pint?'"

"Sure, mate, the pocket will still be there tomorrow. We started for the boozer, but first – and I should have known something funny was going on – he told his little girl to run over to Bernie Bingo and tell him his stones were ready. I didn't realize that the Bingos knew every claim in the district from Archer the Cop's registrations. Didn't cross my mind what they were up to. Bernie came in almost as soon as we got to the pub, and Chuck the Cutter talked to him a while. I thought it must be about Bernie's stones. Bernie left for a few minutes, then came back all smiles."

"Chuck introduced me and asked if I'd like to show Bernie my three stones. Sure. He held them up, one at a time, turned each one around and over, slowly. Then examined them outside though it was almost dark."

"'Nice color, good shape, flake pattern, domed; worth a couple hundred quid anyway,' he said with a smile. 'At least a couple hundred, but let's scrutinize them carefully.' He handed them around the bar. 'What'd yer think, mates?' Being a real sport, 'e was. We were all mates having a pint together, looking for a fair price. Buddies, as a Yank would say. Takin' 'is time, 'e was. Real slow. Two pints. Three pints. Handed them to the blokes at the tables. 'What'd yer think? Two hundred quid?'"

"'Aye, at least.'"

"'Three hundred?' Heads nodded. Now he had my attention. I'd never had that many apples in me hand before. I should have been onto 'im, Bernie was shoutin' the beer. After a few more pints and opal stories about the old diggers, he said, 'Four hundred' and slammed his glass down on the table. 'That's it, 400,' and he pulled out a fat wad and counted it out 40 ten-pound notes, one at a time. Piled 'em up on the table. 'My shout,' I said. I left a few quid on the table and stuffed the rest in my pocket. This was just the beginning. I had a big pocket of stones to dig out the next day. Maybe two, three, five thousand quid? Who knows? I bid my new mates g'day and stumbled out to my pickup. Blotto, I was."

I was puzzled. "This doesn't sound like the Bingos I know. He offered you a good price by the sound of it. What's the lurk?" He passed the bottle back to me again.

"The lurk is that he paid me a fair price for the stones he bought but nothing for the ones he stole. He made sure I was as full as a goog[95] so I wouldn't go back to the claim that night. The next morning I was in no condition to dig and didn't get down my shaft 'til noon. What I found then was a pile of loose clay that almost filled the drive. Must have been three or four blokes at it. The whole pocket was gone, three feet by four feet dug out, leaving only a pile of tailings."

"Bernie was in the pub with you. You got any idea who did the ratting?"

"I can guess by who wasn't in the pub that night. Your mates weren't there. Neither was Shadow," he said.

"Ten Pins never stays home at night," I said. "The Mad Pom does about half the time. They were both in on buggering me, so they're prime suspects. Shadow is a sure bet. He's in on any swindling or ratting."

"Well," he continued, "I didn't know what to make of it. All I knew was that someone had ratted my claim. Then little by little I put it all together. I had told the Chuck the Cutter I was on a pocket. He told Bernie, and Bernie got me tanked while his mates ratted me claim. It's that simple. By late afternoon I was sure. I wanted to knock Bernie's block off. I found him at the bar in the pub, called him a rotten bastard and went for him, but they were waiting for me. Archer the Cop got between us. Archer's big and used to blueys. I bloodied his nose, but that was it. He had me on the floor in cuffs before I got a second swing. Bernie sat there smiling through the whole thing. Then after a lecture on how to control my hot head, Archer took off the cuffs and locked me in

---

95 Full as a goog – Drunk

the Shearin' Shed. Said we'd talk about it in the morning after I cooled down."

"Shearing Shed?" I asked.

"Aye, mate. The jail. Six by eight clapboard shack with a bench and a small window. Not far from the Final Shaft Cemetery. Anyway, I waited 'til after dark, kicked the door off its hinges, got in my pickup and went home."

"Didn't Archer come after you?"

"Nah. Haven't seen 'im since. I haven't been back to the pub. Stayed away because if I see Bernie again I'll slam into him, the bleedin' gallah gink bastard. That'd do me no good, just more trouble. I took a drive to Walgett, bought several bottles of whiskey and two cases of dynamite. I needed time, maybe a lot o' time, to think about what to do. I had to stop the ratters."

"How?" I asked. "By blowing up your claim?"

"No, by droppin' a stick down the shaft. I'll show you how to make a primer; might come in handy sometime."

He opened a World War II ammunition case and pulled out a shiny tube the size of a bullet. "This is a blasting cap," he said. "This goes onto the fuse, like this." He pushed it onto the fuse and crimped it with pliers. "Yer gotta be careful. Squeeze too hard and it'll blow your hand off." Next he made a hole through the dynamite stick with the tapered handle of the crimper and another diagonal one lower, pushed the cap through it and into the stick. "This is a primer. Ready to use. I'll show yer how. I'll leave two minutes of fuse." He snipped the fuse, took another swig of whiskey, and we got into his pickup.

"I named the claim Denmark. That's where me sheila's grandfather came from. It makes her feel a little more comfortable about my being here." It was less than a mile away, but he drove like a wild man, dodging between the mullock heaps. We skidded to a stop by a tailings pile. He jumped out, lit the fuse and dropped the primer down the hole. We stepped back. After a couple minutes of fizz from the fuse, a "Kaboom" sounded. Debris and dust flew up out of his shaft. He smiled. "No blood this time, but we'll check." The heads of two diggers popped up out of nearby holes and looked around. He waved at them. "They think I'm crazy." I followed him down the shaft. He lit a candle and looked around. "They might try rattin' again. This is a good claim, so I do this a couple o' times a day. If any bloke survives the blast and climbs up the shaft, I'll whack him back down with a pick handle and drop in another stick. Then I'll hire Niggly Neville as my defense lawyer," he said and laughed.

Back at camp we had another cuppa and several more swigs. I decided he'd make a good friend or a worthy enemy and opted for the first. We talked about the Bingos and decided to stay clear of them and wait for the right moment, rather than do something rash. We had a mutual enemy and time to plan.

"Fixed for a sheila, mate?" he asked.

"No, I'm alone."

"Me sheila, she's in western Aussie near Perth. Waitin' for me to come back with a fortune." We talked for a while about opal, and then I felt it was time to move on. I set out, more than a little wobbly, for Bruce the Banker's camper trailer.

He was having tea, his evening meal, fried Spam and eggs. I should teach him to make stew, I thought. I sat on a log and waited. He told me Angus and his cutter lived in a wood humpy[96] on the north end of Three Mile Flats. Bruce said he wanted to puddle a mullock heap and asked if he could use my puddler for a day or two

"I'll bring it over in the morning and show you how to run it." Then, after a pause, I added, "I just came across a digger camped not too far from here. Real Aussie. Didn't think to ask his name."

"He's called Dynamite Dan, or Dyno Dan. Got the Wallies. Thinks someone's ratting his claim. Keeps dropping sticks of dynamite down his shaft."

I didn't comment. We'd talk about it later. I went home to a quiet evening with stew, a Dr. Pat and a cuppa by the fire. The Odds were out for the night. Having Dyno Dan for my new ally eased my mind, and I turned in to dream of my Valkyrie and the opals I was certain to find.

The Odds returned late, laughing and singing. I'd never heard them sing before. "Twas on the good ship Venus, my god you should 'a seen us. The figurehead was a whore in bed, and the mast an upright penis." They sang drunkenly through

---

96 Humpy – Shanty, shack

several more verses. I didn't get up or light my mantle lamp but wondered what was going on.

"Shhh. Be quiet, Edward, you'll wake the Yank, and he'll start waving his arms and singing at you again."

After they quieted down, I went back to sleep.

Chapter XIX
Puppy Rain

August 26, 1965

Fifteenth Week

The next morning I went to Bruce the Banker's camp. We drove the puddler to the mullock heap on Three Mile Flats. A puddler is easy to set up and use. Just start the engine, put the rotor in gear and shovel in the tailings. He took me back to camp, and I left for my Yank's Dig. The Odds didn't stir.

Harold Blake walked up from his claim, smiling, and asked if the Odd Mates got home all right. "They were drunker than usual when the Buffs broke up last night."

"Buffs?"

"Short for Buffaloes. A social group. We get together to have a yarn and a pint, sing and tell jokes. Care to join? It's a good mob."

"Aye, I'll have to think about it. Yeah, they got back to camp all right, singing like drunken sailors. Not a sound out of them this morning." After a pause I asked, "Do you know of a bloke called Dynamite Dan? Camped in the Jungle?"

"Aye, mate. A real hothead he is. Some say he's got the Wallies, but I think he just likes a bluey. Bloodied the Copper's nose he did. Archer tossed him into the Shearing Shed, but he kicked his way out. 'He wanted to get out that bad,' Archer said. 'I'll let him go. But he better stay away from the Bingos. They couldn't have ratted his claim. They were in the pub with him.' Why, yer know 'im?"

"I just met him. Curious. Seemed like a decent bloke."

Harold looked dubious but nodded.

I dug for a couple hours then went to the pub for a pint with Bobby and asked him about Dyno Dan. "Aye, mate, he's one of us, a fair-dinkum Aussie. Yer don't want to sling off at him. Yer'll be in a bluey and come a cropper faster than yer can rap yer billy.[97]

---

[97] You'll be in a fight and in big trouble faster than you can settle your tea billy leaves

The Bingos buggered 'im good, but she'll be right, mate, she'll be right. He'll give 'em the drum.[98]"

"If he's right with you, he's right with me, mate," I said and looked over at Bernie Bingo, smiling, at the bar. I raised my glass. "We'll stone the bloody Bingo bastards together."

Bobby looked at Bernie's nefarious grin apprehensively. "Aye, mate, together."

"They still on you?"

"They want Sarah to ban me, wantin' to get me stones. She won't, now that I've got a few quid. Ta, mate."

"I'll have a word with him."

"Good on yer mate. Me and me stones is fine. She'll be right."

Two-Bob Bobby seemed a little more relaxed than usual. I walked past Bernie as I left and said, "We were just 'avin' a yarn about Niggly Neville and Cocky Bowman. Some blokes just don't know how to be fair dinkum." Bernie just smiled and took another drink from his pint. Okay, Bernie, I thought, your day's coming.

The Odds didn't come back to camp that afternoon, just stayed in town. Maybe they didn't dig at all and spent the day in the pub. The Digger's Retreat was more home to them than camp. I was seeing less and less of them, and we talked little. Edward wandered around to other sites now that he was alone so much but usually stayed when I was around.

I snipped my nobbies, had evening tea and settled by the fire with a cuppa and a smoke. Little puffs of dust started coming up out of the ground. Puff, puff, puff, dust, dust, dust, here and there, more and more. I was puzzled until a few drops fell on me. Raindrops were falling on ground so dry they kicked up dust. Then suddenly it poured – poured buckets, sheets of water. I was wet before I got to my tent. Edward scampered into Pom's tent.

What a storm! I had not seen rain since New Zealand more than nine months ago. It rains in Wallangulla just once or twice a year, I was told. But what a downpour! Water three inches deep poured through my tent. I put my footlocker on the cot along with other vulnerable items. By now I had acquired a wooden chair. I lit my mantle lamp, took off my boots and sat down to enjoy this unusual event. Then I heard a puppy barking and yipping frantically.

---

[98] He can handle himself. He'll pay them back

I lit my lantern and followed the yips to Marco's tent. A tiny puppy was in an eight-inch-high cage with no top. He was trying to climb out, standing in water half way up his belly. I picked him up, took him back to my tent, wiped him dry, wrapped him in a hand towel and set him on the cot next to the footlocker. He looked happy and had as friendly a smile as I have ever seen on a dog's face. His long ears hung down over his paws. I petted him while we waited out the storm. Now six inches of water poured through the tent. The clay ground absorbed no water. Fortunately, our camp was on high ground, if only by a few inches. The water ran off.

So Marco has a dog, a tiny puppy that he leaves alone in his tent for hours and hours. Marco's hardly ever here. How long has he had it? Why didn't he tell me? I could have looked after it. I hadn't heard it bark before. What would Niggly Neville, the dog lover, do about this? I didn't know Marco well, but neglecting his dog was just wrong. I braved the storm to get a carton of milk out of the hanging canvas cooler. I was wet anyway. I poured a saucer of milk for the little one. He lapped it up greedily.

I was beginning to dislike Marco more all the time. Conniving in lurking my opal was one thing but mistreating a puppy was in a different realm. No reason to do that. Marco would not want me going into his tent for any reason and would certainly not want me handling his puppy, even to rescue it from drowning. I didn't care. Meanwhile the torrential rain poured down. Then I thought of Edward. I wrapped the puppy tight, grabbed my lantern and made a dash for Pom's tent. Edward was lying on Pom's cot, looking guilty. "Good dog," I said, patting Edward's head. I had never been in either tent, and Marco and Pom had not ventured into mine. On the Wally, private property is sacrosanct. No locks and often no doors.

Marco shouldn't have a puppy, I thought. He won't care for it. He'll just keep it in its little cage. Then what? I balanced the footlocker precariously on the chair, wiped my feet and took the little dog into my sleeping bag with me. The downpour continued and water six inches deep flowed through my tent as we drifted off to sleep.

Morning brought warm sunshine over a steaming landscape of mud. I put on dry socks from my footlocker; knocked out my boots to make sure no scorpions had crawled in, and lit a fire. Sandalwood flares up at the touch of a match, but today I had to split it with a hatchet to get to the dry center. Then it burned nicely over a few pieces of gumwood. I leisurely fried up a nice breaky and walked through the mud with my cuppa back to my tent, where my new little friend was sitting contentedly on the cot. After a saucer of milk we both felt ready to face the day. No use trying to get to my claim.

What to do with this smiling, floppy-eared little puppy? That's what I'll call him, Floppy. It fits. I couldn't put him back in the water-soaked cage. After another cuppa and a hand-rolled smoke, the solution came to me. I wrapped him up in the towel again, grabbed my carton of milk, and set out with him through the mud to Bruce the Banker's campsite.

He wasn't up. I banged on his trailer door, "G'day, mate. Got something for yer." He didn't seem happy to be disturbed but put on his boots and came out.

"Must be important to get a bloke up in mud like this."

"Need your help. Got a neglected puppy here that needs looking after for a while. Just say he washed up in the flood if anyone asks. I call him Floppy, but you can call him what you want. He responds to anything." Floppy wagged his tail and looked wide eyed at Bruce."

Bruce didn't ask any questions. I handed him the puppy and set the carton of milk on the table. He gave the pup a pat. "She'll be right, mate," he said.

"Too young for anything but milk, I think, but he'll soon determine that for himself." He put the pup inside his trailer with a dish of milk.

"Got time for a cuppa?"

After some opal talk I left Bruce and Floppy for a game of chess with the Professor. Puddles of water stood in the low areas, and mud covered everything. I slogged through it and yelled, "Kookaburra. Care for a game?"

The Prof came out of his tent, "Sure, if you don't mind getting your ass wet." He could be civilized even when mildly vulgar. We set up the pieces on a wet board on a wet table and sat on wet chairs.

"No humidity here. We'll be dry in no time."

I didn't ask him where he had been, and he didn't mention it. The Prof was often gone and said nothing about it. None of my business. It was a good day for chess, nothing else to interfere. He won more than half the games. I mentioned Dynamite Dan. "You two have something in common; he'll be a good ally."

"Yeah, I'm glad to have him on my side."

"Be careful. He jumps into blueys too hastily. Plan ahead."

But plan what? I couldn't think about retaliating at the Bingos until I found my pocket of opal.

The Odd Mates still hadn't returned when I got back. Had I known, I would have kept the puppy another day. I set the footlocker on a couple of faggots to keep it out of the mud and spent a quiet evening reading and writing letters. My correspondence was falling off, less news to report and fewer contacts. I was becoming more isolated from the outer world. I went to sleep thinking of Helga and opal.

The next morning brought a new world. Green grass everywhere. Did it grow in the dark? I had noticed some green yesterday, but now it was everywhere, and it kept growing. By afternoon it had reached six inches. Dormant grass seed waiting patiently for a year? Two years? Then frantically shooting up to reproduce more seed that would patiently wait for one, two, five, or maybe even 10 years for the next rain. The desire to live, to reproduce, to become immortal is phenomenal.

Two humans in their 30s or even 40s, composed of aged cells, can somehow produce a baby of totally new cells. Youth out of age. Here, isolated in the desert, one can entertain such thoughts and still not have a clue.

The Odds returned. I was cutting firewood and came back with an armload as they got out of Marco's Holden. I wondered where Pom's pickup was.

"G'day."

"G'day." Marco untied his tent flap, went in, came out and looked around. He walked around Pom's tent and looked inside.

Pom didn't notice, and I was busy building a fire. Then he walked around my tent and looked inside. He walked around the whole campsite, trying to look casual and said nothing. "Shall I put your billy on?" I asked?

"Ta," Marco said as he walked around. Finally he gave up and sat down. He never mentioned the puppy.

A box turtle ambled by the firepit. "How did he get here?" I said. "The nearest warrambool[99] is 10 miles away. Turtles need water."

"The desert comes alive after a rain. Yer'll see new things for two days, then back to normal," Marco said, almost friendly. The three of us had tea together without saying a word. A salamander scooted through. Frill-necked lizards busily gobbled up crawlies. The desert was indeed coming alive.

I had been planning for some time on leaving the Odd Mates but didn't want to stay in the Jungle and hadn't found a satisfactory place elsewhere. I didn't want to be around either one of them but didn't want to move and then have to move again. Besides, if my presence bothered them, so much the better.

A quiet week passed. The grass disappeared, the clay dried and dormant life awaited the next rain. Pom's truck had a wet distributor that dried out in a few days. I found Angus and had his cutter, Garbhan, cut and polish my mug stones. Angus paid a fair price for them. He seemed honest and competent. I trusted him. With him on the Wally why would anyone go to the Bingos? Just having another buyer improved my attitude and life.

Bruce the Banker and Floppy got along fine. "I take him with me underground. He's a good dog, already knows his name. He runs around and digs but comes back when I call him."

"His name is?"

"Floppy, as you suggested. He's growing fast. I'll have to figure out what to do when he gets too big to carry down the shaft. But for now things are fine. Hope you don't want him back."

---

99 Warrambool – Similar to a billabong, but drier, more like a marsh than a swamp

"No, glad you like him. He's yours. How's the puddling going?"

"Too slow. I'm thinking of buying a wet puddler. You can go through a ton of clay in an hour."

I had heard of wet puddling. "Where do you get the water?"

"Puddling tank a couple miles north of the pub. About 75 feet square, clay banks and a pool of water in the center. You pump the water through your puddler washing the clay, and it flows back into the pool to be used again."

"Doesn't the puddler rust away?"

"Aye, it wouldn't work on a dry puddler. Has to be waterproof, specially made. I ain't got the guineas[100] now, but a few more stones, and she'll be right, mate." I was learning new things all the time.

We took my puddler back to Newtown. I had lunch with Bobby four times that week. He seemed happier. He even smiled at Bernie Bingo, which surprised both Bernie and me. I was glad to see my mate in good spirits.

---

100 Guinea. A gold coin worth 21 shillings. Not used anymore

Chapter XX
Two-Bob Bobby's Sheila

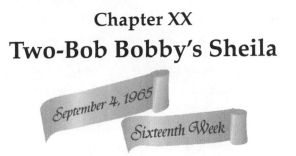

Tourists stopped by my claim from time to time, looking for mug stones or just to visit. My Yank's Dig was less than a quarter-mile from the pub and easily accessible. Sometimes they bought a mug stone or climbed down and had a look at the diggings, but usually they stayed only a few minutes. Going down a shaft was unnerving, but it let them brag that they'd been in a real opal mine.

One day about noon as I came up for lunch, a small man with a broad smile greeted me. "G'day, mate." His Aussie was so bad I didn't even ask him about kookaburras. He had all the characteristics of a Yugoslavian immigrant. I had worked with many Slavs on the Khancoban Dam in the Snowy Mountains. "Dobra utrum," I said ("good morning" in Serbian). He beamed. "Cocka say," (How are you?). His English was adequate for small talk only. He told me he had worked on construction projects for the past year and now wanted to see Australia. I was surprised that he traveled alone, because all the other Slavs I had known stayed in groups.

"I have tent and pots. I camp," he said proudly. "I want find for opal." There was an aura of innocence about him. For the past weeks I had followed my channel, hoping to find another pocket, putting off digging toward the other shaft. He might help.

"Would you like to work with me?"

"Yes, yes," he said with enthusiasm.

"Come, I'll show you my claim."

He followed me down the shaft and into the drive. I lit the candles. He looked a little uncomfortable, but put a brave face on it.

"You okay?"

"I fine."

"Okay," I said. "We dig."

He was a good worker. I forgot about lunch, and we continued digging and hauling up for the rest of the afternoon.

"I camp here?" he said, indicating my claim.

"Sure, you camp here." I showed him a level place to pitch his tent and dug a small firepit in the clay.

"Good. Tomorrow I be here." I bid him good day and left.

The next morning he had his tent up, a fire burning and was rubbing something on the rocks around his tent. "Dobra utrum" he said, finished what he was doing and showed me what he had in his hand.

"Snakes not like this."

I looked. "That's garlic."

"Yes. Snakes away. I not like snakes by tent." I told him that he was not likely to encounter any snakes here with or without garlic but he felt more comfortable with the garlic nostrum.

I hung a rope down the other shaft, and we climbed down using the toe kicks dug into the side of the shaft. The previous owners had gotten about six or eight feet into the drive toward the other shaft. I explained that I wanted to connect the shafts. "You dig here," I said, pointing emphatically. "I will dig in the other drive. Then we'll meet." "Okay, okay," he said, using that universal word that has invaded every tongue. (The German sailors I worked with claimed it stood for a man named Otto Kraus, a German inspector. If his initials were written on an item, it passed customs without further inspection. His work was so thorough that OK came to mean very good. But I digress.)

I showed him how to pack the dug clay under the shaft. We could carry the windlass to this shaft when necessary to haul up the tailings. "Mario," he said, pointing at his chest. "Yank," I answered. We shook hands. I gave him a pick and a shovel and left him to it.

Mario was one of those people who, I felt, couldn't lie, cheat or steal. He struck me as innocent and honest. He was independent, cooked and ate by himself, and lived in his tent. It looked like a promising arrangement.

Two-Bob Bobby was in good spirits. He had not accepted any money from me for the last week or two, saying, "She'll be right, mate." I thought the tourist business must be good, although there never were many tourists. He talked more than usual, just small talk about who's on opal and who got into blueys. Then, "I'll show you me dig, mate."

"Good on yer. Like to see it." At last I would get to see where he camped, how he lived.

"Maybe next week," he assured me. "Then I'll be on me way. Me sheila wants me back. I'm humpin' me bluey, mate, goin' back to shearin." I looked at his smiling face, somewhat puzzled. His sheila wants him back? After 10 years? How does he know? Did she write him a letter? He obviously was happy so I questioned him no more.

Several days passed pleasantly. One morning as I arrived my Slav was already down digging. He climbed up and handed me a nobby with color on the edge. "Look, Yank. I have opal." I showed him how to snip it and rub it on the wet stone. Sure enough, it had color, maybe cut a stone.

"Here. For you." He handed it to me.

"No, for us."

I waved my hand back and forth between us. We hopped into my Morris Minor and went to see Garbhan, Angus' cutter. It cut a nice little mug stone, Angus gave us 15 quid, which we split Mario was very happy. "Already I make money."

This partnership was working out fine. He had dug several feet in the drive. We could connect the two drives in a week or so.

About the fifth day of our partnership, we stopped to have a cuppa after hauling up his tailings. He was always happy. "How you get claim?"

"Well," I said, "you can stake out any area 100 by 100 feet and register it with Archer the Cop, and it's yours. Or you can buy a claim. I liked this claim and bought it from two Yugoslavs who wanted to get to Sydney and gamble on horseracing." Mario looked serious. "Serbian?"

"No. I think they were Croatian."

"I must go. They come kill me." I knew from Khancoban and from what I had read in the Sydney papers that Yugoslavian immigrants were killing and blowing each other up, but I didn't know the details. During World War II the Croats sided with the Germans to escape the Communists, and the Serbs got caught in the Communist takeover of Yugoslavia. Their common language is Serbo-Croatian, but the Croats claim they can't understand the Serbians. Now they had carried the war with them to Australia.

"No, Mario," I said emphatically, "This is Australia. Australian law. Australian government. This is my claim. I own it. The Croats have no authority here. They sold it to me. It is mine."

"You not understand." He shook his head.

"Okay," I said. "Let's dig some more and think about it later."

We went back down our separate shafts and finished out the day. Mario had a woebegone look on his face.

"Its all right, Mario. This is my claim, and I want you to stay here and work with me. We're partners. The Croatians won't be back. We'll be fine. Not to worry, mate; she'll be right," I said, hoping to make him feel at home.

I patted him on the back. He smiled a sad smile. I waved as I drove off leaving him standing there, looking apprehensive.

The next morning he was gone. Packed everything into his Holden and drove off. Nothing left but the firepit and the drain ditch around his tent site. He was right. I "not understand."

Marco spent less and less time at camp, some nights not coming back at all. Must be getting serious with Shadow's daughter, I thought. Pom was growing stranger and more uncommunicative, spending less time by the fire and more in his tent.

"They'll see. They'll see, Edward, we know what they're up to. We'll get them," he said to his attentive dog. He was deep in the Wallies, and I needed to find another place to camp. I paid Dyno Dan a visit and told him Pom's shit-can-man story, about the outhouses in England that use a bucket instead of a hole. I said I thought the Mad Pom soon would crack up completely.

"Wanna blow 'im up, mate? Help yourself to the sticks and caps. We owe 'im one." Dan was joking, but Pom was getting dangerous.

"We'll see what happens. I'm not ready for a confrontation right now."

I missed my Serbian. At the Digger's Retreat I found Bobby in good spirits and ordered our usual pints and pies.

"'oweryergoin, mate?"

"She's right, she is."

"Good on yer." I raised my glass. He smiled as though he were truly happy. I hadn't seen him in such high spirits. "You look like you've found yer sheila," I joked.

"Aye, mate, spot on, spot on. Shearin' time, it is. I'll be a jackaroo again. Had 'nough of bludgin' mate, 'nough of the Wally. Me stones'll look good on me sheila. Meet me at Hart's Four Mile tomorrow, and I'll show yer me digs."

"Righto, mate, I'll be there. I'll give yer a ride into Walgett for the train." I would have to borrow the Professor's Land Rover, but that would be okay.

We had another pint to celebrate the event. I knew nothing about Bobby's life outside the pub. We never strayed far from the subject of opal and news of the Wally. But today, when we finished our pints, he motioned for me to come outside. He opened his hand and held his opals in the sunlight. What brilliance! Purple, yellow, red, green, gold. I resisted the desire to grab them and hold them myself. I had seen them only once before and then only momentarily. They flashed and sparkled. What beauty! I understood why he would rather starve to death than part with them, why the Bingos were crazy to get their hands on them and why he kept them close to his body. After letting me gaze at them for a long while, he said, "Tomorrow, mate. Tomorrow at me digs. Then she'll be right."

"Righto, mate, tomorrow."

I didn't know what he had in mind, but he was the happiest I had ever seen him. What was his camp like? How would he get to Hart's Four Mile with his game leg? Well, not to worry. I'll find out tomorrow. And where was he going? Where was his sheila?

Next day I got to Hart's Four Mile early, overly eager. Bobby was nowhere to be seen. Hart's Four Mile consisted of only a few claims, five shafts total. This small field never produced much. I walked around and finally sat down. What could be keeping him? He didn't say morning, just tomorrow, but he should have been here by now. Out of curiosity I looked down the shafts. In the third one, there he was, lying on his side at the bottom of a 25 foot hole. I couldn't manage the toe kicks without a rope, so I drove back to camp for a rope, pick and shovel and returned as fast as I could.

At the bottom of the shaft, I saw he had a smile on his face. His fist was closed and next to his cheek. I felt his neck. He was cold, dead for hours. Did the Bingo Brothers get to him, threaten him? Did they push him down the shaft? Unlikely. He was smiling in death. The Bingos would have taken his stones. Then I remembered our conversation weeks before. "Will you shovel me under, bury me when the time comes?"

"Righto, mate," I had said. "That I will do."

I sat down and put my head in my hands. "Why? Why did you do this, Bobby? You could have done something else; we could have worked it out together. We've got enough money to live on. You could stay in town or camp with me. Why this? Why now?"

He looked comfortable as he was, so I let him lie. Once up the shaft, I scanned the area, then took the cribbing logs from around the shaft, threw them in the hole and shoveled in the tailings. When the shaft was full, I leveled the ground to make it look like no hole had ever been there. I had never buried anyone, never even been close to a corpse except in a funeral home, but Two-Bob Bobby was me mate, and I fulfilled my promise.

He was me first mate, maybe me only mate. We were close, though we never spent much time together outside the pub. Now he and his stones rested in the ground together, safe from the elements and the Bingos. At rest with the vision of his sheila. At peace at last and forever. I took my hat off and stood in silence for a moment. As tears rolled down my face, I said, "G'bye, mate, she'll be right," and drove back to camp.

I sat by the fire and thought a long time. Bobby had had a vision of the happiest time of his life and was returning to it. He was again a Jackaroo with his sheila by his side. His opals were buried with him. The eyes of Ooluhru, the devil-serpent, had been returned to the ground. It is over. "She's right, mate. She's right."[101]

I told no one. This was between Bobby and me, a private matter, a promise I had made and kept. No need for the law. Bobby had taken his own life; he had the right to do that. I had shoveled him under; I had the right to do that. He was at peace now with his Radiant Opal in his fist. They had returned to the earth together.

I kept to myself for more than a week, avoided Pom as much as possible and didn't see the Professor or Dyno Dan. I didn't visit the Digger's Retreat and parked my panel van on the far side of the slope, out of sight, when I worked my claim. I was truly alone. I had not seen Bobby that much, but having him as a mate had been a great comfort.

I dug. I picked, shoveled, hauled, puddled, snipped and rubbed. Pom hardly talked to Edward anymore. Sometimes we sat by the same fire for hours without him saying a word to Edward or me. While the Mad Pom was getting deeper into the Wallies, I was withdrawing deeper into myself.

Then one morning Harold Blake showed up at my claim. "Haven't seen you in some time, mate. Been away?"

"No, just doing things differently. Getting any color?"

"About the same, just enough to keep a bloke goin'." Then after a pause, a long pause, "They said you did it."

I looked up, surprised. "They said I did what?"

"The Bingos. They say you killed Two-Bob Bobby and pinched his stones." I was speechless. How did they know he was dead or where the body was? And why blame it on me? I stood there dumbfounded.

---

101 Everything is as it should be

"Two-Bob's body was found on the Three Mile Flats with his right hand chopped off. The Bingo Brothers said you were the prime suspect. You were mates, and you knew his stones. Archer the Cop was ready to haul you in for questioning when I happened to go to Chuck the Cutter with a few mug stones. I saw Two-Bob's stones on his table. They were pale and colorless, worthless, but unmistakably his. The size and shape matched perfectly. I had seen them only once, but they were unforgettable. I asked Chuck where they came from. He hemmed and hawed, finally said the Bingos brought them in. I told Archer the Cop he better have a look. They should have been more careful. Now they had to blame somebody, and you were his mate. Archer's questioning the Bingos but not getting any answers."

Fatal Radiant Opals lose all color and become worthless when the cursed possessor dies. The Bingos should have learned that after the fiasco about the Goat Colonel. Questions flooded my mind. Had I been followed? I hadn't seen anyone around anywhere. Who did this? They might have pulled him out through a drift from another connected shaft, but that's still too much work for the fat Bingos. Two or three others must have been in on it. The same ones who ratted Dynamite Dan's claim and lurked me? The Bingos had violated Bobby's resting place – another count against them to be avenged when the time comes.

Archer never did question me.

Chapter XXI

Mad Pom Goes Hunting

September 20, 1965

Fourth Month

Completing the drive to the second shaft became my main concern. I had to put the whole Two-Bob Bobby issue out of my mind. It was too puzzling, too emotional, and I couldn't do anything about it right now. Settling accounts with the Bingos must wait. Since I stopped going to the pub, my main news source was Harold Blake, and he didn't stop by often. Thoughts flooded my mind. What information had Archer gotten out of the Bingo Brothers? Who knew where to look for Bobby's body? Who dug it up? For two weeks, three weeks, there were no answers, just questions. Dig, dig, dig, shovel, shovel, shovel.

At last my driving pick broke through the clay wall of the second shaft and let in light and air, opening up a new world. The windsock brought good airflow. This breakthrough was a major accomplishment. I should have done it weeks earlier, but I had been sidetracked. Now I could follow the channel both ways and look for the geyser blowhole that's often near pockets of opal.

I kept to myself, quietly sitting by the fire in the evenings or reading in my tent. Marco seldom came back to camp now, and Pom sunk deeper into the Wallies and kept more to himself. I did see the Banker or Dynamite Dan occasionally. I said to Dan, "Pom might have been happy as a shit-can-man in London."

"Maybe," said Dan, "But he probably would have ended up mad as a hatter anywhere. I'd hump me bluey, mate, if I were you. He's too loose with his rifle. I've seen him walking around shooting at anything. Pistols ain't legal in Aussie, or he'd be have one on his hip like a cowboy." Dan laughed.

"I've been meaning to shift camp but haven't found a place. I want to get out of the Jungle, but that can wait. Lately Pom hasn't said people are talking about him, hasn't said much about anything, as a matter of fact."

One day I climbed up out of my claim and into a fierce wind that I hadn't noticed underground. It almost blew my little car off the road but lasted only 15 or 20 minutes. Marco's heavy canvas tent survived upright, but my eight-foot square tent was half blown over, and Pom's tent was nearly flattened. I reset the guy lines and made the walls straight again, but I left Pom's tent as is. I didn't want to get into trouble for messing with his property. He and Marco must have been underground during the wind. When Pom came back, he was alone. He looked at his tent and got very angry.

"What's the Yank up to now, Edward? Pushed our tent over. Pushed it right down he did."

"No, Edward, a big wind came through and blew both our tents down," I said. "I set mine up again." I felt silly talking to a dog, but that seemed to be the only way to communicate with Pom.

"A big wind, Edward, a big wind blew our tent down, but not his and not Marco's. Maybe the Yank is the big wind, eh, Edward? We'll find out, we'll find out."

I just sat back and watched him put his tent upright. I could have helped but thought better of it. Pom wasn't adept with the guy lines and stakes, which is why the tent blew down. I had a quick stew with fried bread and went into my tent to spend the evening reading.

Next day Harold Blake told me that High-Rise John's humpy blew off its eight-foot poles. "Left the poles and the floor but blew the walls and roof clean off. Blew off his wife, too. She got a broken arm and went home to her mother, took the boy with her. About 10, he was." Not to worry, Harold assured me. "John picked up the pieces and put it back together. He's staying, wife or no wife." Harold laughed.

"Does the wind come often?" I asked.

"Just like the rain, mate, once or twice a year. The big one, years ago, took half the town with it."

As luck would have it, another big wind came through three days later. Pom returned late, alone and drunk, after a Buffs meeting. His tent was down again. I didn't get up.

"Another big wind, Edward? Did you see it? Blew our tent down and left the Yank's up." Not true, I had had to reset mine.

"Did it huff and puff just like the Yank, Edward? Only one way to stop the big wind."

I heard him rummaging through the fallen tent and come stumbling out. "Only one way to stop the big wind, Edward. With a bullet."

Immediately he pumped three shots into the tree next to my tent. "Only way to stop the big wind." I rolled off my cot onto the ground. The next shot went through my tent; I could hear the canvas tear. I didn't move. Edward was pawing around, looking for a bird to fall out of the tree.

"That'll put a stop to the big wind, that'll do it."

I lay perfectly still. After more rummaging, he got back into his car and drove off, leaving Edward sniffing around.

I waited a few minutes, making sure Pom wasn't coming back. Then I lit the mantle lamp. The bullet that went through the tent would have hit me in the butt. I got dressed and drove to Dynamite Dan's. He was still up, reading an American western. "Yer right, mate. It's time to hump me bluey. The Pom nearly put a slug in me butt." I told him the story and asked if I could spend the night at his camp, in my van.

Dan laughed. "I heard the shots, thought it must be roo skinners.[102] Now you want the Mad Pom to follow you over here and blast me camp?"

"I figure you'll blow him up. He's looking for the big wind, you know. The big Yank wind." Dynamite Dan's barricade of branches were scattered. "I see the big wind got you too, mate."

"She'll be right, mate. Have a swig and relax." He handed me the bottle of whiskey. "Just reading about the Old West. One drink speeds you up, two slows you down."

"You're living in the Old West," I said. "Here's to the Bingos, the Odds and their mob. We'll meet them at the OK Corral some day, mate. Some day."

"Fixin' to shoot 'em up, Yank?"

"No, we have to do it with more finesse, like fair-dinkum Aussies."

We passed the bottle back and forth. Then I crawled into the back of my van and slept soundly. Next morning Dan came back

---

102 Roo Skinners – Hunters who shoot kangaroos for their hides and leave the carcasses after skinning them out

to camp with me. He looked at the shots in the tree and the holes in my tent and shook his head. "He might of put the final bluey on yer, mate."

The Mad Pom had not been back; his tent was still down. I packed up all my belongings and put them in my van, surprised at how little I had.

"Ta, mate," I said, not wanting to hang around till Pom returned. "I'll be back o' the Black Stump." This was the boundary of civilization, nothing beyond but sand and desert. To go "back o' the Black Stump" meant you wanted to be away from everybody and everything.

"Righto, mate. See yer after shearing,"[103] he said, understanding it would be a while before we met again.

I stocked up with groceries at the general store, filled two five-gallon water cans, tanked up with petrol and started driving, first northeast toward Collarenebri, then straight south. Nothing but sand. Northeast through the Three Mile Flats and Hawk's Nest mining districts; too crowded with mullock heaps and tailings. Next I headed due north out of town through Bald Hill. Gentle slopes made the ground here more interesting. I left the mining trails and drove across the desert sand, good as any road, and drove and drove. After following a solid line of bushes for a couple of miles, I came to a lone coolabah tree. I looked out across the rolling plains and saw a troop of 50 or 60 jumping kangaroos, flowing like a giant wave across the desert. My first sighting of wild 'roos. "This is it," I said. "This is where I camp."

The coolabah was 50 feet in front of a solid line of eight-foot high bushes, too thick to see through but spaced far enough apart for walking, if you were careful. I walked into the dense bushes and made my first acquaintance with a "waitawhile" shrub. I had heard tall tales of these shrubs but didn't believe they could move across the sand at will and attack innocent wanderers. They can. This one grabbed me. After carefully, laboriously and unsuccessfully attempting to pick each prickle off my pants, I struggled for half an hour to free my shirt. Thankfully there are not many waitawhile bushes.

I made my way back to the coolabah and set up camp. After pitching the tent, placing the chair, small table and cupboard,

---

103 After everything has settled down

and hanging the canvas-cooling bag on a tree branch, I drove three miles back to the mining area for a load of big rocks and firewood. Everything was in order long before sunset. I built a fire in my new rock firepit and had styk 'n eggs for supper. Ah, this is good! A glass of wine would have topped off things nicely, but a digger can't have everything.

Independence gave me a feeling of freedom: no Mad Pom, no Bingo Brothers, no ratters. Five or six miles from town and three miles from the nearest mining trail may be out of the designated mining area, but who cares? Not the station owner. My camp doesn't interfere with his sheep; they have thousands of acres to forage. The government doesn't know I'm here, not even Archer the Cop. "Not to worry, mate, she'll be right."

Has anyone lived here? Has anyone set foot on my little half acre? The Aboriginals must have passed by here in their nomadic life. Roo hunters may have driven their slaughter vehicles through here. Maybe wild camels have foraged the bushes. But now I am here, alone in the great Outback. What isolation, what freedom!

I understand the delight a swagman must feel looking out to endless desert with a cuppa and a hand-rolled Dr. Pat. The quiet, the isolation, the peace. My first visitor, an 18-inch stump-tailed lizard, meandered through as though this were his personal territory. No more, mate, yer've got company. We'll share the space and the insects; just don't let's bite each other.

With my mantle lamp on the cupboard, I read a little Schopenhauer, but he was inappropriate. His elaborate method of arguing is interesting but too civilized, too much another world. Then I remembered the book of poetry, the *Rubaiyat of Omar Khayyam*, that the professor insisted I have. Half an hour into it, I knew Omar would be my companion for life. He fit. He understood. He sought the quiet and tranquil.

> *With me along some Strip of Herbage strown*
> *That just divides the desert from the sown,*
> > *Where name of Slave and Sultan scarce is known,*
> *And peace to Sultan Mahmud on his throne.*

This 11th century Persian poet is as timely now as he was 1,000 years ago. I read this romantic philosopher as the night cool set in and realized I should have moved here months ago. We can't know depth of life and thought without searching, without adventuring, without experiencing. I thought of Helga:

Ah, Love! could you and I with Him conspire
To grasp this sorry Scheme of Things entire,
Would not we shatter it to bits – and then
Re-mould it nearer to the Heart's Desire!

If she were here, I would quote Omar and offer her a tin cup of wine and a slice of fried bread. Would she like it here this isolated? I miss her, but when we are together again it must be near culture: opera, theater, symphonies. I could live with her anywhere, but there is little room for intellectual growth in the Outback. Ah, how nice it will be to someday discuss opera and the arts with her. But I must keep my mind on the present task, that of making my fortune. Then Helga. I fell asleep in the arms of my Valkyrie and dreamt of flashing colors.

The first Screecher landed in my coolabah and loudly proclaimed the dawn. His mates followed quickly. These pesky little green screamers with big yellow beaks seem to be ubiquitous. My coolabah, the only tree for miles around, was the official stopping place for all tree birds and, as I later found out, even the ground-feeding apostle birds. I crawled out of my cot and threw a few stones through the tree, which scattered the Screechers, a routine I would follow daily until I resigned myself to the inevitability of it all and learned to accept them.

I spent a day leveling the living area, building an elaborate firepit, securing the tent against a big wind and then relaxing. No news from the outside world would clutter my mind, no worries, no schedule, no events to attend. No newspapers, no magazines. My whole world is here, to live and dig for opal. I took a few days off from digging, puddled a little, snipped nobbies and rested.

My first morning back at my claim, Harold Blake was there. "Your mate's copped it[104] this time," he said.

"What happened?"

"Shootin' up the pub 'n all," he said, "You don't know?"

"You talking about the Mad Pom? I shifted camp days ago. He's got the Wallies, almost shot my butt off."

---

104 Copped it – Done something serious, got into trouble

"You don't know then?" He looked a little puzzled. "Last night late he waltzed into the pub with his rifle and put a hole in the ceiling. 'Where's the big wind?' he said. 'I know he's here. The trees told me. Where is he? I have to stop him. Only my bullet will do it. I want him now.' He raised his rifle and looked around the pub, probably 12 to 15 of us there. Nobody said a word. Archer the Cop walked away from the bar and eased up to him. 'I'll take care of it. I'll get the big wind for you. You don't have to worry about it, mate, it's my job.'"

"Mad Pom insisted he had to be the one to stop it. 'Only me. I have to stop him. You can't. He blew my tent down twice. He'll blow down the whole town if I don't stop him. The trees told me he's here. Trees don't lie.' He kept talking about the wind like it was a man."

"Where was Marco?" I asked.

"Crouched behind the bar, whimpering. Anyway, Archer went with the Pom to look around the pub for the big wind. Then, when he saw his chance, he knocked Pom down and took his gun away." Archer's six-foot-four and 15 stone,[105] much heavier than the Mad Pom. Harold went on with his narrative, telling how Archer handcuffed Pom and with Harold's help hauled him 300 miles to the loony bin at Orange. Usually Archer locks up Wallies in the Shearing Shed for the night and hauls them off in the morning. But this one couldn't wait. Pom kept ranting about the trees saying the big wind is in the pub and he had to shoot him. 'It's up to me.'"

"He said everybody was talking about him, but he isn't the shit-can-man. Went on like that, cuffed up in the back seat for the whole trip. Took us all night and most of the next day. Good thing I thought to bring some beer along. Like to drive me to the Wallies."

I said, "He earned his Mad Pom name before I got here, but he got worse. The wind blew his tent down a couple of days ago, and he blamed me. Put some bullets in a tree and one through my tent. That's when I humped me bluey."

"Well he won't be back, ever. He's gone, mate. You can come home."

---

105 Stone – Fourteen pounds. Aussie weight measurement

"Reckon I'll stay back o' the Black Stump. Don't know Marco that well, and I like being out of the Jungle."

"Righto, mate." And Harold was off.

Sounded to me like Dan had a hand – or a tree voice – in this. He'd get a kick out of it. I'll have a yarn with him about it while passing the bottle sometime. Good on yer, mate. One down. Five to go? Six? Patience, mate, patience.

Chapter XXII
Bruno

October 7, 1965

Fifth Month

I was content to be a part of the desert. I needed to get away from it all. The little green Screechers woke me up every morning. The gentle songs of the ensuing groups of birds enhanced the camp. The kookaburras' obnoxious laugh could be annoying, but they kept their distance, usually heard but not seen.

The first week was peaceful. A breaky of bacon, fried bread and boiled eggs started each day off nicely. I was relaxed and spent more time cooking, knowing I had plenty of time to look for my stone. Not to worry, mate, she'll be right. With a jam sandwich and a gallon jug of water, I set out for the claim. After digging underground in two shifts of four hours each and an hour or two above ground shoveling tailings into the puddler, I returned to camp, snipped nobbies, had a bit of stew, a cuppa and my evening Dr. Pat. Life was wonderful. I could contemplate the dancing flames, listen to the birds and hear the gentle rustle of frill-necked lizards darting after insects. What more could anyone possibly want or desire? I found enough mug stones puddling to keep me in tucker and had enough left over to pay the blacksmith for pick sharpening.

Underground in my Yank's Dig is a pocket of opal just waiting for me, waiting patiently for millions of years to be brought into the sunlight. By me, me alone. The curse is pure nonsense left over from the ancient Aboriginals and has no place in our scientific world. When the time comes, I will sell most of my stones, keep a few to show friends and return to Minnesota a rich man. No hurry. If it takes 20 years, so be it. But 20 years is too long. Helga will be busy for a couple of years, visiting her sister Valkyrie and writing her paper, so I have some time. She might join me here again, but I would prefer to have a fortune in opal so we could live where we want. But then she may find her wounded warrior and forget about me. Not to worry. Opal is my first love.

As I snip each day's nobbies, a rattle announces the arrival of a troop of scorpions, just as in the other camp. I stand up and let them pass at a leisurely pace, never understanding why, when attracted to the lantern light, they pass through and keep going. Maybe when I'm wealthy, I'll commission a biologist to study this enigma, but for now it will remain one of the mysteries of the Outback. Meanwhile, I explore the poetic wisdom of Omar Khayyam.

One day I returned to my camp to find four huge, grey horses rummaging through my belongings. They had tipped over the stew billy and knocked down the cupboard, scattering the contents, eating what they could and breaking the rest. I jumped out of the car, yelled and threw stones and chunks of firewood at them. They were big. I knew from the horses on my uncle's farm in Minnesota that they weighed 1,600 to 1,800 pounds each. Fat workhorses, freely wandering around thousands of acres, browsing and ransacking at will. They should be shipped off to the dog food factory. Cocky Nolan, the station owner, probably hasn't used them in years, maybe even forgotten about them.

I chased them off and straightened things up, pounded stakes into the ground around the campsite and strung a clothesline with rags tied to it. That should take care of the horse problem. Nope. Next day I returned to find them back, the clothesline down and a huge grey horse butt sticking out of my tent. Now I was angry. I slammed him in the rear with a rock from the firepit. He reared up and took the whole tent half way across the paddock with him, leaving a shattered jam jar on my flattened cot.

I repitched the tent and straightened things up again. This time I strewed bottles, stones and firewood around my personal territory, along with the clothesline and rags. Just to make sure, I squashed garlic around the tent. My next stew, without garlic, would taste flatter, but sacrifice is necessary.

They returned the next day. This time I chased them away gently, not wanting to have to repitch my tent. My stew was gone, the bread, bacon and butter out of the canvas-cooling bag had been chewed up, wrapping and all.

I sat by the glowing embers with a cuppa and a smoke, pondering for a long time. What would Schopenhauer do? Not his type of problem; he lived in the abstract. What would Omar do? His poetry covers only beauty and wisdom. What would Victor Hugo do? Plan revenge for years. No. I had to find my own solution.

I could get a guard dog, but I didn't want one. Sitting in the shade of my coolabah tree with a cuppa at dusk and listening to the laughing kookaburras would not be enhanced by a dog chasing around. I had enough wildlife to keep me company: kangaroos loping by like a giant wave, a rattling horde of scorpions walking through each night, ugly and obnoxious six-foot emus wandering about and gentle echidnas passing through with their needles clicking. No place for a dog. What would a dog do all day when I was underground at my claim?

But I was here to make my fortune in black opal, not to fight off wild horses. A dog was the only solution – a big, snarling, ferocious, salivating, mean beast that would rip the flesh off a horse's ankle, bring him down and tear into his neck before I called him off.

I hadn't been in the Digger's Retreat for some time, but the pub was the best place to get information. The downside was you couldn't just have a pint and leave. Fortunately I found a small mob. After a few "G'day, mates," "'oweryergoings," and "Findin' any color" I asked about getting a dog. Jake the Wasp suggested I talk to Broken Bill, who had acquired his nickname by falling down a mineshaft. That was the information I needed, but I still had to stand my shout. "A bloke what stands 'is shout is right, idn't 'e? Only a rotter is off." It was another hour before I got away.

Broken Bill was at his campsite. "G'day, mate. You're the Yank. Been waitin for yer." Pub news travels fast. "Got a mongrel I've been trying to put off on somebody for months. Keeps coming back. Jumps up on me at sunup every morning. Should shoot him but can't do it. Might, though, if he comes back again. Name's Bruno. 'E's a stupid, worthless, good-for-nothing mutt. Can't be trained, but 'e's yours if yer want 'im."

The deal was done. Broken Bill wasn't a great one for small talk. Bruno was medium-sized, lean, with a mottled brown coat, four white socks and white splotches on his nose and chest. Not exactly what I had in mind but friendly and, of course, trainable. Any dog could be trained. I could do it. Bill just didn't know how to handle dogs. I opened the car door, Bruno jumped in and we were off.

Back at camp I gave Bruno some three-day stew to make him feel at home. He sniffed it and backed away. Well, life was tough. He'd have to eat what I ate and learn to like it. We took a walk. He stayed just ahead of me, anticipating turning left or right with me, as Outback dogs do, and kept the same pace. This avoids stepping on the most poisonous snakes in the world.

As promised by Broken Bill, Bruno was up with the first Screecher, jumped on my cot, and got yelled at and pushed off. The Screechers were bad enough. Later, when I got up, he timidly stayed back until I assuringly patted his head. This morning, after breakfast of tea and reheated stew, which Bruno once again declined, preferring a drink from his water bowl, I put a rope around his neck and tied the other end to the coolabah. He looked bewildered. I figured he had never had anything around his neck, let alone been tied to a tree. I told him about the horses and assured him that once they were driven off he would be let loose to roam the full expanse of the Outback. The sight of a barking dog, even a stupid, timid mutt, would keep the horses away. He howled pathetically, straining at the neck rope as I drove off to work my claim. "She'll be right, mate," I shouted out the window.

At noon, curious to see how things were going, I drove back to camp. The horses back and had knocked everything over, having a wonderful time of it. Bruno was stretched out at the end of his tether, wide-eyed, whining and trembling with fear. He could have scared them away just by barking and standing his ground but had let them raze the place. I yelled and threw anything I could lay hands on at the horses.

Once they were gone, I untied the quivering dog and chased him away. "Go back to Broken Bill you stupid, worthless, good-for-nothing mutt. Maybe this time he'll shoot you. Good riddance." Bruno cowered and ran when I picked up a stick. I threw stones in his direction. "Beat it! Go! I don't ever want to see you again." He stayed a stone's throw away but didn't leave, lying there with his chin on his outstretched front legs, looking scared and remorseful.

My day was shot. After putting my tent back up and the camp back together, I drove into the trees to gather firewood and do some puddling. When I returned, Bruno had moved closer to the coolabah. I threw a few more stones and chased him away again; using Aussie Outback expletives he would be more likely to understand. Finally he was gone from sight, over the rise 100 yards from the bushes.

The next morning he was back at the call of the first Screecher, gently nudged me with his nose, backed off and looked dejected and pathetic. Now I understood why Broken Bob couldn't shoot him and why he wanted to get rid of him. Bruno lay there with his nose on his stretched-out forelegs, ready to bolt if need be. I shook my head and went back to sleep.

He was still there when I got up. He was pathetic. I cooled off a little and gave up. "Okay, you are a stupid, worthless, good-for-nothing mutt, of no value to me or anyone else, but you can stay." He wagged his tail a little, something he rarely did, and even ate a bit of three-day stew to appease me. I never did find out what or where he ate regularly, but it wasn't my stew.

Fortunately, the horses never came back, and Bruno and I settled into a routine. He got up with the Screechers, nudged me and was off, returning when I rapped the tea billy. After breakfast we went to the claim, a six-mile drive. Bruno ran just ahead of the front bumper of my van. How he learned to do this I don't know. The alternatives were to drop back 150 feet because of the dust or run alongside the van, but that required stopping to remove the thorns he picked up along the road. With a thorn in one paw, Bruno could keep running on three legs. With thorns in two or more paws, he had to stop. Mostly he ran ahead of the van. When I speeded up, he speeded up. When I slowed down, he slowed down. It made me nervous, but he seemed to know what he was doing.

While I was underground he ran the quarter-mile into Wallangulla to associate with the local mutts. After work each day I drove through town to find Bruno, and he either jumped into my van or ran ahead back to camp. When he rode with me, he sat upright in the passenger seat and darted back and forth between the open car windows, barking and threatening all the dogs in town. Once as he jumped across my lap, giving an ear-shattering bark at the biggest dog in town, I had enough and pushed him out the window. There, with tail between legs, nose to nose with a dog twice his size, he backed away and ran home in the dust. We were learning to live together, but his habits did not change.

The desert, that looks so dead at first glance, teems with life. Bruno got to meet our stump-tail lizard – you can't tell if he's coming or going – and tried without success to stare him down, sometimes from the wrong end. This slow-moving, harmless insect eater out waited Bruno. He also followed the scorpions, pawing at them from time to time and watching curiously as I knocked out my boots each morning. When the kookaburras laughed a little crazily, Bruno looked curious but was never brave enough to go into the bushes looking for them. Nor did he show any interest in chasing kangaroos.

One day I looked up and saw a herd of Cocky Nolan's sheep. Bruno was stalking them. If he decides to have a leg of lamb, I thought, I'm in big trouble. But Bruno didn't move, just stood with his nose to the ground like he was grazing. Two sheep stared at him suspiciously, but after a couple of minutes they went back to grazing. Bruno moved slowly closer to the herd. A couple more sheep looked up, and again he pretended to graze. For a long time they stared, and he stood still. Again they went back to grazing, and he moved closer. I thought, 'What is this stupid mutt up to, pretending to be a sheep, or does he think he is a sheep?' This went on until Bruno was so close that one of the sheep – not the world's brightest animals – realized there was something different about him and bleated. The whole herd bleated and ran, Bruno running along with them. I didn't see him again for an hour. When he returned he had no blood on him so I assumed nothing had happened. He had a real Aussie sense of humor.

In October the heat starts to build, 90 to 110 degrees Fahrenheit during the day but still cool at night. The hot summer was still a couple of months off. I was happy to be away from even the few people in the Wallangulla area. The fewer people I saw, the happier I was. Now Bruno was my companion and made life better, stupid mutt that he was.

Absolute silence 25 feet underground sharpens the sense of hearing. The quietness of the desert is captivating. I could hear every subtle sound: the crackling of the fire, the midnight yap of a distant dingo,[106] which always brought Bruno up with a start, ready to cut and run – and the rattling quills of an echidna that sometimes came through at night. Like Pom's dog, Bruno tried to chew the quills with his mouth sideways, trying to pull off enough quills to find flesh to bite. Meanwhile the echidna dug furiously, straight down, to escape into the clay. To rescue it, I shut Bruno in the van and attached a wire loop to a pole to slip over the echidna's body. I needed a bar to pry the echidna up from the hole. Once the echidna was securely in the loop, I hung the pole out the van window to keep the critter safe from Bruno, drove a couple of miles off and released it.

Bruno slept under my cot, where he dug out a little den. One night he was restless, up and pawing, down, up again. "Lie down, and go to sleep," I said. Finally I struck a match and lit my mantle lantern. I discovered that Bruno had been lying on a poisonous six-inch red and silver centipede. I moved the critter a good way into the bushes.

Sometimes during the night I had to get up to relieve myself and usually didn't bother lighting my lantern. Bruno always got up with me. On one such occasion he got ahead of me and wouldn't let me out of the tent. "Get out of the way," I said and nudged him with my knee. He didn't move. Sensing something was wrong, I lit the lantern and found a black snake just outside the tent opening. The snake was deadly poisonous but probably too cold from the night air to move fast. Nevertheless, I got a shovel and dispatched him. It's likely this stupid mutt saved me a few toes, or maybe my life. "Ta," I said, and patted Bruno's head. He didn't make a big deal of it – just an Outback dog doing his job.

The horses were gone, and snakes were seldom seen, but the emus were the ubiquitous scourge of the Outback. Big, ugly, smelly, ungainly, flightless and obnoxious, emus have long necks and could poke their beak into everything. Not as damaging as horses, but more persistent. Now that Bruno and I were on good

---

106 Dingo – Wild dog of the Outback, seldom seen and only heard from a distance

terms, I assumed he was developing a sense of territoriality. I took it upon myself to teach him to chase away the emus that strutted into camp as though they owned the place..

"Bruno," I yelled, "Get 'em out of here. Sic 'em." I ran toward the emus, and they ran for a short distance, then stopped. After many tries, Bruno finally ran after them when they turned to run. Eventually, he caught on that he was to start them running. At the shout, "Bruno, emus," he took off and chased them into the bushes, but returned almost immediately.

I wanted the emus farther away, so one time I ran after Bruno yelling, "Get 'em Bruno, go after 'em." I went full speed, chasing through the bushes, trying to keep up with them, only to meet Bruno returning with his tail between his legs. Before I could stop, I was face to face with the emu that was chasing Bruno. We almost collided. I yelled, the emu straightened up and made a startled, funny noise. Both of us retreated.

Despite the emus, it was a pleasant, never dull life. The Outback was filled with subtle sounds, the companionship of a truly unremarkable mutt, and the promise of a fortune in beautiful gems just underfoot. Bruno never showed any desire to be petted but sometimes got petted anyway. He did want to be in on things, though. We left together each morning, returned together each afternoon, sat by the same fire, and perceived the same world from different perspectives.

We were mates.

Chapter XXIII
A Gift For The King

October 21, 1965

Fifth Month

Space is a primary ingredient of freedom. Having access to space is to have freedom of movement. Aboriginals have no concept of enclosed space. The world is theirs to roam. I can imagine living like this permanently. I can understand the swagman waltzing Mathilda.[107] Immanuel Kant said that God, freedom and happiness are indefinable. However, we use the terms in conversation and each of us has his own understanding of their meaning. Freedom for me consists of access to physical space, unrestricted movement and unconstrained thought.

We roamed the desert, Bruno and I, and thought by the open fire. What he contemplated I don't know; but my mind pursued any idea freely, no matter how esoteric or offensive it might be to the civilized world. Henry David Thoreau said, "If a man does not keep pace with his companions, perhaps it is because he hears a different drummer. Let him step to the music he hears, however far or distant measured." I never was a fan of Thoreau; he was too pompous, but he had his moments. There were many drummers beating in my mind: Mozart, Verdi, Wagner, Schopenhauer, Omar Khayyam, but I stepped to my own beat, free of tyrants.

To be isolated, alone and not dependent on anyone is another component of freedom. If I worked today, I might eat tomorrow. If I didn't work today I might not have the funds for tucker tomorrow. My choice. My struggle. If I kacked off[108] in my camp, how long would it be before someone found my body? Does it matter? If I were injured, I would have to look after myself and live or die without help. This is independence. This is freedom. This is what I loved.

---

107 Waltzing Mathilda – Walking about the Outback freely, with no schedule or destination; the tune by the same name later became the Australia national song
108 Kacked off – Died

In this isolated environment, there is no obligation to do anything. I could live like this forever. Maybe I'll get the Wallies, but that's not a bad way to go. Ah, to be a swagman, waltzing Matilda, roaming the desert at will. I pondered, idly, will I ever again sing in a concert and, still in my tux, have a steak Dianne at a fine restaurant, sitting across the table from a well-dressed, intelligent woman? Will I ever again play the piano? Or, with my friends, sing something other than *Waltzing Mathilda*?

I was writing fewer letters, becoming more and more detached from the world, but I still kept in touch with several old friends. One of them wrote that he is in debt for the next 20 years. "Maybe then," he writes, "maybe then I can do what you are doing."

No, mate, you have to strike when the iron is hot. Twenty years is too much to escape from. But, if you kack off, at least they will easily find your body and bury you. My life is here; I don't want to leave. My time, life and work revolve around nature's schedule, not someone else's whim. I am closer to nature than to people. I like it that way.

My goal now was to find the blowhole, the ancient geyser spout, and radiate out from there looking for pockets of nobbies. I was shoveling clay out of the channel in an awkward position and developed a painful hemorrhoid. I climbed out of my shaft and rapped on the door to the bush nurse's modest office near the pub, just off Main Street. A smiling, pleasingly plump woman of about 30 invited me in. Soon I was laying bare-assed naked on her examining table, spreading my cheeks with both hands while she, with rubber gloves and ointment, was pushing the offending lump back where it belonged. Once my pants were back on, she asked if I would care for a cup of tea. Only in Aussie, I thought, would a nurse who had just put your anus in order offer you a cup of tea. Very casual. I like her.

"Ta, mate. Right on." She left the room to wash her hands and put the kettle on. We chatted. Aussies like to talk to Yanks, a carryover from the war.

The kettle whistled and she returned with two mugs.

"Do you like being a bush nurse?" I asked.

"Yes," she said with a warm smile. "It's challenging. I'm on call 24 hours a day. Besides reinserting hemorrhoids, I sew up wounds, set minor breaks, diagnose illnesses and prescribe medicines. I even delivered Flint's wife's last baby. The flying doctor didn't get here in time."

"Flying doctor?"

"Yes. Anything that's too big for us to handle we radio for help."

"Sounds like an interesting life, but don't you feel out of touch?"

"No. I like the Outback. I'm here for two years, then can choose where I want to go next. Better than being forever stuck in one place, and my work is gratifying."

We finished our tea. She offered me her hand said, "My name is Nell. You're the Yank. You are in the local pub news."

"Yes, I suppose. You probably know more about me than I know about myself." I thanked her and left with a more comfortable posterior. She was nice. I hoped we could talk again sometime.

Several days went by quietly and uneventfully. Then one evening I was reading the *Rubaiyat* and waiting for the billy to boil when I looked up and perceived the most beautiful woman I have ever seen. She was standing opposite me across the firepit. She wore a light, loose, pale-colored dress over her graceful body, a body like the Venus de Milo. She smiled at me enticingly, white teeth contrasting sharply and stunningly with smooth black skin. Her black eyes pierced my soul. She was elegant and savage, majestic and wild, beautiful and feral. I was hallucinating, getting the Wallies. My entire being responded to this perfectly formed enchanting beauty, radiantly beaming at me. I shook my head to clear my mind. She didn't move, just stood there – smiling.

After a quick glance around, thinking there may be a tribe of Aboriginals surrounding us, my eye caught a man's movement some 60 or 70 feet away by a saltbush fire. I smiled at my Venus, lifted the billy and rapped it, nodding and holding it in such a way as to invite them both for a cuppa. I poured three cups carefully and motioned for them to sit on the log and the chair. Instead, they took their tea squatting while I sat on the log. Why was I so concerned about spilling when they were just two unsophisticated Aborigines on walkabout, freely roaming the Outback?

She was encompassingly beautiful. That's why.

We sipped slowly for a long time. I thought of my Aboriginal friend, Nardoo. He said little but exuded warmth. Sometimes he came in quietly and squatted on the floor of my room while I was writing letters, then left without saying a word. I surmised we were communicating, but he was naturally much warmer and more emotive than I could ever be. I felt close to him. Now I felt that same warmth. I had come to accept the belief that Aboriginals had mystical powers and could communicate over hundreds of miles.

My mind wandered erratically. I saw her as part of our college chorus singing *Daphne e Chloe* with Antal Dorati and the Minneapolis Symphony – I in my tux and she in an elegant gown. Maybe dinner at Charlie's Café afterward. No, that doesn't work. Too social.

Then Omar came to mind.

Here with a Loaf of Bread beneath the Bough,
A Flask of Wine, a Book of Verse – and Thou
    Beside me singing in the wilderness –
Ah! Wilderness is Paradise enow.

No. Omar doesn't work either. No bread here, no wine, no singing verse; just a tin cup of tea and passionate silence. My mind kept imagining. Walking arm and arm along the seashore? No. Too aimless.

Digging for opal? No. Too constrained, she belongs above ground, in the sunlight. I couldn't put us together anywhere.

They finished their tea. While the man sat looking into the fire for a long, comfortable time, she continued to smile enticingly at me. As darkness set in, they walked off into the night. Through all this Bruno did not stir. Before I turned in, I saw the glow of a saltbush fire in the distance.

I relived this bizarre event in my mind for several days, dying to tell someone about it. Then my hemorrhoid popped out again, and I returned to the bush nurse for another treatment.

Once again, after the cheek-spreading ointment routine, Nell offered me tea, this time English style – first hotting the pot and then taking the pot with tea leaves in it to the kettle of vigorously boiling water. Very cultivated. We sipped from small cups, difficult to hold in my workingman's hand.

"Something unusual happened the other night," I said.

"You saw a dingo!"

"No, but just as rare."

"A wombat? Camel? A sober digger after 10? Sarah shouting the pub?"

I laughed. "I am camped way out, up north by the bushes. I saw the most beautiful woman smiling at me from the other side of the firepit. An Aboriginal girl, maybe 18."

She set the pot down roughly, and a horrified look spread across her face.

"It's true," I said. "I'm not making this up. I haven't got the Wallies. She was really there."

Nell looked up. "Did you...?" she started. "Did she...?" she started again, "I mean, were you...?" She stopped.

"Well," I said, "I saw her father. I think it was her father off in the distance so I invited them to join me for a cuppa."

Nell smiled a little and said bluntly, "Did she offer herself to you?"

I was surprised by her question but went on, "She smiled at me like I was the swagman's jumbuck,[109] but I was so taken by her beauty that I didn't even think of sex. Do you know something about her? They had a cuppa, squatted a while by my fire and left. That was it."

"Thank God," she said, almost under her breath. "If you had invited her into your tent, she would have gladly spent the night. In the morning the man in the distance, who really is her father, would have joined the party and asked if you could spare a couple mug stones. They're professionals. They work the Outback."

---

109 Jumbuck – In the song, Waltzing Mathilda, the sheep that the swagman grabbed with glee

"You mean I missed a chance to have a naughty[110] with the most beautiful woman I have ever seen," I said shaking my head in mock remorse.

"If you had, hemorrhoids would be the least of your problems. She has every venereal disease that I've heard of. Archer tried to bring her in for treatment when they were here a year ago, but they're too canny. He couldn't find them. I'm surprised she's still well enough to ply her trade. Tell me where you saw them and when, and I'll get Archer on it. She infected seven diggers last time through. Four are still in treatment. You're one of the few who resisted her."

I gave her what information I had and left as she went off to find Archer. Things were starting to fall into place, and I had an idea. Back at camp I picked up the few mug stones I had and set out searching for my Black Venus, hoping to find her before Archer did.

Fortunately, I found Harold Blake pulling tailings at his claim. I wouldn't have to go into the pub for information. After a round of "Oweryergoings and gettin' any color" I turned the conversation to who was digging where.

"Aye, Skinner and the Wombat are working on Hatter's Flat. Jake the Wasp and Wee Willy are pulling a shaft by Deep Bellars." He went on and on about diggers I didn't know. Finally I had to ask, "What's King Tut doing these days?"

"Funny you should ask. He's pulling a claim by Becketts with your old mate, Marco. They teamed up after the Mad Pom shot up the pub."

I smiled at the mention of Marco and kept the conversation going for a few more minutes, like I was just passing the time, then let him get back to work. He was a nice bloke, and although he had lived on the Wally for years, he still spoke standard Aussie.

Becketts was on the edge of the mining area, bordering the great dessert. My Black Venus and her father would stay away from the central claims for fear of discovery by Archer the Cop. Becketts is a good place for a secluded saltbush fire and a night's rest. But first I had to find them.

I drove around the mining perimeter, avoiding trails and mullock heaps, south of Frog Hollow and Snowy Browns, then

110 Naughty – Aussie slang for sex.

north of Darbys and New Year's Rush. After miles of searching, I found the remains of burnt saltbush east of Pumpkin Flat. I roamed around Angledool and found the pair just north of Bald Hill, squatting under a gum tree.

Parking some ways away, I walked over. I tried to be nonchalant, but her smile again stirred all my primitive desires. I squatted with them. They knew I had something in mind, and I'm sure she thought it was she. But after a quiet while, I pulled out my three mug stones, which caught her attention. We had not spoken before. I said only "Becketts. Tomorrow morning," showed the stones, and then took them back. They said nothing. Her father kept the same, inscrutable expression, not looking at me. I said nothing more. I looked back once as I left. Her smile followed me.

I went back through town to pick up Bruno, who had spent the day with his mates, and had a nice evening anticipating success in my little venture.

In the morning I drove around the Outback side of Becketts and parked some distance away. It must be 10, 12 miles from where I saw them yesterday, a short walk for Aboriginals. They were squatting by a small saltbush fire on the knoll that overlooked the field. What do they eat? I thought. Where do they find food? What do they cook it in? They must have more possessions somewhere.

Her smile greeted me. Her father looked out over the field. We waited some time in silence before we saw King Tut and Marco pull up in a pickup a considerable distance away from us. The two diggers were busy setting up a power windlass so I didn't worry about being spotted as I pointed them out.

"A present," I said, "for the King," and put the three mug stones in her father's hand. He looked at me. I pointed to his daughter and said, again, "for the King," and indicated the shorter of the two diggers. She took hold of my arm. I could feel her soft breast pressing against me. Her smile and her eyes pierced my soul. Her smooth black completion and graceful, lovely curved body moved enticingly. I peered into her lovely eyes one last time, touched her arm, turned, and walked away, not daring to look back.

My scheme had been set in motion. Now it was up to them.

Chapter XXIV
Mud Humpy

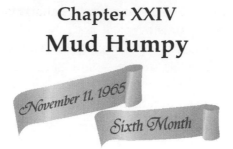

November 11, 1965

Sixth Month

It was some time before my hemorrhoid popped out again. The same ritual followed with Nell, the bush nurse, only this time while we were having tea she said, "It's much larger. It really needs to be cut out."

"Is that something you can do?"

"No, beyond my talents. But I can radio ahead and arrange an appointment with the doctor in Walgett."

"Is he good?"

"He's different. Outback doctors have their own way of doing things. He'll do just fine on this." This didn't inspire a lot of confidence in me.

"How long will it take?"

"Not long. Just an office visit. I'm going into Walgett for supplies next week; you can ride along."

"Good, that'll be fine."

After a long pause, she said, "Archer found your Black Venus. She agreed to be taken into Brisbane for treatment. She may come through okay, but it will take months. Thanks for your help." Then as I sipped my tea slowly, not wanting to show undue interest, she said, "She did infect two more diggers. I can't tell you who they are. It's a curious thing."

"It's okay," I said, "I won't turn you in to the medical board."

She thought, and finally said, "One is the bloke who works in the pub evenings. I believe he's your former campmate." I set my teacup down carefully, trying to hide my delight.

"Oh," I said. "That is curious."

"Who was the bloke you bought your puddler from? The bloke who charged you four times its value?" she asked. She knows everything, I thought.

"I think it was Tut or something like that. I never knew him well. Was he one of the victims?"

"Yes. It's sad, with a wife and three little children. She'll also have to be examined." This caused me some remorse. I hadn't thought of the secondary consequences. But she probably will not get infected and will caution her husband to be more prudent in the future. "Tut is in Brisbane with Marco now, being treated. Modern drugs might work, but it will take time."

I could hardly contain myself. I had hit two Gigs[111] with three mug stones. Vengeance brings joy to the soul! The Count of Monte Cristo himself couldn't have done better or enjoyed it more. "Well," I calmly pontificated, "that's what happens to men who can't keep their pants buttoned."

"But it's odd that your Black Venus and her father went so far to seek out diggers with others nearby. Tut and Marco were 8 miles away. Took Archer two days to find her." She looked puzzled. I just shrugged my shoulders, smiled and indicated I'd like another cup of tea. Three down. How many still to go?

My odious ploy had been successful. I felt bad about King Tut's wife having to suffer for his escapade and be tested. She was a nice woman and a good mother. I hope the King will act a little more royal now. My account with him is settled. And Marco? He betrayed me when I had reason to trust him. This is a serious enough offense to land him in the eighth layer of Dante's hell, to spend eternity with used-car salesmen and politicians. Maybe I'll call it even with him, maybe not.

It was a quiet time for me: digging, Omar, Bruno and the fire. Fifteen feet down the channel from the main drive I found the blowhole from an ancient geyser. I dug out the dome, which went up three feet and had a five-inch-wide hole at the center. This surprised me; I had expected a much larger hole for the waterspout of a geyser. Now I explored around it for other channels, not expecting to find any pockets close to the blowhole.

---

111 Gigs – Scoundrels

The week passed. I sponged myself off and accompanied Nell to Walgett. She was always pleasant company and didn't mention the infected diggers. "That's Ten Mile Warrambool," she said, as we passed an area with termite mounds, some six feet high. "Be a nice place for a picnic if you're interested." I looked. Standing pools of water left from the big rain, a couple of trees, some dry grass and plenty of termite mounds to sit on. It went on for a couple of miles.

"Sounds like fun. I need a little diversion. I'm spending too much time underground."

"Then it's settled," she said with a smile. "I'll see when I can get someone to cover for me for a day off."

The ride to Walgett wasn't bad in her late-model Holden, and it took less than two hours. The young doctor was casual, a fair-dinkum Aussie, my kind of bloke, with a hand-rolled cigarette hanging from his mouth as he greeted the bush nurse. His office had not been cleaned recently, possibly never. One chair in the corner had a leg missing, drawer handles were loose and piles of debris lay everywhere.

"G'day, mate," he said, turning to me. "Righto. Let's 'ave a look at your arse then." I didn't see a table to lie on so I just dropped my shorts and bent over. He took a quick look, then said, "Put yer head against the wall and spread yer cheeks."

I had no idea what Nell was doing. I could see only the unswept floor and my feet. After some feeling around, the doc said, "Open wide and grit yer teeth, mate. It'll just take a minute."

The thought crossed my mind that in America a doctor might offer a painkiller shot or at least an aspirin. Here I would have settled for a shot of whiskey. I felt the knife cut in. Did he sterilize it? I gritted my teeth but didn't make a sound – I'm an Outback Aussie now – and felt the needle as he stitched it up. He was right; it took just a few minutes. I pulled up my shorts, glad it was over.

"'ere yer go, mate." He handed me a tissue with my hemorrhoid on it, a red blob the size of my little fingernail. "A souvenir from Walgett. Save it to show your grandkids." Aussie humor. I smiled, thanked him and that was it. Finished. Paid for by the National Health. He and Nell were discussing something so I went outside, able to walk with almost no pain.

I put the tissue in my pocket, resolved to toss it at the first opportunity. We stopped at the chemists, the grocery store and the butcher, where I picked up some lamb's fry hoping Nell would fry it up with potatoes and onions when we got back to the Wally.

"Well, what do you think of National Health Service?" she said as we left Walgett.

"Seems to work. Less overhead. No fancy machines with flashing red lights and nothing completely sterile. Helps build up an immunity to germs."

She smiled. "You'll be fine. No more hemorrhoid."

"Oh, I've still got it. Do you want to keep this to show your patients?" I showed it to her. She shook her head no, so I tossed it out the window.

She did fry the lamb's liver with potatoes and onions, the best meal I'd had in weeks.

"We'll picnic on Sunday. Flint the Ratter's wife will cover for me."

And we did. Nell drew me away from my life of solitude, and I was enjoying it. It was friendship, not romance. We both understood that. I quoted passages from Omar's *Rubaiyat*, and we talked about Dickens, whom I love, and Jane Austen, whom I had not read. Bruno was having the time of his life splashing through the puddles of standing water, cavorting around the termite mounds while we ate delicately prepared chicken sandwiches with condiments. It was good to be in civilized company again.

As we were leaving, walking back to the car, I did something impulsively that was entirely out of character. I was distracted by our discussion of *Bleak House*, contemplating Dickens' dislike of lawyers, and without thinking, I jumped up on a two-foot-high termite mound, raised one leg and farted loudly. Even Bruno stopped splashing. I stood there on one leg, mortified.

She was smiling. After enjoying my embarrassment for a minute or so she said, "You mustn't strain too much; you'll get another hemorrhoid." She took my arm and we continued on back to the car, leaving the discussion of *Bleak House* unfinished.

Back to digging. The opal layer of clay around the blowhole was a different texture, smoother and softer, easier to dig. Then I noticed my candles burning brighter, six-inch flames, and I smelled the opal aroma, maybe methane gas. My heart beat faster; I felt the clay get gritty as I dug carefully. Then out came little nobbies the size of peas. Next the size of hazelnuts, then marbles, but no color. With sweat pouring into my eyes and candle flames a foot high, I pried the lumps out one by one with my jackknife, more that a dozen in all. When I was through the small pocket, I shoveled tailings back into the face to discourage ratters and left.

Back at camp I snipped the nobbies carefully around the edges first and then farther in if no color showed. Six had color, and four looked promising. I took them to Angus' cutter, Garbhan. He polished the four into nice little stones. I paid him and examined the stones in the sunlight. One with a rolling flash, one pin fire, one jelly opal and a flake pattern that looked really good. Three precious opals, and one gem. I showed them to Angus. "Nice color, nice stones. Come back tonight, and we'll see how they look under artificial light."

"I'll just leave them with you and come back tomorrow," I said. We shook hands, and I started back to my van. Angus and Garbhan lived in the larger of two roughly built wood humpies. The two younger Scots, Rab and Gordon, lived in the smaller humpy. They were all mates, working together. Rab and Gordon had finished for the day and were sitting under the bough shed having a beer.

"G'day, Yank. Care for a wet one?" Rab had learned a bit of Aussie.

"Ta, mate," I said. "Good time for it."

"Another couple weeks and the temperature'll be up to 130 or higher. You got a humpy?"

"No, just a tent. I'm out back o' the bush line under a coolabah."

They shook their heads a little. "You'll have to stay underground for a couple of months." They laughed.

"That's what I intend to do. It cools down to 90 at night, so that's not too bad."

"But the days are real killers," Gordon said. "You can sit in the shade and drink till you're bloated and still feel thirsty. You might want to have a look at our mud humpy." He pointed at a vacant, ratty-looking hut not far away, with a junk VW parked by it. "It's been around for 20 or 30 years. Some old digger built it out of sticks and mud and then either made a fortune or went broke, and left. Next digger moved in and did the same. Be nice to know the whole history of the place. We acquired it from the Dane a year ago."

He swigged his beer and went on. "The Dane staked an old claim that had been called Old Eddie's. He was working it on a share basis with two other blokes when they hit a huge pocket that went on and on. The stones were medium quality, but a lot of 'em. He started thinking, 'This is my claim, and I'm only getting one third of the stones.' He talked to Angus, we looked at it and bought it for thousands of quid, everything we could lay our hands on and borrow, and promised him more after we dug it out. He said we could have the mud humpy as part of the deal. He pocketed the cash and left."

"That's when the trouble started," Rab said. "His two digging mates said the mine was theirs. So we showed them the Dane's registered claim deed from Archer, with only the Dane's name on it."

Gordon continued the tale. "Bunko, one of his mates, started yelling and cursing and calling us mangy bastards. He got a .22 rifle out of his pickup and started toward us."

"Well, what happened?"

They both smiled. "Not much," Gordon replied. Bunko is a Skite, all talk, no backbone. He got so nervous when Garbhan walked toward him that the gun went off and shot into the ground. Garbhan took it away from him and hit him over the head with it, knocked him down. Then he unloaded it and while Bunko was still on the ground, laid it on his chest. He told him in graphic detail what he would do with the rifle if Bunko tried that again. That was pretty much the end of it."

Rab said, "Two of us had to be underground in the claim all the time to keep Bunko and his mate Beesly from ratting it. Sixty feet deep, that was tough. The four of us worked it day and night for a week."

"It was dangerous, too," Gordon said. "Old Eddie had dug his drifts too wide 40 years ago, and it wasn't safe. Two big cave-ins blocked the main drive. We had to dig them out. But we did it and came out good on the stones, good enough to buy a tractor, a generator, a wet puddler and an old flatbed truck."

"And build a 300-gallon water tank to catch roof rain water," Rab said. "That was a real step up for us. Four years ago we had nothing. We ate 'roo meat."

"Even the Aborigines don't eat 'roo," I observed. "Too wormy."

"Yeah. The Aussies make soup out of it, can it, and sell it to America. Worms and all." They both laughed.

I made a note never to buy canned 'roo meat soup.

I asked, "Did all of you leave Scotland together?"

"I worked in a coalmine," Rab said. "Like my father. Made six quid a week. But after paying my mother for room and board and other expenses, I had 10 bob left over for spending money, just enough for a few beers. I might have married and toughed it out, like my friends, except for a scare. Coalmining is dangerous. One day we were cleaning a freshly dug area, and the ceiling started coming down. Just moving slowly down, from eight feet to four feet, then it stopped. No one had ever seen this happen before. A half dozen of us crawled out and made it safely back to the elevator and went straight up to the surface. What the other five did I don't know, but I resolved never to go underground again. I had a few quid saved and borrowed some from friends for passage to Aussie, and here I am."

"And here you are working underground," Gordon pointed out, laughing.

"But this is safe mining; no one here gets killed by cave-ins. And I get to keep my own earnings."

"If there are any. Remember, we used to eat 'roo."

Gordon told me he was from the islands and fished with his father. "It was a good life. We rowed our boat out in the morning, cast our nets, pulled them in, gutted the fish and sold them at market. Then one day a storm came up fast; that happens at sea. We were too far out, farther than we should have been, but the fishing was good, and sometimes we took the risk. It looked real bad. We left our nets and rowed with all our might, while the wind picked up and the waves rose and spilled over the gunwales."

Here Gordon stood up and walked around. "We rowed hard. Our arms were aching. The storm worsened, the sky turned black.

We didn't think we'd make it. My mother couldn't even see us. She stood on shore waving a lantern frantically and yelling, 'This way! Over here! Here I am, come this way!'" Gordon was silent for a few minutes. Then, "Somehow we got to shore. We made it, and I said I would never again go to sea."

"And the next day you bought a ticket for a ship to Australia," Rab said.

"That's different. Ships don't sink."

"And opal mines don't cave-in."

They both laughed and handed me another beer. I liked these blokes.

"I'd like to have a look at the humpy," I said.

It was a mess. The mud walls, three feet thick, were crumbling. Someone had covered the whole thing with aluminum foil, probably to reflect the sun or keep the rain off. The inside was full of junk, broken furniture, pick handles, and debris. The clay floor was uneven, worn down in front of the stone fireplace. Ah! But the stone fireplace is what made it all livable. Imagine being able to cook over a fire at waist height. No more squatting, bending or kneeling. Just stand up, build a fire and cook "I'll take it. How much?"

"No charge. You'll make a good neighbor," Rab said. "The place needs a little fixing up. But there's one other thing."

I waited.

"Bunko says it's his and he'll shoot anybody who tries to take it."

"But we don't think he has the guts."

"Unless he's full as a goog, but then he couldn't hit anything anyway." Rab said with a laugh.

"Where's he live?" I asked.

"About a half-mile over the ridge by Herbert's Rush."

I thought: Is this worth facing a dill, a no-hoper with a rifle? Just Bruno and me? Without a gun? I looked at Bruno lying there with his nose on his paws, ready to bolt and run at the first sign of danger. Then I thought of the coming hot weather and the waist-high fireplace. Yes, it's worth it.

"She'll be right," I said, and the deal was done. We shook hands.

Chapter XXV
Bunko's Choice

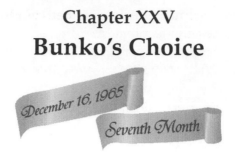

December 16, 1965

Seventh Month

Angus had my opals on the table the next morning and discussed each one. It was rewarding to deal with a buyer who described the stones' value rather than just say "yes" or "no" to a sale. "Opals have a hardness of six and a half, compared to a diamond's 10," he explained. "They're a soft stone and scratch or break easily. The moisture content can be as high as 20 percent; that makes them mortal. They don't last forever. In time they dry and crack. But with proper care they can last a century."

Angus went on to say that opals are judged by their size, color, shape, dome, clarity, clearness, trueness and pattern, which can be harlequin, pin fire, flame, flash or any combination of these. Opals are ranked from worst to best as common opal, mug stone, noble or precious opal and gemstone. Gemstones vary a great deal; the brilliant are more valuable than diamonds or any other gem.

We went out into the sunlight. "Let's start with the jelly opal. It's small, just large enough for a ring. Like two of the others, it's the same under artificial light. This is good. This jelly gives off flashes of greens, yellows and blues as I turn it in the sunlight, but it isn't true."

"True?" I asked.

"'True means it faces up – looks good from any angle. That's a rare characteristic that even many gem opals don't have. See, as I turn it, many areas are just dead. This detracts from its appeal and value. Have a look at the rolling flash in this grey[112] stone. The flat surface isn't as desirable as a dome, and the rolling flash is predominantly blue, not the best color. But it looks good." Angus turned it, and the rolling flash moved with the stone. "But it dies

---

112 Grey – Denotes the color of the potch. Black potch reflects the colors brighter than grey.

under artificial light, making it just a day stone. Difficult to sell an opal that doesn't look good at night."

He examined the pin fire opal. "Harlequin is the prized pattern, squares or diamonds of colors that dance in the light. Next come the flame and flash patterns. Pin fires have the same pattern as the harlequin, only smaller, tiny, so all you see is dots. This is the least desirable of the four types. But it is precious opal."

"This one is a gem." He turned the flake-patterned opal in the sunlight. Reds, yellows, golds and greens shot out. "It's true. Notice how it looks at you from any angle and becomes a different stone each way you turn it." He placed it on my ring finger. "It's just the right size. This four-carat stone is good day or night, has a nice dome, good shape and is true. It faces up nicely with only a little cloudiness around one edge. Three of the four are precious opal. This one is gem quality."

I was happy to learn what buyers look for. This opal, a gem, couldn't compare with the stone I had sold to Bernie Bingo for 180 quid, but it was nice. Angus went on, "The day stone will have to be sold for less."

I asked. "How much are they worth?"

"I can give you 550 for the gem stone or 800 for the parcel, but you should get another bid."

"No. I don't want another bid. Your price sounds fair. I don't trust the other buyers. I'll sell the gemstone and keep the others for a while, just to look at."

He counted out 55 ten-pound notes. I thanked him and left. Rab and Gordon were driving away when I came out. "We'll meet you in the pub for lunch. Got something to tell you." They were laughing, as usual.

"Righto," I said and Bruno and I left for my claim.

Five hundred fifty quid ($1,125 American)! More money than I had ever held in my hand. My claim had just paid for itself, and I could cut Willis in on the profit. It felt good to climb down my shaft with a wad of bills in my pocket. Very good. I hoped this was just the beginning. I dug out in four directions from the blowhole, even though the channel continued on straight. Dig, shovel, tote, haul. Dig, shovel, tote, haul. Dig, shovel, tote, haul. More encouraging now that I had found another pocket of opal.

I was late for lunch, and the Scots were standing at a table with Bunko and his mate, Beesly. I nodded at the Scots, but joined Wombat and Skinner at the next table, preferring the odor of dead sheep to Bunko.

"G'day, 'oweryergoing?" Each of them had drained a pint so I stood my shout and made polite conversation while listening in on the Scots' conversation with Bunko.

"The Yank's coming in three days," said Rab. "He's moving in. You ready to protect your property?"

"He doesn't have a gun," Gordon said, "but his dog is fierce – can't be stopped once he tastes blood. I heard he can rip a 'roo to shreds in just a few minutes."

Bunko listened wide-eyed. Beesly just sipped his beer; this wasn't his dispute.

"You know once he moves in, it's his," Rab pressed on. "That's the law of the Wally; the man who claims a vacated humpy owns it. It's his by right of possession."

"You'll have to be there to stop him. Bring your gun. You can probably scare the Yank away, but you'll have to shoot that wild dog."

"Be careful. That beast doesn't bark or growl, just attacks without warning when his master is threatened. Look around; you never know which direction he might charge from. Shoot first; ask questions later," Rab advised.

Beesly obviously didn't want to get involved. "I'm off, mate. See you back at the puddler," he said, leaving Bunko standing there with an apprehensive look on his face. He left without standing his shout.

Wombat looked at me quizzically. "They talking about the mutt you got from Broken Bob? He wouldn't attack a bird."

I smiled. "Not to worry, mate, she'll be right."

"We have to get back to work," Gordon said. "Remember, Bunko, three days from today. Once he's in, it's his forever."

Bunko hadn't noticed me or uttered a word. As the Scots started for the door, he blurted out with beery bravado, "I can take care of meself, mate. I'll be there. I'm ready."

I shifted so my back was toward Bunko. I didn't want him to see me. Skinner smiled and said, "Yer movin' into the Scots' mud humpy? I wouldn't worry. Bunko's about as brave as a dead sheep." Nodding to Sarah, he declared, "Another round. We're fixin' for a bluey."

Bunko left. I had a pork pie and shouted another round for Wombat and Skinner. I needed another pint to figure out what the Scots were up to. They knew Bruno would be off at the first sign of trouble. But why tell Bunko to bring his rifle? To make him think it was dangerous? I wondered. So dangerous that he might get hurt? So dangerous that maybe he should let it go without a fight? What are they getting me into?

I'm moving in three days. It must be true; I heard it in the pub. I will be rejoining the digger's world, no longer isolated. Six weeks in the bush is probably enough. Normal people start getting the Wallies or hearing voices after two weeks of isolation. That hadn't happened, but I should return before it does. I decided to take the afternoon off and visit me old mates. Bruno stayed in town.

Dynamite Dan's pickup was by his hole. I yelled down the shaft, "Look out down there, you ratters. Fire in the hole!"

He yelled back, "You bloody Yanks don't know a ratter from a gink. Jump in, and I'll show you how a real digger works."

I grabbed the rope and climbed down. His claim was about 35 feet deep with good toe kicks. "Oweryergoin'? Ain't seen yer in three fortnights. Thought you mighta hit a pocket o' nobbies and gone back to Ameriker. Or got yer hand chopped off by the Bingos. Or got tossed in the Shearing Shed for messing with Abo sheilas."

"You heard?"

"No, it just seemed odd that she would approach those two in broad daylight. Too risky. Out of character. Then I heard you were the one that tipped Archer the Cop. But not till after you had set the whole thing up," he said with a big grin. "Good on yer."

"Marco was in on ratting your claim, and I owed you one," I told Dan. "The Mad Pom hearing the trees tell him to look for the big wind in the pub sounded a little too fortuitous to be pure chance. You must have had to dodge bullets to pull that off."

"Not so bad. He was shooting wildly, all over the place, wasn't sure which tree was talking to him. But we're on our way, mate, got the Pom and Marco, and I know who two of the other ratters are."

I cocked my head.

"Want it to be a surprise," he said, still grinning.

We sat down and rolled a cigarette. "Getting any color?" I asked.

"Not much, but the slope of the ceiling looks good. I might hit something in a week or two. It's a good claim."

"Any ratting?"

"Nah. It's the dynamite. They think I've got the Wallies; that helps. I've been tying a thread across the shaft, a thin thread that breaks easily. No one's been down here in weeks. I still drop a primer once in a while, just to keep up appearances. And you?"

"Found a small pocket of medium grade, got 550 quid from Angus the Scot. I like the Scots; moving into their mud humpy in a few days. A bloke called Bunko says it's his, but he's a bull artist. I don't think it'll come to blows."

"Count me in, mate. Haven't been in a bluey for a couple o' months."

"It's been interesting being isolated. It gave me a chance to sort things out. I'm back now. You stopping at the boozer?"

"Not yet. I'd slam into Bernie first chance I got and end up in the Shearin' Shed again. Maybe Archer would run me out of town this time."

"Well, hang in there, mate." I said. "I've been doing a lot of thinking and planning. See you in a few days when I'm settled in."

Bruce the Banker's pickup was parked by a mine on Three Mile Flats. His dog, Floppy, was lazing on the tailings but stood up when he saw me. He bounded into my arms, fur flying, and licked my face. He remembered our rainy night together. While he ran around and barking, Bruce's head came up out of the shaft.

"G'day, mate," I said. "Your watchdog's doing his job."

"I see he attacked you. Didn't know if I'd ever see you again. How's life back o' the Black Stump?"

"Nice. But I've returned. Moving into the Scots' mud humpy for the hot weather."

"Good. Floppy missed you. Been some changes, too. Found a couple good nobbies, Angus bought them for over 400 quid. I now have a wet puddler."

"Good on yer, mate!"

"A banking friend of mine is here for a couple weeks. We're pulling an old shaft on the Pony Fence. Had good stones in the old days." Bruce paused. "I owe you for the use of your puddler and for Floppy. Feel free to use my wet puddler. I'll show you where it is and how to run it."

"Good on yer mate. I'd like that. Be good to get out of my hole once in a while. I'll toss you a couple mugs if I have any luck."

We talked for a while, and then I stopped in town, picked up Bruno and drove to the Professor's. We were in luck. He was home. I got out and said, "Kookaburra."

"Give it up, Yank. You'll never get it right."

"What yer mean, mate? I'm considered a fair-dinkum Aussie by some."

"Well, you better be careful what birds you talk about. Pawn to king's four," he said before we even sat down.

"Like you to meet my new mate, Bruno." The Professor gave him a nod; clearly he wasn't a dog man. Bruno crawled under the table.

We discussed a lot of things, including Omar Khayyam and Schopenhauer, interrupting the chess game when necessary. Once again I drank too much rum and tea. The nice thing about Outback driving is you only have to miss the trees; there's nothing else to run into. Somehow Bruno and I made it the several miles back to our coolabah camp.

My isolated life had been fulfilling, but it was good to see my mates again.

The Scots had promised Bunko I would move in within three days. I came over two days early to clean out the debris and fix things up. I had only glanced at it before. It was full of junk. No one had lived in it for years. I built a fire outside, burned broken chairs, an old sofa, pick handles and assorted trash. My humpy needed more than just cleaning. The roof poles sagged two feet in the center, the clay floor was uneven, and the walls were crumbling in places – still, not bad for a mud humpy built 30 years ago.

The Scots had an abundance of equipment. I asked Angus if I could use the floor jack, stepladder, Swede saw and other tools. "Help yourself to whatever you need. Just put it back where you found it."

First the roof pole. I found a 12-foot tree, five inches in diameter, in the woods used for mining timbers. I cut it down and drove back to the campsite with it sticking out of my passenger-side window. Using the ladder I fastened one end of the tree to the roof beam with a loose wire twist. Wire twists are a handy device. Double a two-foot piece of flexible wire, loop it around what you want to fasten, put a screwdriver through the loop and twist till it's secure. I propped up the pole to the center of the roof beam and put on another twist, then several more on that half. Next, with a pole cut to fit under the sagging beam, I jacked it up till the beam was level and wire-twisted the two poles together. Voila, I had a straight roof. I was proud of my good day's work. Bruno and I went back to the coolabah and had a cuppa and a smoke.

Next day I watered some mud in the Scots' cement-mixing trough and plastered the inside walls with fresh mud. After filling in the holes and leveling the clay floor, I got piles of old newspapers from Petula at the post office, overlapped them, one sheet at a time, on the floor and covered them with three layers of tar paper. The stick and bark door would be okay for now. I was ready to move in.

I stepped outside for a breath of air and heard two gunshots. "I'm warning you, Yank. Stay out of my humpy." Bunko was a ways off, brandishing his rifle pathetically. I picked up a faggot from the campfire and ran toward him. He jumped into his car and drove off shouting, "I'll be back tonight. You better be ready to hump your bluey."

"I'll sic my dog on you, you dill gink," I yelled and threw the faggot at his car. It hit the rear fender, which was already dented. I looked around for Bruno. He had taken refuge in the humpy.

We went back the coolabah and broke camp. I had accumulated more possessions, enough for two trips. The young Scots were there when I got back and helped me set up.

"Bunko came by for a few shots and a warning."

"Aye, we thought he might." They both smiled. "Not to worry, she'll be right, mate." They were taking all this lightly, so I said, "I see you have a shower bag. I might clean up before I move in. Then if I get shot you'll have a clean body to work with."

They smiled again. "Righto, mate. Help yourself. Use our water."

I filled my water can from their rainwater tank, lowered the canvas bag on its rope, filled it with water and pulled it up again over the tree branch. I got a bar of soap and turned the large showerhead. Water poured over me. What delight! I hadn't had a shower in the months since I arrived on the Wally. Five gallons is a lot of water. I stood there until the bag was empty. Now I wished I had clean clothes to put on, but my other shirt and pants had aired out for a couple of days, and I felt like a new man.

The waist-high fireplace made cooking a breeze. Styk 'n eggs to celebrate. The downside of my new home was the lack of a ground fire in sight at night and no stars to be seen as I dozed off. But I'll live with it.

I recalled Dynamite Dan's thread idea and strung a thread in the humpy's doorway, just above ground level, and connected it to a heavy pot above the door. If someone broke the thread, the pot would fall, making a racket. After reading late, I sat on my cot with a pick handle between my legs, waiting. Bruno stayed up, too, with his nose on his paws, ready to cut and run at the first sign of danger. We waited until I finally dozed off.

Next morning Rab broke my thread, and the pan fell with a bang. He stuck his head in the door. "Ah, mate. You're still here. Glad you decided to stay." He was off without another word.

I got up, had a leisurely breakfast and ambled down to my Yank's claim, now only three miles away; a shorter run for Bruno.

I joined the Scots for lunch at the Digger's Retreat. They always smiled, but now they were beaming. "A pint for the Yank, Sarah. He won the shootout. He's the fastest draw on the Wally."

Wombat and Skinner at the next table laughed. "Some shootout," Wombat mumbled.

"What's the celebration?" I asked. "He never showed."

"Aye, Bunko had a choice to make, perhaps the most important choice of his manly life – whether or not to protect his property at the risk of getting ripped apart by a ferocious dog and beat up by its owner."

"Or shooting the dog's owner and getting tossed in the slammer for life," said Rab.

"He might beat the rap. A man's mud humpy is his castle – says so in the Bible," said Gordon, laughing wildly at his own joke.

"The important thing is, he made the expedient decision, the one he could handle," said Rab, "a decision that was in accord with his philosophy of life."

Gordon raised his glass. "Hear, hear! I'll drink to that."

Gordon had the attention of the whole pub and everyone raised his glass. I, too, raised mine and waited. These Scots milk every humorous possibility to the hilt.

"What are you on about?" I finally asked, realizing I was the only one not in on the joke.

"He chose to get drunk," said Rab.

"And beat up his wife," added Gordon. "Archer locked him in the Shearing Shed and took his wife to Walgett. She's waiting for the next train to Brisbane."

"Here's to Bunko, the man who follows through with his threats," said Rab, laughing and raising his glass.

"And," said Gordon, "to the Yank who stood his ground and didn't cave in to threats of violence."

"Or maybe to the Yank who stood his mud," Rab said.

This whole thing was an elaborate joke. Everyone knew Bunko would do something stupid, not courageous. I smiled at the Scots' sense of humor.

Chapter XXVI
Wally Tales

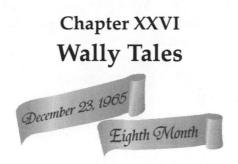

December 23, 1965

Eighth Month

Fly season starts in November. Sand flies. They don't bite but come in unbelievable numbers. Jokes abound. "Aye, mate, I heard 100 'roos leaping by, but the flies swarming around my head were so thick I couldn't see 'em." "There were so many flies on 'is back yer couldn't tell if he had a shirt on," and so on. To eat stew during fly season, I would constantly wave my hand back and forth across the plate, quickly get a forkful of stew, then go *pfft* to blow the flies off just before putting it in my mouth. You must wave your hand in front of your face continually, or they will crawl into the corners of your eyes, up your nose, and into your mouth. (They don't go for the ears – no moisture there.) Blokes walk stiffly, trying not to disturb the settled flies. Better to just leave them be.

Fortunately fly season is short, a month or so of everyone hand-waving. One must learn to live with it and stop waving when it's over. Blokes who keep waving are getting the Wallies. Fortunately flies don't come around after dark. A tent attracts spiders and a lot of small critters. Now that I had an enclosed humpy, I hung mosquito netting to keep them off me at night.

Christmas came. It's difficult to celebrate at 130 degrees, but the Scots made the effort. It was Angus' idea to keep up the old traditions. "Bethlehem's climate is closer to Wallangulla then it is to Glasgow's," he pointed out. They decorated a small saltbush with a few mug stones waxed to a string, and that was it. We didn't sing carols.

The contrast between life by the coolabah and my mud humpy was significant. Now I was really alone only when underground.

After evening tea I often joined the Scots under their bough shed to learn the local gossip.

"Do you know Flint the Ratter?" I asked, "How did he earn his name?"

Rab and Gordon bantered back and forth, telling the story as one person.

"He and Denny Strayman sunk a monkey[113] and tunneled under the Leaning Tree claim next to their claim. Then they dug back up to the first opal level and ratted the claim before the owners, Buttons and Turk, got to it. It took weeks, but when Buttons and Turk dug into that open area, it was obvious who the ratters were. Archer the Cop fined Flint a quid per foot, 15 pounds total."

"Flint said, 'It'd be cheap at twice the price.' He did well on the job. Everybody likes Flint. He gets into blueys when he's had a pint too many, but outside of that he's good natured."

"A bloke called Territory Burt came all the way from Darwin just to have a go at Flint the Ratter. He was huge, filled the whole pub door when he came in, smiling. 'I'm Territory Burt, and I'm lookin' for the Ratter,' he said, 'Is he 'ere or off hiding somewhere?' Flint was standing at the bar having a beer with his mob. He looked up at this huge bloke and said, 'Sarah, a pint for the bull artist who came a long way just to get thumped.'"

"It was all very cordial. They each had a couple pints, then stepped outside to have a bluey. It didn't last long, Flint had him on the ground in short order, went back into the pub and said, 'Sarah, another glass for the big bloke when he comes to. The Ratter stands his shout.' That was it. He went home."

"The next morning Flint heard a loud banging on his door. It was Territory Burt. 'I 'ad a bit too much to drink last night, mate. You can't take me when I'm sober.'"

"'Righto,' the Ratter said, 'but let's walk away from the house, I don't want my kids to see me fighting.'"

"The Ratter thumped him real good this time, and that was the end of it. He humped his bluey back to Darwin, a beaten man."

Gordon handed me another beer and looked at me quizzically. "The stories about the Ratter are endless. You game for more?"

---

113 Monkey – A shaft down to a lower opal level

"I've got all night. Carry on."

Gordon continued, "Flint's wife, Fiona, is still a beauty, even after three kids and 10 years in the Outback. She won several beauty contests as a girl. She's the one with the temper."

"One night, after a few pints at the pub, they stumbled home and got into an argument. They didn't hit each other, but she got so mad she tore up his only white shirt. So he tore up her best dress. The destruction went on until Flint was disgusted and sat down at the table and put his head in his hands."

"Seizing the opportunity, Fiona picked up a piece of firewood and clunked him on the head, knocking him out. 'Oh, my God,' she said, 'I've killed him. I've killed my husband. Oh, my God.' She ran into town looking for Archer the Cop, which took a while; he wasn't in the pub."

"In the meantime Flint came to. He was still a little groggy, but he ambled down to the pub for a pint to cure his headache. The wife, meanwhile, dragged Archer up the hill to their house, only to find Flint gone. Now she was really mad. She picked up the same piece of firewood and went down the pub where he was standing at the bar and clunked him again."

"She did what no man was able to do: knocked out her husband twice in the same day. But, as we said, Flint the Ratter is always smiling and good-natured. A nice bloke. Garbhan partnered him a few times; they pulled a couple o' holes together."

"How did you meet Garbhan and Angus?" I asked.

Rab said, "In a pub in Sydney. We were having a pint, wondering where to go and heard the Scottish brogue at the next table. We introduced ourselves and got to talking. They invited us to join them and become millionaires, simple as that."

"Here we are. We're mates, but we don't know them well. Angus is gone a lot, buying or selling opals. Garbhan is quiet and stays to himself. We all do what we can and get along well. It was tough the first couple o' years, but we're fine now, settled in, so to speak."

I never did find out what their financial arrangements were, but they all seemed satisfied.

In summer, December to February, 130-degree midday heat and 90-degree nights were not unusual. My thermometer went up only to 128 and often topped out in the hot season. It is amazing how adaptable the human body is. The desert heat is dry and more comfortable than a humid climate; no sweat accumulates on the body. The comfortable time to work is early morning, while it's still less than 100 degrees.

Dynamite Dan and I decided to take advantage of Bruce the Banker's offer to use his wet puddler. We both needed a break from digging alone. I stopped by Bruce's trailer and was greeted by Edward, wagging his tail. I patted him on the head as Floppy came running out of the trailer and jumped up on me excitedly. Bruno stayed back but touched noses with the two mutts.

"You know that one?" Bruce asked, indicating Edward. "He just showed up one day and stayed. Easy to get along with and likes to take walks."

"He belonged to the Mad Pom. Never got a lot of attention. I'm glad he found a home. His name is Edward."

"Oh. Glad to find out he has a name. Floppy about drives him wacko, wanting to play all the time, but I think he likes it here. Stays at camp when I'm digging. I never knew much about the Pom; a little odd, I thought."

We drove to the puddling tank, and he showed me how to use it. For hauling, the Scots let us use their old flatbed truck with no brakes. "Just keep shifting down, and when you're in low gear, turn off the key. It'll stop." Sounded okay to us, nothing out here to hit or damage anyway.

Dan had acquired a power winch to use in place of a hand-cranked windlass. A small gasoline engine was mounted on a pole with guidelines. It had a three-foot arm with a pulley that let the cable and the bucket on a hook go down the shaft. Dan picked a hole on the low side of Three Mile Flats. I didn't like the look of it; it had been filled with water at some time, and the shaft had caved in 10 feet from the top.

"Wombat said this hole had yielded some good nobbies in years past," Dan said with enthusiasm.

"Why don't he and Skinner pull it?" I asked.

"They think it's too dangerous, might cave in on them."

"Why wouldn't it just as easily cave in on us?"

"She'll be right, mate, I know how to pull a wet hole."

I didn't like it, but he was me mate. We set up the power winch, and I let Dan slowly down the hole and then lowered the bucket down the two-by-four shaft. He filled the bucket with wet clay in short order. I pulled it up, dumped the tailings on the flat bed truck and lowered the bucket again. After a few buckets he yelled up, "Have a go, mate, it's nice down here." I pulled him up, and he lowered me into the shaft. We were down five more feet, and the newly exposed shaft walls were wet and crumbly. I filled the bucket several times. Then one side of the shaft caved in a little, burying my foot up to the ankles. I had a hard time pulling them out. "Righto, mate, pull me up, I've had it with this wet mud. Too chancy."

"You bloody Yanks," he said, "Nothing but galas, ginks and poofters. I'll dig the whole bloody shaft myself. You stay up here where your feet won't get wet," he said with a disgusted look. I let him down and he slammed into the wet clay with a vengeance. One foot, two foot, five foot. He dug with the fury of a madman. Then the other side of the shaft caved in, burying him up to his knees. This was serious, you can't just pull your feet out, and there was no place to throw the clay except into the bucket. He dug frantically, knowing another cave-in could bury him up to his neck. I could do nothing but empty the bucket and let it down again. There wasn't room for both of us in the shaft. It took four buckets before he could free his feet. I pulled him up, and without discussion we took down the power wench, loaded the bucket and shovels and drove off to the puddling tank.

I invited Dyno Dan over for New Year's Eve. The Scots decided to get New Year's drunk at home this year, and Angus came up with two bottles of Scotch whiskey. After several spirited toasts – none of them to the Queen – Angus and Garbhan in their kilts did a Highland fling. They asked us to join in, but it was more fun just to watch. None of the rest of us knew the dance. They were entertaining, jumping from one foot to the other waving their arms. We sang Auld Lang Syne several times and talked into the wee hours. One of the topics was the Helen Shapiro movies that the town ladies rented for 10 quid ($22.50) and showed in the town hall every Saturday night. Imagine! Movies in the Outback. Sounded interesting. Ten bob admission ($1.15). Helen Shapiro was a plump Jewish girl from England with a nice voice. The movies had little plot, but they were affordable. John Wayne and Tarzan movies were too expensive. I vowed to go with them next Saturday night. Dan and the young Scots passed out under the bough shed. I managed to get back to my humpy. Best New Year's Eve I had ever had.

Everyone was more subdued the next morning, and the world returned to normal. The next night I was back under the bough shed having a beer with the Scots, getting more news. Garbhan and even Angus joined us from time to time, busy as he was buying opals and going to Sydney to sell them. I was now part of a mob, the Scots Mob.

"You know Hungry Hank the Hatter?" Rab asked.

"We've howdy'ed, but we ain't shook," I said, using the quaint Texas expression and not wanting to discuss my bluey with him.

"He's an interesting character. His wife left three, four years ago. Said he was as mad as a hatter. Left him with their four kids. Rumor has it she ran off with the piano tuner when he hit the big lolly.[114] Hank's oldest daughter was 12 and had to look after the younger ones. They all took the school bus to Walgett with the six other kids from the Wally."

"Hank poked around a little in old claims but didn't do much but drink," Gordon added, "Then a new young bloke called Winston came through and met Hank in the boozer. They teamed up and did a few digs together."

"Gossip says he was more interested in Hank's 12-year-old daughter than he was in opal. Anyway, this went on for some time. Then one day Winston accused Hank of swinging a stone on him."

"Seems Bernie Bingo, after a few beers, was bragging about the price he got it for, and someone told Winston."

"The upshot is that Hank had a black eye, and Winston was gone."

"Didn't take the 12-year-old with him, just left."

---

114 'The big sweet.' Found a pocket of opals

Rab and Gordon bounced off observations like a verbal tennis match.

"Hungry Hank went back to serious drinking. The town ladies looked after the kids and fed them even though Hank told them to mind their own bloody business. Hank was living on bread and treacle, nearly starving."

"Then one day the locals heard a blast and saw dust and debris shoot into the air."

"It was Hank's humpy two miles out of town. The local volunteer fire department, which consists of whoever is in the pub at the time, swung into action."

"The fire truck was one of those the Yanks left after World War II. How and why it got to the Wally is a puzzle. It hadn't been started in years, and the battery was dead. These half-potted blokes started pushing it but gave up on the hill just out of town."

"It didn't matter. The truck holds 500 gallons of water, but the tank was empty, and the pump ran off the engine, which didn't start."

"Some kept walking, and a few went back to the pub to get more beer for the firefighters."

"The bed mattress was up in a tree. Hardly anything left of his smoldering humpy by the time the fire brigade arrived. They pulled out a few pots and pans, but most everything was destroyed. So they sat down and had a beer and argued about how many sticks of dynamite were involved."

"His 12-year-old daughter was gone, presumably with Winston. The younger children were at school. The local women brought a tent and supplies, and took the younger kids but Hank never got into life again. And he wouldn't sell his stone."

"I saw it once. I felt sorry for the poor bloke and bought him a pint and a pie. He pulled it out of his pocket and let me have a quick look. A real beaut: a Radiant; purple with reds, greens and yellows, flake pattern. Worth tens o' thousands. Back in his pocket it went. Angus was interested, so the next time I saw Hank, I asked him if he wanted to sell. He denied ever having had a gemstone."

Dyno Dan and I went back to mining our own claims, but planned to pull another hole. I invited him to join me and the Scots under the bough shed evenings to hear the Wally stories, but he didn't want to be away from his claim that long. He still drops a stick of dynamite down the hole daily. Stories bounced back and forth between Rab and Gordon.

I told them, "I heard about some Yugoslavs who hit it big on Duffer's Dag, but I don't know the details. I've been isolated from Wally news for some time."

"It's a classic story. About a month ago two Croats walked into the Digger's Retreat and announced, 'We buy beer. We want find opal.' They shouted the pub. We were there, sipped our pints slowly, knowing Aussie humor would come into play. 'We work construction, have money, now want dig hard for opal, be rich.'"

"Shadow was the first to get into it, while greedy Bernie Bingo contemplated how to shear these sheep. 'Aye, mates, yer've come to the right place. If yer ain't afraid o' hard work, we'll set yer up and tell yer where to dig. You'll be rich in no time,' 'Thank you, thank you,' they said and closed in on Shadow intently."

"Some of us were embarrassed but said nothing. Sometimes blokes, especially immigrants, set themselves up; there's no helping them. 'First,' Shadow said, dripping with sincerity, 'you'll need equipment: tents, shovels, picks, water cans, cooking pots and...' 'We have tent and pots' one of them cut in, but Shadow hushed him, 'Yer've gotta have the right equipment, or yer'll end up broke or dead in no time.'"

"He was so sincere I was starting to believe him myself. He sent Wombat and Skinner to the general store with a list and said, 'Now, remember the prices; we don't want to overcharge our new mates.' King Tut jumped in, 'I've got a puddler I can let you have for a hundred quid ($225).'"

I said, "That's the mangy bastard who sold me a puddler for four times its worth."

"We heard the story. His venereal disease is in remission, last we heard," Rab said with a laugh. "You puddled him good." There are no secrets on the Wally, I thought. "Continue."

"Marco offered them a kerosene refrigerator for 50 quid, but both that and the puddler would have to wait; their pickup truck was too small to carry all the stuff for sale. Someone else had a windlass he could part with and a tent, picks and shovels. By the time it was over, Shadow and his mates had put the fang into[115] these two blokes for a couple hundred quid – and several shouts. Even Sarah saw the light and charged them double for the beer. Bernie just stood at the bar with Chuck the Cutter, not quite knowing how to get in on all this. They dealt in opal, and there was no opal – yet."

"I've never seen two happier faces. Here they are, strangers, and everyone is sacrificing to help them become rich. 'Thank you, thank you' they said, over and over. The upshot of all of this is they sent them out to the Duffer's Dag. Duffer's Dag, 35 miles away in the middle of nowhere, got its name because it had never produced even a dozen mug stones. It had a brief run several years ago when a few blokes sunk four or five shafts, but they gave it up as a bad go. Potch and color with sand was all they got."

"Shadow drew the Croats a rough map to get there and told them how to mine. The whole pub turned out to see them off. We just shook our heads and went back to digging, leaving a happy, laughing mob of drunks in the pub. For the next few days they speculated whether the Croats would die of thirst or exhaustion or get lost in the desert. If they found Duffer's Dag, how long would it be before they realized they had been had and give it all up? Would they return to the Wally or just light out for Sydney with their tails between their legs?"

"But I heard they did find opal," I said. Rab and Gordon smiled.

"Hard physical work is what they wanted. So they went at mining with an entirely different attitude. We pieced the facts together without knowing the details. The shafts were 30 feet deep to the opal clay level. To save hauling up tailings, diggers make as small a drive as possible. The drives left by the diggers on Duffer's Dag were 4 feet high by 4 feet wide, standard size. As you know, opal on the Wally is found within six inches of the sandstone ceiling. Sometimes an odd stone will show up lower but that's rare."

"These Wogs didn't want to crouch down. They were free men now, away from the terrors of Yugoslavia and determined to

---

115 Put the fang into – to take advantage of someone like a snake does to an unsuspecting victim

walk upright. So they dug the drives two feet deeper and hauled out tons of dirt. Lo and behold, the opal layer was underfoot. Within a week they hit a pocket. They came back to the pub with a bucket of nobbies, dumped them on the bar and couldn't thank Shadow and their new mates enough. Sarah drew pints for all and charged them double as before. They were rich."

Gordon chimed in, "Beesly ran out to tell Bernie Bingo and Chuck the Cutter the good news. The pub was soon full. Chuck and Bernie poured over the nobbies with open glee."

"Many good nobbies were cracked and broken by careless digging, but they had a small fortune."

"'We'll get these cut and priced for you right away,' Chuck said. 'I come with you,' one of the Croats said."

"Bernie, smiling, took him by the arm. 'No need for that, it's best to let the cutter work alone, in peace and quiet.'"

"'I not make noise,' the Croat said seriously."

"'No, no, you just stay here and have a beer with me and Shadow. We have things to discuss.'"

"Shadow reminded them several times that he was the one who put them onto the riches and they promised him a share. Bernie talked about the quality and pricing of opals and assured them top price."

"After several hours Chuck came back with a bowl of cut stones. Bernie examined each one in detail. When all was said and done they got 15,000 quid. We figure they broke more than half the good stones digging them out and Chuck kept half the stones he cut. Bernie got the rest for half price or less. Shadow was awarded 1,500 quid with many thanks and offered his 13-year old daughter, Chickie, to them as a cook. They accepted, and the next day the three of them, with food and fresh cans of water in the back, once again set off across the Outback for Duffer's Dag."

"But not alone. Wombat, Skinner and half a dozen other blokes packed up supplies and staked claims on the Duffer. Two weeks later they all came back. Too much work digging a six-foot deep drive and looking for stones under foot. Too far from water, food and supplies. Too far from the pub. For all intents and purposes it looks like the Croats stumbled on the only opal in the area. One claim. They came back last week with another tin of nobbies but this time stayed with Chuck while he cut, and counted the stones carefully."

"And told Bernie they wanted to sell the stones in Sydney. He promised to pay top price and offered them twice as much as he had a few minutes earlier. The Wogs were learning. They sold him a few stones but kept the rest. They're staying at Lenny's and plan to leave next week. They have enough money for now and can't wait to get back to Sydney and bet on the horses."

Having enough money and wanting to gamble fit right in. These blokes will soon be fair-dinkum Aussies, I thought. Then an idea hit me. I had to have a yarn with me mate, Dynamite, to see if we could get in the game.

Chapter XXVII
Yanks, Croats And A Bluey

Bruno adjusted nicely to the new surroundings of the mud humpy. He slept under my cot on the tarpaper floor that now had a dusting of dirt. No Screechers to awaken us at our new location. He still got up with the sun and gently touched me with his nose to let me know he was off for his morning inspection. As always, he came back when I banged the billy. He ran ahead of my van to spend the day with his dog mates in town. Evenings he stayed close to the bough shed but not close enough to be petted. He was an Outback dog. We were mates but seldom touched.

Dynamite and I worked our own claims now during the hot weather. Most days hit 130-plus, but by 9 p.m. the temperature dropped to a comfortable 90 to 100. I told Dan my plan to help the Croats lurk Shadow, since they now realized his real intentions. The Croats had decided to give Duffer's Dag one more shot. This was good news; we now had time to work it out and could talk to them when they came back in a couple of weeks.

"Hello down there. We're looking for the Yank." I crawled back to the shaft and looked up. "We're Americans. We're living in Brisbane. Here for a holiday. Heard about you and wondering what the hell a Yank is doing in this god-forsaken place. Got time to talk?"

I climbed up the shaft. Gerald Fisher, his wife and two small children, a boy about 10 and a girl, 8, were happy to see me. "G'day mate," I said without thinking, "Oweryergoin'?"

"Are you the Yank?" he asked, puzzled.

"Righto, mate."

"Well then, drop the damn Aussie lingo and talk American. We ain't talked American in three months."

"I'll give it a try," I said. "I've been here a while and gone Outback. I even eat with the fork in my left hand." I decided these were nice folks. "Want to have a look at my claim?"

"Righto, mate," he said with a smile. "You kids stay up here and noodle. Your mother and I are going underground." His wife looked a little apprehensive but smiled gamely. I put both hands on the cribbing and slipped into the shaft.

"Hold onto the rope with both hands and find the toe kicks one at a time before moving on to the next one. Take your time. It's a little tricky."

I went down and Gerald followed with little difficulty. It wasn't so easy for his wife. He talked her down, and she looked relieved to be at the bottom. Then she realized she was in a hole. Looking down the drift quickly she said, "I've seen enough. I'm worried about the kids up there all alone. I better go look after them," and started back up with difficulty. After some time she made it.

"I heard it's bad luck to have a woman in a mine. Maybe its just as well," he said.

"She's not the first one," I replied, and suddenly had a flash thought of Helga kneeling beside me. Bad luck? Maybe.

Gerald was enthusiastic and wanted to dig. He said his wife and kids were just fine, even in the heat. The car was air-conditioned, and they could go to the pub or the café if it got too bad. I gave him a pick, and he went at it enthusiastically. We talked about how and why I was here and his job for an American company in Brisbane. He liked the idea of independently digging for precious stones, but he did have a family to support. He came back the next morning, and the one after that. Fortunately we found a small pocket of mug stones. Garbhan cut them, and each Fisher got one. They beamed.

"We have to go, now," Gerald said on the fourth morning. "But if you ever get to Brisbane please feel free to stay with us. You can have Joey's room; he won't mind. Stay as long as you want." Joey smiled proudly and showed me his opal. Gerald put a folded paper in my hand with their address. "Just rap on the door, anytime." Then, trying to sound Aussie, he said, "Ta, mate," as they got into the car.

"I might just do that," I said, knowing it was a genuine offer of hospitality. "I might just do that." And they vanished into the Outback dust.

Once in a while, just for company, Dynamite and I decided to dig together in our own claims, now that we were mates. The understanding was: Share mug stones and precious opal; gemstones belonged to the claim owner. This worked out okay. We did not make an old-time miners agreement: "If I swing a stone on you, mate, I want you to put a bullet in my head, right here," one miner says and points to his forehead. "Because if you swing a stone on me, that's what I'm going to do to you." That would show a lack of trust.

Some days we dug together, some days alone, depending on how we felt. I was driving in a new run off his shaft while he dug the other way down his primary drive. "I got something here," I said. "The opal dirt is getting gritty." We excitedly poked and prodded out several black nobbies, all without color, before finding a large round nobby with color. Quickly we dug out the rest of the dirt and took our find to the top. Dan snipped it, brushed it and licked it. Good color shone through. This could be a gem.

Garbhan carefully cut and polished it: a beaut. A round stone the size of my thumbnail with flares of color that faced up. Angus looked at it, turned it in the sunlight. "Nice stone," he said, "Good color, bright, true." Then, "Bad size, bad shape."

What? He's rubbishing our stone, I thought. I looked at it again. Sure, it was large and round, shaped like half a shooter marble. But it had good color. Angus placed it on Dan's ring finger. Way too big to be comfortable. Then he placed it on my chest. Stuck out too far to be a necklace, too clumsy. Then on his wrist. "I don't think a lady would want to carry this on her arm, no matter how beautiful." He paused. "What can you do with it? A paperweight? A desk ornament? A knick-knack? This is a hard stone to sell. Someone will buy it, but that someone may take a while to find."

"Are you saying it's worthless?" I asked.

"No, it has value; it's a lovely stone, but the most I can give you is 200 quid." Dan and I looked at each other and thought.

"You might try another buyer," Angus suggested.

"No, we've tried other buyers," Dyno said. "Two hundred seems fair to me. What'a yer think, mate?"

"She'll be right," I answered.

"What I will do," Angus went on, "is give you half of anything I get over 250 quid."

We agreed, and he counted out 20 10-pound notes. We celebrated by having styk 'n eggs at Lenny's.

The Croats returned after a couple of weeks when their water supply ran out. They had another tin of nobbies, sure this time they had the last of the stones from Duffer's Dag. None of the other diggers who went there found anything, not even one mug stone. This time the Croats brought their nobbies to Garbhan for cutting, and he invited them to stay and watch. Angus examined each stone, and explained their value. They seemed to understand. Several were precious opal but no true gems. They had been burned the last time around and decided to keep most of them. Still the number they decided to sell was worth over 5,000 quid. Angus counted out the pile of 10-pound notes.

"We buy beer. We make shout," they said and invited us to join them at the pub.

"Me Dragan," one said, pointing at his chest.

"Me Mirko," said the other. We all shook hands formally.

It had been some time since Dynamite and I had been in the pub.

"Don't sling off at Bernie," I said. "Save him for later. We'll concentrate on Shadow for now."

"Digger's price this time," Angus said to Sarah, with just a hint of contempt. "The hooly-dooly is over." Sarah raised her head with a look that said, "Who are you to tell me what to do?" But she didn't overcharge Mirko. The pub was nearly empty, too early for lunch, but Shadow's wife and two daughters, Dovey, age 19, Marco's intended, and Chickie, 13, whom Shadow had sent up to cook for the Croats, were having a pork pie at one of the sitting tables in the corner. Mirko's eyes strayed to the younger one.

"You like Chickie?" I asked.

"She beautiful. I love her. But too little." He meant too young, of course. Chickie was physically mature.

"Maybe Dragan and you like to take sisters with you to Sydney to gamble on horses."

"Me like," Dragan said. But Mirko just shook his head. "Chickie too little."

"Take the mother along with the daughters," Dynamite suggested, innocently. Both Dragan and Mirko looked up with anticipation. "Offer them a nice opal," and with this he indicated the small bag in Mirko's pocket. Mirko took it out, and Dyno poured a few on the table. He held one on his ring finger and another on his chest. By now the daughters and the mother were looking at us. Angus and Garbhan looked bemused, knowing something sinister was afoot. "They go," he said as he put a few opals in Dragan's hand. "They go."

Eagerly the two of them, beaming brightly, walked over to the ladies table and said something to the effect of, "We go Sydney, gamble horses. Stay in best hotel. You want come?" With this they placed opals on the girls' ring fingers and held one in front of Shadow's wife's neck. She asked simply, "Me, too?"

"We all go," Dragan said, circling his hand around the five of them. By now they were all smiling, obviously interested in this unusual offer.

Dan said, "There's a bit of the bull artist in them. This might work out. My shout, Sarah."

Before the ladies could answer, Shadow walked in with a bloke I hadn't seen before. A new sheep about to be sheared by an expert, I thought. Shadow looked at the group and surmised the two he had bilked were up to no good, having found him out.

"Ah, Mister Shadow. You tell us where find opal stones. You make us rich. Thank you. Now we do for you, take family to city, gamble horses." He's a natural con man, Dan said under his breath. After a pause Mirko said, "You come, too?"

"Quick thinking," Dan said, again under his breath. "I could get to like this bloke."

Before Shadow could answer, his wife chimed in "He doesn't like horse racing. He'll stay here and look after things. The three of us will ride the school bus into Walgett tomorrow morning and meet you at the airport." Shadow didn't know how to respond. He just stood there with a stupid look on his face. Dragan and Mirko smiled at him and rejoined us.

"My shout, Sarah," I called out, "Four pints for us and two for Shadow and his cobber." Shadow scowled at me. His offsider just looked at us, then back at him.

"You mangy bastards had a hand in this. I'll see to you." Then, to his new mate, "I don't drink with gigs," and they walked out.

Angus raised his glass, "To a successful caper, though I'm not quite sure what it's all about." We all tipped our pints. Dynamite clicked his glass against mine and nodded to the Croats. "Good on yer, mates."

The two Scots were under the bough shed, into the beer earlier than usual and not looking happy. The conversation bounced back and forth between them.

"We won't do that again."

"Aye, once is enough."

I opened a can, sat down, and waited. And waited and waited. Finally I asked, "What happened?"

"Wombat and Skinner said he was the fastest driver on the Wally."

"Aye. Six feet a day, they said."

And waited.

"So fast that we asked Garbhan to help us. With him digging, me shovelin' back, Gordon loading the buckets and Garbhan tending the windlass, we thought we could keep up and drive through to the other shaft."

"Aye, and we did."

These two blokes who usually didn't stop talking were bogging down on this tale. "Who is 'him'," I finally asked, "And if you did keep up, what's the problem?"

"The problem is him, Slammin' Sam, the fastest driver."

"It's him, not us. Garbhan wasn't in the hole; he didn't see it. There was nothing we could do to stop him'"

"Get on with it before we run out of beer and the sun comes up," I said somewhat testily.

"We hired him, gave him 15 quid for the day. 'Just dig', we said. 'Just dig.'"

"Aye, that was the mistake right there, it was. We should have filled in a few details. He said, 'I dig'. And he did. The whole seven feet to the other shaft."

I was getting a little impatient. "If he did what you hired him to do, what's the problem?" Another long pause.

"The problem is he hit a pocket of nobbies."

"A big pocket."

"'Look at the pretty colors,' he said and handed me a handful of broken nobbies, chips of gold, red, green, yellow. 'Stop,' I said. 'We're on opal.' He looked at me and at the chips. 'Stop,' I said again. 'Pretty colors,' he said and started slamming into the clay again. 'Stop,' I said the third time. He looked at me and said, 'I dig,' and slammed on through the whole pocket, leaving nothing but chips in his wake."

"By the time I got back from the shaft, it was all over. We went through the chips and found nothing worth saving. He's real dill. He's had a bit of hard kack with his wife running off with the painter, or was it the bricklayer? Anyway, we couldn't stop him 'til he broke through the second shaft, seven feet in one day, probably a record."

"We had to keep shoveling and filling the buckets, or we would have been buried in tailings. Garbhan saw the colored chips and got upset. He doesn't understand. Slammin' Sam is a huge bloke and determined. Impossible to stop once he's digging. It's not our fault."

"Now Garbhan says it was a mistake to invite us up here in the first place. We're not working out. He wants us to leave – right away."

Angus appeared, smiling. "It's okay," he said, "I know about Slammin' Sam. It's not your fault. I talked to Garbhan, he understands." He paused a moment and saw the relieved look on the young Scots' faces. Then he smiled. "Don't hire him again."

The heat eased off a bit in the first part of February. Dynamite and I decided to try wet puddling again. Instead of going to the pub to get information on claims that were once rich, we decided to drive around and pick claims at random. The first one we selected was on Newtown, not far from my Yank's Dig claim. We set up the power winch over a shaft that was open down to the opal level – no more cave-ins. Two of the drifts were filled with tailings. We dropped three buckets down, and I filled while Dan ran the winch. Much easier than the first shaft we had tried. In a few hours the flatbed truck had as much dirt as it could hold.

We drove to the puddling tank and parked by Bruce the Banker's wet puddler. The tank was about 75 by 50 yards, dug out of dirt pushed up into banks to hold a pool of water in the center. The water hose was coiled around the water pump. We uncoiled it and ran the hose down to the pool, started the pump motor and then started the tractor that ran the puddling cylinder. All this was a noisy business. Once set up we shoveled our tailings into the puddler. The water rushed over them, washing out the clay and leaving just the nobbies.

Everything was working fine, but it was so noisy I didn't hear Flint the Ratter's truck go by below us. I noticed our hose jump when he ran over it on his way to the far end of the puddling tank. No way to go around it, and no harm done. I just smiled and waved, but Dan's mouth was going a mile a minute, yelling at Flint and his mate, Wild Denny Strayman. Dynamite was a hothead and often yelled. Wild Denny yelled back as they passed. I couldn't hear what either of them was saying. I didn't pay attention and went back to shoveling. After a few more shovels I noticed I was alone on the flatbed. Looking up I saw Dynamite on Flint's truck, 50 yards away, wrestling with Wild Denny. Now what? I got down, shut off the puddler tractor and the water pump and started toward them to see what was going on. They fell off the truck, landing on their shoulders, and got up, their fists flying.

Wild Denny, like Flint, had been caught ratting, and Dynamite thought he was one of those in on ratting his claim. I thought he would wait for revenge until we had time to plan things out, but he was a hothead.

Then I noticed Flint walking toward me. Now I was in for it. My mate had picked a fight with his mate, and he was coming for me. The law of the Wally – your mate gets into a bluey and you're into it with his mate. Flint was a good-natured, happy man, but still the best fighter on the Wally. It wouldn't do to turn and run or fall on my knees and plead for mercy. If I became known as a skite or a poofter, I would have to leave the Wally.

Going up and down a 40-foot shaft several times a day with just a rope and toe kicks uses every muscle in your body. Shoveling, winding a windlass and dumping 125-pound buckets of opal clay builds muscle. The body becomes a unit of equal, well-tuned muscles that work together. No backaches, weak ankles and wrists or pulled muscles. Body builders create bulging muscles that have to be overcome to perform the slightest physical task, but a work-toughened, integrated body can take a lot of physical stress. It is a wonderful feeling. My body was unified, but so was Flint the Ratter's, and he was a fighter. I knew nothing about throwing or ducking a punch.

My mind focused quickly under stress. I could not hope to win this fight; no lucky punch of mine could hurt him, but a punch from him could easily leave me brain dead. I had to acquit myself honorably. I planned. At close range I would take two quick steps, rise off my left foot, bring my right arm down from high over my head with all my weight behind it and plow my fist into his nose before he could raise his guard. Then afterwards, in the pub – or maybe at the Digger's Final Shaft – they can say, "Aye, the Yank did all right, he did, before gettin' done in. Bloodied the Ratter's nose. Not many blokes could do that."

The paces between us were closing. Ten, nine, eight. My body was taut, my mind clear, resigned to the inevitability of it all. Closer, right arm straight at my side, fist solid, left foot ready for the quick step. Then at the last moment, Flint threw up his arms in a futile gesture.

"Have yer ever seen anything so foolish? Two dills fighting over nothing. Let's me and you sit down, have a beer and watch this." My body immediately relaxed. I resisted the impulse to hug him, smiled and said, "Righto mate, a brew would do nicely."

We walked back to the fight, turned over a couple of buckets, sat down and popped a beer. Never have I enjoyed a sporting event so thoroughly. Dan and Wild Denny were taking a breather, having exhausted themselves while doing no real damage. Wild Denny's shirt was torn, and he had a spot of blood at one corner of his mouth. Dan had a bruised cheek. Fights usually last only a few minutes, but neither of these blokes had landed a decent punch and were obviously looking for a way to end it without losing face.

"All right," Dan said, "Apologize, and I'll let you off this time."

"I'll not bloody well apologize to you. Flip me a quid for a new shirt, and and I'll quit beating you."

"I'm not bloody well flippin' you a quid for anything." Punches flew again.

"Crouch, Dan," I yelled, "He's swinging high and leaving his midriff open."

"Jab, Denny," Flint said, "He can see your roundhouse coming a mile away."

It was over before we got into the second beer. They just tired out, sat down and had a beer with us. Dan's animosity subsided. Pummeling a bloke does that. But he was still on our list.

The day ended for us with a few mug stones, nothing to get excited about, but worth the effort. I quite liked Flint the Ratter. He liked a bluey and a joke. My kind of bloke, as long as the joke was shared with me and the bluey with another bloke.

I checked for mail with Petula at the post office. "You can't beat the Aussie postal service," she said and handed me a letter addressed simply to: "The Yank, Wallangulla, Australia."

"Is your Swedish sheila coming back?" Petula asked with an inquisitive smile. "What in the world is she doing in Iceland?"

Nothing's private on the Wally. Petula had been suspected of steaming envelopes open, reading the letters and resealing the envelopes. Everyone in town would soon know about my letter. I didn't want to tell her to mind her own business. I simply said, "She'll be right."

Chapter XXVIII
Gained And Lost

February 10, 1966

Ninth Month

Helga wrote:

I miss you, the Wally, the expanse of the Outback and its freedom of movement. It is now a part of me. I found the Valkyrie settlement, Oskulden, on a small Icelandic island. They have carried on the tradition from mother to daughter for 1,000 years and name the eldest daughter after her grandmother, making it possible to easily name all their ancestors. Eyeborg Bjarteydottir, Bjartey Eyeborgdaughter, Eyeborg Bjarteydottir, etc. The tradition carries on, but its more difficult now to find wounded Viking warriors. The flickas search England, Ireland, Russia, Norway and Sweden for men who would have been warriors in the Viking era.

They must be wounded; that's the difficult requirement. But many of them have been eaten up by the modern world and are languishing when our maidens find them and nurse them back to health. Some flickas stay in the warrior's country, so the village of Oskulden hasn't grown very large. But still they raise their daughters and sons in the old Viking manner. My goal is to find more Oskulden settlements and put them in contact with each other to make it easier to carry on the ancient tradition. I will continue with my research until my warrior is wounded and needs me.

I will be busy for some time. I think of you and wonder if you have found your stone. Write, if you wish. I will be here for a couple more weeks.

I wrote back. "It has been nearly six months since you left," I began, "and a lot has happened." I went on to tell her about Dynamite Dan, Bruno, Two-Bob Bobby, the Mad Pom and my mud humpy. "I still think of you often and realize it wouldn't work for us, but it was wonderful to hold you in my arms for a short time. I have not yet found my stone, but it is down there waiting for me. By now you must have found your warrior. I wish you both happiness."

Petula examined with interest my letter addressed to Iceland. I wanted to say, "Don't steam my letter open," but I just smiled and paid the postage.

Dynamite and I wet puddled two or three days a week and found a few nobbies the old-timers had missed, enough to make it worthwhile. On other days I dug on my Yank's Dig. Bruno and I settled into a routine that suited us. I missed the quiet of the coolabah camp and the dancing flames of the open firepit but enjoyed the evenings under the bough shed and the gossip. I went to Helen Shapiro movies on Saturday nights in the Wally's old clapboard town hall. Weeks passed quietly. We heard nothing about the Croats and Shadow's wife and daughters.

Marco shot dirty looks at me in the pub but stayed away. Shadow said to the Scots and me, "Yer'll get yers. Archer is looking into the complaints and drawin' up the papers now, and Slammin' Sam is ready for a bluey. Yer'll be run out of the Wally. Yer time is comin'."

"How's your wife and daughters?" Gordon asked. "Haven't seen them around lately. Are they working a claim on Duffer's Dag?" Shadow scowled, turned and walked on. These cheeky Scots are going to get me into trouble. But it'll be worth it. They got Bernie between them at the bar: "'oweryergoin, Bernie?" Rab said. "Chopped off any hands lately? Here's one you might want to have a go at. Might be a stone in it." He held his fist across the bar in front of Bernie.

"Be sure to chop it off below the wrist or you'll have to pry the stone out with a screwdriver, like Two-Bob Bobby's," Gordon said.

Bernie said, "You'll all come a cropper. We're going to run the lot o' you mangy bastards out of town, and that includes the Yank and Angus. Bunch of rotters, you are." He slammed his glass on the bar so hard it broke, spilling the beer.

"Fair go, mate," Sarah shouted. "You'll have to pay for the glass." Bernie shook his head in disgust and stomped out.

Nothing of any value surrounded the blowholo in my claim. I dug in all directions to no avail. Weeks passed. It was discouraging, but I continued. Then one day, driving through the clay below the opal dirt level with my heavy pick, a lump fell out. It was in a place where you don't normally find nobbies. I rubbed some clay off and saw a glint of color. Then more clay off, more color. I wiped it hard, and a burst of color shot out. I rubbed it, licked it and held it close to the candle. Sweat poured into my eyes; my heart raced. Yes, this was the stone I'd been looking for all these months underground. This was *my* stone.

It was in the clay, not the opal dirt. No opal smell. No candle flames burning a foot high. Just there all by itself, a loner, waiting for millions of years for this moment. Waiting for me to bring it into the world, to let the light shine on its brilliance, to give it life. And it waited to give me life. At last we were together, fated to be united. I clutched it tightly in my hand. I had been put on earth for just this moment. All desire was sated. I was filled with life. It is mine, mine alone! No one will ever take it from me! No one else will ever see it!

I must rub it on my whetstone. If only I were still living isolated under the coolabah, I could rub it in privacy with no danger of being discovered. Yes, that's it! I picked up Bruno in town, got my whetstone and a can of water from the mud humpy and went back to our coolabah. Bruno looked around timidly for horses, then settled in under his tree.

I watered the whetstone and rubbed the thin layer of porcelain off the surface of my nobby. Brilliant violet leaped out, and red, yellow, green, gold, chartreuse, blue and shades between. My Radiant. A harlequin pattern. The quintessential black gemstone, my Radiant Opal. It was nicely domed, as such a stone should be, though not symmetrical. I snipped around the color to shape it. Cut and polished, it would be magnificent. But it will not be cut, just roughed in and hand polished. It is mine and mine alone. I turned it in the setting sun, with the light coming over my left shoulder, moved it around and around. A different array of color, a new stone at each turn. Sensational!

After a time I showed it to Bruno. He looked at it, then at me. I got the impression he would rather chase an emu. I folded a handkerchief around it and put it in my pocket. We went back to the mud humpy.

Finding your Radiant takes a bloke out of the struggle. I carried it with me at all times. I thought of the Goat Colonel, who stopped digging; of Two-Bob Bobby, who started bludging; and Hungry Hank the Hatter, who turned to drink. None of those things will happen to me. I am in control. Now I can plan revenge on the gigs that lurked Dan and me.

The general store had a freshly slaughtered bullock hanging in the back. A chunk of that fried up with eggs and bread made a nice supper. Cooking at waist level was so easy, just lay out the green gum tree faggots, cover them with sandalwood, strike a match and you're in business. Then a cuppa and a Dr. Pat.

I didn't join the Scots that evening. I looked at my Radiant in the firelight, then by candlelight, then under the mantle lamp. It was good in all lights, an outstanding gemstone, a true Radiant. I named it Chungula. I had the urge to show it to the Scots, but no, it was too personal and sacred. Best to keep it private.

Frog Hollow came to mind, full of beautiful stones that crack the day after being dug and exposed to air. I had heard that soaked in kerosene they last another day or two before cracking. I had to find out more. Real potential here, I thought. With a gallon of kerosene and Bruno, I spent the next day at Frog Hollow, gathering easy-to-find nobbies. I dug out a dozen nice ones and dropped them in my can of kero. A day later, I washed off the kero and asked Garbhan to cut a couple. "Nice stones," he says, "very nice. Angus will like to see these."

"No," I said, "They're from Frog Hollow. I'm just curious. They'll crack tomorrow," and left them on his shelf. They did. Then it occurred to me that my friend, Willis, was now a chemical engineer. I wrote him asking if he had any ideas. I had been sending him small amounts of money from time to time and told him I had found the big one and would settle later.

His answer came in just a few days. "Butyric acid. It's mild, but after soaking your opals in it for a few days, wash them thoroughly. It's not dangerous, and the stones will be safe to handle. Quite expensive but the right thing for the devious plot you have in mind. Good luck."

I had to get to the chemist in Walgett. My van was not up to it. Fortunately, one or two of the Scots went in for supplies almost weekly. It was Garbhan's turn. We left the next morning. The chemist had it in stock and looked puzzled when I asked for a quart: ten quid. "It's for a science project," I said, jokingly. Garbhan got his supplies, I bought some groceries, and we started back. Garbhan is not a talker, didn't ask me why I went to the chemist or fill me in on any new gossip.

Bruno and I made another trip to Frog Hollow. I soaked the nobbies in the butyric acid for several days, then washed them off well, hand rubbed them and set them on my shelf. Meanwhile I joined the young Scots under the bough shed for their usual ping-pong conversation.

"Hungry Hank the Hatter finally gave up drinking." I knew them well enough now not to get caught up in one of their jokes, so I waited quietly for the punch line. "Some blokes say the Bingos helped him quit the habit. Said it was bad for his health, they did." I waited.

"He quit for good."

"Aye, that's for sure. Jumped down a 30-foot shaft with a 20-foot rope around his neck. He'll never touch another drop. That was his last drop." They laughed at the pun, but it didn't strike me as funny.

"Did he jump, or was he pushed? Who got his stone?" No answer. Hank was the third bloke I knew who had a Radiant and met an untimely death. Could that happen to me? No. They all had the Wallies. I am in control. But I need to have a yarn with the Professor and a game of chess. It had been too long.

He was reading. I never knew what he did, where he went, why he was here or where he got his money. Didn't matter; we were friends, and he would tell me if he wanted me to know. I didn't even say "Kookaburra," but just sat down at the table behind the black pieces, giving him the first move. Bruno took his usual place under the table. The Professor marked his place with a bookmark and pulled up a chair. We didn't talk, just played, until he said "check" and then "checkmate."

We set up the pieces again, and I moved pawn to queen's four. After a few moves, he said, "He had a vision, a vision of returning to the happiest time of his life. He would once again be joined with his wife, making hats in his own shop, surrounded by friends and family."

The Professor was always ahead of me; he knew me well. "Are you saying that Ooluhru, the Aboriginal god of the opal, has the power to give visions, even to non-Aboriginals?"

"Only through the Radiant opal. We create our gods in our own image, to help us make sense of life's mysteries, to help understand the imponderables. It is believed by some that the power of the gods depends on the number, the unity and the intensity of their believers. The ancient Israelites believed that gods were territorial. The Yahweh that led them out of Egypt was wonderful. They thanked him profusely but turned to the worship of Baal once they got to the Land of Canaan. The Vikings had great conquests through Thor and Odin, but then Christianity was forced on them. Pagan gods served the ancient Greeks well; magnificent temples were built in their honor. The Greeks greatly increased the world's knowledge and thought. When Greece was conquered and their best minds went to Rome, their pagan gods fell from favor and lost influence to the more powerful Romans. In turn, the Christian god superseded Rome's gods, and the number and intensity of Christians rules the world to the present day. We still have Lucifarians, Druids and various occultic believers, but their numbers are too small to give their gods any real power."

"But Ooluhru? The Colonel, Two-Bob Bobby and Hungry Hank didn't believe in him," I said, trying to understand his point.

"They worshipped their Radiant opals. They prized their stones more than life itself. This was Ooluhru's eye peering into their soul. This gave him power over them. If you believe the legend, Ooluhru gave them a vision of a happier life, a vision of heaven, but to reach that happier life they must die. In this way his eye was returned to earth, his earth. For Hungry Hank that heaven was a vision reached at the end of a 20-foot rope down a 30-foot shaft. He now rests in peace."

"Are you saying no man can resist this vision? No man can sell his Radiant, smash it, give it away or bury it to be free of this curse?"

He looked at me intently. "I have neither met nor heard of the man who could. Once in possession of his fatal stone he dies with it in his hand. That is the curse of the Radiant opal, the scourge of Wallangulla."

"What absolute rubbish! Only a fool or an idiot could believe this nonsense!" I swept my hand across the chessboard, knocking all the pieces to the ground. I stood up and stomped off into the woods muttering to myself, "That will never happen to me." I clasped my hand around Chungula in my pocket and walked. "I will give it away, sell it, or smash it up with a hammer, but I will not jump down a hole with a rope around my neck." As I muttered angrily, Bruno, who usually walked ahead, stayed some distance behind.

I was disturbed and aimless. I passed Bruce the Banker's camp without stopping. Edward wagged his tail but didn't get up. I came to Pom and Marco's old campsite. No trace of anyone ever having lived there except for the fire pit, the remains of the bough shed and the old kerosene refrigerator standing by itself. Bruno paid little attention. We went on. I collected my wits and walked back to the Professor's camp. He had replaced the chess pieces and was back to reading Schopenhauer.

"Sorry," I said.

"I understand," he replied. And he did. By now he had surmised that I had a fatal stone in my pocket. I wanted to ask him if he also had a cursed stone and could not leave the Wally because of that, but I didn't. I didn't want to know. It's a personal thing; his way of dealing with it is none of my business. I got into my little van and drove off, head swirling with imponderables.

Two days later Dan and I were on our way back from the wet puddler. Dan was driving. Bruno, as always, was running just ahead of the front bumper when we met the Scots in their other truck. We waved, they waved, and Bruno turned his head in recognition and hesitated just a moment. Before Dan could stop, Bruno was under the truck. We had run over him. When I got back to him he was making tight circles in the road as if chasing his tail, then fell over dead. He lay there while I called, "Bruno, Bruno," and shook his lifeless body.

The Scots stopped. It wasn't their fault. A stupid dog insisted on running just ahead of the truck. Dan felt terrible. It wasn't his fault. I picked up Bruno's warm body and carried him the half-mile back to the humpy, tears streaming down my cheeks.

I put him in my van and took his body to the coolabah camp. My heavy pick cut deep into the red clay to bury him safe from dingoes. There I laid him, still warm, in the shade of the coolabah with his nose resting on outstretched forelegs, ready to cut and run should the horses return. I would like to say he died performing some act of courage, but that would have been out of character. He was a stupid, worthless, good-for-nothing mutt. He was me mate.

No stone encumbers his grave. No marker restricts his venue. He is now a part of the great Outback that was always so much a part of him. I could never again camp here under the coolabah without Bruno. Too isolated. Too quiet. Too alone. I had me stone; I lost me Bruno. I would trade to have him back.

Chapter XXIX
Worldly Hope

March 3, 1966

Ninth Month

I awoke with the sunrise slipping clandestinely through the open door of my mud humpy, the same sunrise that used to flood my tent with brightness. It was time for Bruno's nose nudge that meant, "I'm off for my morning tour, and you're missing the best part of the day." "Get out of here, you stupid mutt," I said out loud, but he wasn't there, and I couldn't get back to sleep. When I did get up and rapped the billy, I felt the lack of his unobtrusive presence, lying there with his nose on his front paws, watching me fry eggs and bread. If he were still here, I would have tried harder to entice his taste buds. I never did see him eat; he must have eaten in town. Anything was preferable to my three-day stew. I had to learn to live with my Radiant and without my Bruno. Life was changing.

I looked at my magnificent stone several times a day, surreptitiously, and kept it wrapped in a clean handkerchief in my pocket. *It* is why I am here. *It* is why I gave up my other life, why I dug in a hole for months, ate three-day stew and lived an isolated life. Now I held *it* in my hand, the colors flashed in the sunlight. The stone was worth a fortune. When I sell *it*, I will live leisurely, travel and eat well.

Omar Khayyam's words were a comfort to me. I memorized many quatrains of The *Rubaiyat* and thought:

The Worldly Hope men set their Hearts upon
Turns ashes – or it prospers; and anon,
   Like Snow upon the Desert's dusty Face
Lighting a little Hour or two – is gone.

My worldly hope is in my hand. Will it turn ashes or will it prosper? Both of us are mortal and in time will return to the earth. But for now, "Not to worry, mate, she'll be right."

With that happy notion I could turn my thoughts to other things: Shadow, the Bingos, Chuck the Cutter, Marco and even Pom, who won't return soon, if ever. It's time to have a yarn with me mate, Dynamite Dan.

Dan drank whiskey, which I don't handle well. "All right," he said, "if the time is come, I say let's blow up the lot of 'em. We can get them to rat one of our claims. If I'm in the pub with one of 'em, and they think I'm on a pocket, they'll feel safe ratting it. You drop half a dozen sticks of dyno down the hole, and Whamo! That's it."

I took another swig from the bottle. My throat burned, and I wished we could at least mix the whiskey with tea, the way the Professor does.

"There's a few things wrong with that idea," I countered. "Bernie's our main gink, but he isn't going to crawl down your shaft. He's too lazy, too scared and too fat. And some of the ratters may just get conned into doing it for a few measly quid; they don't deserve the death penalty. And finally, we could get permanently locked up in some Shearing Shed that we can't bust out of. But if it did work, and we got the lot of them, it's all over. It's too crude; too..." I struggled to find the right word... "too unsophisticated, and we would always be suspect."

I took another pull on the bottle. "I'd like to give them the opportunity to do themselves in, devise their own downfall, and have plenty of time for remorse as we remain blameless bystanders."

He took a swig and smiled. "You've been thinking. I'm listening."

"There's a fortune waiting for us in Frog Hollow."

He shook his head. "Can't sell 'em; they crack. We'll get caught sure. That's a dill idea. It'll never work."

"We won't sell them; we'll give them away."

"What then? Take a tax write-off? We don't pay taxes. You've had too much to drink." He put the bottle on the table and laughed. "We'll talk about it tomorrow."

"No," I said, "Now. How much did they lurk us for? My stone may have been worth 10 thou ($20,000). Your pocket of opal probably was worth about the same. But let's say 15,000 quid each. We'll put the fang in for 30,000. If we're going to lie, lie big, like politicians, or no one will believe us. A good lurk must look like a hooly-dooly. Would your sheila be happy if you came back with 15 thou?"

"Aye, reckon that'd be tops with her. But you can't expect to gink them with Frog Hollow crackers.[116] It won't work. They won't buy 30,000 quid of dag stones, no matter what you tell them."

"We won't sell them. It'll be a gift. We'll just give them the opportunity to steal the stones. What they do with them after that is their business."

He took a long draught and handed me the bottle.

"Butyric acid," I said. "Butyric acid will give us the time we need." I took a couple of lovely opals out of my pocket. "These came from Frog Hollow three weeks ago. They'll last another week or two at least." Then I laid out the scam in detail.

We spent the next two days in Frog Hollow digging out pockets of nobbies only two feet under the clay. Ironic that the pockets with the most stones were the easiest to get, but maybe that's the way it was in the early days. These got left because they crack. We had to work fast. Into the bucket of kerosene they went, dirt and all. Once back at Dan's site, we washed and sorted them, saving those with color in the butyric acid. Then, after snipping, we hand-rubbed the ones that might cut a stone.

"Nice nobbies," I said. "Many of these will cut precious opal, good quality." We were in business.

We had a coffee tin of stones that would keep indefinitely in the acid and for at least two or three weeks after they were cut.

---

116 Crackers – Opals that crack when cut and shaped into gems

They looked worth 30 or 40 thousand quid, the biggest find on the Wally in years.

The Scots were comfortably settled on the couch under the bough shed. "This is roughing it?" I asked. "You blokes are getting soft. What next? Hire a waitress to open your beer cans?" "Not a bad idea, Yank" Rab replied. "A bloke shouldn't have to work himself to death."

Gordon chimed in, "Haven't seen you in some time. You've been avoiding us. You're up to something."

The two of them were full of curiosity. "You can tell us. We can keep a secret. Involves a sheila, does it? We heard Sarah's sister was visiting at the pub."

"Or maybe the bush nurse. Been rumors about you two."

I sipped my beer slowly, enjoying their curiosity. "Her sister a good looker?"

"Well, not right away, but after a few pints they say, she's attractive. We heard one bloke was sweet on her." Rab looked at me quizzically.

I still sipped my beer slowly. "No, nothing that romantic," I said. "Dynamite and me are thinking of hiring Slammin' Sam to sink a monkey for us, and I wanted to get your advice."

They sat up with a start and stammered, together, "But he'll break…" "We told you…" "He can't be stopped…"

When they settled down, I explained, "Just to sink the monkey through the sandstone down to the second opal clay level. Once down there, we'll do our own driving. It's a tough job so we'll try to get Wombat and Skinner to help us clear the tailings."

"You're going in a hole with Skinner? He stinks worse than a whole herd of dead sheep."

"We'll keep him on the windlass, up in the open air," I said. "Just Slammin' Sam in the monkey. I'll shovel what he digs into the trolley, Wombat will wheel the trolley back to the shaft, and Dynamite will fill the buckets for Skinner to wind up and dump. What did you pay Slammin' Sam? Did you say 15 quid a day?"

"Yeah," said Gordon, puzzled. "Wombat and Skinner will work for 10 or 12. Why the monkey? It'll take a week and cost a couple hundred quid, and you'll still have to dig and move the opal clay once you get to the lower level. That'll be a lot of work for just the two of you."

I said, "Dynamite had a vision that a big pocket of nobbies is waiting for us down there. Not to worry, mate, she'll be right."

"What does he call his claim? Denmark? Methinks there be something rotten in Denmark that smells worse than Skinner. You two are up to something not fair-dinkum, and I can't wait to find out what."

Gordon said to Rab, "If you're going to quote the Bard, do it right. 'Something's rotten in the State of Denmark,' was what Marcellus said, 'not rotten in the opal claim named Denmark.' And you can't wait to find out because you want to tell the boozers."

"I'd tell one or two and tell them to tell only one or two others. I know the Yank wants to keep it secret."

These two Scots, who were kicked out of school at the age of 13 because they were working class and didn't need additional education, are more familiar with Shakespeare than I am with a college degree. I paused a moment, then changed the subject. "You two have very suspicious minds. You wouldn't trust the queen herself."

"Hear, hear," they replied, "To her majesty," and hoisted their beer cans. I laughed and said, "Dynamite Dan and I are just two hard-working, honest, trusting diggers trying to stand our shout, hoping to find a few good stones and take a step up in life; to rise to a higher level and give up eating 'roo. That's all. No more, no less."

They laughed.

I joined Wombat and Skinner in the pub and stood the first shout. "Getting any color?" I asked.

"We be in hard kack," Wombat said. "Not a tint. Like a Helen Shapiro movie, all black and white."

"Aye," Skinner added, "and only three dead sheep all last week."

He shook his head. "We'll be on bread and treacle before Turk gets called away."

Turk was a digger who lived in a well-constructed wood humpy. He had the only outhouse outside of town; it was placed over an abandoned shaft. He claimed to be from a wealthy family that owned mines in Europe and said he was the only one who knew how to run the business properly. The family would have to call him back very soon, he was sure. His parting comment always was, "I probably won't be here next week. I could be called away any minute." He had been saying this for 15 years; hence "before Turk gets called away" had come to mean "before next week."

"Well, Dynamite and I might put you back in tucker," I said. "We're sinking a monkey and need three hands for a week or so. You interested?"

"Do he blast his way through?" Wombat said apprehensively.

"No, no blasting. Slammin' Sam will do the picking, and the four of us will tote and haul."

They looked at each other.

"How good's the tucker?"

"Twelve quid a day, paid daily, and lunch at the Digger's Retreat, but only one pint; my shout."

"Righto, mate, yer on," Skinner said. "Sarah, another pint."

Sarah knew they were short on a quid and looked at me. I nodded and she brought three more pints. Two smiling faces promised to be at the Denmark day after next. I caught a glimpse of Sarah's sister. She resembled Sarah. Yes, it would take several pints to make her attractive. I looked around the pub but saw neither Dan nor Slammin' Sam. I hoped Dan had found him; I didn't want to pick through sandstone myself.

I left and parked my puddler by a mullock heap near Dynamite's camp. I'd rather puddle tailings than just sit and wait. He came in late afternoon.

"Thought I'd never find him. He's working for Dirty Douglas three miles west of Old Nobbies. Did you know he never digs on his own? Always hires out?"

"No, I didn't," I said, 'but it's not surprising. He'd break all the nobbies."

"He's sinking a shaft, be done tomorrow, and Dirty Doug doesn't want him in the opal clay. We have to pick him up; he sleeps wherever he works."

"I heard he sleeps in Harold Blake's shed."

"Only when he's in town."

"We'll bring him back to town each night. I don't want him at the claim if we're not around. We're employers," I said to Dan. "This is big stuff for me. I've never had to meet a payroll before."

"Aye, mate."

Dynamite Dan picked up Slammin' Sam the following day. "He was sleeping on a piece of tarp," Dynamite confided to me. "He used his jackknife to open a tin of something for breakfast, had it with a swig o' whiskey. He lives close to the earth."

Sam looked disheveled even by Wally standards. His thin shirt had several holes, and his shorts were ragged. No socks protected his feet, and one toe was exposed.

Wombat and Skinner showed up on time. Smith was already down in the hole. I gave him a heavy driving pick and pointed at a spot midway down the drift.

"Dig here," I said.

"I dig." And dig he did. Chunk, chunk, chunk; his pick smashed into the clay. Before long he was two feet down and hit sandstone. Now it went slower. The sandstone was harder to pick and shovel, but he kept digging.

The Slammer shoveled tailings out of the hole. I shoveled them into the trolley, Wombat dumped them at the shaft, Dyno Dan filled the buckets, and Skinner pulled them up with the power winch and dumped them away from the cribbing. As the hole got deeper, we used a bucket on a rope. Wombat and I switched off.

Noon came. "Dinner time," I said to the Slammer. He kept picking. "Dinner time," I shouted. He looked at me. "I dig."

"No, now we eat. We eat at the pub."

He didn't like being interrupted. He took a pull on his bottle and crawled out of the hole. I hadn't realized how large he was. Even crouched, he filled the drift. It felt good to climb up the shaft into the sunshine and fresh air. I reassured myself that my

Radiant was still in my pocket and climbed into the back of Dan's pickup.

Sarah knew what we drank and brought us two middies, two new beers and one old, along with five pork pies. A happy crew. We were doing well, although my idea of a one-beer lunch doesn't fit in with the Aussie way of life. After three pints we climbed back down the hole. Slammin' Sam took a pull on his bottle and went after the sandstone. How could a man who sleeps on the ground, lives on tinned food and drinks whiskey straight out of the bottle work so hard?

At 5 p.m. we knocked off, which surprised our hard-working crew. They expected to work another hour or two since we're paying by the day. We dropped them off in town, and I paid each one in cash and offered to shout for tucker at Lenny's Café. The Slammer declined, saying he didn't like to eat sitting down. He went to the pub.

Lenny is slow, and the Skinner stunk up the whole café. We won't do this again, I thought. One of the other three tables had customers, probably tourists. They tried not to stare, but Dan and I both knew they were trying to figure out which one of us stunk.

The next morning we picked up our crew in front of the pub, and the day went like the first: three more feet of sandstone and a three-pint lunch. But no more Lenny's. Dan and I had styk 'n eggs at his camp. I showed him how to make fried bread. We had a cuppa, a Dr. Pat and talked. Things were going well.

Day Three went as planned. That evening Dan said, "Be good to see my sheila again. She wants to have a family." I noticed the faraway look in his eye. He was ready to go back to her right now. I had to keep his mind on our current project, so I said, "Thinking of taking an office job?"

"You got the Wallies? I don't work inside."

"How you going to support your family? Stake a gold claim? Mica claim? Kinda iffy business. It'd be tough for you to work for someone else. You'd best not think of your sheila right now. We have to concentrate on pulling off our scam so you can go home and be independent."

"Righto, mate. Righto. I'm back."

The next day, Saturday, was the end of the workweek. Aussies don't reckon a bloke ought to work on Sunday. The day went well, and the 10-foot-deep monkey bottomed on opal clay. How the Slammer could dig! I paid them all off and said we'd keep going on Monday. Dan and I went back to our own camps, and in the evening I went to the Helen Shapiro movie with the Scots, who were curious about what Dan and I were up to.

"Marcellus will find out," was all I had to say.

I took Sunday off to think and relax. I had stopped distinguishing the days while working alone, but now, with the Saturday night movie and Sunday off, I felt almost civilized. How long had it been since I had done nothing for a whole day? I looked at my stone several times and hand-rubbed some of the Frog Hollow nobbies, but that was it. I missed Bruno. We would have spent the day together, walking or doing nothing. I felt so alone without him.

On Monday Dan picked up the crew in town. I drove directly to the claim. Once there I found both shafts had six-inch spaced iron bar grids over the holes, with eight-inch strap hinges lag-screwed into the cribbing inside, where they couldn't be reached with a spanner when the grid is closed and padlocked.

"What on earth is this?" I said angrily. "Archer must have locked up our claim. The Bingos are behind this. Now we are going to break out the dynamite and blast the lot of them."

Dan was laughing. "Not to worry, mate, she'll be right." He pulled a key out of his pocket, unlocked the grid and swung it open. Wombat and Skinner were laughing; the Slammer took a pull from his bottle. I had never seen a claim with an iron grate, and neither had they. I said no more about it until later, when we could talk.

"What are you doing?"

"What are they going to do when they find out we're on opal?" Dan said. "I can't drop dynamite sticks down the shaft 24 hours a day. The grate will keep them out until we want 'em in."

He was right, of course.

Digging through the opal clay was easier and faster. Wombat and I kept busy pulling up the buckets. The next day the Slammer started a horizontal drive and went five feet west. That night Dan and I talked by his fire.

"One more day with Slammin' Sam; then we dig ourselves. Bring the Skinner and his mate back in two days?"

I smashed up some Frog Hollow stones and put the chips in an empty Dr. Pat tin that I could stash in my pocket and pull out without raising suspicion. I washed the butyric acid off a third of the rough nobbies and put them in a coffee tin. That night I slept with Chungula in my fist under my head and dreamt of flashing colors and flying through the air on Voltronga in the arms of my Valkyrie.

ſ

Chapter XXX
Boomerang

March 15, 1966

Ninth Month

The next day dawned bright and clear as always, under an azure sky. I dispatched two six-inch red and silver centipedes on my stone fireplace and planned the day. My opal chips were ready.

Once at the claim, I told the Slammer to dig east into the opal dirt. I pulled the buckets, and Wombat pushed the trolley to Dan under the shaft. The morning went nicely with the Slammer driving more than three feet. Back in the drive after our leisurely three-beer lunch, I pulled out my tin of colored chips while Wombat was off with the trolley and sprinkled some on the tailings.

"Aye, mate, we're on opal," he said.

"There's no stopping the Slammer," I said. "Just keep on the lookout for nobbies."

No more chips appeared in the tailings until late afternoon. I sprinkled generously when no one was looking. Wombat dug through the tailings with his hand. Late in the day I tossed in a couple of rough nobbies.

"Look at this!" Wombat handed them to me.

"Good on you, mate; you just made double pay."

We went up the drift and showed the nobbies to Skinner and Dan.

"Good color, might cut a stone."

I slipped Slammin' Sam some colored chips. "Aye, look at the pretty colors," he said.

"You might want to save them to show in the pub," I remarked casually.

We paid all three workers double, thanked them, and, after Sam was gone, told Wombat and Skinner that we would need them again in a few days. Fortunately, we could afford to do this because of the 200-quid nobby we had sold weeks earlier. Now we had to plan carefully.

For two days we dug hard to get enough tailings to call back Skinner and Wombat. The Frog Hollow nobbies were too clean after being soaked for weeks, so we packed them in mud, let it dry, pulled them out and brushed off excess dirt and debris. When the rest of our nobbies from the coffee tin were in the new drive to the east, we were ready.

I avoided the Scots whenever possible, and when I did see them, we talked about banalities. They knew something was afoot but enjoyed the intrigue and knew they'd find out sooner or later.

Now the plot unfolded. I dug, Dan pulled up the bucket, Wombat shoveled our tailings into the trolley, and Skinner windlassed and dumped. This kept all of us busy until noon. Over our pints and pies, we let Wombat and Skinner know we were on a pocket but swore them to secrecy. After lunch I handed up a tin of nobbies for Dan to show Wombat. He's properly impressed. We finished out the day and once again paid them double for their secrecy.

Dan took the tin of nobbies to Chuck in the evening and waited while he cut and polished them. They were mostly precious opal, just a few mug stones. Chuck knew the claim, having ratted it once for the Bingos; but these opals were different. He was impressed.

"We sunk a monkey; these are from the second clay level." This satisfied Chuck's curiosity. Dan told him he had a run-in with Angus and won't sell anything to Bernie Bingo because Bernie lurked him before. "These stones are all going to Sydney." He gave Chuck a few extra quid to keep it secret. Chuck asked if he could keep one of the stones for a day or two, just to look at it closely.

Is he suspicious or just curious? He'll ask Wombat, and we figure Wombat will spill the beans, making us fair dinkum. Then he'll show the opal to the Bingos.

It took a couple of days to pile up tailings. Then we hired the mates again. I handed up another tin of nobbies for Wombat to see. This time he called Skinner down to have a look. Dan pulled out his packet of cut gems. "A fortune!" Wombat yells. "A fortune!" Skinner was more subdued but very impressed.

Then Dan showed them where he kept the tin of stones buried, in a side shaft, covered with tailings. He winked, "You're the only two who know where they are. They're safe. No one can get through our iron grate. But don't say a word." We paid them triple this day.

Again Dan went to Chuck at night, saying he doesn't trust anybody else in Wallangulla. Later he told me the story.

"Whad'yer think they're worth?" Chuck's cuttin' and polishin'. He's real friendly. "I'm ready to quit mining," I tell him. "I don't care if there's twice as much still down there. I want to get away from here and see me sheila before I get the Wallies."

"Chuck's examining the stones real carefully. He hands back the one on his shelf. 'Good quality, all of them' he says. 'They ought to be worth 50 thou easily.'"

"I tell 'im a bloke from Sydney's interested in me claim so I sent him a sample. He's talking 40 thou – for the claim only. I'm keeping the stones."

"He's sweating, almost drooling. He looks at me funny and says, 'Just the claim? Not the stones?'"

"No," I say, "I'm keepin' the cut stones for meself. They're safe, buried in the mine in a tin, under tailings. No one can get at them with the grates over the shafts. Plus I check regularly. You and Wombat are the only two who know that. Well, Skinner, too."

"Chuck's thinking, planning, scheming. I go on. 'Once he has a look, I'll sell for the 40 thou cash and leave the next day, after we register with Archer. The deal is this; I collect my cut stones just before I go. I don't want to be robbed.'"

"'This deal set?' he wants to know. 'If someone else comes up with more, say 50 thou, would you sell?'"

"I fake surprise. 'You know someone with that kind of tucker?' I say I'm suspicious of the Bingos and wouldn't sell to them for twice that!' and slam my fist on the table."

"'No, not the Bingos. I know this bloke in Walgett,' Chuck says. 'Give me a day. I'll see what I can do.'"

"I'm acting real wary. I say, 'This bloke's gotta do it just like I say; I keep me cut stones underground until I'm ready to leave. We sign the agreement with Archer, and I get time to retrieve me stones.'"

"Chuck says, 'Righto, mate' so I promise to meet 'em day after next in the pub."

Two days later we take Slammin' Sam and Wombat to the claim. "You're a witness," Dan says to Wombat. "You're gonna come back to town with us and swear that you saw the cut opals here." To Sam he says, "I want you to guard the mine. Stay here as long as it takes. I should be back before nightfall." Dan unlocks the grate and swings it open. We climb down the shaft, and he shovels some tailings aside in the drift to show Wombat two large tins containing cut gemstones. "Here, hold them so you know they're real." Dan casually dumps some in Wombat's hand. Wombat's hand is shaking; he's never seen anything like it before. "May be twice as much left down the monkey, ready to be dug out," Dan remarks as he reburies the tin in the tailings.

Dan, Wombat, and I were standing at a table drinking. Dan looked distant as he poured down hard liquor, a lot of it. The whole pub knew something was going on. Then Chuck walked in, carrying a large shoebox, big enough for boots. He joined us. Dan scrutinized him but didn't talk. Finally I said, "You got the tucker? We're ready to sell."

"Your stones still in the mine?" he asked Dan.

"I seen 'em meself," Wombat blurts out, "buried in the tailings. We come here together. Slammin' Sam's guardin the claim. They safe."

Chuck, very sure of himself, nods to Archer at the bar. Archer came over with some papers. "This is a bill of sale. Chuck is buying the Denmark claim for one Australian pound and other considerations, contained in the box. This one is a claim deed transfer. This here paper gives you the right to retrieve your stones from the claim until midnight tonight. Only you, yourself, alone."

I tried to look at the papers, but Dan grabbed them out of my hand. "This doesn't concern you. It's my claim."

"Rubbish. We agreed to share our claims equally. We're mates. We work together."

"Bloody 'ell. We were mates 'til we found the stones. It's my claim. Now we're loners." Dan gave me a sinister grin. "You're out of it, Yank. You keep your claim; I'll keep mine." He laughed at me. I had never seen him like this before. For a moment I just stared at him, and he stared back. Then I lunged, fists flying. He was on the floor, his nose was bleeding, and I was slamming my fists into his face. They pulled me off.

"All right, Yank," Archer growled. "It's the Shearing Shed for you." He quickly had my hands behind my back and cuffed. I yelled at Archer, "We had an agreement! It's half mine!"

"That's between you and Dan," Archer said. "My job is to keep order." He's strong. I was surprised he had handcuffs with him. Did he anticipate trouble? But Dan was right; I am out of it. Archer half carried me to the Shearing Shed, threw me in and took off the cuffs while I was face down on the floor. The shed is six-by-eight clapboard with one small slit for a window, a bench just long enough to sleep on and a tin chamber pot in the corner. The window doesn't face the pub; it looks out over the great expanse of Outback.

I had never been locked up before. I wanted out. I kicked, shouldered, and even butted my head against the door to no avail. The new door was stronger than the one Dan had kicked down a few months before. I put my hand in my pocket; my stone was secure. I sat on the bench with my head in my hands, still raging.

After some time – I have no idea how long – a face appeared at the window. "'oweryergoin." It was Harold Blake wearing a sad look. I just nodded. "Archer sent me. I'm here to let you out. I want you to know ahead of time so you don't come crashing into me." He smiled. "Dynamite's eye is swelled shut, and his nose is crooked. You thumped him good, mate. He had it coming. I'll come around now." And with that he opened the door. You're out early because Archer needs the shed for the one you thumped. I looked toward the pub and saw Archer and several other blokes carrying the cuffed Dynamite. He was badly beaten.

"Archer says you aren't to come into town for two days, and you have to stay out of the pub for a week. Any more trouble out of you, and you're off of the Wally for good. Sorry, mate. Leave now," Harold walked part of the way toward my van with me and wished me good luck. I didn't look back. I didn't want to see Dynamite or whoever was with him. I had enough troubles of my own to worry about.

I examined myself, once back in the mud humpy. A lump on my head that I couldn't account for and several bruises. Fortunately, I had wood for fire and yesterday's stew. I was hungry. I built the fire, ate the stew and sat at the table for a long time with a hand-rolled Dr. Pat and a cuppa. I wished Bruno were there; he would have gotten petted, like it or not. Now I was now so alone.

After a while, a knock at the door. I looked up. "Nobody knocks on an open door. You must be tourists." My feeble attempt at humor didn't cheer the Scots.

"May we come in?"

"You two are getting awfully polite. Am I going to have to rap on your bough shed and ask permission after this? Of course you can come in."

Rab sat on the cot and Gordon on the footlocker, quietly. I was glad to have their company, good mates. After a long, comfortable period of silence I asked, jokingly, "How's Marcellus doing with the rot in Denmark?"

"He's a bit puzzled," Gordon replied. "Double, double, toil and trouble. Knows who's stirring the pot, knows what's in the stew but knows not Macduff."

Rab stood up, waving his arms and projecting like an actor. "Aye, but he'll have to wait for the last act, won't he? Marcellus will wait patiently, advising caution, but in the end he will know what rots in Denmark."

"But it is not a time for frivolity. Our combatant is wounded," Gordon said.

"'Tis but a scratch," I said, theatrically noticing for the first time that my arm was bloodied. "'Tis but a scratch."

"We'll leave you be, just wanted you to know your mates are here if you need us."

"No, stay," I said. "Polonius would advise it. How did you find out about the fight?"

"We came out of the store just as Archer was tossing you in the Shearing Shed. So we went into the pub to find out what was going on."

"Your mate, Dynamite, was..." Rab's voice trailed off.

"Not his mate anymore," Gordon said, "or at least, not at that time ..."

"Righto. Dynamite was making some sort of deal with Chuck. Arthur was handing papers to both of them."

"Dynamite looked terrible, and he was as full as a goog. We heard later that you'd thumped him."

"Good and proper, it looked. His face was all puffed up. Teaches us not to sling off at you, mate. So, Dynamite had a pencil in hand and was about to sign the papers when he said, 'This doesn't mean you're guaranteed to find opal. It's a good claim, but new ground is always a gamble.'"

"Chuck said, 'I know that.' Then Dynamite said, very seriously, 'and I get to take my stones out.'"

"Archer said, 'Yer've got till midnight tonight. It's in the agreement. After that its Chuck's claim.'"

"By now the whole pub was gathered around, watching the proceedings. Chuck handed him the shoebox tied with string. A one-pound note was on the top under the string. Dan opened it. It was full of tenners in bundles. 'You want to count it?' Chuck asked. Dan went through the bills quickly and said, 'It's all there,' and tied it back up."

"Then Dan signed the paper and said, 'I'll say goodbye now. I'll be out of the Wally in an hour. And happy to be gone. Happy to be rid of the lot of yer.' He staggered toward the door with the box under his arm, but Bernie and Benny Bingo, Shadow, and now Chuck, blocked the way."

"'There's something you should know, Danny Boy,' Chuck said with a sneer, 'You've been hit with a boomerang. The Bingos own Denmark.'"

"'Chuck got the tucker from us,' Bernie said. 'Think about that while you're humpin' the bluey. It's all ours. Legal.'"

"'Legal,' Shadow said and took a step toward Dynamite, as though to provoke him."

"Dan dropped the shoebox. 'You mangy bastard ginks,' he said. He hit Shadow, knocked him down and then went after the fat Bingos, who were already headin' to the door. Chuck kicked him in the stomach, and as Dan bent over, he kicked 'im again in the face. Wombat and Skinner grabbed Chuck but couldn't hold him. Now Archer was in the middle separating the lot of 'em, and the whole pub got into a bluey. Never saw anything like it. Must have been 30 blokes all bashing each other."

"Yeah, I wanted to bash somebody myself." Rab said.

"But you didn't. Afraid they might hit back. Archer cuffed Dynamite and dragged him off. 'I warned you before. This time I'm locking yer up until you can control your temper. Then you're off the Wally for good.'"

"Dan was shouting, 'But me stones, me stones. I'll take them and leave now. I'll be gone for good. No more blueys.'"

"Archer said, 'You've been nothing but trouble. You ain't going nowhere 'til tomorrow, and then I'll escort yer out of town myself.'"

"Archer tossed Dan in the shed roughly, slammed the door and padlocked the hasp. We could see it from the pub. The bluey was still in full swing when Archer got back. He bashed a few blokes around to get things settled down, ended up with a bloody nose himself."

"But something strange happened," Rab said. "Soon after the bluey started, Shadow grabbed the shoebox off the floor and handed it to Marco behind the bar. Marco put it on the shelf above the kitchen door, like it had all been planned out ahead of time."

"It probably was," Gordon said. "Nobody would pay thousands for a mine when they can stake a claim next to it for 10 bob. They wanted the stones and bought the claim thinking they could grab the box back in the scuffle, have Archer keep Dan in the shed overnight and steal the stones. All planned out by a mob of gigs."

"Archer had to be in on it to make it work. That's what we think." They both looked at me.

"I missed all the excitement. I was the first one out." I lamented. "I missed out on everything."

"Too bad about the claim, mate, but legally it was registered to Dan. That's the same way we bought our big find – legal but not ethical. Too bad it was you who got stuck this time."

"But there's more to the story. Remember the box with a quid on top? How much was in it? Some say 50 thousand. Well, during the bluey that we were trying to stay out of, Skinner jumped over the bar and slugged Marco. Skinner! Of all blokes! He never gets into anything. He slugged Marco, Marco fell against Sarah, and both of them went down on the floor."

"Then Skinner took the box off the shelf and handed it to Wombat. Wombat had crawled under the bar lid to get in. They fumbled with it for a minute. Then Skinner decided to put it back where it came from on the shelf."

"Strange," Gordon said. "What were they thinking? That they could run off with all that tucker and get away with it? Then decided it wouldn't work and put it back? I don't think anyone else saw this; everybody but us was fighting. Marco and Sarah didn't get up for some time, and when they did Marco checked to see that the box was on the shelf. After the bluey, Shadow looked at the box. There it sat. All very curious."

Rab looked up. "I forgot that half of this is yours, or should be. Sorry."

"It's all right, mate. It's over and done with," I said.

"The whole business was the talk of the pub once things settled down. I counted half a dozen bloody noses. The Bingos, Shadow and Chuck left right away."

"Wombat said the agreement gave Dan 'til midnight tonight to get the stones out of the mine, but he's locked up 'til tomorrow morning. It all depends on Archer. Wombat saw the stones. A fortune, he said, a fortune. Now the Bingos copped the lot. They got it all. Dan got hit with a boomerang, right in the groin. Oh, and you, you got hit worse. You don't have anything."

Rab started "You don't suppose Archer would let you..."

"No," I said. "I've been ejected from town, banned for two days and from the pub for a week and told to stay away from the mine. The claim was in Dynamite Dan's name, and now it's the

Bingos'. I'm out of it. But," and here I smiled a little, "I could use a beer."

They looked puzzled but said no more. We sat under the bough shed. It was a beautiful starlit night. I drank too much. If I remember correctly, they carried my body into the mud humpy and dropped me on the cot, my good mates, and left shaking their heads in bewilderment.

Chapter XXXI
Aftermath

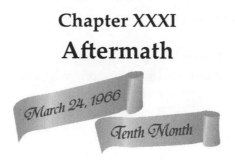

March 24, 1966

Tenth Month

My head throbbed at first light. Where's my Bruno to yell at? An hour or two later I had the last of my eggs and slices of fried bread. I couldn't risk going into town, even for groceries. Archer would use any excuse to lock me up again. He must have been in on the Bingos' scam. I'm sure Chuck and the Bingos never planned on that money ending up in Dynamite Dan's hands. But I don't know if Dan got the shoebox this morning or even if he's alive. Would the Bingos and their gig mates murder for 50,000 quid? Righto, mate, if they could get away with it.

Is all this worth it? I had my stone. I took it out and looked at the dancing violet, chartreuse, red, gold, green, yellow and blue flashes pouring out. I held it close. What beauty. Yes, it was worth it.

Our plan was to meet at Dan's camp and divide up the swag, but that changed when both of us got tossed into the Shearing Shed. If all else failed, we would meet safely at my old coolabah camp; only the two Aborigines knew where that was, and they were both gone. I drove to the coolabah, staying safely away from town and Archer, but found no sign of Dan ever having been there. Then I drove the long way around to my puddler parked by Dan's camp. His camp was gone. Nothing but a hole left with scattered fireplace stones and debris. I looked around for body parts, thinking they may have blown him up, but found nothing. His pickup was gone; maybe he did make it away, but I had doubts.

I got up my nerve and drove to the Denmark claim. The sites around the claim were already marked and registered; these old sites had been partially worked and left. This area had never been a great producer, at least until Dan and I got to work on it, just a pocket here and there. But now the diggers were going down to the second level hoping to find new pockets. I laughed at the thought.

"What the bloody 'ell you giggling at?" said Flint the Ratter, working the next claim with his mate, Wild Denny.

"Sometimes things are so bad you just have to laugh," I said, surprised. "I had a bad day yesterday. Trying to get over it. Gettin' any color?"

"Not yet, but this area puts out the big lolly," Flint said with a laugh, "as you well know." I nodded and walked over to the Denmark claim. The grid had been blasted off. Flint understood ratting, but did he condone lurking? I had ginked out of one bluey with him and didn't want to get into another.

"Be careful," I said, "the Bingos are professional ratters. They'll have your claim before Turk gets called away."

"Not if we tunnel into theirs first. We're better underground than they are."

I towed the puddler back to the Scots' camp, not knowing where else it would be safe. Will the Bingos' mob trash my equipment, too? I lolled the remainder of the day, reading *The Count of Monte Cristo* while I pondered our scheme.

I finished off the stew. I had run out of tucker before. I still had quid but couldn't go into town for another day. I asked the Scots to pick up a few items, and, thankfully, they did.

Next day I needed physical exercise so I puddled nearby mullock heaps and found several nobbies with color. I was anxious to find out what happened to Dynamite Dan.

The following morning after a quick breaky, I went to my Yank's Dig, now permitted to move about unless Archer changed his mind. I parked my car next to the windlass as Harold Blake walked up from his claim.

"Gettin' any color?" he asked, despite knowing I hadn't been there for a while.

"Just red blood."

Harold smiled. "You'll want to know what happened," he said. "I help Archer when he needs it. He wanted me with him to escort Dynamite Dan out of town. Too much cash involved, too much animosity, too many tempers ready to explode, too many things to go wrong. We carried pistols, first time for me, and I didn't like the idea. But that's the way it was. Archer didn't like the idea either. He had me pick up the shoebox full of tenners from Marco in the pub. It had been on the shelf out in the open since the night before, and he didn't want to touch it."

I was nervous and couldn't help shifting from one foot to the other as Harold talked. "We got Dan cuffed and out of the Shearing Shed without incident, no one around. Then Archer took the key to the grid padlock out of Dan's pocket, and we drove to the Denmark claim. Dan was quiet; he'd been badly beaten. I followed in his pickup."

I sat down on the mullock heap and waited. Harold smiled a little, noting my anxiety. After a long pause, he went on. "The grate had been blasted off Dan's claim. Slammin' Sam was there with his swag, just sitting on the mullock heap. 'I be here all night guardin'. I not stop 'em. Too many, too fast and dynamite. 'Get the bloody 'ell away' they say. Boom! Boom! I no stop 'em, Danny, they's too many, too fast.'"

Harold took a deep breath and walked around. "The stones were gone. Chuck and Shadow had gone down the shaft and brought up two tins of cut opals. 'Pretty colors' Sam said. 'I tell Yank and Danny I guard, but they's too many, too fast.'"

"Archer told Dan there was nothing to be done about it; it was all legal. Dan had had the right to collect the stones up until midnight, but he couldn't collect them; he was locked up. Now the Bingos legally owned the claim and the stones. A little less than legal, I thought. I wondered how deep Archer was into this."

"'Mangy bastards,' Dan said, and that was it."

He looked at me. I shook my head. "It's over. One way or another I'm out of it. The Bingos boomerang landed squarely on Dan."

"'I want Slammin' Sam along when I pick up my gear,' Dan said. 'I owe him a few quid. He did as much as he could.' Archer nodded. Sam grabbed his swag and got in with me."

"Dan's camp was trashed and scattered; I don't know what they were looking for. He shook his head and muttered 'mangy bastards' again. Archer uncuffed him, and I gave him the shoebox. The Slammer stayed with Dan while he made several trips to his pickup, carrying small items, kicking away the broken stuff. He took a long time packing the pickup, fiddling with little things. I thought he did this just to irritate Archer."

"He came back to Archer and said, calmly, 'They used *my* dynamite to blow up *my* claim and steal *my* stones. I've decided to finish the job and blow up my camp. I just set a primer with a five-minute fuse on the last half-case of dynamite. In four minutes my camp will be leveled, and the rock fireplace will be scattered all over. You may want to observe it from a little farther away.' Slammin' Sam was laughing wildly and jumping up and down like a gleeful child. They both jumped into Dan's pickup and roared off."

"Archer and I took a quick look. The fuse was burning. We left in a hurry and were still moving when a horrendous boom shook Archer's car. Rocks fell all around us. Fortunately, we didn't get hit, but Archer was really mad. 'I'll throw him back in the Shearing Shed and haul him off to Orange. He should be locked up for good.' He spun his Holden around and drove like a wild man, darting between the mullock heaps, trying to figure out which way Dan had gone. We drove around for an half an hour with no luck. Dan made a clean getaway. 'I'll use the bush nurse's radio and get the Walgett police after him,' Archer said."

"'He probably won't go through Walgett.' I said, 'And once word gets out that a criminal is on the loose, every fair-dinkum Aussie in the Outback will protect him. He's gone. Gone for good.' That was the end of it. I had the feeling Archer didn't want any outside investigation into the whole affair."

Harold sat down on the tailings. His storytelling had worn him out. "So Dan's gone," I said. "What happened to Slammin' Sam? Doesn't he sleep in your shed?"

"Aye, when he's not working a claim. But I haven't seen him since he left with Dan. Dunno what happened to him."

I thanked him for filling me in and promised to shout him a pint. Once down the shaft, I sat on a bucket and rolled a Dr. Pat. Dynamite Dan got away with 50 grand that easily. Hard to believe. But where is he? And where's my half? And what do I do now?

The Scots had brought me a nice steak. After tea I joined them in the bough shed, hoping we wouldn't get into Shakespeare again. They were quiet tonight, not smiling.

"All right," I said. "What's up? What's the latest news? What's the gossip?" They sat, not smiling.

Rab said, "Reckon we ought to tell him?"

More silence

"He'll find out anyway," Gordon said, after a long silence. "We're his mates; better to find out from us than in the pub."

"Okay. They're all gone. The whole kit and caboodle of 'em. Gone."

"Off to the Big Smoke. With a fortune in your stones, cut and ready for sale. They blasted the grid off the claim before Dynamite Dan was out of the Shearing Shed. We thought maybe Dan would share with you, once it was all over, but he's gone, too."

"I know," I said. "I had a long talk with Harold Blake. He helped Archer see Dan off. They saw the blasted grid. The stones were gone, but Dan did get away with the shoebox – though not before blowing up his campsite and scaring the hell out of Archer."

"Aye, we heard the boom."

"Aye, the boom." I waited. These two blokes knew how to drive me to distraction. "The boom and the shoebox."

"Aye. Yer our mate, and had a bit of hard kack with Dyno Dan, but still we hoped he'd get off with the Bingos' quid."

"He did," I said. "Harold Blake gave him the shoebox himself. He drove away with it in his pickup." What's going on? I wondered. What do they know that I don't?

"We were having a pint and a pie in the pub yesterday when the whole mob of lurkers came in – the Bingos, Shadow, Chuck and Marco. Bernie Bingo opened a tin of polished opals and dumped them on the bar."

"Finest parcel we'd ever seen. Looked like they were worth 100 thou anyway. Bernie said 'Drinks for the diggers, Sarah. Dynamite Dan's treat.'"

"'And the Yank's,' Shadow said. 'Don't forget the Yank.' Blokes crowded around for a look at the stones. Bingo stepped back and smiled. Then his brother Benny, the quiet one, said, 'And that's not all. Marco, let's have the shoebox, the *other* shoebox, he said with a sneer that only a gink could do justice to."

My heart skipped a beat. "The *other* shoebox?"

"Aye. The *other* shoebox. Marco took it out from under the bar and handed it to Benny. 'The deed for the sale of the claim stated that the price was one Australian pound and other considerations to be found in the shoebox. It happens that there was more than one shoebox, and the one Dan got had fewer considerations in it than the one we have here.'"

"He untied the shoebox and opened it. It was filled with tenners. 'Who would be stupid enough to think we would pay 50 thousand pounds for a claim.' He laughed until tears ran down his cheek and almost fell over. He closed the box and tied it up neatly with the pound note on top, as it had been. 'He ginked his own partner to get lurked himself.'"

"All of them were laughing now, Shadow, Marco, Chuck and the Bingos. The rest of us didn't think it was funny. Rab and I had had enough. I wanted to slam into them, but we just left. So did the other diggers. It was over. They had pulled it off. They no longer cared what we thought of them. They didn't need us, anymore; they had their fortune."

"Shortly after that they all left for Sydney. The lot of them humped the bluey together."

So the Bingos had outlurked us, after all the careful planning by my mate and me. They had the crackers, but we came away with – how much was in the other shoebox? Not much, I bet. Just enough tenners on top to look good. Questions flew through my head.

"Where was Archer during all this?" I asked.

"He was back in the corner. Didn't say anything. It was all legal; the Bingos made sure of that. The bill of sale, 'for one pound and other considerations' is commonly used when no one wants the price known."

"Still, Archer said nothing and didn't laugh. We think he must be in on it. It all went so smoothly."

Too smoothly indeed, I thought. Too smoothly indeed. Gordon was thinking. "Still, questions do float into one's mind, he mused. "Why did Dan have Chuck cut the stones and not Garbhan? Why offer to sell the claim to Chuck, who's in tight with the Bingos and had lurked him before? And why cut you out? You were his mate." They looked at me, questioningly.

"Ah, mates. Who knows? As my friend Omar says,

The Moving Finger writes, and having writ
Moves on: nor all thy Piety nor Wit
Shall lure it back to cancel half a Line,
Nor all thy tears wash out a word of it."

We had lurked the Bingos' mob. They planned not only to rat the stones, but also to steal the shoebox with the cash. That was why they were so happy to make the deal. It would cost them nothing to acquire the claim and the cut gemstones and probably get Dan and me run off the Wally at the same time. All this was contingent on the bluey at the pub door. They knew a drunken Dyno Dan would bash the Bingos once he heard they were the legal owners. Then one of the mob, Shadow or Chuck, could grab the shoebox and hand it to Marco behind the bar, who could easily switch it with the second shoebox, giving them the claim, the money and the stones.

It was over. They had the cash and the stones. We had only their sale of the crackers to look forward to. I hoped it would be a fiasco, but I now doubted everything. They were too slick for us. We were amateurs. Poor Dan. What's he going to tell his sheila when he opens the box and finds only a couple hundred quid? It's time for me to leave the Wally for a while. When the crackers start falling apart, especially the stones sold to other buyers, the mob is going to come looking for Dan and me. I'd be a target, even though I was essentially out of it.

Since I was leaving on holiday this week, I thought I would risk Archer's wrath and have lunch in the pub with the Scots. Dan and the mob of lurkers were gone, so I was no longer a threat. The Scots were at a table with Jake the Wasp and his mate, Wee Willy. "I think they got money from several blokes. Fifty-thousand quid is a lot to come up with in a few days," Jake was saying. "Archer's been ready to slam into anybody who looks at him wrong, and Sarah looks like her last dog died. She doesn't smile anymore. They're worried about their investment. If I know the Bingos, they'll say or do anything to get what they want. I don't know much about Benny; he's gone most of the time and doesn't talk when he is here, but they're mates as well as brothers. I reckon they told these blokes to put in everything they could get their hands on, that they'd get it all back in a few days and be partners in a valuable claim. That's what I think."

"My shout," I said, being new to the mob. Sarah nodded.

"You really copped it," Jake said, turning to me.

"Aye, mate. But I'm glad to be out of it, I could have come a cropper dealing with that mob. As it is, I'm lucky not to be seeing stars at midday.[117] Them's a lot of apples."

"Who else is in the scam?" Gordon asked Jake. "Wild Denny? Flint? King Tut?"

"Wild Denny, if he had the chance, but not Flint, he's too proud," Jake maintained. "King Tut has been minding his Ps and Qs ever since his wife found out about the Abo. Sarah, I don't know about. Chuck's wife doesn't like the way she looks at him. But who knows? We'll find out in time."

Slammin' Sam came in. "C'mon over, mate. I owe you a shout," I said, motioning to Sarah.

"G'day, mates," he said, all smiles. "Good on yer."

We continued to speculate on the events until Archer came through the door. He was greeted by silence. He walked directly up to me. "You're lucky to be out of the shed, Yank. You'd still be there if we didn't need it for Dynamite Dan. Should 'a put the two of you in there together and let you kill each other." He pointed his finger at me, almost touching my chest. "One more incident, and…"

Before he could finish the sentence, the Slammer stepped between us. He grabbed Archer by the arms, just below the shoulders. Rab later said that he lifted Archer off the floor. Archer was big, but the Slammer dwarfed him.

"The Yank's me mate," he said. And that was that. He let go, and Archer just backed off and walked out.

"Ta, mate," I said to the Slammer, feeling much better. "She'll be right."

The conversation tapered off, but it was plain that I, because of the Slammer, had the envy of every bloke in the pub. "With a

---

117 It is said that in a deep enough shaft you can see the stars at midday. True or not, the implication is that you are down deeper than you want to be, not of your own volition

mate like that…" I heard someone say, "You could rob the whole bloody town and get away with it." I hoped that was true. We had tried, and it wasn't over yet. The Scots looked at the Slammer in a new light.

I had to leave soon. It was nearly a week since the sale, and the cracker stones were drying. I must be off the Wally before they started to break. I needed a ride into Walgett.

The Professor was playing chess with Artie. I poured a cuppa and sat down quietly. It was a tense game; these two are serious players. Finally the Professor tipped his king over.

"Remember the Yank?"

Artie nodded and smiled. "Aye, thanks for the shout." I cocked my head questioningly. "We were in the Digger's Retreat the day after the big bluey."

"The Bingos shouted the town," the Professor said. "'This one's on Dynamite Dan, who got hit with a boomerang,' Bernie said and laughed. 'We got his claim for a few quid and all his stones.' And the Yank,' added Shadow, raising his pint. 'He got blasted by Dynamite.' Real wits, these two. Bernie dumped a tin of stones on the bar. True gemstones, worth 100 grand or more."

"It was the gloating that got to me," Artie said. "They pulled the biggest lurk anyone remembers and wanted the whole world to know about it. Then they pulled out the scam shoebox. Chuck said, 'It's a good claim; we got for a few quid. A lot of good stones came out of it. I know, I cut 'em all.' 'Even the ones Dynamite Dan never got to see,' Bernie said. They all laughed."

"We were about to leave – I didn't like the taste of Bernie's shout – but Chuck kept talkin'. 'The second-level stones are the first I've seen of that type from that field. Different composition, as you can see,' he said, pointing at the opals on the bar. 'But they are good. Very good. A fortune in Denmark, just for the digging.'"

The Professor poured us a scotch. Artie sipped his scotch, looked at me and waited. I smiled and sipped my scotch. "Something doesn't sit right in my mind," the Professor said. He walked around trying to piece the story together. "The Bingos ginked both of you before, ginked you good." He seldom used Outback slang. "And Dyno Dan buggers you out of the deal at the last minute. You're mates. I don't know the Dyno, but I do know you. This all is highly unlikely," the Professor declared. "Then to believe that these shysters would pay 50,000 pounds for just the claim is incomprehensible. They must have set it up with Archer to make sure they got the cut opals and not Dyno. They sell the stones and make a huge profit, and they own the claim, too." He paused. "And you're out. I can't make it work logically."

"You've been reading too much Schopenhauer," Artie said. "You're losing your belief in the basic badness of mankind. Go back to Dickens."

"Something just doesn't smell right."

"Something fishy in Denmark?" I asked innocently.

"Ah, he knows *Hamlet*," Artie interjected. The Professor smiled a little.

"Well, maybe there is more to the story. It ain't over till the fat kookaburra sings," I said, "or laughs."

"This conversation is degenerating. I'm going back to Adam Smith," Artie said and got into his Holden and drove away.

I reset the chess pieces. "Black or white? You're up against a clever player here."

"Very clever, I suspect. I'll keep my ear out for the fat kookaburra."

We played in silence. He knew he wouldn't get any more information out of me. He was off his game, and I maneuvered into a position where a queen sacrifice would win the game for me.

"That's a stupid move," he said, "I can capture your queen."

"Look closely. You take my queen, I have checkmate in four. You don't take my queen, I have checkmate in three. Sometimes one has to sacrifice a thing of value to win the game. It's not always obvious."

He poured us another scotch and tipped over his king. "Not my day."

"I'm taking a holiday and need a ride into Walgett. You going in soon?"

"Day after next. Need to get away for a while, do you? How long will you be gone? I can pick you up in Walgett if you know when you'll be back."

"I'm not sure, two or three fortnights.[118] Maybe more, maybe less." I enjoyed tweaking him. "I'd like to leave my van here in the Jungle, if it's okay."

"Will your van involve me in anything sinister or illegal?"

"Probably not," I said, laughing, "but you can always feign innocence."

"Will the fat kookaburra sing before you get back?"

"Not to worry, mate, she'll be right." I laughed again.

Now he laughed. "See you day after next."

---

118 Four to six weeks

Chapter XXXII
Holiday

April 1, 1966

Tenth Month

I stopped to say goodbye to Nell. "I'm off to the Big Smoke for a holiday. Just thought I'd let you know my hemorrhoid is fine."

"Did you want me to have a look at it?" she said with a mischievous smile. A mother with a small child was in the waiting room, so I said, "See you in a few weeks" and started for the door. She followed me out and gave me a warm hug. "Too bad you lost your mate and your money and your stones," she said sadly.

I answered with a phrase I had been using a lot, lately, "Not to worry; she'll be right."

"You're taking this all very lightly," she said, perplexed. "We'll have to talk when you return. Have a good time at the track." Aussies assume you will visit the racetrack anytime you get to the Big Smoke.

I left her in the doorway and went to the pub for a pie and a pint. "Where is everybody?" I asked Jake the Wasp. Only three blokes at the bar and five at two tables.

"They're all digging at the Dyno's Rush."

"What?"

"Eight new claims surrounding the Denmark. It's grated up again, until the Bingo's mob comes back – if they ever do. They may have enough tucker to stay away for years."

"The Dyno's Rush?"

"That's what Flint the Ratter called it, and it stuck."

"Maybe it should be called the Dyno's Dag," I mumbled. Fortunately I would be gone when they find out it's a scam.

"You know the area and didn't stake a claim."

"Too many bad memories. I just want to be away from here. I'm off to the Big Smoke for a holiday." He nodded.

Next day with Chungula in my pocket and 500 quid in my swag, I climbed into the Professor's badly dented Land Rover, and we left for Walgett. He didn't prod me for more information. We talked mostly about Omar, our poet. As I was boarding the train he asked, "Are you going to stop at Wee Wah and see the new Yanks?"

"I hadn't planned on it. Who are the new Yanks?"

"A Yank tourist from Texas came through several years ago and thought it would be a good place to grow cotton. So he bought thousands of acres and sold it to his friends back in America. They moved down here and planted cotton. That was three or four years ago, and they've had nothing but crop failures. If the crop fails this year, they'll go bankrupt and will all have to go back to Yankland. I'd like to know how they are doing. It should be about harvest time now."

"Righto," I said. "I'm in no hurry; I'll have a look."

After nearly a year on the Wally I was apprehensive about going to the Big Smoke with its people and noise.

Already I wanted to crawl down my hole to escape from it and have a smoke. Getting to the small town of Wee Wah on the train did not take long, less than 100 miles. The first thing I saw impressed me: A cocky with a horse-drawn cart was selling fresh milk out of a pail. He ladled it into people's containers. This would be illegal in America, I thought. Why? Seems to work fine here. A plump teenage girl in a railroad uniform was closing the doors on the passenger cars of the freight train.

"G'day. Can you direct me to the hotel? And the cotton gin?"

"We don't have a hotel, but my gramma takes in boarders, and the gin is that way," she said, pointing down the street.

"That'll be fine. I'll just be here for a day or two."

She escorted me to her grandmother's house, and a smiling old lady showed me a small room with cot, chamber pot and water basin. I dropped my swag, rinsed my face and started down the street. Thievery in Outback Aussie is nonexistent. Even the larger hotels' rooms don't have locks. My swag was safe.

The cotton gin was a couple of miles out of town. A huge metal building standing in the middle of nowhere had a half-dozen 16-wheel wagon racks full of cotton waiting to be processed. The door was open so I looked around and stepped inside. A short, plump bloke with the ambiance of a bull artist was walking around checking things. "G'day," I said, "'oweryergoing."

"Howdy. Y'all lookin' for work?"

"Righto, mate," I said impulsively. That was it. He took me out to one of the huge racks with a large pipe hanging down into it. "Climb up there. When the blower comes on, y'all move the pipe around 'til all the cotton's gone." He went back inside. Not a highly skilled job, I thought. There were two blowers. The bloke manning the blower on the next rack was nearly finished; his rack was empty. I climbed up and grabbed the 18-inch-wide, 15-foot long tube hanging down from a larger tube overhead. It started sucking up the cotton. I moved it around until all the cotton was gone, which took about 30 minutes, and then it shut off. In the next lane a bloke had pulled the empty rack away and brought in another full wagon. When that blower came on, the other operator, who had been sleeping in the loose cotton, jumped up and started moving it around. I crawled out while the "runner" – his job title I later found out – drew another wagon in for me. The least skilled, easiest-to-get-job I ever had. And fun.

Between wagons I went into the plant and talked to the manager for a few minutes at a time. "Y'all know you Aussies could have been growing cotton here for the past 50 years," he told me, "but you had to wait for us Yanks to show you how."

"Aye, mate. Is it turning a quid?" I said in my best Aussie.

"Three bad years, but now a bumper crop. We can pay off everything: land, gin and equipment, with this crop. Yep. Y'all gotta wonder."

"Yer own a block of land?" I asked.

It took several wagonloads to get the story. Turns out he owned nothing. His sister married one of the blokes from Texas, and he came along hoping to get a job. He was a bull artist. To hear him tell it, he had made and lost several fortunes and was about to do it again.

At 6 p.m. two new blower blokes came to work. The gin ran 24 hours a day during harvest. The manager paid me four quid cash for the half day and asked if I'd be back. "Righto, mate." Twelve hour shifts, 6 a.m. to 6 p.m., eight quid a shift. I needed the diversion and stayed. Intending to meet some Yanks, I went to the pub for a steak and kidney pie and a pint, and lingered. Yanks drifted into the sitting room, males and females together. After a few beers one went to the piano, and started playing *Deep in the Heart of Texas*, *The Yellow Rose of Texas*, *Home on the Range*, and other western favorites. It was awful. Texans are different from Minnesotans. Their pride and arrogance came out in the singing. I had no desire to sing with them or even meet them. I stayed at the bar with the Aussies.

One day drifted into the next. My landlady fixed breakfast: rasher of bacon, banger sausage, egg and cold toast. She packed me a lunch, and off I went at 5:15 a.m. for my walk to the gin. After 6 p.m. I had a meat pie and a few pints in the pub, and my day was over. I was on a working bloke's schedule, just what I needed to divert my mind and prepare for the Big Smoke. Sleeping enclosed in a small room took some getting used to, and the steel springs in the old cot were worn out. The center dipped so much I had to sleep on my back.

In two weeks the harvest was finished. I paid my kind landlady, gave her a few extra quid, packed my swag and hopped on the train for Brisbane with some notes on Wee Wah to give to the Professor when I returned to the Wally.

Once in Brisbane I didn't want to visit the Fishers until I had cleaned up a bit. I checked into a hotel. The hot water shower felt wonderful, my first in a year. Next morning I went down to breakfast to find I needed a jacket and tie to be admitted. I was lucky to have a shirt. So I found a little eatery and had a typical Aussie breakfast: eggs sunny-side-up, banger sausage, slice of fried tomato, cold toast and a rasher of bacon. First order of business, since I looked like a swagman, was to buy new clothes and shoes, get a haircut and have my beard trimmed. This took most of the day, but I felt presentable. That evening I went to see *Mary Poppins* in color at an elaborate movie theater. Sure beats the hard chairs and a black-and-white Helen Shapiro movie. The Big Smoke does have some advantages.

The most urgent thing was to get a letter off to the Dyno. I didn't know where he was. We separated unexpectedly before we had worked out all the details, but I knew he was near Perth. He wouldn't chance writing to me in Wallangulla, and I wouldn't send a letter to him through Petula at the Wally post office. So I sent it to Dynamite Dan, care of GPO Perth, hoping it would get to him. I gave my return address as "Jack the Yank, care of GPO, Brisbane." How clandestine this was getting! But we had to avoid any contact that could be traced.

> *Dear Dyno,*
>
> *Sorry about the bloody nose, but I had to make it look good. The gigs really worked you over, from what I hear. Sorry. I didn't expect to get tossed in the shed and thought we would meet before you left. No such luck. Archer later threatened me. Fortunately the Slammer got between us; he's our mate now. But it's not over. I heard about the other shoebox and how they gave you the one with only a few quid in it. My apologies to your sheila.*
>
> *Now our only hope for revenge is that they will do themselves in selling the stolen crackers. Things haven't gone as planned for us so far, so I don't expect much. We took on some real pros, and it looks like they buggered us. The Denmark is surrounded by new claims. They call it Dyno's Rush – you're notorious.*
>
> *I'm staying away from the Wally for a few weeks to let things cool down. I could be in for it when I go back, but I must find out how it all comes out. I'll try to write again, later.*
>
> *Your mate, the Yank*

The Fishers had no idea I was here, so the next day I waited until after supper before taking a taxi to their address. I knocked on the door. The little girl, Susie, answered and yelled, "It's the Yank," and jumped up into my arms.

"Don't jump up on men," her mother admonished, but she greeted me with a hearty, "Welcome to Brisbane!" They had been expecting me to show up for some time. Joey took my swag and showed me to his room, which was now mine. I thanked him and unpacked some of my new clothes. The Fishers were casual, and I felt as comfortable as an Outback Aussie can in the city. The most difficult adjustment was remembering to flush the toilet. In the great Outback you squat, wipe and walk away. In the city you have to remember to push the flush handle. After a couple of days Joey said, "Don't worry, Yank, I'll check for you," and he did. I forgot about half the time but got better toward the end of the week.

We had a beer on the back patio. Gerald and Ruth were here for three years, two of which had already past. He was an engineer for an American corporation. I don't know what kind or which one. We talked about opals and Aussies. I told him how Dynamite Dan and I had been lurked and gave him a brief summary of our retaliation, without going into too much detail. He talked about city life in Brisbane. They had been grabbed up in a mob that consisted of just under a dozen couples. "We'll have a party tomorrow night so you can meet our mob."

"Ta, that'll be nice," I said not really wanting to be in a big group.

"Then the next night, or the night after, the Fosters will throw a party."

"Oh," I said, "Two parties in the same week?"

Gerald smiled. "A day or two after that it will be the Walkers. Next the Allens, the Parkers, and so on until the whole mob have done their duty. It's the way they do things. As you'll hear, our mob does things right; we're the best mob in the city. Not like those other mobs that don't have a clue."

My hand went into my pocket and grasped Chungula. Two weeks of parties was more than I had bargained for, but I was a guest and "when in Rome..." The next day I helped prepare for the bash, which went nicely. About two dozen happy, beer-drinking Aussies showed up and enjoyed the party. Questions about Wallangulla kept me busy all night. I passed my half-dozen opals around for all to examine, but I never mentioned my Radiant. Several couples wanted to retire and dig for opals. "Nice mob," I said when it was over. "You'll get to know them better" Gerald replied.

And so it went, night after night. Sports were the main topic of conversation. Several of the men in their late 30s still played rugby. A couple of the blokes played cricket. The wives played bridge and mahjong. Aussie houses have 12-foot ceilings. One of the sheilas, after a few beers, liked to stand on the fireplace mantle and free fall into the waiting arms of the mob. The parties changed little, and I had had enough after the first week, but there was no escape.

Meanwhile I went into the city by bus every day to check the mail at the general post office and give Ruth some breathing space. It was difficult for me to spend time idly. I read the newspaper without interest. I tried the library and the parks. I caught a few matinees. But I was just killing time. I felt my Radiant often and thought of Helga. I realized I would never see her again, but the memories were pleasant.

Eight days after I arrived, I received an answer from Dyno.

> G'day, Mate,
>
> The bloody nose wasn't as bad as the kick in the face from Chuck. We owe him one, so if you get the chance... The swelling has gone down, and my sheila says "ta" and is happy I'm back. We'll discuss everything over a beer sometime. For now, be careful. They're rat bags who will stop at nothing. I won't give you any details about what you don't know. The less you know the better off you'll be for the next few weeks. The Slammer is our good mate. As you may have heard, he helped with my getaway and enjoyed the dynamite blast. When everything cools down ask him to show you the dead sheep.
>
> Ta. Danny

What don't I know, I thought? I got the whole story from Harold Blake and the Scots. And why ask the Slammer to show me a dead sheep? That doesn't make sense. Skinner knows where the dead sheep are, not the Slammer. There was no time for more correspondence with the Dyno. A lot of questions remain but, like the Scots and the Professor, I'll just have to wait.

Not much more to say about Brisbane except that Joey is determined to move to Wallangulla as soon as he can leave home, which, to hear him tell it, might be in a year or two. When the party ritual was over I bought a used Holden[119] for 300 quid cash, thanked the Fishers for their hospitality and lit out for Sydney with a fortnight to kill.

I bought a few supplies: a Swiss army knife, a pair of large boots, and a good sleeping bag for the Slammer; new mosquito netting and a pick and shovel for me; and a bottle of scotch for the Professor. The 500-mile drive to Sydney is on smooth blacktop. I could drive 60 miles an hour and not bounce off the road. Having had my fill of sleeping inside a house, I pulled off onto a side road and slept on the ground with my jacket for a pillow, just like a year ago. It felt good. Soft beds don't let you rest properly.

Sydney doesn't have avenues, only streets. It can be confusing. At the end of the second day, I found my way to Kings Cross in Darlinghurst. From there it was a short hop to Hardie Street and Madam Baker's rooming house, where I had stayed the first two weeks after arriving on the German freighter. It was a large two-story house of eight spacious rooms with 11-foot ceilings

Madam Baker was 82 years old, always wrapped in a heavy shawl and had a tic in one eye. On my first visit, several men, construction workers mostly, stopped in just to say hello and talk to her. This was curious. As I had an upstairs room, I didn't see her that often. Once while coming down the hall, I heard *Dream of Manon* playing on her phonograph. I had learned the tenor aria in college, so I sang along. The next day she invited me to tea to make my acquaintance. Her tea manners were impeccable and her teapot and cups beautiful. The lace tablecloth spoke of better times. She was a charming old woman, not pleasant to look at, but she exuded warmth.

Madame Baker enlightened my intellect while we became friends. She had emigrated from France as a young girl, hence the French opera and the bond between us that my singing created. We discussed music and composers: Debussy, Offenbach and Saint Saens. Most of my opera training had been in Italian and German. I had read Hugo, Voltaire and Dumas in English but with little understanding. She thought Rousseau a degenerate,

---

119 Holden – A General Motors automobile made in Australia

and I couldn't agree more. Anyone who would put four of his own illegitimate children in an orphanage certainly fits that category.

Not only was Madame Baker a music lover but also a knowledgable punter. In the evening we sometimes walked to her bookie down the alley and made a few select bets for five shillings each, never more. "Odds too short." "Not a mudder, doesn't run well on a wet track." "Not the right jockey." She bet carefully, and we won almost every time. I got excited. "I'm going to bet five quid this time," I announced. "No," she said. "If you bet more than five bob, I won't give you any more information. Betting has to be fun, not hazardous."

One day she showed her picture at age 17. She had been a fantastic beauty. This explains her attraction to men and men to her. She had always been comfortable around men and vice versa. Her Aussie husband had been a publican and died in his forties after being pricked by a rose bush. "I should not have gotten old in Australia. It's difficult here, but too late now." The rooming house earned just enough for her to survive.

I knocked on her door and Madam Baker welcomed me back warmly. It had been a year since I was last here. We had a polite tea, made from just the tips of the tea leaves, and a civil conversation. How different from the month previously when I served billy tea to a beautiful Aboriginal woman and her father around an open fire, squatting and silent. Madam's dog, Musso, had a growth on her neck and didn't have long to live. "I shall not be far behind," Madam said. I replied simply, "I'm sorry to hear that. I will miss you."

I stayed for two weeks and resumed my old pattern: Lunch at the Yugoslav immigrant's stand, steak and French fries 4/5, (four shillings and five pence), less than 50 cents American. Supper at the Greek's little café 3/5. "How can you serve roast beef or lamb meals with potatoes and another vegetable so cheaply?" "My children help," he said. "If I had two more kids, I could do it for 2/5."

The time passed quickly, I felt comfortable here, although the house was no longer clean, and my mousetraps were full every morning. Some days I played chess on the three-foot-high chess set in the park. Someone always was ready to have a game, but it's not as much fun if you have to carry off the piece you capture.

My passport had been packed in my footlocker, but I took it out for the trip. I noticed that my Australian visa had expired two months previously. I went to the immigration office and found I needed a new picture. The new picture showed how much I had changed – eyes glazed, somewhat addled expression. I was getting the Wallies; it's time I left the Outback, I thought. But I can't, not with Chungula. I felt my pocket several times a day to assure myself the stone was there. I couldn't leave without it and couldn't take it away from the Wally, but I have other problems to think about now.

When my third fortnight away was finished, I bade farewell to my good friend, Madam Baker, and started back to Wallangulla apprehensively.

Chapter XXXIII
Boomeranged

May 13, 1966
Eleventh Month

I stopped by the Khancoban Dam where I had worked for several months. It was nearly a mile long and was finished. Work still was going on at the seven million yard cut two miles away. The dam was a work of art. The project manager had an eye for beauty and function. The dam was designed to fill and empty twice a day. The dry side had smooth grass, nicely laid. The riprap rocks on the waters edge, some as large as a water buffalo, were carefully placed and set. The manager could have saved a lot of money by having a crane drop each rock on the batter. Instead, the crew carefully laid each rock. It was his last project before retiring and a monument to his skill and sense of aesthetics. I was pleased to have been a part of the project.

It's a long drive to the Wally, and I took my time. With more than 100 quid left in my pocket, I stayed two nights at small hotels. Travelers can eat well at them. As the owner of one hotel, sitting across the table from me while enjoying his meal, said, "They don't stint on the food here." Aussie is a world of individuals, not yet taken over by the Hilton and Sheridan corporations. Each hotel reflects the pride and personality of the owner.

As I passed through Walgett, my apprehension increased. Drawing nearer I recognized the scent of the Wally – not a bad scent, not a good scent – but it smelled of home and gave me a comfortable feeling. The young Scots were gone when I parked my Holden by the mud humpy. Everything appeared unchanged. I tossed Slammin' Sam's new sleeping bag in a corner and set his Swiss army knife on the shelf. My swag of new clothes went into the $5 footlocker. I boiled the billy and tossed in handful of tea leaves, the brand Madam Baker used, expensive, but what the hell, life is short; why not enjoy the finer things? Then out in the sunlight, I turned my Radiant, admiring the sparkling colors, sipped my tea and enjoyed a Dr. Pat. When I heard the Scot's truck, I quickly rewrapped my Radiant, secured it in my pocket, and tried to look relaxed.

They bantered, as always: "The Yank's back."

"And with a new car. Must have found a sheila in the Big Smoke that had a few quid."

"More likely he hit the horses. I can't imagine a sheila spending money on the likes of him."

"He's back just in time for the hanging. Too bad. If he had let us know we could have warned him off."

"What hanging?" I said smiling.

"Yours, mate. The meeting's tonight in the town hall. The Bingo mob already bought the rope, a new one so you have nothing to complain about."

"Aye, they swore out a warrant for your arrest. You and the Dyno pulled it off, mate. It's a beaut! Gemstones are cracking from Hong Kong to London and all parts between."

"You have our unabashed admiration. 'Lay on, Macduff, and damned be him who first cries, 'Hold! Enough!'"

"What's rotten in Denmark's claim now taints the gigs, the ginks and the galahs. Benny Bingo is in the slammer, and his brother is lying to save his skin."

"Aye, it's not his fault. The Yank and the Dyno sold them crackers – took advantage of their trust and honesty."

"Where will it all end? If you can't trust the blokes you steal from, what's the world coming to? Let's have a beer, mate; you deserve it. You have a few scalps hanging from your belt."

It was still afternoon, and this was a lot for me to digest. "Benny's in jail?" I asked, surprised.

"Aye, he's the one who sold the crackers. To the International Opal Syndicate, no less. They were shipped all over the world." Both Rab and Gordon laughed uproariously. "Ah! Lay on Macduff! The boomerang they thought hit you, did, as boomerangs will sometimes do, come around full circle and smacked the hurlers." Rab handed me another beer.

"I haven't had a chance to sip the first one, yet," I said, trying to figure out events. "But I'm shocked! Shocked, I tell you, that you believe I had anything to do with all of this." I waved my hands in the air. "I was locked up in the Shearing Shed. I'm innocent, completely innocent. How could anyone believe these lies?"

"Well, you'll have the chance to prove your innocence tonight at the meeting. The New South Wales mining inspector and Sergeant Taylor from Sydney are here to sort out things. They've been looking for you."

"They've been out here several times. The Bingos and their mates have them convinced that you and the Dyno grabbed the money and skedaddled, after selling them 50 grand worth of crackers. By the by, now we know why you had Chuck cut the stones instead of Garbhan. Garbhan was miffed at first, but now he understands."

"And sends his thanks."

"The meeting is tonight?" I asked, trying to absorb it all.

"In the town hall," Rab said. "More fun than a Helen Shapiro movie. They are determined to get to the truth. We're glad you're back to put things right."

How am I going to put things right against that mob? Slammin' Sam's words floated back to mind "They's too many, too fast."

"I better go wash up and put on some clean clothes," I said. As I walked back to the mud humpy, Gordon said, "Not to worry, mate, she'll be right."

"I hope so," I muttered to myself. "I hope so."

Things had gone farther than Dyno Dan and I had planned. We didn't want to destroy the opal market, just stick the Bingos with some crackers. The Bingos were trying to cover their backsides. A warrant for my arrest? For what? And why the meeting? Didn't everybody already know what happened? I ate a sandwich left over from my trip and had a cuppa and a Dr. Pat.

We drove in together, the Scots and me, but I waited outside, away from the main door, not easily recognizable in my new clothes and hat. The small hall was nearly full, about 40 people, a larger audience than any Shapiro movie. The mine inspector and Sergeant Taylor were seated behind a table at the front. Bernie Bingo and his mob were in the front row, looking uncomfortable.

"As you all know," the inspector began, "the opal market has been affected by a large number of stones called crackers. Mr. Benny Bingo sold these stones to a worldwide distributor, the International Opal Syndicate. Over a period of weeks they were distributed to dealers in Hong Kong, Tokyo, London, New York and several other cities. Fortunately, none of them had yet been sold to jewelry stores, so they didn't get into the hands of customers. All of them are being recovered. Mr. Benny Bingo is in custody and being questioned about the origin and sale of these stones. He is refusing to pay restitution to syndicate. He says opals crack, and the risk is the buyer's. This will be settled in court."

"The purpose of this meeting is to find out how this happened and how to ensure that it does not happen again. Mr. Bernie Bingo has asked us to issue warrants for the arrest of two diggers, one called Dynamite Dan and the other the Yank. He claims they sold him and his brother the stones for 50,000 Australian pounds, knowing they would crack and break, and then they both ginked out and haven't been heard from since. We understand that many of you saw the transaction take place. We want the details and the whole story. We will begin by asking Mr. Bingo to tell what exactly happened."

This was the Wally's biggest event in years. The room was silent, filled with locals and diggers. Some were dressed in city clothes; Jake the Wasp and Wee Willy wore white shirts. As Bernie was standing up, I walked up from the back of the room and said, loudly, "You can tear up your warrant for the Yank. I'm here."

"He's lying," Bernie shouted, obviously surprised. Chuck, Shadow and Marco also stood up. "Don't believe a word he says."

The police sergeant said, "He hasn't said anything yet. Give him a chance to lie before accusing him." The sergeant's humor relaxed me a lot, but everyone in the room was fidgeting, squirming, though some were smiling.

"May I speak?" I asked the inspector.

"He's lying," Bernie shouted again. "Don't let him go on with this. Ask Chuck the Cutter or Archer the Cop what happened. They'll tell you. Don't listen to the Yank; he's a gink!"

"You are the Yank?" the inspector asked.

"Yes," I said. "I would like the opportunity to answer the charges just made against me. Here. Publicly."

"He's lying," Bernie shouted, his brows furrowing, his face turning rosy. "Arrest him. Don't let him tell more lies."

The sergeant stood up and took a few steps toward Bernie. "Please take your seat, Mr. Bingo. We are here to gather information. We'll decide for ourselves who is or is not lying." Bernie sat down, still glaring at me.

I walked to the front, surprised at my audacity. My anger rose as I spoke directly to the inspector. "I have been accused of selling crackers to the Bingo Brothers. This is not true. I have only sold one stone, one gemstone, to Bernie Bingo, and that was several months ago. I knew little about the value of gem opal at the time, and my campmate, Marco here" – Marco hung his head as I pointed at him – "suggested I ask Shadow to assess it. Shadow thought it might be worth 200 quid. I had been without tucker for three days and, hoping not to lose the sale, I offered it to Bernie for 180 quid, which he immediately paid. The next day I heard he had gone straight to the pub and shouted the house, saying he got this beautiful gem for less than 5,000. I had been set up. Chuck, Marco and Shadow were all in on it. There was nothing I could do; it was all legal."

I turned to Bernie, "How much did you sell my gem for? I heard more than 10,000."

Bernie jumped up, his voice rising, "What I sell my stones for is none of your business. We're not here to talk about your stupid deal."

"Yes," I went on, "it was a stupid deal, and that is the only stone I ever sold to Mr. Bingo. You can understand why." I paused and looked sternly at my accusers. "The other charge, that I ran off right after the sale, is pure fabrication. During the proceedings, my partner, Dynamite Dan, decided to cut me out of the sale of the Denmark claim, his claim, the only thing for sale, not the opals. This infuriated me. We were mates. I slugged him, knocked him down and was beating on him when Archer pulled me off, cuffed me and locked me in the Shearing Shed. I was barred from town for two days and from the pub for a week. Archer will verify that."

I looked at Archer, who was seated behind the table with the inspector. Archer nodded, reluctantly.

"After feeling bad for a week, I needed a holiday and left to visit friends in Brisbane. Note, inspector, that the stones never were for sale – just the claim. The stones were from another site that we wanted to keep secret, so we made it appear that they came from the Denmark claim. They were beautiful stones. Chuck cut them. Then a couple cracked, which caused us to suspect all of them. We decided not to sell them but wait to see if more of them would crack."

"We've heard enough of this story," shouted Bernie on his feet again, along with Chuck, Shadow and Marco.

"He's going to tell you he's completely innocent," Chuck said. "You've got to believe us."

"You'll get your chance to speak," the inspector said. They stood defiantly for a moment and then sat down, looking disgusted. "You may continue," the inspector said to me.

"Then Dyno told Chuck he was planning to sell the claim, not the opals, for 40,000 pounds. Chuck made him a higher offer, 50,000. This sounded ridiculous to both of us. Who would pay that much for a claim? We thought the Bingos must be in on it and that they really planned to steal the stones. So Dyno agreed to the sale if he could keep the stones. Archer drew up the papers, and we met in the pub. That was when Dyno decided to cut me out of the deal and Archer locked me in the Shearing Shed. I was out of it. That's all I know firsthand."

"Thank you, Yank," the inspector said. "Now Mr. Bingo, you may tell us your story." Bernie squirmed, looked around and slowly rose. He hadn't expected me to show up for this meeting.

"They salted the claim to make it look like it was worth a fortune and tricked us into buying it. They were in this together and planned to split the money. They are gigs." Bernie shook his fat fist at me.

"We were trying to keep our find secret until we knew for sure that the opals did or did not crack," I said, my jaw clenched. "Dyno had Chuck cut them and swore him to secrecy. He also had been lurked out of several thousand pounds by the Bingo Brothers months earlier and wanted nothing more to do with them. I don't know what nefarious methods Bernie used to find out about the stones. All Dyno's dealings were with Chuck. Chuck was the one who offered to buy the claim."

"Where is Dynamite Dan now?" the inspector asked me.

"I don't know. I haven't seen him since Archer locked me in the Shearing Shed. Archer ran him out of town the next morning. It was a nasty parting. I don't think I will ever see him again."

The inspector looked at Chuck. "This is getting complicated. You were the claim buyer? You had that much cash?"

Chuck looked sheepish. "The Bingos gave me the money. I bought the claim for them. We had Archer draw up two sets of papers. One for Dyno's sale and one for my sale to the Bingos."

The inspector sat silently for a long time, looking from Bernie to Chuck to me and finally to Archer. "Do you have these sale papers with you?"

Now Archer squirmed and looked uncomfortable. He hadn't wanted to be involved. "No, not with me. It was so long ago. They are probably filed somewhere. The sale was straightforward and witnessed; I didn't think the paperwork was important."

The annoyed inspector said, "Would you please find the papers and bring them here? We will take a short break."

The meeting hall emptied loudly. I met the Scots outside. "You're doing fine, Yank. You're going to pull it off. The inspector seems to believe you."

"Why shouldn't he? I'm telling the truth." Several others gathered around. Wombat said, with a big smile, "Glad you be back, Yank. The Bingos ginked us too. Time they got done in." Slammin' Sam was smiling ear to ear. "You're me mate," he said. I smiled and ambled away from the town hall.

Rab said, "Did you notice that Shadow and Marco have been beaten? Their faces are bruised, and Marco limps. Rumor is they got thumped good by the Croats in Sydney, but we think there's more to it than that."

"I didn't notice," I said.

"Shadow's wife is back, but the daughters stayed," Gordon said with a grin. "She nags him mercilessly, compares him to the Croats."

"You think his wife beat him?" I asked.

"No, his mates."

"Rab," I said, "It would be helpful if you could tell the sergeant that Harold Blake knows about all this and is an honest bloke."

"Righto." He smiled and went inside.

The hall crowd settled in again. This was the finest entertainment on the Wally since Benny dumped the cracker opals on the bar and shouted the house. Archer set the papers on the table, and the inspector picked them up one by one.

"That's the transfer deed for the claim, from Dyno to Chuck," Archer said. "The next is the bill of sale stating the price, one Australian pound plus other considerations contained in the shoebox." Archer waited while the inspector examined the papers carefully. "The third one gives Dyno the right to remove all his stones still in the claim, but it must be done by him alone before midnight. The last is the deed transfer from Chuck to the Bingo Brothers."

"Mr. Bingo," the inspector said, "you said you and your brother were tricked into buying the opals, but Chuck bought the claim on the condition that Dyno retained the opals. It seems your dispute should be with Chuck."

"It's more complicated than that," Bernie said, shaking his head. "We knew we were dealing with two tricky diggers and had to be a little surreptitious ourselves."

"How did you get the stones?"

Bernie was silent. I could see now that Shadow and Marco had been in a bluey. The two of them said nothing. After a long silence Bernie said, "It got very confusing. Dynamite Dan attacked me as he was leaving the pub, and Archer locked him in the Shearing Shed. The whole pub got into a big bluey, and I don't know what happened after that."

The inspector looked at Bernie and Chuck, then turned toward Archer, who just stared at the table. "Is Harold Blake here tonight?" the inspector asked. Harold stood and walked to the front of the hall. "Would you be kind enough to give us some information? Remember, this is just a hearing. You do work with Archer from time to time, is that correct?"

"Yes."

"And you were in the pub at this time?" Harold nodded. "Would you give your account of what happened?"

"Dyno by now was as full as a goog. He signed the papers, said he was leaving the Wally for good, picked up the shoebox of money and started for the door. The Bingo Brothers, Shadow and Chuck blocked the way. Bernie announced that he and his brother now owned the Denmark claim. This infuriated Dyno. He dropped the shoebox and slammed into them. Archer broke up the fight, but the whole pub quickly got into it. Archer gave me the key to the Shearing Shed and told me to let the Yank out so he could lock up Dyno. I did, and he dragged Dyno over and locked him up for the night. Dyno was protesting up and down."

"Why?"

"He said he'd leave the Wally immediately and cause no more trouble. All he wanted was the shoebox and the opals still in the claim. Archer told him he'd be locked up for the night, and he Archer, I mean – would personally escort him out of town in the morning."

"But the agreement said he had until midnight to collect his stones," the inspector pointed out, emphasizing each word.

"He was a troublemaker," Archer said. "I wanted to make sure he was sober when I got him out of town in the morning. The agreement was between him and Chuck, and he was in no condition to do anything. My job is to keep things legal and restore order, so I locked him up." Archer attempted to look a self-righteous. The inspector shook his head.

"The next morning Archer asked me to get the shoebox of money from the pub and follow him in Dyno's pickup," Harold Blake continued. "He took the key to the grate out of Dyno's pocket and drove to the Denmark claim. The grate had been blasted off. Slammin' Sam, who Dyno had asked to guard it, said the Bingos, Chuck and Shadow had gone off with the opals just after midnight."

"This was all legal," Bernie said, angrily. "After midnight the claim and everything in it was ours. We were within our rights to take them. Don't you see?" Bernie asked. "It was a scam. Dyno Dan and the Yank set it all up. They wanted to sell us the crackers for 50,000 quid."

The inspector looked at Archer and said, "You're stating that they got Archer to lock Dyno Dan up overnight knowing you would take the stones?" Archer, surprised, shook his head. The inspector went on: "Why would they want you to steal the crackers? They could have sold them to you for 50 grand or more and ginked out. Why go though this elaborate hoax? Chuck had already told you their market value." The inspector waited. Bernie remained silent. "The transfer papers stated that Chuck, and ultimately you and your brother, were buying the claim, not the opals. Both the Yank and Dyno have stated they didn't want to sell the opals because they might crack and be worthless. The case might be made that you paid an enormous sum for the claim planning to finagle the stones one way or another and retrieve your investment by selling them."

Bernie replied in frustration, "If they sold us crackers, that's fraud, and we could get the money back and put them in jail. This way it looks like they didn't really sell us the stones, just the claim and now we can't recover our investment."

"You have just said that selling crackers is fraudulent, yet you and your brother are saying that the risk is the buyer's, not the seller's."

Bernie threw up his hands and sat down. Harold Blake was still standing by the table. The inspector said, "Mr. Blake?"

"That's about all of it. We took Dyno and Slammin' Sam to his camp. It had been trashed. Dyno blew up his last half case of dynamite in a final act of defiance, and the two of them roared off in his pickup. We had to hurry away to escape the explosion. That's the last I saw of him."

The inspector turned to his sergeant. "Do you have any questions for these gentlemen?"

"I think we have all the answers we are going to get. Additional questions would just confuse things. I think we have the information we need."

"Mr. Bingo," the inspector said, looking directly at him. "You and your brother will be required to reimburse the International Opal Syndicate for the full sum and added expenses and penalties. My advice would be to repay immediately. If this goes to court, both you and your mates could come a cropper, whatever part they have in all this."

He looked at Shadow, Chuck and Marco and then Archer. They were all uncomfortable. He stood up. "Everything in this affair seems to be legal, too legal for my taste. Suspiciously legal would be a better way of putting it. I wish we could use surnames, but that is not the way of the Wally. The bloke called Dynamite Dan had the legal right to sell his claim and cut out the Yank; it was in his name. I can understand and forgive the Yank for thumping him – not a criminal act. Any Aussie would have done the same." He looked at me and smiled. "Archer had reason to lock him up, legally. The sale of the claim to Chuck the Cutter and his presale to the Bingo Brothers were legal. The sale price of one Australian pound plus other considerations is a commonly used agreement. Legal. The question of who lurked whom concerning the cracker stones puzzles me, but Dyno Dan had the right to the stones up until midnight and couldn't retrieve them because he was in the Shearing Shed. Archer had the right to lock him up and the Bingos, after midnight, owned the stones. Legally. Dyno Dan was free to leave with the money and even blow up his own camp, regardless of how much it irritated Archer. Ethical questions aside, this whole affair is disturbingly legal. And, as far as I am concerned, it is over. Once the Bingos reimburse the IOS, it will be finished."

He looked around the hall. "Does anyone here have anything to add?" Silence. "Then this meeting is adjourned."

Several blokes patted me on the back. "Time somebody got to the Bingos. Good on yer." "Sorry your mate ginked you." "Too bad about the other shoebox." We drove back to the bough shed and had a beer.

"It went well," Rab said. "You and your mate pulled it off. Congratulations are in order. The boomerang came full circle and smacked the lot of them."

I answered, "You're so cynical! Don't you believe the inspector?"

"Aye, mate, we believe everything," Gordon said. "I'm only sorry they copped the other shoebox. You 'n your mate didn't make a quid on the whole deal. Too bad. It would make a much better pub story."

"Still," Rab said, "it may not be over. There might be more to come. Don't underestimate the Yank. Lay on Macduff." They raised their beers.

I raised mine, also. "No, it is over – barring a hooly-dooly. The fat kookaburra is singing." They looked at me curiously. "It's a private joke," I said and smiled.

Chapter XXXIV
Hooly-Dooly

May 17, 1966

Twelfth Month

Everything looked the same as I parked the Holden at my claim. Harold Blake had been watching for me; he wanted to talk. "Interesting meeting. Surprising conclusion. I thought both of the Bingos would be locked up, but it seems like restitution is all the inspector wants. They're out of business, you know."

"No, I didn't know."

"Several diggers and other buyers told the inspector they didn't want the Bingos dealing in stones any more. Asked him to ban them. Be that as it may, no one will sell or buy from them. They're finished."

I was glad to hear that. With Harold I didn't have to say anything to keep the conversation going. He always said what he had to say and left.

"I kept my eye out for ratters on your claim, but nobody came poking around. I'm sorry about the other shoebox. If I had known, maybe I could have done something. I don't like the Bingos any better than you do; they're a nasty mob."

"It's not your fault. They're too slick for any of us." I thought for a minute before asking, "Do you think Archer is in on any of this? He didn't look comfortable at the meeting last night."

"The thought has crossed my mind. I've lived next door to Archer for years. He's a good bloke, I reckon, but he's seen many diggers leave here with a fortune. He may have seen this as a chance to get in on it himself. Some of his doings seem suspicious, but as the inspector said, it's all legal."

I asked: "Are the diggers at Dyno's Rush ready to show me stars at midday?"

Harold laughed. "No, they thought it was a good lurk. Also, you got buggered worse that they did. Flint and his mate hit a pocket on the second level worth a couple hundred quid. It all might turn out well. The Bingos' mob isn't working their claim that they paid – or professed to pay – 50 grand for."

"Where's the Slammer these days? He got thrown into the middle of the mess. I brought him a sleeping bag and a Swiss army knife."

"He's sinking a shaft for a bloke two miles beyond Three Mile Flats. Not much going on out there; you should be able to find him. He'll like the knife and bag. He's a bit simple but a good bloke. I heard he got between you and Archer."

"Yeah, saved me a broken nose and maybe another night in the Shearing Shed."

"Well, Archer'll think twice before he slings off at you again."

With that, Harold went back to his claim, and I crawled down my shaft. All I had left it were my picks, shovels and trolley. I dug with little enthusiasm. I couldn't get my mind into it, even though I was getting short on a quid and must do something soon. We had planned to split the 50-grand, but Dan went back to Perth with only a few hundred. The Bingos were out of business but not suffering enough to please me.

I gave up digging after a couple hours, went to the general store, bought a half dozen tins of Dinty Moore beef stew and set out to find the Slammer. He was neck deep in a new shaft, smiling as always. "G'day, mato, 'owei yergoing?"

"G'day, Yank," he said as he crawled out.

"I brought you a couple of things from the Big Smoke." I unrolled the sleeping bag and showed him how to unzip it, but I knew he most likely would sleep on it closed up. He put on the new boots with a big smile. They fit. He was very appreciative. I forgot to get socks. Then I gave him the tins of stew and brought out the Swiss army knife. After showing him all the blades, I pulled out the can opener blade and opened a tin of stew. He was thrilled and opened another tin and then another.

"Ta, mate, ta. Good on yer." Then I showed him the tweezers and the toothpick on the knife. It was the best present I could have given him.

"Looks like you'll have a big dinner today," I said and pointed at the three tins.

"She'll be right, mate, she'll be right. Ta. We mates, Danny and me and you," he said, waving his hand between us.

"I'll let you get back to work then."

He was still waving and smiling as I drove off. I felt better about life. Dan really must have made contact with him.

The next night I caught up on the news from the young Scots. "Sorry we spoiled the opal market," I said.

"Aye, mate. Didn't hurt it a bit. Angus is glad to have the Bingos out of it. They were always trying to pull something. Angus gives a written money-back guarantee for all opals to insure against breakage."

"Righto. The Bingos are out of it. Benny is in the slammer and Bernie sits in the pub with Chuck wingeing."

"Why don't they leave?" I asked. "They've got 50 grand."

"Ah, they can't leave just yet. Seems the inspector still has some more questions. Archer, Marco, Shadow and Chuck were in on it. It's rumored they all put a lot of money into the Denmark sale, even Sarah, and God only knows who else. You'd think they would have split it up by now, but you know the Bingos."

"Marco complains about having to tend bar fulltime to pay back some bad loans he made."

"Where's the money?"

"Interesting question. Who knows?"

"Do you know who pulled a bluey with Shadow and Marco? They look pretty bad."

"Just more rumors, mate. Maybe something to do with the 50 grand. It's all still a puzzle."

"Where's Macduff now that we need him?"

The next day I dug again with little enthusiasm. Helga crowded into my thoughts. I gave up and drove to the Pom's camp in the Jungle. With my fatal Radiant opal, Chungula, in hand and Helga in my heart and thoughts, I walked to the gum tree that we stood by on that memorable night so long ago and reminisced about my Valkyrie in my arms.

I couldn't shake my lethargy, the first symptom of the Wallies. I drove to my coolabah camp where Bruno is buried and looked out across the plains. It always used to be such a comfort. Now it didn't help.

That night, May 19, I told the Scots I had been on the Wally for exactly one year. We talked about their four years here. I thought, "Do I want to stay that long? Do I have a choice? Dan and I put everything we had into the Denmark scam and got buggered by the Bingos. Now I'm really short on a quid. It may take months to find enough stones to pay my way back to the States. Unless I sell my Chungula, but I'm not ready to think about that." Another beer for now.

I spent the next few days alone, either by the coolabah or in the Jungle, reading cheap paperback novels. I had mates now but missed Dan, Bruno and Helga.

The Scots asked me to the pub for lunch and tried to cheer me up by baiting Bernie and Chuck who were standing morosely at the bar.

"You thought they were honest diggers and stole their stones only to find out they're crackers. Who can you trust? What's the world coming to if you can't trust the people you steal from? Get out your papers and get your money back!"

"They ginked us," Bernie said. "Sold us crackers."

"But didn't you steal them? That's what it looks like."

"Your mate, across the bar there, was in on it."

I couldn't resist saying, "I'm innocent. It was Dan's claim. And what stones are you talking about? Dan sold the claim, not the stones. You stole the stones. I'm shocked! Shocked that you would even think I'd sell a cracker. I would cut off my hand before doing such a dishonest thing." Bernie looked away, disgusted. He was a beaten man.

I went on. "How much did you sell my gemstone for? Was it 10,000? More? And how much did you rat Dan's claim for? 10,000? More? Well, now you have time to think about it. Lots of time." I smiled at Bernie and Chuck, who said nothing.

Later, "Ta, mates," I said to the Scots. "I needed that."

For a few days I dug lethargically and hit a small pocket of nobbies. Garbhan cut six nice stones, worth several hundred quid, he said. I decided to keep them for now; surprised that he thought Angus would even offer to buy stones from me. I had a roast beef supper at Lenny's to lift my spirits.

I joined Wombat and Skinner for lunch the next day. Skinner didn't smell so bad. Either he quit skinning dead sheep, or I was losing my sense of smell. I looked around. "Where's Archer? I haven't seen him for some time."

"He be gone," Wombat said. "Gone to new place. Sergeant Taylor come."

So Archer's gone too, I thought. Chuck and Shadow were talking loudly at the bar. Shadow and Marco behind the bar, looked like they had taken another beating.

"It's the bloody Yank," Shadow said, almost yelling. "He's behind it all. He's got the money. He's the one we have to beat it out of." I smiled, uncertain what was afoot. I turned back to Wombat and Skinner. "What's that all about?"

Before they could answer, Shadow and Chuck charged around the bar, knocking over chairs. They grabbed me, threw me to the floor, and kicked me in the head and gut before I could roll over. As I covered my face with my arms, I glanced up and saw a huge figure that came out of nowhere. It was the Slammer. He picked them both up and slammed them against the wall with a cracking noise, and as they lay on the floor, the Slammer announced to everyone, "The Yank's me mate." He helped me up off the floor, smiling as always. "We mates," he said, "Danny and me and you."

Shadow and Chuck scrambled to their feet and hurried out the door, Shadow holding one arm as if it were broken.

Bernie was at the bar. "This wouldn't happen if they hadn't taken Archer away." The Slammer took a few steps toward him and said, "The Yank's me mate." Bernie cowered and backed out the door. Marco and Sarah looked apprehensive but said nothing.

"Ta, mate," I said to the Slammer. "Join us for a pint."

My nose was bleeding, and my belly ached. Thank God for my huge mate.

"What was that about?" I asked Wombat and Skinner. They gave me a "Should we tell him?" look.

"You and the Dyno done right by me 'n Skinner. We didn't want to say, mate. Dyno ginked yer," Wombat said.

"She'll be right. Dyno's still me mate."

Wombat looked a little apprehensive and continued, "When yer in the shed a big bluey broke out. Archer grab Dyno Dan.

Shadow grab shoebox." He lowered his voice and looked toward Marco.

"Shadow give box to Marco. We sees it, Skinner and me."

"Aye," Skinner said. "Marco has another box like it under the bar. He grabs the box from Shadow, sets that one under the bar and puts the other one up on the shelf where every bloke sees."

"Aye," Skinner says emphatically.

"We sees it all." My huge mate, the Slammer, just stood there smiling, like he knew the story.

"Skinner, me mate," Wombat says proudly, "jump over the bar and wallop Marco who falls over Sarah. They both on floor, and we switch boxes back. They up to no good. No one sees we do it." He looks at Marco who is busy drawing a beer. "No one sees. Dyno got quid, not Bingos."

It took a minute for me to catch my breath. "They never got the money box?"

"Aye," Skinner said with some pride. "Nobody sees."

I said quickly, "Dyno's me mate. Still me mate. And yours." I circled my hand to the three of them. "Yer fair-dinkum Aussies. Bloody good on yer. Sarah, another shout." When she left, Wombat said, "Archer, Chuck and Bingos beat Shadow and Marco, for losing money box. Knocked them down and kicked them almost to death. Sarah stop them. They much mad."

"Not always honor among thieves," I muttered and smiled.

For several days I pondered this. Dan got the 50 grand and kept it for himself? Hard to believe. We were mates. He didn't mention money in his letter. I dug, shoveled, pulled and pondered, trying to make it all fit. Then I got his letter out of my foot locker and reread it:

> G'day, mate,
>   The bloody nose wasn't as bad as the kick in the face from Chuck. We owe him one, so if you get the chance... The swelling has gone down, and my sheila says "ta" and is happy I'm back. We'll discuss everything over a beer sometime. For now, be careful. They're rat bags who will stop at nothing. I won't give you any details about what you don't know. The less you know the better off you'll be for the next few weeks. The Slammer

is our good mate. As you may have heard, he helped
with my getaway and really enjoyed the dynamite blast.
When everything cools down, ask him to show you the
dead sheep.

Ta. Danny

What dead sheep? Whose dead sheep? I drove out to where
the Slammer was sinking the shaft. The claim owner was pulling
buckets for him, now that the shaft was deeper. "G'day, mate.
Like to talk to the Slammer."

"Bloke here to see yer," he yelled down the hole.

"It's the Yank," I yelled.

He came up on the rope, digging his new boots into the toe
kicks. His huge body filled the two-by-four-foot shaft.

"G'day mate."

We walked away from the shaft, leaving his employer standing
there with a puzzled look. "Danny said I should ask you to show
me the dead sheep."

"Dead sheep!" he said gleefully, and clapped his hands.
"Dead sheep! We go."

"Not now," I said. "You're working. I'll come back later."

"We go now."

He went back to the shaft, climbed down and came back up
with his shovel.

"Sorry," I said to the digger, "We'll be back."

The Slammer pointed, and I drove, without a clue where we
were going. After several miles of dodging mullock heaps, he
pointed to a heap of tailings around a shaft abandoned years ago.
On the tailings were the bones of a dead sheep, picked clean, with
bits of wool scattered around.

"Dead sheep," the Slammer said, smiling. He got his shovel
out of the car and said, "I dig."

"No, it's okay. Leave it be," I said. "The sheep has been dead
a long time. No need to bury it."

"I dig," he said. And he dug and dug. It was a big pile of
tailings, and he was well into it when his shovel hit metal. He dug
out a World War II munitions case and handed it to me. "Danny,
me mate, say for you."

It was heavy. I brushed off the dirt and unlatched the cover. It was filled with bundles of tenners. Now I understood. This was a hooly-dooly!

"Good on yer, mate," I said. He smiled. I wondered that he had kept the secret that long, but Dan must have told him to wait till I asked for it. He pulled a wad of tenners out of his pocket to show me.

"We mates," he said, and waved his hand between us. Dan had paid him well. I dropped him and his shovel back at the shaft and drove away with a new understanding of how things really were and a new feeling about life. The coolabah camp was just the place to count my new wealth. I laid the tenners out on the clay, 25 bundles of a hundred each. I shouted madly with joy! I danced around wildly trying to do a Highland fling. I couldn't resist unwrapping a bundle and flinging the whole wad into the air to catch in the breeze. I knew I could easily find the bills on the flat desert floor, no mater how far they blew. What a great feeling to fling money into the open air.

I laughed. Then a large emu and three smaller ones raced out of the bushes and started to gather and eat my bills. These stupid, ugly, stinking, pesky nuisance birds picked up the tenners and gulped them down. I hadn't seen an emu in months and had forgotten they existed. Now I was chasing after them shouting like a madman. One of the smaller ones picked up a bundle of a hundred. Fortunately it dropped the bundle when I almost had him by the neck. I chased the others away, gathered up my loose tenners and put them and the bundles all back in the munitions case. I could only find 78 of the loose bills. My fling had cost me 22 tenners, 220 quid, enough to live on for months, eaten by bloody emus. What a pub story this would make. I shook my head and laughed.

The next day, June 2, I surreptitiously drove into Walgett and booked a hotel room. How much should I send Willis, I wondered? His grubstake had made it all possible, and while the claim had yielded just over 1,000 quid in sold opals, I had a Radiant in my pocket that he doesn't know about, worth perhaps 40 or 50 grand. Or much more. But it's not for sale, not yet. We'll talk about that later. I'll give him half of the big take in cash, minus 5,000 in expenses and wages. Ten thousand pounds Australian is $22,500 American. Not a bad return on a grubstake of $400.

I bought an American cashier's check for 10,000 Australian pounds, wrote a long letter to Willis telling what had happened and promising to fill him in on the whole story when I next saw him. Then I spent the evening writing to Dan. What a story! I described everything, even the town meeting and the dead sheep. I apologized for not having yet slugged Chuck and promised to do it at the first opportunity. "Don't address a letter to me; write to the bush nurse using the return address of a hospital in Perth. She'll get it to me. Petula, the postmistress, has been known to steam letters open. Ta. The Yank."

With a hot shower and a good breaky, I wandered leisurely through the Walgett shops for hours before my rough ride back to the Wally. The bush nurse was having a slow day. We talked about my holiday and my bluey with Shadow and Chuck. She had heard about it and had set Shadow's broken arm. I warned her, "One more is coming with Chuck. I owe him for kicking Dan in the face." I asked her to join me on another picnic, sadly without Bruno. I promised to tell her the whole story if I could use her as a mailing address. She smiled and said, "Sunday, day after next."

"Fine, I'll pick you up. That'll give me a day to settle with Chuck."

Chapter XXXV
Wallies

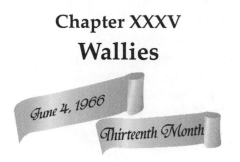

June 4, 1966

Thirteenth Month

I had to start the bluey with Chuck myself, something I had not done before. It's unsporting to just walk up and slug a bloke, though it happens regularly. I will call him out. He spends most of his day in the pub now. It must be in the morning, before lunch, when he's sober. Later than that, the whole pub might get into it, and if I wait until night, somebody might go down and get kicked, and it might be me.

I got to the bar a little after 10 a.m. Sarah, who never made small talk with me, put down my middy and said, "Gettin' into it early today?"

"I need to have a yarn with a bloke," I said with a smile. "Ah, here he is now." Chuck came in with Bernie, gave me a dirty look and ordered a pint.

I got right to it. "I owe you a kick in the face. Do you want it here or outside?"

He looked around, "Your Slammer waitin' out there to do your dirty work?"

"No, just me. To even the score."

"Right, mate, yer on."

He looked too confident. I'm not a fighter and thought I might end up with a kick in the face myself, but I had to go through with it to fulfill my promise to my mate. He stepped aside to let me go out first. I moved quickly, I didn't trust him behind me. We squared off. I just waded in, not knowing how to go about it. My body was all muscle; he had spent his years sitting on a stool cutting nobbies. He hit me a couple of blows, which rocked me but had little effect. I never realized how difficult it was to land a punch. I swung futilely several times and nearly lost my balance. We parried and danced around. He had been in blueys before and kept moving his head back and forth and hitting me with straight lefts. I was in better condition and finally connected with one blow that knocked him back against the pub's wall. Then, like I knew what I was doing, I hit him again. A blow to the stomach bent him over, and I finished with a solid kick to his chest. He fell to the ground groaning. He deserved a kick in the face, but my sense of fairness intervened. I turned to fat Bernie, who looked apprehensive. "You want to get into this?" He shook his head and backed off.

I went back into the bar, finished my pint and said to Sarah, "The Yank stands his shout – drinks for the house. Last time the Bingos paid with my quid; this time I pay myself." I laid a tenner on the bar. Sarah looked around. There weren't half a dozen blokes in the pub. "Use it when they come in," I said.

My self-instigated bluey was a success. I could get to like this. Then I remembered seeing blokes get knocked down and kicked by a mob full as googs and decided to avoid blueys. I was about to leave when I felt a hand on my shoulder, "Archer warned me about you. Said the Yank was nothing but trouble. We better talk." It was Sergeant Taylor; he was smiling. "I'm filling in until they find a replacement for Archer." We left the pub and walked down main street. I waited for him to speak.

"The inspector's still trying to sort out what happened up here. Benny's in the slammer and doesn't want to give back the money, but he will. Even at that he might be in the slammer for some time. The Bingos ginked a lot of blokes, but you and the Dyno did them in. I have to admire that. The inspector will never know all the details; it involved six or eight blokes, including Archer, and they all tell a different story. Maybe you'll give me the full yarn sometime over a pint. My shout." He smiled, turned and walked away. This bloke is okay, I thought.

It had been two months since I last saw the Professor. He was at his table, reading. My Morris Minor was right where I left it.

He looked up. "The fat kookaburra is singing, says it's all over. The final bluey was this morning, and you got thumped good," How could he know? Pub news travels fast, but this had happened less than an hour ago.

"Never laid a hand on me. Copped it in the first round, he did."

The Professor laughed, something he didn't often do. He went into his tent and came out with a shaving mirror. (He was one of the few in the Wally who had a mirror or shaved.) I looked into it and saw a black eye; a shiner.

"Aye, he may have landed a lucky punch or two," I admitted, "but he was soon down for the count." I paused a moment, set the bottle of scotch on the table and said, "It is over, all over." We set up the chess pieces and had a leisurely afternoon playing, talking and drinking rum-laced tea. I filled him in on the details. He enjoyed a good scam, especially one on the Bingos.

"Good on you, mate. Well done. You had me stumped. I'm glad to hear you ended up with the tucker. That was iffy for a while."

Then later on, "I started your Morris every week to charge the battery. It's fine."

"I'm not sure what I'll do with it. Can it stay here a while longer?"

He nodded in agreement. I told him the news about Wee Wah.

"Too bad about the bumper crop," he said. "Now they'll never leave. But their children will learn to speak Aussie and settle in. There is always hope for the next generation."

After a couple hours of chess, rum and tea, I said, "I have to leave the Wally. My time here is finished."

He pondered this. "It's not that easy to leave," he said. "What do you do with it? Where do you keep it? Or hide it? Can't destroy it. Can't leave without it. Can't leave with it." He, too had had a lot of rum and tea, and his mind was meandering – talking not about me but about himself. I knew now that he also had a Radiant. I felt my pocket; mine was secure.

"It's not over," he said as he got up and walked around. "It's never over. Never. You'll be back. Some day you'll be back."

The next day Nell was waiting for me with a lunch basket. "I hope you made chicken sandwiches again," I said with anticipation. The general store usually had beef and lamb but not chicken.

"I did," she said, and we were off to the 10-mile Warrambool. This time I vowed not to do something stupid. We walked through the termite mounds and spread the blanket on a nice flat surface.

"It's not the same without Bruno splashing through the water," she said.

"No, I miss him greatly."

She laid out the food. How nice are the simple things of life. The sandwiches, chockos, carrots, pickles, apples, oranges and brownies exemplified life in abundance. Aussies always live in abundance, even when short on a quid. We ate.

"I can't help but notice that you had your bluey with Chuck – our former cutter." Interesting. Seems Chuck is out of business, also.

"Aye, I didn't think Chuck had done any damage until I stopped at the Professor's for a game of chess. He has a mirror and enjoyed showing me my shiner."

"Ah, the Professor. The most interesting bloke on the Wally." Then she caught herself, "Except for you, I mean."

I laughed. "He's way beyond me. I've played a lot of chess with him, but I still don't know what he is doing here."

"He's quiet about himself, but Petula – she who analyzes the mail – says he has a lot of correspondence with universities. He's a friend of mine." She paused. "He likes to talk to someone outside the pub once in a while."

"Has he told you why he left the academic world to live in the Jungle?"

"No, she laughed. "But everybody here has a story from the past. I've heard the rumors about some illicit sexual encounter and his dismissal, but I don't believe it." After a thoughtful pause, she added, "He said he came up here for a holiday several times and decided to take a year or two off and have a look for opal."

"That sounds familiar," I said. "Now maybe he can't leave."

She looked perplexed. I skipped the whole thing about being obsessed with a fatal opal. "Great sandwiches! Baked chicken on homemade bread with lots of butter topped with homemade mayonnaise, salt, pepper, and a leaf of lettuce. You are a wonderful cook."

"All this praise. Does that mean you'll marry me?" she said with a smile.

This was dangerous territory, and I quickly changed the subject. "No, but I will think about it while I have another sandwich and a glass of lemonade." I went on. "He taught metaphysics and must have been great. He says Immanuel Kant was an isolated thinker, and Schopenhauer is more social. Schopenhauer said Kant told it all in one book, and the rest of his books are redundant. Few understand enough to criticize Kant and the Prof likes Schopenhauer, who explained great ideas in ordinary language."

Nell and I went on to Dickens and English literature. It was a pleasant afternoon, and she was good company. On the way back to the car, I jumped up on a termite mound just for the fun of it. She smiled.

For the next few days I tried to dig, but acute withdrawal and paranoia had set in. I suspected everyone of talking about me, conspiring against me. I knew this was absolute nonsense, but the thoughts kept crowding into my mind. My hatred of the Bingos was gone but I was losing my love of life. Mozart was no comfort. Brahms, Schubert and Mendelssohn had become distant. I couldn't even conjure up Berlioz, but I could still tune in mentally on the *Ride of the Valkyrie*. My Radiant, which I looked at several times a day, gave comfort but did not cheer me. This is the Wallies: lethargy, animosity, acute withdrawal and paranoia. I promised myself a year ago that I would leave when that happened, but a voice within me said, "You can't leave. You are home where you want to be, where you belong. You are here with your Radiant. Gemstones lie under your feet. There are no opals under the Big Smoke."

I found Wombat and Skinner in the pub having a pint and a pie.

"G'day, mates. 'oweryergoin'?" I shouted another pint and ordered a pie for myself. "If yer got the time, I'd like to have a yarn by my Yank's Dig later this afternoon."

"Righto, mate. We be there."

I found the Slammer and told him the same. Then I had Sergeant Taylor draw up some transfer papers. When they showed up, I took them down the shaft. "This claim has produced some good gemstones. I'm leaving the Wally and giving the claim to the three of you; we're mates."

"Aye, mate, take another holiday. We need yer here."

"No. It's time to hump me bluey. I'll miss me mates." I gave Wombat the transfer papers and told them where I thought the next pocket might be. "When Wombat says dig," I said to the Slammer with a smile, "You dig. When he says to stop digging, you stop. That means you are on opal and need to be careful."

"Aye, mate. I dig. I stop."

I gave them each a wad of 500 quid. They almost had tears in their eyes, but Outback Aussies don't cry. Just a simple, "Ta, mate."

"I'll say goodbye, then. It's all yours. Now, if you'll all come with me, Skinner can bring the dry puddler up here, and I'll take Wombat to the Professor's and give you the Morris Minor. It won't make it into Walgett, but it'll get you around the claims."

Only a short time ago I camped under the coolabah and had one mate. Now I have several blokes to bid goodbye. We dropped Skinner and the Slammer at the puddler, and I showed them how to start it. Then I took Wombat to the Professor's, gave him the keys to the van and bid him farewell. He left.

Then to the Professor: "One last game of chess before the fat kookaburra sings again?"

"Okay, Yank. I'm sorry to see you go. I don't know how much longer I'll be here myself." We played several games with little conversation and much rum. It's hard to say goodbye to good mates. I carefully guided my Holden through the trees, knowing I would never see the Professor or the others again. It was over.

The next day I stopped at the bush nurse's office and told Nell I was leaving. "I never mentioned how nice you look in your new clothes," she said and started crying. She always wore a white nurse's uniform and looked good, if no one had recently bled on her. "I have a letter for you." She handed me a letter from Perth and started crying again. I held her in my arms a long time. She was a good friend. I would miss her softness of character and body. I kissed her on the lips for the first time and hurried out the door.

Next the Scots. "I've decided to rent out the mud humpy to a family from Brisbane with seven kids. I told them how much you two like children and would be happy to help take care of them." I had never seen the Scots silent before. I opened a beer and sat down casually.

"Ah, c'mon, mate. Don't be a gallah. We can get enough hard kack on our own."

"It won't be so bad. They can afford to pay two quid a week, and I told them you'd help out with the groceries and beer and give the father 15 quid a day to help you mine."

They both jumped up like a scorpion had stung them. I couldn't help but laugh. Then they knew they had been had. We all laughed. I told them I was leaving. They had expected as much. I also said goodbye to Angus and Garbhan. We had another beer but not much conversation.

"You'll be back, Yank," they said. "You'll be back."

My stone. My Radiant. My fatal opal. My Chungula! I contemplated selling it to Angus. It easily would bring more than 50,000 quid. Over a $100,000 American, when going wages were under $5,000 a year! I could live where I want and do what I want. It's just a stone. Sell it. Dump it. Get rid of it. Think of life on a South Sea island with native girls in grass skirts dancing around a fire. Ah! Why not?

I looked at my Radiant, long and carefully. Next morning I packed up my few belongings in a duffle bag and left the five-dollar footlocker filled with non-essentials for the Scots to dispose of. With one small shovel, I drove to my coolabah camp where I had been so content camping with Bruno. After looking furtively in all directions to make certain no one was around, I looked for the last time at my Chungula, then packed it carefully, surrounded by ready-rubbed tobacco, in a Dr. Pat's tin, and buried it next to Bruno. That was it. It was over. I had rid myself of the fatal opal that could have destroyed me like the Colonel, Hungry Hank and Two-Bob Bobby. They were weak-willed and suffered from the fatal greed of possession. They let Ooluhru steal their soul. They showed their stones to others, which increased his power over them. But not me. No one else on earth had seen my Chungula; it was mine and mine alone, and I alone determined its fate. Now it was back in the ground and had no power over me. Ooluhru could no longer peer into my soul. I was free. Free to return to the real world, the world of people. Free forever from Ooluhru and the curse.

I felt elated as I departed my Radiant, my Bruno and my coolabah. "Goodbye to the three of you. Rest in peace. I will see you never again."

As I drove toward Walgett, colors appeared in the windshield, the flashing violets and golds of my Radiant. "Give up, Ooluhru," I said out loud. "I'm out of your territory, out of your reach, and your eye is buried in a tobacco tin. You no longer have power over me."

The colors lessened with the miles and were gone as I neared Sydney.

Chapter XXXVI
Homeward

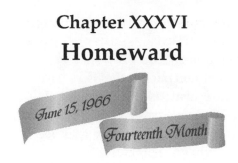

The Professor's words haunted me. "Once in possession of his fatal stone, he dies with it in his hand. That is the curse of the Radiant opal, the scourge of Wallangulla." But he was wrong. I have escaped. And in time I also will be free of the Wallies. I wended my way to Kings Cross, then to Hardie Street in Darlinghurst. Madam Baker's door that always had been open was locked. I rapped. Then rapped harder. A second-floor window flew open, and a woman stuck out her head.

"What'd yer want?"

"I'm looking for Madam Baker."

"She died." Slam, the window came down. That was that. My first friend in Australia was no longer. The woman next door, Mrs. O'Connell, also ran a rooming house, which Madam Baker had said was a brothel at one time. She had an empty room. Fat, coarse, crude and ill kempt, she was Madam's opposite. I hauled my things in and read Dan's letter. He was glad things had worked out well. We had pulled it off. He'd purchased a piece of land, married his sheila and planned on starting a family. All thanks to the Bingo Brothers. He was a good mate, but now that too is over.

The next day I went down to the docks to see what ships were in port. By sheer coincidence, the M/S Belgrano occupied Dock 5. I climbed on board. The young seamen I had known were gone; they had signed on for one trip before settling down in their trades back in Hamburg. I would have enjoyed working my way back on the ship, but the boatswain, steward and cook, whom I knew from the voyage here, said the ship no longer took workaways.

Back at Mrs. O'Connell's, I told another roomer my story. He said, "I signed two months ago to work my way back home on an American ship."

"I didn't know you could do that. I thought you had to have seaman's papers."

"No. Seamen jump ship, get sick or fake an illness. The company has to fly them back to San Francisco and fill the vacancy with anyone who's available in port. An Australian girl at the American Embassy said I was twelfth on the list and would have to wait my turn. I told her I already had been waiting a month. I'm an American citizen. She better get me on the next ship, or I'll have her fired. She'll be right, was the only thing I could get out of her, whatever that means. They shouldn't have foreigners working at the embassy. It's not right."

The next morning I went to the American Embassy and found the young lady. "G'day. 'oweryergoin'. I'm just off a year on the Wally. If a bloke had a spot on a Yank ship, she'd be right and I could show me stones." I sounded like Two-Bob Bobby.

"Good on yer. Not to worry, she'll be right."

"Know a pub with good tucker?"

"The Pig 'n Whistle's nice. I stop after work."

"Righto."

I said nothing to my fellow American at the rooming house. The sheila and I had steak and a few pints at the Pig 'n Whistle. I showed her my parcel of opals and gave her a small mug stone. She was nice. I never knew her name. Three days later I got a telegram: USS Sierra, Dock 10.

The 400-pound chief steward interviewed me and said I could have the job of third cook, but my beard would have to go. Fine.

"What happened to the third cook?" I asked.

"He was from Watts and just got tired of working. Said he didn't feel well. They'll fly him back to Los Angeles. Happens every trip."

Thanks to him, with a job and union dues paid, I could get seaman's papers.

Three happy, laughing, young, Italian immigrant barbers greeted me at the door of the barbershop. Business was slow. They took turns cutting off parts of my beard, standing back and laughing. Finally they got it all off. Then they laid me flat back and covered my face with hot towels. I thought of the opera, *The Marriage of Figaro*, and almost started singing, but they would have joined in, and then I'd never get out of there. The straightedge razor, having been stropped, flowed gently and expertly over my soaped face. It was my first barber shave. Safety razors had brought a change to the social life of men, who now shave themselves. I would have enjoyed the barbershop companionship of the old days.

I boarded the USS Sierra on June 21. My forecastle mate was steward to the officers. He was a poker player, and we seldom saw each other. My bunk was port to starboard, with straps for rough seas. The third cook, me, makes breakfast, peels vegetables, scrubs pots and pans and helps out wherever necessary. I was bent over the sink, scrubbing pots, when the second cook, Wesley, came up behind me and whispered in my ear, "You wouldn't have bent over in front of me like that 25 years ago." I straightened up. He laughed. He was a poofter but past the active age, and turned out to be helpful. He showed me how to make pancakes and fluffy omelets, poach eggs, fry eggs sunny-side-up, over easy, medium and hard, and boil four-minute eggs exactly right for the captain's breakfast (or he sent them back). The captain was fussy but had no authority concerning food on a union ship. He ate what the seaman ate. If he wanted a special dish, he had to buy one for every man on board, so that never happened.

The first cook prepares the meats and the soups. He stuck a long meat fork into his knee to show me his wooden leg, the result of a motorcycle accident. The second cook is the baker and cooks the vegetables. They both had a sense of humor. I settled in quickly.

As we set out for Tasmania and Melbourne, the weather got rough. I rapped on the first cook's door and asked, "Should I close the windows in the kitchen?"

"You may secure the ports in the galley," he stated pointedly.

One day at sea is much like the rest, and all days soon became routine. We left Melbourne in mid-August. "How long have you been down here?" Wesley asked.

"A couple years. Why?

"You'll be surprised at how much has changed. A professor at Harvard, Dr. Timothy O'Leary, has found God with a drug called LSD."

"How does he know it's God and not the devil?"

Wesley smiled. "And how do we know he's not crazy? But LSD is now the big rage. We also have permanent press pants, just wash and wear."

"Sounds like someone is trying to put mothers out of business."

"Motherhood is another thing," Wesley went on. "Birth control pills are in common use. Mothers may cease to be."

I had some catching up to do.

My tin of Dr. Pat tobacco was used up. I bought a pack of cigarettes at the commissary; filter tips. They were awful. "What are they doing to cigarettes, Wesley?"

"Nothing different than before you left. You're just not used to them. With filters they use cheaper tobacco and chop up the stems as well as the leaves. The stems are where the pesticides are heaviest." He laughed. I threw my pack overboard and quit smoking.

Ships make constant noise. I missed Helga, the quiet of the Wally and Dr. Pat smokes. The crew of 50 was old compared to that on the Belgrano, due to seaman's union seniority in hiring. The higher wages and union dues spawned more seaman than jobs. Three days before docking in San Francisco, the crew started drinking. I said to Wesley, "I would think they'd want to be sober coming into the home port with their families and friends."

"Most of their wives got tired of waiting and left years ago," he explained. "If you go to sea often enough and stay long enough there is nothing to come back to, friends or family."

The first cook was currently on his third wife, but he hit the bottle heavily just out of port. "She'd better be there," he muttered. "She'd better be on that dock when we pull in," he said to no one in particular.

"The day will come when 'she' is not there either," Wesley said. "It happens sooner or later, no matter how many times you marry." As it turned out, she was there, waiting at midnight when we pulled into the dock.

We were paid in cash at the homeport, as is customary, in $100 bills. The next morning I took a bus to Santa Rosa and was welcomed so warmly by my shirt-tail relatives the Boratchiks that I stayed two weeks. Walt Boratchiks, his wife Evie and their five children heard more about my trip and opals than they wanted but were kind listeners. The weather was always nice, and the house was crowded so I slept on a cot in the backyard with their dog, Frocious.

I had to pick up the pieces of my interrupted life. It was too late to teach school this year, so I bought a 10-year-old Frazer automobile and set out to visit Willis on the other side of the country. Reno, Nevada, my first stop, was located, like Wallangulla, in the middle of the desert, but it was filled with casinos. I gambled several hundred dollars away and sampled the food on Virginia Street. Harold's Club was my favorite, and Harold Smith's book, *I Want to Quit Winners*, became part of my library. It is a simple book about a very average man who became a millionaire by running an honest casino and almost lost it gambling in Las Vegas. Omar Khayyam took a back seat; he doesn't fit in *this* desert.

After several days I shoved off again on the new freeway system, "one long road going nowhere." Roads became more crowded and people less friendly as I went east. It was hard to find Willis. His street address was common in several other villages around Media, Pennsylvania, and there is no way to tell when you leave one village and enter another.

Willis had married, settled and led a busy life. He thanked me for the money. I told him it would not have happened without his help. I gave him and his wife a few opals but said nothing about the Radiant. He was pleased to have been a part of the successful scam. After a few days I left for Minnesota, apprehensive about going home.

My parents were happy to see me. "Sonja is married," my mother said sadly. "She didn't think you were ever coming back."

A big sigh, then, "Such a lovely girl." I thought; good for her. I have enough problems. My mother had the jelly opal I gave her set in a ring, and the black gem became my father's tie tack.

My mother said, "It's too late this year to get a teaching job, but we hope you find a good school for next year. We're so glad you're back. We hope you got that traveling out of your system. You belong here, with your friends and family. Your brother wants to see you."

My brother lived close to our parents in the little town of Maples, 30 miles out of Minneapolis. He yelled into the living room where his four children were watching television, "Your Uncle Anskar is back from Australia." No answer. He tried again, "Your Uncle Anskar spent a year in the Outback of Australia mining opals." No answer. "He has some opals to show you that he dug up himself in Australia."

The oldest boy said, "Yeah, we saw a program on Australia a couple of weeks ago." That was it. How life had changed! My generation, as children, sang and talked whenever we got together. If someone had even been as far as South Dakota, I sat in rapt attention and devoured every detail of the trip. Now a trip halfway across the world can't compete with television. No dancing flames or flashing opals for them, just moving blobs on a TV screen. God help us.

My friend from college, Grant, had an apartment in Minneapolis with two bedrooms and invited me to stay with him while I went about the process of finding myself. We had sung in many choral groups together as well as the college choir that sang with the Minneapolis Symphony. We frequented the numerous piano bars in Minneapolis. My tenor blended well with his bass. I was asked frequently, after singing *Waltzing Mathilda*, what a jumbuck, billabong and coolabah were. Swagmen and waltzing Mathilda were more difficult to explain, and I sometimes choked up. But it was good to sing again, even in bars. Sometimes we found an alto and soprano to harmonize with to fill out a quartet.

Nothing permanent appealed to me. I didn't want a long-term commitment, so I got a job at the post office on Central Avenue in nordeast Minneapolis and settled in. Work started at 6 a.m. and finished at 2:30 p.m. I was a sub carrier, filling in for other carriers on their days off. Not a bad life. I pigeonholed the letters, tied them in bundles called splits, put them in storage boxes along the route, then walked door to door, house to house, through sleet, rain, hail and snow. On cold mornings, round, friendly Polish women reached out through doors that were never locked and pulled me inside, insisting that I have a glass of wine and a piece of apple pie. The children of these warm, friendly people had prospered, and the next generation was moving to the suburbs.

Grant was a good friend and understood why I cried out at night, dreaming, when my razor-sharp pick nicked a nobby and the brilliant, flashing colors poured out in the candlelight, 30 feet underground. And why I twisted and turned in my sleep, prying stones out of the hard clay.

Still, I could not even tell him about my Radiant, my stone that could support Helga and me in comfort for the rest of our lives. My stone that would have looked so delightful around her lovely neck. My stone that I could still visualize in every detail, the beautiful harlequin-shaped patches of seven different scintillating colors, dancing in the light, changing with each turn. I could see it so clearly.

"You can leave the Wally," the Professor had said, "but the Wally never leaves you."

I miss the dancing flames of the fire, the quiet, the stars overhead and the isolation. Here I am never alone, devoured by noise and crowds. Life is indoors. Television is a substitute for dancing flames to gaze into. No gemstones to examine and talk about. How can I live without a struggle, without passion, without hope? Can I live here as a teacher?

My life is empty. One day is just like the next. Week after week, month after month. I can't draw my Viking sword and run the Skraelings through; they are not to be found. An unseen enemy is destroying me. I look at those around me and asked, "Are they the ones doing this to me? Are they the enemy? Do I want to be like them?"

I have no wealth. Wealth is family, friends, community. Wealth is loving and being loved. I do not fit into this life marked only by a biweekly paycheck. Tomorrow's dig will yield the same as yesterdays: no gemstones, no surprises and no fortune. That life is gone and I cannot return to my previous life, which is also gone. I have nothing. My Radiant is buried in the Outback, and my Helga has found her warrior and is waiting for him to be wounded so she can heal him.

Grant married. His life changed, and so did mine. I stayed on in the apartment after he and his wife moved into a house, knowing I would have to do something soon, but not knowing what.

Then, almost miraculously, I received a letter addressed to The Yank, Wallangulla, Australia, that had been forwarded to my parents address in Minnesota. Petula kept track of everything.

> *Dear Yank*
>
> *Just wondering how things are going for you in your new life, or maybe I should say, in continuation of your old life. I am still finding Oskulden settlements in Iceland. Interesting reconnecting with new friendships that go back a thousand years. I spend a lot of time in the Sagas.*
>
> *Love, Helga*

> *I answered:*
>
> *Dear Helga*
>
> *My return to my old life is empty. It doesn't work. I must escape. I want to live as an Outback Aussie and die like a Viking. You will not hear from me again. I hope your Viking warrior is soon wounded so you can heal him.*

She answered:

Dear Yank

> *You dill. You are my Viking warrior, and you have*
> *been wounded in the battle with an unseen, devastating*
> *enemy — the Skraeling who does not show his face. You*
> *want to live as an Outback Aussie and die like a Viking?*
> *I will join you, my love. I will join you forever.*
>
> *Your Valkyrie*

I crawled into my old Frazer and fled west across the mountains to the vast Pacific that leads to the Wally.

Chapter XXXVII

Valhalla

Later...

I wasn't noodling. I was pretending to noodle while looking for Chungula buried under the coolabah, near Bruno. I scraped and dug, furtively glancing around into the bushes and out across the great Outback, watching for those who would take her from me. They are so many and so determined. I must be constantly alert. My shovel hit metal, the Dr. Pat's tin. I brushed off the clay and opened it, freeing my Chungula, locked up like a common criminal for nearly a year, glowing, surrounded by tobacco.

The setting sun flashed out of her Radiant colors: violet, red, gold, chartreuse, yellow, green. I clasped her to my bosom, happy to be reunited, never again to part. The Professor was right; I did return, but I didn't talk to him – too risky. I don't think he is one of them but I can't chance it. I cooked a stew, boiled a billy and rolled a Dr. Pat from the tobacco that had encompassed my Radiant for so long. How good to once again taste the full rich flavor of prime tobacco. I sat back and gazed at my Chungula sparkling in the firelight. I have found myself. I know who I am and why I am here. I am at peace.

The future is destined. Tonight with Chungula tightly in my fist, my jacket rolled up for a pillow, I will sleep under my coolabah. Soon Helga will join me; life will be complete. We will have a breaky of styk 'n eggs and fried bread, a nice cuppa and a Dr. Pat. Then arm in arm, with Chungula securely in my hand, we will walk out across the great Outback until we come to the day of Ragnarok. Then, joining our fellow Vikings, we will fight the final battle between good and evil. As has been foretold, we will fight bravely and die cheerfully: a heroic death in a hopeless cause.

Here is what will happen.

I, with my sword, and Helga, with her spear will plunge into the thick of the battle, slashing and impaling. But there are too many of these damnable Skraelings. Hundreds, thousands of evil little dwarfs coming at us from all directions. Again I am flat on my back, bleeding from many wounds, trying to protect Helga, slashing out to keep the Niebelungen at bay. I want to die in Valhalla, not on this bloodied field of Niebelungen. Will Voltronga arrive in time to save us?

I hear *The Ride of the Valkyrie*. Violins swoop in on the first glissandos, then the horns and the rich, full-throated trombones make their majestic entrance fortissimo. The third trumpet soars into the heavenly sphere, announcing the Valkyrie. The music trembles the earth as our maidens charge through the celestial sphere to reclaim the fallen warriors. Hy Yah Tow – **Ha**, Hy Yah Tow – Ha, Bruinhilda and her sisters sing as they pass overhead. Helga leaps up shouting Hy Yah Tow – **Ha**, Hy yah Tow – **Ha**, brandishing her spear. The Niebelungen flee. Again she is my Valkyrie.

I see the magnificent black mare, Voltronga, her mighty wings piercing the air. I hold up my flashing Chungula to guide her on her quest. She alights forcefully, stomping and snorting, her powerful wings beating down the Niebelungen. My Valkyrie smiles, touches my wounds, which stop bleeding; kisses my forehead; gathers me up in her strong arms, and mounts. "Fly, Voltronga. Fly elegantly," she says. "It is the day of Ragnarok, our final battle. We will depart with dignity and pride. Wotan awaits us." Chungula's brilliant colors flow through the night sky as we majestically leave the field of battle for the last time.

Valhalla is ablaze with torchlight. The earthshaking horns of Gotterdammerung fill the great hall, joyously heralding our coming demise. The Viking warriors are gathered for the ultimate toast. "Not to worry, mate. She'll be right," I say to myself as I hack off chunks of roasted wild boar and fill our stoups with mead. I gaze at Chungula, shinning brightly, and look into Helga's eyes. We are together: my stone, my Valkyrie and me, surrounded by Viking warriors. Life is accomplished.

As midnight nears we gather in the center of the great hall, solemnly waiting for the clock to strike. At the first bong we raise high our stoups and shout, "Skula Wotan, Hail to the chief of the Viking gods," as the walls come crashing down.

Bong, bong, bong. Again we raise high our stoups and shout, "Skula Ragnarok, Hail to the final battle between the forces of good and evil," as the castle of Valhalla crumbles around us.

Bong, bong, bong. Finally we raise high our stoups and shout "Skula Dauoa! Hail to death, an end to it all" as the hordes of evil Niebelungen pour over the rubble with their bloodied swords slashing furiously at all and sundry.

With Chungula between our palms, my Helga and I clasp our weapon hands together in the Viking farewell and press tightly for the final knells: bong, bong, bong. Then it is over. Helga will be with her Valkyrie sisters. Chungula will return to the earth and again be an eye of the half-devil, half-serpent, Ooluhru. And I – I at last shall be rid of my fatal stone, free from the Curse of the Radiant Opal.

The End

Helga's Epilogue

Later still...

It was a difficult trip. I had a hard time finding Anskar and was late getting there. Anskar had been camped by his coolabah for a week or more before I arrived. He had run out of food, was short on water and in a frenzy.

"Thank Wotan you made it. I was afraid they had you, and I would have to walk to the day of Ragnarok alone."

I thought, "Who are *they*? And how can you walk to the day of Ragnarok, and why would you want to?"

"We must be careful," he said waving an imaginary sword. "The Niebelungen are all around us. They are after my Chungula. Hurry. We must get to Ragnarok and join the battle."

I realized my chosen Viking was quite mad and living in a fantasy world he had concocted in his demented mind. "Ragnarok cannot happen without us; the battle will wait," I said, nonsensically. "We must eat first and prepare for the big fight." He was deep into the Wallies. Can I save him? Will he ever recover?

I hadn't known what to expect so I came fully equipped with firewood, sleeping bags, camp stools (I never was fond of sitting on a log), a canvas water bag to hang from the coolabah tree, bread, steak, bacon, eggs, tins of food, cans of water and even a couple of bottles of rum. He relaxed his sword arm somewhat as I unloaded the supplies.

I started a fire, boiled the billy and fried steak and eggs. He looked at the food as though he hadn't eaten in days. I handed him his plate of steak and eggs and fried two slices of bread. He ate greedily, furtively looking around like we were in danger of being attacked at any moment. He was frightened and disoriented.

"Don't worry," I said. "We are together now and have time to prepare."

"No," he said. "There is no time. We must go. Now!"

"Ragnarok can not happen without us. We are Ragnarok." I blurted out this twaddle not knowing what I was saying nor why, but the only way to talk to a madman is with gibberish. "We must eat, rest and get ready for the battle." He settled down.

What could I do? I didn't know what was going on in his head. Will I have to become crazy like him to reclaim him? Will I have to wield an imaginary sword in an imaginary battle? If he were bleeding, I could dress his wounds. If he had a broken arm I could set it. But he was ranting balderdash. Maybe a change of subject would help.

"I haven't seen your Radiant opal." He looked apprehensive and then decided he could trust me. He reached into his pocket, pulled out a white handkerchief and unfolded it. Bright colors shot out, beautiful, vivid hues sparkling in the sunlight. I had an overwhelming urge to grab it, hold it and take it for my own. I leaned forward.

He drew back. "No, it is mine and mine alone. I will carry it to Valhalla and die with it in my hand." He folded it back in his handkerchief, returned it to his pocket and sat moping by the fire. I now had an inkling of the power a Radiant wields over its possessor. I also understood that this stone is the key to his madness. I can't compete with its beauty. I must destroy it to break its hold on him. But how can I do that without destroying him?

"Let's take a walk," I said. He had written me about Bruno. "I'll fill in for Bruno and watch for snakes." He didn't find this amusing. I said no more. We walked for half an hour, with Anskar continually glancing around to make sure *they* weren't following us. I wondered, "How am I going to heal my broken Viking?"

He sat quietly for the rest of the day. After a tin of stew and a cuppa, I spread the sleeping bags under the coolabah, and we lay down separately, his stone, Chungula, closed tightly in his fist under the jacket he used for a pillow. This was not the man I knew. This was a stranger. I must get my Viking back. I drifted off into a fitful sleep.

After breaky and a cuppa, I noticed his car, an old Holden. "Is that a rental?" I asked.

"No, it's a junker. I just needed something to get me here, a one-way trip." I looked at him quizzically. He smiled. "Ragnarok is the way to Valhalla, and Valhalla is the final triumph. The glory of a heroic death awaits."

He really is mad, I thought. I got up to walk around and clear my head and looked into the car. "What's the box in the back seat?"

"Just my writings. With so much time here and such a different life, I wrote down everything from the first day I arrived on the Wally, planning to write a book someday. I'll leave my writings here. Maybe someone will find them and mail them to my friend back in Minnesota. His name is on the box, in care of our college."

His writings might explain what is going on, I thought.

"May I read them?"

"Go ahead. It doesn't matter now; it's all over."

I opened the box and started reading tablet after tablet written in longhand in pencil. I read all day, then the next day and half of the third. He grew impatient, but I convinced him to keep watch for the Niebelungen, and I plied him with food and tea spiked with rum. "We must be well fed, strong and clear-headed when we march into battle," I said, stalling for time.

I discovered that he had worked out an elaborate mythology centered on Chungula, his fatal Radiant opal, and me, his Valkyrie. He had created a fantasy and sunk deeper and deeper into his delusional world. He even wrote about our demise. He plans to take Chungula and me into battle and death, a fulfilling death for him, like the Goat Colonel, Hungry Hank and Two-Bob Bobby. For him death is only one battle away, and he is eager to get on with it. Now I understand. He cannot part with his fatal Radiant and must die with it in his hand.

After hours and hours of reading, I realized it's not only the curse of his Radiant opal I have to contend with; he is also deep into the Wallies. The Wallies I can cure with good food, love and the company of friends. That can wait. I must first free him from the Curse of the Radiant Opal. A plan formed in my mind.

He was sitting by the fire smoking one Dr. Pat after another. "You've wasted two whole days," he said irritably. "We must march to Ragnarok and our destiny," he said as his imaginary sword swept out over the desert.

"Yes, it is time," I answered. "We will rest today and march into battle tomorrow morning." He wants a battle, I thought. I will give him a battle. According to his plan we walk into the desert until we come to the day of Ragnarok. Then, defeated in battle and near death, my winged mare Voltronga will carry us safely from the field of battle into Valhalla, where we will die surrounded by Vikings. In reality we will expire of thirst and exhaustion in the endless Outback while having delusions of grandeur.

Not if I can help it!

He was sitting by the fire smiling and looked content for the first time since I arrived. I pried a hubcap off his junker auto and slashed four slots in it with the hatchet. I ran one of my belts through the slots and buckled it to make a shield. I cut a hefty branch off the coolabah. The small end became a sword, his sword; the heavy shaft a spear, my spear. I sharpened it to a point. "For tomorrow's battle," I said, waving the weapons. He nodded but really wasn't interested. His imaginary battle needed no paraphernalia; he could fight the Skraelings with an air sword.

After a hearty supper of steak, eggs and fried bread, I again served him many cups of rum tea and talked about the thrilling days of the Sagas. I wanted my wounded Viking to sleep soundly and not be fully awake in the morning. His fist held Chungula tightly inside his rolled-up jacket pillow as he fell into the world of Morpheus.

I awakened him at dawn, shouting, "It is the day of Ragnarok! The battle awaits us!" I threw his shoes at him and said, "Hurry!" I strapped the hubcap shield to his arm; his clenched fist still held Chungula. He was in his skivvies, the way I wanted him. I handed him his swordstick. Then before he was fully awake, I ripped off my blouse. He was stunned, having never seen my naked body before. I picked up my sharpened spear, yelled "Follow me!" and ran off into the Outback. He followed, stumbling, in a state of bewilderment.

He was weak. I continued to run until he fell down exhausted. Lifting him up I yelled, "Look out; they're behind you!" As he turned I banged his shield, swatted him with the spear and stuck him with the point. "Now they're over here!" I yelled again and swatted and stuck him again. "They're everywhere, all around us! Look out! Don't you see them? Hundreds of Niebelungen charging from all directions!" He kept turning in confusion. I dragged my spear point over his body to make sword slashes and stuck him many more times. I kept this up until he was in a state of shock, still waving his swordstick in the empty air.

Then with the thick end of my spear, I hit him on the head so hard it knocked him down unconscious. My wounded warrior lay bleeding on the ground at my feet. This is the man I love; the man I have lied to, deceived and beaten to a pulp. His world was imaginary. His wounds were real.

As he came to and started to move, I brandished my spear. "Hark! Voltronga is coming! I hear the beating of her mighty wings." He was completely baffled, seeing nothing but believing everything. Using his words but not knowing how to sing them, I brandished my spear overhead and shouted like a Valkyrie, "Hi Ya Tow, Ha. Hi Ya Tow, Ha."

I bent over him and said in a soft voice, "Your Valkyrie is here. You are safe now. We are together." I brushed his hair from his forehead and kissed him gently. I gathered my poor, confused Viking up in my arms; he clung to me. I carried my dazed warrior back to the shade of the coolabah and dressed his wounds with ointments. He slept.

When he awoke, still bewildered, I said, "Your Valkyrie is here," touched his wounds to heal and comfort him and then eased him back to sleep.

Much later he awoke again. I touched his wounds again, kissed him and made love to him for the first time. Again he slept.

Later, when he awakened more consciously, I made love to him again. He smiled and seemed to be rejoining the real world. Now I knew I must act quickly.

"Open your hand and look at your stone!" I commanded.

"No," he said, pulling his hand close to his body, "No, It is mine."

"Open it!" I commanded again. He looked sullen but put his hand forward and opened it. The stone was dull and lifeless. He gazed at it in disbelief. "I am your Valkyrie; you are mine now. Give that colorless stone back to Ooluhru. Fling it to the dingos. It is worthless."

After a long pause he looked at the stone, then at me, then at the stone again and back at me. He sat upright and flung the worthless gem into the great Outback. It was finished. I had my Viking. He had his Valkyrie. The battle of Ragnarok was over. Now we will create our own Valhalla.

Still later, on the Icelandic Isle of Oskulden.

Anskar and his new Viking mates are building our house on a promontory just up the mountain from the village, overlooking the great rolling expanse of ocean. From here we can see both sunrise and sunset.

I will make him happy. He will be a good husband and a caring father. We will name our first son Baldur, after the bravest, wisest and most handsome of the gods. Our first daughter will be Freja, the goddess of love. I will teach her the healing arts, so she will be prepared to rescue her own fallen Viking.

Our rescued warriors row out to sea in longboats to fish and come home fulfilled and happy. Or they go up the mountain with spears and bows to hunt the wild boar. My sister Valkyrie and I tend the cattle, milk the goats, make cheese, gather honey for mead and laugh and sing together with the playing children. Evenings we gather around the fire, eat roasted wild boar, tell tales of the Sagas and toast Wotan, Thor and Freja with stoups of mead.

Life is complete.

I typed Anskar's memoir and read it to my sister Valkyrie while our mates were off hunting. It is a good story, and the time has come to send it to his friend in Minnesota. I know it is time because this morning he put his arms around me and said, "You are the most precious thing I have ever held. Here I will stay with my Valkyrie, forever."

His old life is over. We have our new life together. His fatal stone, the Scourge of Wallangulla, is no more, and we are free of the Curse of the Radiant Opal.

Glossary

A

Aboriginals	Native Australians
Apples	Money. Currency. Cash

B

Back 'o Burke	Far into the Outback, beyond the last pub
Battler	Someone, usually likable, who struggles very hard but never gets on top of things. 'E's 'ad a bit of 'ard luck, mate'
Billabong	A swampy area with standing water where animals drink and swagmen camp, as in the song 'Waltzing Mathilda'
Big Smoke	Sydney, Brisbane or any big city
Bit of a Dag	Unusual, interesting person, different. Usually meant as a compliment. Also see dag
Black Stump	The last marker, imaginary, beyond which nothing grows. This side 'o the black stump is civilization. Back'o the black stump is nothing but desert
Bloke	Male, man, guy
Bludge	To sponge off other blokes
Bludger	One who begs or sponges
Bluey	Fist fight, altercation
Bob	Shilling; coin worth twelve pennies
Boozer	The pub
Bot	A drinker who can't stand his shout but still manages to stay drunk
Buckley's Chance	No chance at all. Buckley advertised in newspapers for partners for his 'Back 'o Burke' mining operations. He always returned with minerals but without his partners. They never returned. He left them buried in the diggings. Hence Buckley's Chance is no chance at all
Bugger	To cheat
Bull artist	A braggart, boaster

C

Chasing Dingos	Pursuing something impossible to catch. Running after a dream
Chungula	Name of Anskar's Radiant opal
Cobber (Kah'ber)	Offsider, mate, working or drinking partner
Cocky	Farmer, rancher
Come a Cropper	Get into trouble, fail
Coober Pedy	Opal mining area. In Aboriginal language means man in a hole
Coot, Silly coot	Mild reproof
Copped it	Had bad luck. Got into trouble
Copped the lot	Got it all, whether good or bad
Crackers,	Opals that crack, or have a tendency to crack when cracker opals are cut and polished
Crook	Ill, sick
Cuppa	Cup of tea

304   The Curse of the Radiant Opal

D

Dag	Dirty wool around the rear end of a sheep. Must be cut, cleaned and processed separately from other wool. To be called a dag is not complimentary. See 'bit of a dag'
Dill	Idiot. Dull witted, dumb
Dingo	Wild native Aussie dog. Slang – someone who does not accept his social responsibilities
Drongo	Less than human
Duffer's Dag	Mining site 35 miles from Wallangulla, so named because it had yielded no salable opal

E

Ear basher	Talks on and on, usually about nothing important

F

Fair-dinkum	True, real, genuine, authentic
Fair go, mate	Ease up. Be reasonable. Give me a break
Fang	Put the fang in – bite. Take advantage of
Final Shaft	Miner's burial grounds
Fortnight	Two weeks
Frog Hollow	Mining field. Opals from this field crack when exposed to air.
Full as a goog	Drunk

G

Gallah	Noisy parrot. Considered useless
Gig	Scoundrel
Gink	Cheat. A cheat
Gink out	Leave without paying

H

Hard Kack	Bad luck
Hooly-Dooly	Bit of unexpected good fortune. Serendipity
Humping the Bluey	Following work across the Outback from station to station. What shearers do. Similar to Waltzing Mathilda
Hump me bluey	Leave. 'I ain't humpin' me bluey' – I'm not leaving
Humpy	Shack, shanty. Hut made of wood, stones, mud and sticks or whatever available

I

Itie	Italian

J

Jackaroo	Ranch hand being trained to manage
Jungle	Wooded area where most diggers camped

L

Lolly	Sweet. Candy. Hit the big lolly – have good luck, find a pocket of opal
Lurk	Cheat
Lurked	Cheated

M

Mates	Friends, working partners. Sometimes used loosely for blokes in general
Me	Aussie word used instead of my

Mob	....	Group, as in a social or drinking assembly
Monkey	....	A shaft down to the next opal level not under the main shaft, off one of the drifts
Mug	....	Fool, simpleton.
Mug stone	....	Poor quality opal only a fool would buy
Mullock heap	....	Pile of tailings around shaft

N

Naughty	....	Slang for sexual encounter
Nobby (nah'bee)	....	Lump of potch that might cut an opal.
No hoper	....	Will never get anywhere, no matter how hard he tries
Not worth a Zac	....	Worthless

O

Off me tucker	....	Off my food. Not eating. Not feeling well
Offsider	....	Cober, mate, partner, friend
Oululuu		Aboriginal name for half-devil, half-serpent that lives in a hole in the ground and lures men with flashing opals
Opal types	....	Basic opal stone is potch, white or black, and of no value. Potch with color may cut a mug stone, worth little. Next in rarity is precious opal with a variety of patterns: Pin Point–tiny little points of color; Flake–larger patches of color; Flame–streaks of color like fire; Flash–colors that change when stone is turned. All of these come in different patterns, shapes and sizes, making opal difficult to value. Every buyer will offer a different price for the same stone. Gem quality black opal is more brilliant and very rare. Radiants are the rarest of all
Outback	....	The interior of Australia, the desert

P

Parcel, 'Pahsel'	....	Collection of opals of different quality sold together
Poofter	....	Homosexual
Potch	....	Common opal, no value. May be white, black or grey
Pound sterling (L)	....	English or Australian unit of currency. One pound consists of 20 shillings or 240 pennies. Guinea=21 shillings. Crown=five shillings. Florin (two bob)=two shillings

Q

Quid	....	Slang for Australian Pound, $2.25 American

R

Radiant	....	Highest quality black opal. Rarest of all opals. Said to glow in the dark
Rat a claim	....	Pilfer, steal from someone else's mine
Rat bag	....	Someone who is insulting; has poor behavior. Despicable
Ratter	....	A bloke who pilfers opal from another's claim, the one doing the stealing. In the old days a caught ratter might have the shaft filled in on him
Roo	....	Kangaroo

Rotter ....No good. Not trustworthy or reliable

Royal Gem ....Top quality precious black opal. So named as being worthy of Queen Victoria. Very rare stone. More valuable than diamonds, rubies or emeralds

S

'She'll be right' ....Common term with various meanings: Everything will be okay. Don't worry about it. Don't bother me. I'll take care of it. Whatever

Shearing Shed ....The local jail. Six by eight clapboard shack with a bench and a small window. Located near the Final Shaft Cemetery

Sheila ....Woman, female, girlfriend

Short on a quid ....Without funds, no cash

Shout ....Buy a round of drinks

Skite ....Same as bull artist; one who brags and boasts but has little backbone. Not brave enough to stand his own in a bluey

Stars at midday ....It is said that in a deep enough shaft you can see the stars at midday. True or not, the implication is that you are down deeper than you want to be not of your own volition

Stand your shout ....Buy a round of drinks when it's your turn. 'He stands his shout' – He can be trusted to do the right thing

Station ....Outback Ranch, some as large as American smaller states such as Delaware or Rhode Island

Sundowners ....Blokes, sometimes families, who arrive at a station in time for the evening meal, ostensibly looking for work. But after being fed and housed for the night, leave in the morning before anyone else is up. Fly by nights

Swagman ....A vagabond who lives in and wanders the Outback with a sack (swag) on his back

Swing a stone ....Pocket an opal instead of sharing it with your mate

T

Ta ....Thanks

Ta-ta ....Goodbye

Tailings ....Refuse left after nobbies have been removed from opal dirt. Piles of clay around shafts, called mullock heaps

Tenner ....Ten pound note. Largest Aussie currency

Treacle ....Sweet syrup

Tucker ....Food. Sometimes money, cash

W

Wallies ....The crazies that inflict diggers and locals of Wallangulla, caused by too much isolation, obsession with opal, beer, and too little food.

Waltzing Matilda ....The process of wandering the outback with all your possessions in a swag on your back – what a swagman does. Also known as 'humping the bluey'

Warrambool	...............Similar to a billabong, but drier, more like a marsh than a swamp
Winge	...............Grumble, bellyache, snivel
Wog	...............Bug. I picked up a wog; I'm ill, can't work. Also slang term for foreigner

Y

| Yarn | ....Chat. Idle talk or serious discussion |

Z

| Zac | ....Sixpence. 'Not worth a Zac' – worthless |

Mining Terms

Shin cracker	...............A hard layer, similar to cement, just under the red desert clay. The top six inches to two feet of cement-like material which flies off against the shin when struck with a sinking pick
Sandstone	...............Just under the shin cracker, 10 to 30 feet deep.
Opal dirt	...............Sandstone. Clay level beneath the sandstone. Clay and sandstone alternate every ten to 50 feet for a thousand feet down. The deepest opal mines on Wallangulla are 80 feet, but most are less than 50 feet
Shaft	...............The two foot by four foot vertical hole straight down, used as access to the mine
Drift	...............The horizontal tunnel through opal dirt just under the sandstone level
Drive	...............A drift in the making. A digger may 'drive' towards another shaft for ventilation. When it's finished, it's called a drift
Monkey	...............A shaft, offset from the main shaft that goes from one opal level to the one beneath it
Potch	...............Milky white or shiny black nodules that may contain color and cut a gemstone. Black potch comprises the backing for all black opal.
Nobby	...............Any hard lump found in opal dirt. Some may contain potch and color
Color	...............Any color found in a nobbie. Some snipped nobbies are sold to collectors as potch and color
Mug stones	...............Lesser quality opals that are sold for a few quid each. Mug equals fool in Aussie slang
Face	...............The front of the drive that is being dug. The working area
Muck	...............Dug out dirt to be removed and disposed of as part of the mining process. Also called tailings
Trolley	...............A 25 gallon drum cut in half lengthwise and set on wheels. Used to haul muck from the face back to the shaft

Grapple Hook	................Three hooks welded together in such a way that a bucket handle is easily snagged from the top of the shaft
Windlass	................A wood cylinder with a crank handle used to wind up a rope that lifts buckets of dirt out of the shaft
Windsock	................A sheet-like air scoop, 20 to 30 feet long, hung above the shaft to direct a downward flow of fresh air into the drift
Ratting	................Stealing opal from someone else's claim. To sneak down into someone's claim and dig out his opal is to 'Rat the claim'
Ratter	................The one doing the stealing. As, "I was on opal, mate, but they ratted me." In the old days a trapped ratter might have the shaft filled in on him

Diggers and Locals

A

Angus the Scot	Opal buyer
Archer the Cop	The law in Wallangulla
Artie	Chess playing friend of the Professor's

B

Barcoa Jack	Found hand in tailings
Beesly	Bunko's mate
Benny Bingo	Brother, opal buyer
Bernie Bingo	" " "
Blacksmith	Local. Has shop just out of town
Bough shed	An open shelter with branches and leaves on top for shade
Brady	Horizontal Bill's mate
Broken Bob	Gave me Bruno
Bruce the Banker	Quit banking for opal mining
Bunko	Claimed he owned mud humpy, mate of Beesly
Bush Nurse	Resident medical
Buttons	Russian George's mate

C

Cocky Bowman	Jackaroo who dragged dog to death
Cocky Nolan	Station owner of mining land
Chickie	Shadow's thirteen-year-old daughter
Chuck the Cutter	Cuts stones for Bingo brothers

D

Dragan	Croat, mate of Mirko
Dynamite Dan	Digger also lurked by Bingos

E

Edward	Pom's dog
Elly	Bush nurse

F

Flint the Ratter	Got caught ratting claim. Has a wife, Fiona, and family. Mate of Wild Denny Strayman

G

Garbhan	Angus the Scots cutter
Gerald Fisher	American living in Brisbane with family. Visited Anskar's claim. Son Joey, daughter Susie, wife Ruth
Gentle Mike	The local blacksmith
Goat Colonel	Veteran from WWII British Army
Gordon	Scot, mate of Rab, Garbhan and Angus
Gunther the Kraut	Digger

H

Harry Hutchen	Opal buyer, seller, bull artist. Met at pub
Harold Blake	Local. Had claim on Newtown. Anskar's main source of local news
Helga, also Valkyrie	Anskar's young lady from Swedish Embassy
High Rise John	Built his humpy on stilts
Horizontal Bill	Wouldn't dig new shaft, only use existing ones.
Hungry Hank the Hatter	Had a Radiant opal, went hungry rather than sell it

J

Jake the Wasp	Digs small drive. Mate of Wee Willy
Jimmy the Snake Catcher	Used to catch and sell snakes for medical use

K

King Tut	Sold me a puddler at four times its value

L

Lenny	Owns Lenny's Café

M

Marco, or Ten Pins	Pom's mate. Father came from Italy, family name Polo
Mario	Serb who worked Anskar's claim for a few days
Mirko	Croat, mate of Dragan

N

Nardoo	Anskar's Aborigional friend
Niggly Neville	Shot Cocky Bowman

O

Old Otto	Starved with Radiant in hand
Old Sam	A bot. Can't stand his shout
Old Weber	Buried in Final Shaft Cemetery

P

Petula	Post mistress
Piano tuner, Wally	Hit the big lolly, left for the Big Smoke with Hungry Hank the Hatter's wife.
Pom or Mad Pom	Marco's mate. From England
Professor	From Canada, lectures

R

Rab	One of the Scots with Angus
Russian George	Has house and machine shop. Button's mate

S

Sam the Barber	Left with a small fortune
Sarah	Barmaid at Digger's Retreat pub
Scots	The four blokes, mates who work together
Sergeant Taylor	Policeman from Sydney
Shadow	A local scoundrel, in with Bingos and Chuck
Skinner	Wombat's mate. Skinned dead sheep to support mining
Slammin' Sam Smith, also the Slammer	Fast digger, six feet per day
Snookie	Shadow's eighteen-year-old daughter
Sonja	Anskar's fiancée in Minnesota

T

Territory Burt	From Northwest Territory. Got thumped by Flint
Two-Bob Bobby	Bludger with Radiant opals

V

Valkyrie, Helga	Anskar's young lady from Swedish embassy
Vertical Bill	Afraid to work underground. Just sinks shafts

W

Wee Willy	Mate of Jake the Wasp
Wild Denny Strayman	Flint the Ratters Mate
Wombat	Skinner's mate, has short arms and legs and perpetual smile

Made in the USA
Charleston, SC
23 May 2013